PRAISE   JAPROV

'Amanda Prowse is the queen of contemporary family drama.'

Daily Mail

'A tragic story of loss and love.'

Lorraine Kelly, *Sun*

'Captivating, heartbreaking and superbly written.'

Closer

'A deeply emotional, unputdownable read.'

Red

'Uplifting and positive, but you may still need a box of tissues.'

Cosmopolitan

'You'll fall in love with this.'

Cosmopolitan

'Warning: you will need tissues.'

Sun on Sunday

'Handles her explosive subject with delicate care.'

Daily Mail

'Deeply moving and eye-opening.'

Heat

'A perfe⸺ . . . a real tear-jerker.'

9030 00006 2083 2

Sunday Mirror

The Coordinates of Loss

OTHER BOOKS BY AMANDA PROWSE

Anna

Theo

How to Fall in Love Again: Kitty's story

The Art of Hiding

The Idea of You

Poppy Day

What Have I Done?

Clover's Child

A Little Love

Christmas for One

Will You Remember Me?

A Mother's Story

Perfect Daughter

Three-and-a-Half Heartbeats (exclusive to Amazon Kindle)

The Second Chance Café (originally published as *The Christmas Café*)

Another Love

My Husband's Wife

I Won't Be Home for Christmas

The Food of Love

OTHER NOVELLAS BY AMANDA PROWSE

The Game

Something Quite Beautiful

A Christmas Wish

Ten Pound Ticket

Imogen's Baby

Miss Potterton's Birthday Tea

The Coordinates of Loss

AMANDA PROWSE

LAKE UNION
PUBLISHING

LONDON BOROUGH OF WANDSWORTH	
9030 00006 2083 2	
Askews & Holts	04-Oct-2018
AF	£9.99
	WW18008798

Published by Lake Union Publishing, Seattle

www.apub.com

Amazon, the Amazon logo, and Lake Union Publishing are trademarks of Amazon.com, Inc., or its affiliates.

ISBN-13: 9781503904958
ISBN-10: 1503904954

Cover design by Emma Graves

Printed in the United States of America

This book is for my brother, Simon Ward Smith,
The funniest, sharpest person I know – Simon, you
have been making me laugh my whole life and I am
thankful that you are my brother.
Amelie is so very lucky to have you – the best dad in the
whole wide world!
I borrowed one of your walking routes for this book.
And I dedicate The Coordinates of Loss *to you.*
With love now and always
Mandy xx

THE COORDINATES OF LOSS

My tears do sea diamonds make.
Each tiny drop of heartache woven into the great
blue that lies between my world and yours;
this fractured sea.
With hollow heart and red-wrought eyes I look
back at the trail I have left and see
nothing,
But cresting waves, shot through with life, lost to
a current that takes you further and further
into that regrettable abyss.
And should I twist my aching head on fragile neck
to look towards the horizon I see nothing,
But the vast, azure and navy canvas, stretching to
infinity; leading me further and further away
from a place I crave.
The place where my happiness used to lie with
you on the other side of the sea. For now, I
feel nothing.

For I loved you.
I loved you.
I will always love you.
And now I live for eternity in deep, blue grief.

ONE

Rachel always thought it felt like a gift to wake up smiling.

Today was no different.

She stretched her tanned arm over her head and took a deep breath, considering that this, the gentle rocking of a boat, was quite possibly the best alarm clock in the whole wide world. Her mind flitted to the cold winter mornings of her youth when her dad whistled through the flimsy bathroom wall as he shaved, rain beating on the double-glazed picture windows and the smell of toast wafting up the stairs of her mum and dad's flat-fronted 1970s house. It had been a struggle to heft her body from the warm nest of duvet that covered the dip in the mattress where she liked to curl. A struggle and a chore, the promise of a loo floor, chilly underfoot, and the long walk to school along grey pavements, avoiding the spray from speeding lorries, no real incentive to get on with the job.

This morning, she nestled back on to the soft mattress and took another deep breath that developed into a yawn. Slowly she opened one eye, closing it again quickly. Sunlight filtered in from the hatch above their bed in the rear berth, warming the air into a pleasant fug that cocooned them in this tiny space. There was something unique about sleeping like this, in a boat out on the ocean. It felt like an island, an oasis, away from the pace of real life; away from everything. Safe and sound, away from traffic, machinery, people and all the things that might bring them harm. It was as close to heaven as she could imagine.

It always took her one night to settle into the pace of life on the boat, and as she lay there, after the first night of three out at sea, she knew she had arrived. The rest of the trip stretched out ahead of them like a promise and she could barely quell the leap of happiness in her gut.

What's on the agenda for today? Spot of fishing. Swimming. More swimming. Supper on the deck, maybe a bottle of fizz or a cold beer, as we watch the sunset . . .

She smiled and turned on to her side, running her finger over the strong, tanned back of her husband.

'I am not prepared to wake up yet. So you can cut that out,' James groaned, in the groggy voice she knew meant that they had gone one bottle too many in the champagne stakes last night.

She laughed her throaty chuckle. 'I told you we should call it a day after that first bottle, but no.' She leaned forward and kissed his skin. 'Come on! Life is for the living! That's what you said.'

'You win. You were right. But that doesn't help me right now,' he moaned.

'Plus' – she flicked her long, chestnut hair over her shoulder and sidled against him, lifting her leg and wrapping it around both of his as she pulled against him – 'you should be glad I still want to disturb your beauty sleep in this way after eight years of marriage.'

'I am glad,' he whispered. 'But can you let me show you how glad after a bit more sleep? Just five more minutes.'

'It might cure your hangover,' she suggested, kissing the back of his neck and running her hand over the flat of his stomach, reaching down.

'Is the door locked?' He turned and lay back on the bed, glancing at the varnished oak door. 'I can see you're not going to take no for an answer.'

'That's right.' She nodded and climbed on to him, bending to kiss him full on the mouth, this beautiful man she got to wake up next to every day . . .

◆ ◆ ◆

'Coffee?' She yawned again, slipping on her vest and calf-length, cotton PJ bottoms, as James sat on the side of the bed and scrolled through his phone.

'Oh, yes please, and lots of it.'

'How's your hangover?' she asked cockily.

'Gone, would you believe.' He smiled at her over his shoulder before something on the screen caught his attention.

'Remember the rule, no work while we are out here. This is family time.'

'I'm looking at the footie scores!' He flashed her the screen and poked out his tongue, happy to have proved his innocence.

'I'll let you off.' Rachel fastened the white cotton waffle robe around her midriff and opened the door, treading the single step down into the quiet cabin.

She had half-expected to hear the zany burble of cartoons coming from the wall-mounted TV, or at least the canned laughter from one of the Nickelodeon programmes that seemed to be permanently playing on her son's iPad. She filled the kettle and set it on the stove, igniting the ring by bending low with one finger on the button and her hair coiled and bunched in her other hand as she watched the tick, tick, tick of gas flare into life. A quick glance at the clock told her it was six forty-five. Her boy, usually an early riser, had slept in. *Thank the lord!*

She had enjoyed her leisurely wake-up this morning and even more what came after . . . It was good for her and James to have these stolen moments of bliss away from the busy whirl of life where either one or both of them were permanently dancing in and out of the wide front door with car keys in hand and one eye on the clock. It seemed crazy that they lived in the same house, shared a bed, and yet she missed him, missed quality time with him. It was an irony, how life in paradise came at this cost.

Tiptoeing to the door that sat parallel to theirs, she carefully pushed it open. The second berth, a little smaller than theirs, was warm. She looked up at the hatch and decided to open it right up, get some fresh sea air into the space and remove the smell of a little boy who thought it funny to parp beneath the covers.

'Good morning, sleepyhead.' She eyed the lump of duvet, pale blue and covered in crudely drawn sailing ships; red, with darker blue-and-white striped sails. She'd bought it three or four years ago when he still had one foot in toddlerhood, but now considered replacing the bed linen with something a little more grown up, maybe *Star Wars*? She'd have a look online or get her mum to do it back in the UK; she liked to set her chores that were connected to her grandson, knowing it made her feel involved and less remote.

'Oscar?' she called, softly now. 'It's a beautiful day and I thought we could have our breakfast out on the deck, how about that? Croissants and juice. And before you ask, that is all we have.' She pre-empted his regular request for whatever she hadn't listed. It was like a game to him and one she heard him and Cee-Cee laughing over of a morning.

'I can make you French toast?' the housekeeper would offer.

'Can I have bacon?' his countermove.

'No! No bacon. I've got cornflakes?'

'Do you have Choco Puffs?' and on it went.

Cee-Cee had more time and patience than she.

'Oscar?' she called again. Still nothing. Bending down, she noted that his head wasn't on the pillow. She reached down and pulled the duvet back to reveal her son's bed, empty.

'Where are you, you little rascal?' She looked around the confined area, knowing logically that there was nowhere for him to hide in here, nowhere big enough to conceal a seven-year-old boy.

'Oscar?' she walked back into the cabin and let her eyes glance at the banquette on the other side of the fixed dining table, knowing he sometimes liked to lie on it. But he wasn't there. A similar look around the tiny bathroom revealed it to be empty. Next, she scanned the curved sofa that ran the length of the galley-cum-sitting room, before climbing the steps and pulling herself through the hatch up on to the deck.

'Oscar?' Her tone soured a little now, as the beginnings of anger flared. He knew he wasn't to come up here alone, not ever. She held the port-side guardrail and walked carefully along, scanning ahead to the sunbathing area at the foredeck where he liked to languish with his iPad resting on his raised knees and a cushion under his head. She could see it was empty, but stood there nonetheless, staring at the white vinyl cushions with the blue-piped edging, almost as if she believed that if she looked long enough, he might pop up.

The kettle whistled. And fear started to bloom in her chest.

Rachel turned and looked towards the back of the boat from where the yacht could be steered either with the steering wheel when they were under power, or with the tiller, now resting in its neutral position, when they were under sail. Here there was also seating on either side with storage cubbies below.

The kettle stopped whistling.

Moving now with speed, swinging from the rear stanchion and with her breath coming fast, she jumped down into the rear of the boat and with a sense of urgency yanked the cushions from the seats, flinging them on to the floor before fixing her finger in the brass loop handles and pulling up the base of the cubbies. She stared into the stowage space. Her eyes registered the coiled ropes, a spare fender, a pump and two pairs of flippers, one large and one small. Shielding her eyes with her hands, trying to dampen the glare of the morning sun, she searched the water from the back of the boat. There were cresting arcs of foam, a bobbing blue, plastic rope trailing from the rear deck, and even the flash of iridescent scaled skin – fish on an early-morning hunt.

But no seven-year-old boy.

'Coffee!' James called from below. 'Rach, Oscar! Coffee's ready!'

She stood still, as if frozen and more than a little confused, as she waited for her husband to pop his head through the hatch as he climbed from the galley.

'Coffee, darling!' He raised two mugs. 'Do you want me to bring it up or are you coming down?'

'I can't . . . I can't find Oscar.' She swallowed, using up the remainder of her spit to speak.

James laughed. 'What do you mean you can't find him?' He knitted his brows, still smiling, and yes, she had to admit, it was just as ridiculous as it sounded. They were only three on this thirty-two-foot yacht – a space smaller than their entrance lobby at home and with only so many places to be, and yet she couldn't find him.

Ridiculous.

'Well, he'll be hiding!' He turned back and disappeared. 'You look up there and I'll do down here.'

She didn't want to say she had already looked; better right now to think that she had been outfoxed, searched badly, and that James would extract him from whatever nook or cranny he had managed to secrete himself in. Yes, this was much better, because the alternative . . .

She walked back to the front of the boat, her heart beating loudly in her throat, and began to plead silently under her breath as she removed the cushions that lay flat on the foredeck; of course he wasn't there. Logic should have told her that for someone to hide beneath the cushions, there would have been a giveaway lump, a bump, but there was not.

Please, please, please, Oscar, please come out now . . .

Rachel was not thinking logically; she had entered the beginning of panic.

She ran her eyes over the top of the boat at head height, knowing that had her solid boy been standing on that at any point it would have been obvious, but she looked nonetheless.

Her limbs began to shake and her blood felt simultaneously icy and yet thick in her veins. 'James?' she called.

He appeared on the deck, his mouth wide open, his head jerking and his eyes wide.

'Where is he?' he asked, as if hoping she might have the answer.

She noticed he too was having difficulty catching a breath.

Instantly, and in an almost choreographed move, she raced to the port-side and her husband starboard, each holding the thin metal rails as they peered overboard, scouring the water. 'Oscar!' she called loudly.

'Oscar!' he called louder.

'Oscar!' she yelled.

'Os-caaar!' he bellowed.

All the while their eyes darted about the surface of the ocean, drawn to any change in light, any flicker of movement.

'Oscar!' She was screaming now. 'Oscar!' she screamed again, as loud as she could, her body folded over.

She heard a splash; heartened, she ran to the other side of the boat, but it was only the sound of James, who had jumped in and now bobbed in the water, turning his head this way and that, still calling, yelling with a rawness to his tone that was petrifying; it told her he was out of control, flailing. 'Oscar!'

Taking his lead, she ran back to the other side of the boat and did the same. She jumped, hitting the Atlantic Ocean and not caring that she was in her pyjamas, careless about anything other than finding her son.

'Oscar! Oscar!' she screamed, crying now, her tears clogging her nose and the back of her throat, making shouting harder and blurring her vision. She ducked under, looking as far as she was able at the hull, and then came back for air; nothing. Her hair hung in a heavy, water-logged curtain over her face; she dug at it with her fingers as she trod water, spinning this way and that, looking, hoping and crying, as her teeth chattered in her gums.

She could hear her husband screaming louder than she had ever heard and in a way that was chilling, desperate. His lack of control and fear only fuelled her own.

It was in that moment of realisation that Rachel Croft looked towards the horizon, weakened, weary and with the certain knowledge that her life had changed.

It had changed forever.

◆ ◆ ◆

Someone had wrapped a grey wool blanket around her shoulders, but still she shook – every part of her, trembling and shaking. Her head jerked, her knees jumped and even her eyelids fluttered. She was, despite the warmth of the midday Bermudian sun and the thick blanket, cold. Colder than she had ever felt, as if the chill started in her gut and filled her right up.

Rachel felt like the world was covered in gauze. Everything she looked at was hazy, every voice a little distorted. It was as if she were floating high above, scanning the sea around the boat, watching the coiled shape that was her.

She kept repeating, 'This is a dream. This is a dream.' Followed by, 'It's okay. It's okay.' Worried that if she stopped saying this then she just might give in to the scream that sat at the base of her throat.

At some level she *wanted* to scream, pull out her hair, smash something, and at the same time she wanted to hide. Rachel didn't know what she wanted.

She found it hard to think straight. Her mind jumped from minutiae like the fact that Mr Cardew, the garden man, was coming to cut the grass today and she wasn't sure if Cee-Cee knew where the key was to the back storage shed, to wondering why James, sitting opposite, was crying, folded over on the narrow bench at the back of the police boat, rocking silently, but with thick lines of spit looped in a lacy bib of distress from his lip to his chest. And then she would remember why he was crying, why they were there, and in the nick of time lift the plastic orange bucket to her face and retch into it again. The pain in her stomach muscles reminded her that this was not the first time she had vomited.

It was a significant moment and one Rachel would only ponder in the coming months. Ordinarily, to see her husband, the man she loved, so distressed would have pulled at every thread in her body and she would have leaped to offer comfort in any way she could. It would only be later, much, much later, that she would recognise that in this, his moment of need, she felt nothing. Nothing. It was as if she stared at a stranger.

'So, Mrs Croft.' The officer spoke in a way that told her it was a call to arms, he needed her to concentrate, participate. 'You last saw Oscar at?' he almost prompted, as if he knew the answer.

She wiped her mouth on the damp sleeve of her dressing gown and held the bucket to her chest with both hands. Looking up at the policeman in his immaculately pressed, short-sleeved white shirt, she studied the thin, neat line of his moustache on his top lip. She read his name badge: 'Mackenzie'.

She kept thinking about the day before, throwing on her clothes, grateful for the early-morning hiatus from the heat and excited about their excursion on the boat. A couple of days of bliss to look forward to with the people she loved.

With the large cooler that Cee-Cee had packed in tow, it was with happiness and without any sense of foreboding that she'd trod the open planks of the dock with her bare feet. Oscar's hand sat snugly in her free palm as they skipped and hopped, navigating the gaps, stepping behind James, who walked with purpose, assuming, as he always did, the role of captain before they had even left the shore. He turned to speak over his shoulder. 'Are you sure we've packed enough?' He laughed, rolling his eyes at the large beach bag he had slung about his body and the stuffed knapsack in his hand.

'I've actually pared it down! It's only towels, dry clothes, suntan lotion, snacks; you'd be surprised how much stuff we need.' She smiled at her man.

'You're right, I would!' He laughed again.

She recalled looking him up and down, appreciating the look of him in his khaki cargo shorts with his hands on his hips and his feet inside his battered, tan deck shoes; his mirrored sunglasses hid his eyes, but his wide grin spoke volumes. He had the healthy glow of a man who slept well, ate right and woke every morning with very little to trouble him. A man who was on the right side of happy with all he could ever hope for and more. Lucky.

Oscar broke free from her hand and ran. 'Be careful, darling!' she shouted after him.

The little boy ignored his mum's warning, trotting ahead without looking back.

Fearless.

After they had cleared the marina the boat picked up speed. Oscar wriggled back into the space next to her as the hull bumped on the waves and kicked up spray that peppered their skin with salt-filled droplets.

'Woo-hoo!' her son shouted with his arms in the air, as if he were on a rollercoaster.

Hold on, please, Oscar, don't fall from the seat, don't go over the edge, stay close to Dad . . . She remembered having these thoughts. *A premonition? Why didn't she say anything?*

When the engine changed tone and the boat slowed, it was as if a cloak of peace and well-being enveloped them. Sitting at the mercy of the ocean, with only the faintest lick of breeze, was as quiet and calming as ever.

She and James had looked back from where they had travelled; the beautiful wide stretch of beach was fringed with lush, green plants, spiked through with palm trees. Vast, colonial-style homes painted in shades of sugared almonds sat in grand manicured plots with decadently crafted water features that flowed into infinity pools.

She loved seeing their beautiful island from this vantage point. It had promised to be a perfect trip.

'Mrs Croft,' Mackenzie said her name again, a little more forcefully, and she wondered how long it had been since he spoke; it could have been seconds or hours. 'When did you last see your son?'

'It was . . .' She tried to focus. 'It was when we put him to bed, about eight thirty last night. He usually goes a little bit earlier, but as we weren't at home and there's no school tomorrow . . .' She let this trail.

'You both put him to bed?'

'No.' She shook her head. 'James put him to bed and I called out "Love you" from the bathroom.'

'So you didn't see him in his bed?'

'I know he was in his bedroom,' she countered.

'How do you know that?'

'Because James had put him to bed and he called out—' She broke off, as a fresh batch of tears gathered. 'He called out, "Night night, Mummy" and it came from his berth and I called back.' She stopped and swallowed.

'What did you call back?' he asked with his pen poised.

'Just "Love you . . ." That was it. "Love you."' She pictured holding her hair in one hand and spitting the blue/white foam into the minute corner basin, emptying her mouth to call out of the side, not heartfelt or sincere, but more a reflex, *'Love you!'* Her mind had been on cleaning her teeth, wondering where her perfume was and thinking about her evening to come with James and a glass or two of something chilled . . . *Why didn't you say more? Did he hear you? Does he know how much you love him? Come back now, Oscar, come home to me, darling . . .*

She tried to gather herself. 'You . . . you are still looking? He might be tired, he will be swimming or floating but, but we need to keep looking for him.' She felt a wave of desperation at the idea that instead of sitting here, trapped in this police boat, she would be better off rowing, searching, or in a speedboat in which she could circle around and around, confident that no one would look as thoroughly as her.

She began to shrug off the blanket. 'Can I go now? Can I go and help look for him? He might not answer to a stranger, but I know his voice and he knows mine and I know what his pyjamas look like and he might be listening out for me, listening to hear me call!'

The man answered with a softened tone. 'I promise you that there is an extensive search under way, Mrs Croft. The coast guard, my colleagues, volunteers; there is quite a party out there. You are best off here, helping us build a picture of what happened. And if he is . . .'

She looked up at him now, daring him to speak further. He closed his mouth.

'We need to get to him,' she pressed. 'He will be getting tired. And he might be scared.' This thought sent a fresh bolt of pain through her chest and her shakes increased. She bent forward and let out a high-toned mewl that was visceral, wounded. The other policeman stepped forward and repositioned the blanket around her shoulders.

Mackenzie nodded and waited for her to calm. 'I know this is difficult, but just to clarify this one point, Mrs Croft: neither you nor your husband have actually seen Oscar since around eight thirty last night.'

She shook her head and wiped her eyes, trying to catch her breath. 'No, but if he'd left his cabin while we were on deck, we'd have seen him.'

'We would,' James interjected, his voice raw. 'We were in the seating at the stern, which faces the stairs, almost opposite his cabin, and he'd have to pass through to get to the upper deck.'

Why didn't I check on you, baby? Why didn't I lock the hatch? Why did I not get up the moment I woke up? Where were you then?

She couldn't help the questions that rolled in her mind.

'Mrs Croft?'

'What?' She was again unaware that he had been speaking.

'I asked if you heard anything in the night, any unusual noises, any sounds of movement or another boat?'

She exchanged a look with James, who sat up at this suggestion. 'You think another boat came? Do you think . . . do you think someone came and took him?' Her chest heaved and she closed her eyes, hardly able to process one more piece of information and all the possibilities associated with it.

'I think at this stage we really don't know and so it's good to keep all options open.'

'I didn't hear anything.' She shook her head. 'I had had . . . a drink and the cabin was very warm. I slept heavily.'

She watched Mackenzie and his colleague glance at each other and then back to her.

'Why would someone take him?' she asked quizzically, and then a thought occurred. 'It might have been a . . . a school friend, erm, lots of the parents have boats, they . . . they might have come and got him for a trip or so that the kids could play, they might have forgotten to leave a note, can you' – she swallowed – 'can you check with the school or . . . or with the coast guard, they might know about other boats.' She felt the first glimmer of hope. This could be possible. Her son could right now be playing with a friend or bumping along on an inflatable, or he could be on the beach!

Mackenzie nodded and she saw the flicker of something that looked a lot like pity in his eyes. 'We are doing exactly that, Mrs Croft. Don't worry; we are doing everything we can. And just to get back to the questions, this morning you woke at?'

She shook her head, trying to clear the fog. 'I suppose it must have been about six or quarter past.'

'And you got up and' – he checked his notepad – 'put the kettle on and that was when you noticed your son was not in his bed?'

She could hardly bear to look at her husband, who answered on her behalf. 'We made love and we lay in bed for a little while after. We both got up at around a quarter to seven, sevenish.'

The policeman didn't flinch, but she felt the flame of mortification lick at her throat. It wasn't the fact that they were talking about sex, it was the admission of how they had been so very distracted, pleasure-seeking while their boy . . . Again she bent her head inside the grubby walls of the orange bucket.

Rachel spat and straightened, and wiping her mouth on her sleeve, she looked through the window across the water. Some twenty feet away, she could see officers climbing all over *Liberté*. She thought the boat looked small. No longer the shiny, grand vessel over which James had beamed as he enthusiastically described her proportions, her speed, her electronic wizardry. Their boat had been photographed in a thousand different lights and angles, on a thousand days out, each picture posed, edited, glossed and sent back to friends and family in grey, cold Blighty. *Look what we've got! Look at the life we lead!* It wasn't intended to taunt, but rather make them proud; proof that she had made the right choices. She pictured the photograph of the three of them on board, tanned and smiling, pinned to her parents' kitchen wall.

She remembered the first time she trod on her shifting deck, a girl who grew up in a suburb of Bristol, a girl who thought a brisk walk around the Downs and a hot chocolate drunk on the terrace of the Avon Gorge Hotel with a grand view of the Clifton Suspension Bridge as the sun dipped, was living the life!

And it had been. A lovely life, until she met James. Clever James. Handsome James. James who had a well-paid job working in reinsurance, an industry she had never even heard of.

Do you mean insurance? she had giggled, coyly.

No! I mean reinsurance . . .

James who was heading for the very top. James who wanted to take her with him.

She remembered the first time she had set foot on the boat. Oscar had waved from the deck; he'd only been three and had looked too cute in his tiny life vest. James held his hand. She had quickly learned where to plant her feet. It had been a sunny day with the lightest of breezes, not long after the America's Cup had been held on the island, everyone was boat-mad and she wondered if this were just a phase in which James would lose interest. She pictured the scuba equipment in the cellar and the chassis of the Jaguar E-Type, sitting under a tarpaulin in his parents' barn in Sussex. 'I'll restore it and we shall take it to Le Mans! God, it will be bloody brilliant!' He had leaped around the rusting carcass, hands on hips, smiling, doing what he did best: painting her a picture that would make her fall in love with his idea. 'We can camp! We can stop the car somewhere pretty en route, a bend in a river! And we'll eat good bread and cheese, washed down with a fine red, and we'll lie on a tartan blanket and wear leather goggles! Vintage style! We should get you a fancy silk scarf and some of those flick-up-at-the-side sunglasses!'

She had smiled, bitten by the bug, drawn into his daydream, committed. He stared at the car as if he could actually see it whizzing around the track with the glorious racing-green paint restored and shiny. But the leap between the adventure in his mind and the project in front of him was time-consuming and demanding. James certainly had energy for anything new, but always fiercely underestimated the level of time and commitment required to make it come to life. Far from holding his flights of fancy against him, Rachel loved the fact that her man had this impetuous, spontaneous lust for adventure. It was as infectious as it was thrilling. She often thought of her dad in Bristol, popping pennies in a jar and waiting for the day his life might start – 'When the kids get older,' 'When the weather clears up,' 'When I retire.' As far as she could tell the last time she saw him, over two years ago now, he was still waiting.

As for James's E-Type, it had been mothballed and still sat in darkness, waiting for discovery and its promised trip to Le Mans. As she gripped the handrail on that first trip and felt the slight pull of the vessel, she wondered how one mothballed a boat.

'One hand for you, Rach, and one for the boat. Always, always hold on to something,' he had called. James was instantly at ease on the water, as was his way; naturally adept, competent in everything. He had laughed at her concerns. 'Oscar lives on a tiny island! He practically lives in the ocean! Sailing will be second nature to him, he will love it, our water baby . . .' Determined not to let him down, she had learned to bob with the boat, bending her knees and taking it slowly. Gradually she had quashed the leap of fear in her gut, until spending time on the sleek boat that dipped and rose at the will of the ocean became almost second nature to her.

Quite unexpectedly and very quickly, Rachel had fallen in love with her, finding it hard to describe the sense of freedom she felt when heading towards the horizon with the sun and droplets of sea peppering her skin. Nor could she relay the sense of perfect isolation when the only sound was waves lapping the hull, when, with the salt spray dried in wavy lines all across her limbs, she, James and Oscar would lie under duvets on the foredeck, looking at the dazzling array of stars in the purple-tinged, Bermudian sky. Just the two of them and their water baby.

Now, though, as she looked at the shiny boat being picked over by men in heavy boots and peaked caps in the way scavengers might go after bones, she saw none of the glamour and there was no joy. If anything, she felt a flicker of hatred for *Liberté*, a foul vessel that had brought harm and heartache to her family. To her son! She shot her husband a misplaced look, laden with dislike.

Why did you get this fucking boat? Why did I listen to you? How come you got to put him to bed? Did you tuck him in properly? Did he have Mr Bob with him? He can't sleep properly unless Mr Bob is on his pillow . . .

'Where are you, Oscar? Where are you, darling? Come back now. Come back to me.' She only realised she had spoken the words out loud when her husband sobbed in response. She looked at him, quite unable to help him in his moment of distress. Although they sat on either side of the narrow boat, the distance between them was a million miles. She looked back at *Liberté* and saw a policeman stuff Oscar's duvet into a plastic bin bag.

And once again, she lowered her head and retched into the orange bucket.

'We need to think about heading back.' She heard Mackenzie speak to his deputy. His words were like lava chasing her, and as her heart raced she looked left to right in the confined space, wondering how she could outrun them.

How can I make them understand that I do not want to leave here? How can I? It's crazy to think I could just turn my back and head home – to what? What waits for me there? Nothing!

'I don't want to go back.' Rachel planted her bare feet on the floor and shook her head, adamant.

'Mrs Croft, we need to get you and Mr Croft back to shore and we need to tow your boat back to the harbour.'

She shook her head, 'No!' and a small laugh escaped, not that anything was funny. 'I am not leaving here! Not until we have got Oscar! He might be trying to get back to the boat and if it's gone, can you imagine that?' She heard the high-pitched note of panic in her voice. 'He will be tired, he will be floating and it's going to get cold and dark soon!' She pointed outside, as if this fact might have escaped their attention.

'Rachel, we need to go back.'

'How can you say that, James? How the fuck can you think it's okay to leave him out here on his own?' She was aware her voice was thin and reedy through a disgusting combination of distress and exhaustion.

'I don't, I don't, I . . .' She watched him struggle and give in again to his tears.

'I can't leave him! I won't leave him out here! He's only a little boy! He's only little!' The strength left her legs and they folded beneath her. Her body slipped from the bench and she found herself sitting on the bottom of the boat, weeping and making a noise that was part scream, part wail; it came from a place beyond her consciousness. It was the call of an animal, hurt, cornered and desperate.

'No, no, no, no!' she screamed and kicked.

'Rachel! Rachel! Please!' She was vaguely aware of her husband's voice and then a heavy, weighted blanket covering her, clamping her arms and legs, already weakened by fatigue. It pushed her further into the floor. She continued to whimper, to call out 'Oscar! Oscar! I don't want to leave you! I am sorry, I am sorry, my baby! Hang on, Oscar! Hang on! Don't be scared! Mummy is here! I am right here!' The boat shuddered to life and with a feeling of utter and complete helplessness, she felt it make a turn on the water, taking her back to the marina at Spanish Point, speeding away from the place her little boy now dwelled.

With the movement of her limbs restricted, all she could do was bang her head on the floor and continue to emit the loud wail of distress.

Shock had begun to dissipate her rage and with leaden limbs she was assisted from the boat. Someone, a young American doctor Rachel had never seen before, was waiting on the jetty, at whose request she didn't know. He smiled benignly, avoiding her eyeline, as one of the policemen pulled up the sleeve of her dressing gown. And like a magician revealing synthetic roses from a secret pocket inside his jacket, the doctor exposed the sliver of steel that would slide beneath her skin and deposit the drug into her system. A drug that would round off the edges of her grief, soften the spike, smooth the shards.

A small group of people huddled in the car park, all with horror-struck expressions, witnessing her at her most vulnerable. Not that she cared; she cared about nothing other than staying mentally focused on her boy, willing him to make himself known. *Come home, come on, keep swimming, Oscar. Come back to me . . .*

She felt strangely more like an observer than a participant. With the drug coursing in her blood, she felt a little drunk, a little faded, ethereal . . .

She sat slumped on the back seat, her body yielding to the forced torpidity. Lilting to one side, she lay her head on the cool glass of the window. James, in the front seat, kept looking back at her, his eyes bloodshot and searching, as if she might have the answers.

She looked up at the scrolled, wrought-iron gates of their home, waiting for them to whir open. Her eyes swept to the right and she saw the pool where an outdoor four-poster canopy bed sat strategically positioned. White muslin curtains fluttered in the breeze.

'Beautiful . . .' she muttered.

She remembered lying on that very bed last year with Oscar next to her, his bare feet curled against her thighs and his head sharing her pillow. He smelled of sunshine and was fidgety, kicking her gently as he chattered. She only half listened as he verbally juggled topics as varied as Lego, lunch, swimming, his best friend Hank, sports day . . . she nod-ded and cooed, but she was listening to the hum rather than the actual words. How she wished she had paid better attention. Later that same day, as the temperature cooled, they had abandoned the car at the dock and gone fishing on *Liberté*, and while James navigated the sandbars and reefs that littered the exit route that would lead to open water, she and Oscar had sat on the foredeck, letting the wind batter their faces as they bumped along, exhilarated, happy.

'How much do you love me, Mummy?'

Rachel had paused, looking out over the horizon as she tried to find the words. 'I love you deeper than the ocean and higher than the sky.'

Oscar looked up at her and smiled. 'I think I will marry you when I get older.' He jostled a handful of small shells in his palm.

'Well, how lucky am I?' She cursed the tears in her eyes.

'Why are you crying, Mum?' he asked, his freckled nose wrinkling in the sunlight and his long, tawny fringe falling over his eye.

Because you will change your mind; because how you love me now at six will wane, change and become something different; and because I love you so much that the very thought of that change makes me weep . . .

'I think I have some suntan lotion in my eyes.' She coughed.

'Oh.' Oscar shrugged and despite the bob of the vessel, gripping with his toes, he shifted over towards the starboard side of the boat and hurled his shell booty into the Atlantic.

Rachel didn't recall leaving the car, but evidently she had because she now stood at the foot of the grand, sweeping staircase. She looked towards the kitchen and saw Cee-Cee slumped over the countertop with her head on her arms.

'Cee-Cee,' she called softly.

'Oh! Oh! Sweet Lord in his heaven.' Cee-Cee, whose face bore the evidence of tears, ran from the kitchen and stopped short in front of

Rachel, as if suddenly aware that theirs was not a tactile relationship and remembering her role as housekeeper.

'We . . . we can't find him, Cee-Cee. We can't find Oscar! They made me come back . . .' She spoke with a slight slur to her voice.

'They will be looking, they will.' The housekeeper spoke words designed to reassure.

'Is . . . is he here? Did he come home?' she whispered.

Cee-Cee shook her head and pushed the dishcloth in her hand over her face, whether to hide her own distress or shield herself from Rachel's she wasn't sure.

Time again slipped and Rachel didn't remember climbing the stairs, but evidently she had, because now she stood in the entrance to their bedroom. Exhaustion pulled her to the wide, freshly laundered bed, but she was also jumpy, as if every fibre of her being urged her towards the balcony from which she had an uninterrupted view of the sea.

'How are you feeling, Mrs Croft?' It was the doctor's voice. She didn't know he had come too and yet there he was, magicked from the ether.

How do I feel? She blinked away the tears that gathered.

Like I have just fallen to earth.

And I am made of glass.

She looked at the doctor and realised James was standing next to him. 'I don't know,' she managed.

'I think it best you rest now. Try to get some sleep.' He gestured towards the bed.

Rachel looked at him with a narrowed gaze and softly shook her head. 'My son, Oscar, he's missing. He's out there somewhere.' She pointed at the ocean, because this man must not know or might have forgotten. Surely if he knew of the situation, then neither he nor anyone else would have taken her from the place where Oscar had gone missing and forced her back here to this ivory castle. Her fear, sadness and impotence sat on her chest like a physical weight. It prevented her from taking a full breath. She felt her body crushed beneath it.

'Yes.' He nodded, again avoiding looking directly at her. 'I know, and rest assured there are lots of people out looking, but you getting ill or collapsing with exhaustion is not going to help anyone. Quite the opposite.' His words were blunt, but his delivery kind.

'He's, he's seven. He is seven.'

With a shiver snaking over her skin, she walked with a wobble to the bed and fell on to it. Keeping her eyes on the window and with the glimmer of distant blue stretching for miles and miles, she gave in to the pull of slumber, talking in her mind to her little boy, as she drifted. *Don't be scared, my darling. Don't be scared, Oscar. I will find you. I will. I love you . . . always . . . I'm right here . . .*

Rachel sat up with a jolt, thankful to find herself in her bed. She had had the most horrific dream, too awful to recount.

Oscar! She kept picturing him waving at her from the other side of the swimming pool or the opposite sofa in the sitting room or from the back of the car, but always, always just out of reach.

The instant throb of a headache behind her eyes and the bolt of sadness in her chest told her that it had been no dream.

Gently she pulled herself into a sitting position and swivelled her legs around, pushing the soles of her feet on to the cool floor.

'I'm here.' She looked up at the sound of James's voice, which came from the wide wicker chair in the corner. James, the man she had chosen to marry, the man she believed could fix anything, the man who would always fight for what she wanted, needed. He had let them bring her back to the house, when all she wanted was to be on the ocean, close to her son.

'Is there any news?' She hardly dared ask. 'Have they . . . have they found . . . ?'

'No.' He spoke with what sounded like a throat full of grit. 'Nothing.'

'How long did I sleep?'

'Less than an hour,' he croaked, reaching out his hands, beckoning her to him.

Ignoring the gesture she made her way out on to the balcony and sat, scanning the water. Suddenly, she sat forward and gasped, alerted by a swell of white a few metres from the shore. She pointed, her eyes narrowed and her teeth hooked on her bottom lip. 'What's that? What, what is that movement? Something . . .' She let this hang as she placed the flat of her palm over her heart.

James rushed outside and stood at the balcony edge, trying to follow her pointing finger.

'Where?' It was infectious, this crumb of hope cast in his direction, this comforting diversion, the small swell of optimism in her tone. James appeared to catch the verbal lasso and held it fast as he craned his neck, shielding his eyes. 'Where?'

'There! James, there! Just off the shore. It could be something; it looks like . . .' She jumped up and stood by his side, as if this metre or so might give further clarity to her vision. But she had lost sight of it. It had gone.

'I need binoculars. You need to get me some binoculars,' she whispered.

Rachel stumbled backward and slid into the chair she had only recently vacated. Her tears again fell and she did nothing to stop them. This was her new normal. Her husband walked forward and dropped to his knees; his tears matching her own.

'Rachel.' He seemed to be calling to her, which struck her as odd, as he was so close. 'Rachel,' he cried again.

The telephone on the dressing table rang. She spun around and jumped up, racing back inside.

'Cee-Cee will get it,' James called after her. 'She is pretty upset, but said she wants to stay here. I asked her if she wouldn't mind getting the door and answering the—'

Ignoring him, Rachel lunged for the phone and grabbed the receiver, casting him a look. She didn't want Cee-Cee to get it! Was he stupid? It could be the police! She needed to speak to them!

'Mrs Croft?'

'Yes.' She held the phone close to her face with the lift of hope in her heart.

'My name is Elspeth Richardson and I work for the *Hamilton Daily*. We have heard police reports that your son has drowned somewhere off the coast of Spanish Point; would you care to comment? I know this must be a difficult time for you, but our readers—'

Rachel let the phone fall from her shaking hand. She turned to head for the bathroom. James, on high alert, grabbed the receiver from the floor. 'Who is this?' he asked sternly.

Clicking the bathroom door closed behind her, she heard the rise of anger in his voice, a tone that previously would have made her feel love for him and his assumed role of protector. 'How dare you call me like this? How did you get our number? No! I will not give you any comment and don't you dare print anything about our son, about us – don't you fucking dare!'

Rachel heard the tears in his voice and sat on the toilet with the seat down. She bent forward and placed her head on her knees. She heard her husband yell and then the smash of china against the floor tiles. This she understood, barely managing to contain her desire to smash everything she could lay her hands to.

Standing slowly, she pulled the dressing gown, now dried stiff with sea salt, around her form; it did nothing to warm her. She leaned against the wall and noted the fresh, white, fluffy towels that Cee-Cee had placed on the rail. The glass shower door gleamed and the sinks and mirror were all smear free. She hated the pristine perfection of it all, knowing her boy was in the cool salt water. She decided to change into the pale-grey dressing gown that hung on a hook by the shower, thinking it might help bring warmth to her bones.

Gently, she peeled off the white garment. The sleeves and hem were smeared with marks from having been under the ocean and from whatever muck had gathered in the bottom of the police boat. She ran her palm over the bulges in the two front patch pockets and felt the grind of sand between her fingers and the material, deposited no doubt when she had dived into the sea. Dipping her fingers into the space, she scooped out a slug of damp sand, run through with tiny shells and crushed sea matter. A similar dig in the other pocket yielded the same. She ran the pad of her thumb over the sludge and felt tears thicken in her throat and drip once more from her eyes, which were now swollen and red. This paste cupped in her palm was from the place where Oscar had gone and she was overcome with an urgent, desperate need to preserve it.

With her one free hand, she pulled open the drawers of the vanity unit, yanking out packets of tissues, cotton buds, hotel freebie sewing kits and sanitary items, none of which she was hunting for. The search in the second drawer was equally fruitless. Running into the bedroom, she barely registered James sitting in the armchair in the corner, flopped forward with shards of a vase scattered around his feet and bent flower stems lying forlornly in a pool of water. Sitting down on her side of the bed, she ran her hand around at the back of the shelf on her nightstand and pulled out a Tic-Tac box, about a third full. She flipped the lid with her thumb and disgorged the orange and lime contents, before using the box to scoop the sand, pushing the remainder of it in with her thumb.

Gripping it in her palm, she took comfort from its weight before rubbing the smooth side along her cheek.

Where are you, Oscar? Where are you, my darling?

She made her way across the cool, pale-tiled floor and out on to the balcony. Carefully, as if her limbs were made of fine china, she lowered herself once again into the wooden steamer chair that sat opposite its matching twin with a small table between the two, perfect for a glass of something cold or a novel to rest on when such things had mattered.

Their whitewashed home in the parish of Pembroke was grand by any standards, and like many along this strip on the North Shore Road, owned and maintained by companies specialising in insurance and reinsurance – the largest employers on the island. She remembered when they arrived, four years ago – *four years*? It felt simultaneously like the blink of an eye and a lifetime. That first time she had opened the French doors of their bedroom and walked out on to this most magnificent space with a perfect view of the sea and the big, big blue sky!

'Oh my God, James!'

She had stood with her hand over her mouth and tears in her eyes; this was everything she had hoped for and more. Oscar, a toddler, had run out and walked right to the edge of the balcony, jumping up and down and laughing.

'Don't go near the glass, I don't like it,' she had urged.

James laughed. 'He is fearless, and don't worry, darling; it's toughened. He's not going anywhere.'

He walked slowly towards her and stood behind her with his arms wrapped around her waist as he kissed the back of her neck. 'Didn't I promise you paradise?' She leaned her head back against his chest, inhaling the glorious scent of him. This view. This life. This was the reason she had eventually agreed to leave their lovely flat in Richmond, Surrey, her friend, Vicky, her parents in Bristol, indeed all that was familiar to her. This was to be her consolation: year-round sunshine, a house that she had dreamed of and a view of the big, big blue sea.

'I love you,' she had breathed, turning and kissing his face.

We should have stayed in England. I could have kept you safe there, darling. An ordinary life. A safe life. We would never have been on the boat, never have been at sea . . .

James appeared to her left, casting a shadow. She continued to stare out at the water, looking for any sign of movement.

'Rach.'

She looked briefly towards him and away again.

'I spoke to your parents and I left a message for mine. They were the hardest calls I have ever had to make. It was terrible.'

'You shouldn't be saying anything yet, we just don't know,' she whispered.

'Rach,' he began again, his voice thick with yet more tears, 'I don't know what to do. I don't know what to say.' He spoke with a tremor to his tone before giving in to the sob that robbed him of speech.

She stared at him now. 'I can't even . . .' she began, her mind searching and failing to find the right words, the words that might begin to convey her utter desolation and her complete and total preoccupation with thoughts of Oscar. 'I can't even think of you.'

She would never forget the look on his face, the beginning of realisation that they had both lost so much more than their son.

He rallied a little. 'Mackenzie is downstairs. We need to go and answer some questions when you are ready.'

'More questions?'

'Yes. More questions.' He wiped his eyes on the sleeve of his shirt. 'I'm going to have a shower and then we'll go down together?'

She nodded, her eyes fixed on the ocean. The sun was starting to dull and the thought of the darkness that would blanket the island sent a jolt of fear through her gut.

I can't stand it. I can't stand the thought of you out there waiting for me. I think you will be hungry or cold or scared . . . And just like that she was wailing again, loud and unrestrained, a noise that came from deep within; a desperate, visceral outpouring of her pain.

James, alerted by the noise, ran from the bathroom in his towel, evidently about to jump into the shower.

'It's okay, Rach, it's okay!' Dropping to his knees he held her tightly in his arms, as she screamed.

'It's not okay!' She flailed, beating her fists on his chest, and he let her. 'It's not okay! It's not okay! It's not okay! Where is he, James? Where is my boy? I want him home! I want him here with me!'

'Shh . . .' he cooed, gripping the back of her head with his palm, trying fruitlessly to bring comfort.

Mackenzie had taken a seat at the kitchen table. He had removed his cap and it now sat next to a glass of iced tea. His notepad was open and she noticed the illegible scrawl of notes that he no doubt wrote as they occurred. She pulled out the chair opposite him and jumped as Cee-Cee placed a mug of strong tea in front of her.

Rachel barely noticed the woman's hollow, sad expression. But she heard the sound their housekeeper made, a quiet but continual whimpering, that was interrupted only when she drew a snatch of breath through her tears. She watched as Cee-Cee ran her fingers over the melamine plate on the countertop, a plate with Spider-Man on it, Oscar's favourite and one on which she had placed countless croissants, sandwiches, slices of toast . . .

Thank you, Cee-Cee.

You are welcome, my little darling!

Rachel placed her little box of sand on the table and cupped the mug in her palms. 'Thank you, Cee-Cee,' she managed, glad of the prop.

James stood leaning against the countertop. She thought he looked grey, like a thing once shiny and full, now faded and deflated, and wondered if she were similarly altered in such a short space of time. The look of pity Cee-Cee flashed her told her this was probably true.

'Forensics are still going over the boat, but there is no sign of Oscar on it.'

Rachel stared at him with a crease to the top of her nose; did they think there was any chance that they hadn't searched the vessel front to back and inside out? Of course they had; this was a waste of time!

'They have also said that at this time they can find no evidence of any struggle or distinguishing marks that might indicate an altercation or violence.'

'What do you mean? Why are you saying that to us?' She banged the table with her flattened palm. 'Of course there isn't! We had a lovely evening. We . . . he . . . we had supper and he was laughing.'

'It is standard procedure in any unexplained disappearance for us to explore all possibilities.' Mackenzie nodded. 'We are just doing our job.'

'There wasn't any violence.' She hated the shape of the word in her mouth but thought it best to press the point. 'We woke up and he was gone!' Again, the onset of tears threatened to defeat her. 'We have told you this over and over. He was gone and we need to be out there looking for him!' She pointed towards the water, disliking the croak to her voice, feeling it somehow diluted the strength of her message.

'I promise you, Mrs Croft, we have teams searching and they will resume at first light tomorrow.'

'Resume? They can't stop! They can't stop looking!' She raised her voice. 'That's when he will need us the most, in the dark! You can't leave him out there in the dark! I am begging you, please, please don't leave him out there on his own!'

Cee-Cee left the room, as if this raw outburst were more than she could bear or more than she felt Rachel would want her to witness. Rachel saw Mackenzie and her husband exchange a knowing look and it infuriated her – why wasn't James demanding they stay out looking? She glowered at him as she laid her hand on the Tic-Tac box.

'You said you were looking for other boats, boats that might have come and picked him up, his . . . his friends . . .' She let this trail, unwilling to admit to just how unlikely it sounded, even to her ears.

Mackenzie licked his lips and shifted his position in the chair. 'We can find no evidence of any other boats, either approaching or docking near *Liberté*. We will of course keep checking.'

She didn't believe him and this sent another lightning streak of frustration through her core. 'Did you ask his friends and his friends' parents?' she fired.

Mackenzie nodded and she saw the first etchings of sympathy on his brow. 'We did, but I promise you, Mrs Croft—'

'I don't want you to keep promising me things!' Again she banged the tabletop. 'I just want you to find Oscar and bring him home!' Her voice cracked again. 'Bring him home to me now!'

There was a second or two of hush before Mackenzie turned to James and asked, 'What kind of child is Oscar?'

'He's lovely. Lovely.' She spoke, through her tears, on her husband's behalf. 'He's funny and sweet.'

'Is he boisterous? Does he wander off? Is he impulsive?' Mackenzie waited. It was James who responded.

'He is confident and enthusiastic about the world he lives in. He likes to try everything; he's not one of life's observers.'

Mackenzie gave a single nod. 'Can Oscar swim?'

She watched her husband brighten a little, his lips set in a thin line. 'Yes. He's a good swimmer. We have a pool and he's been swimming since he was little.'

'I took him for lessons when he was a baby. In Richmond where we used to live. In England,' she added. She pictured him in his water-proof nappy, his chubby body snug inside her outstretched arms as she dunked him under the water and watched as he came up giggling, surprised but happy.

Mackenzie made a note in his book. 'Would you describe him as a strong swimmer, a weak swimmer or somewhere in between?'

'Strong.'

She and James answered at the same time. Again Mackenzie lifted his pen.

Her mind raced. 'He *is* a strong swimmer, James, isn't he?' She sat forward, looking at her husband, as a thought formed and her tone bordered on hopeful. 'Mackenzie, you need to find out where the closest boats to ours were and check if he swam to them!' She allowed herself a small smile. 'Or if one picked him up. He is a strong swimmer! He could have got to a boat! They might have him now and maybe, erm, they don't speak English and he can't tell them his name and they don't know what he's saying! You need to check that!' she urged.

Mackenzie blinked and laid his pen on his pad. 'As I said, we are exploring all possibilities.' He drew breath and she instinctively stood, thinking that if she ran away then she wouldn't have to hear what he was about to say. She felt the policeman's eyes on her as she crossed the kitchen and stood next to James, her safe harbour, and she like a little rowboat, sheltered in his shadow from the encroaching storm.

'When someone falls or jumps overboard . . .' He paused. 'There is data, evidence . . .' He paused again, longer this time.

Rachel shook her head and wrapped her arms around her trunk.

'And the data suggests,' Mackenzie continued, 'that a fit adult in warm water can survive for a while, hours, even. But in the cooler Atlantic and if someone has banged their head as they've fallen in or been surprised and taken a breath or is young or old or weak – then that is very, very rare. Data shows that it is far more likely people do not survive beyond seconds, minutes, because of an accident, trauma, shock, and so for a little boy . . .'

Data. Data. Data. Data! We are not talking about bloody data; we are talking about Oscar! My child!

'I think I would know if' – she faltered – 'if he had come to harm.'

I will never use the word

D.

E.

A.

D.

She spelled it out in her head. *I will not use that word.*

'Why do you say that?' Mackenzie looked at her quizzically.

'Because' – she swallowed – 'because I am his mum.' Her voice broke. 'I am his mummy.' Her voice was now barely more than a rasping whisper. 'And I would know. I would feel it.' She placed her hand on her chest. 'I would feel it here, but right now, all I feel is that he needs me.'

'Okay.' Mackenzie reached for his cap and closed his notebook.

'Can I ask you a question?' She wrung her palms, kitting her fingers at her chest.

'Of course.' Mackenzie placed his cap on his head and turned it into position.

'How, how long exactly do these fit adults in warm water survive for? How long can they be in the sea?'

She noticed that he looked first at James, and she again hated the feeling that the two were conspiring. Mackenzie coughed to clear his throat, either to tell a lie or to try for deflection, an embellishment of the truth. She didn't know which. He gave a slight shrug to his left shoulder. 'I think about six hours is a record, but the circumstances were quite unique.' He let his arms rise and fall to his thighs.

Six hours . . .

Rachel took these two words and used them as a solid foundation on which to build hope. She looked at the oversized clock above the breakfast nook. It was coming up to six in the evening. They first noticed him gone at six forty-five that morning.

Eleven hours.

Eleven hours, it was a new record. Please . . . please come home to me, Oscar! Come home now! She prayed silently, looking out of the window into the evening sky.

CEE-CEE

Cee-Cee took a seat at her kitchen table and unscrewed the lid from Grandma Sally's ink pen. Carefully, she folded the top sheet of the notepad over and leaned forward, resting her forearms on the mahogany table.

~~Dear Mr and Mrs Croft~~

She crossed it through and started again.

~~Dear Rachel and James, It is with~~

This was also not quite right, and what had moments earlier felt like such a simple task now seemed almost beyond her means.

Cee-Cee tapped the tortoiseshell pen against her teeth before placing it on top of the notepad and abandoning the idea. Instead, she used an earthenware jug to scoop up the water from the green washing-up bowl in the sink, with which she would water the loquat tree. She was the third generation to lovingly tend its roots. Her reward would be the soft yellow/orange fruit that could best be described as a cross between a mango and a peach.

She thought about the letter waiting to be written and looked out over the clustered fern fronds that lined the roadside, giving way to the view of the ocean.

'I suppose I could tell you both how I felt about little Oscar.' She smiled at the image of the boy who had come into her life, transforming the nature of her job at the big house on the North Shore Road. Her tears naturally followed and she let them fall. It seemed appropriate somehow to honour her broken heart with this physical display. She remembered those first few weeks, when she had got to know the three-year-old a little better.

'So.' She had beamed at him. 'Your name is Oscar and you have come *all* the way over the sea from England to Bermuda!'

He held the duvet up to his chest and nodded, eyes wide. 'On a plane!' He smiled.

'On a plane? Well, goodness me, I have never been on a plane.' Cee-Cee had sat in the wicker chair by the side of the single bed. 'I think you and I are going to be friends. And do you know the best way to become friends?'

Oscar shook his head.

'It's to tell stories! They are the way that people get to know each other all over the world and they always have been. My grandma told me stories and her grandma told her stories and I told my baby stories.' She took a sharp intake of breath, as if something sharp had lodged in her breast, a memory that pierced.

'I like stories,' the three-year-old whispered.

'Who doesn't?' She chuckled. 'When people wave at each other in the street, when they say "How's the weather for you?" or "How you doing?", that's storytelling, catching up, and it's very, very important. Whether written on a page or spoken from your mouth, stories are what joins us all together.'

She looked up at the sound of the bedroom door creaking open. It was Rachel, the young woman of the house, her new boss and Oscar's mother. She was pretty with long, shiny, dark hair and painted finger-nails. Cee-Cee hoped she wasn't a young woman who placed impor-tance on such things. She had no time for vanity or selfishness.

'How are we doing? Are you still awake, Oscar?' She walked in and folded her arms over her fancy red evening frock. 'I think we are going to head off now, Cee-Cee.' She bit her lip. 'Is it okay to call you Cee-Cee? Or is Mrs something better? I . . . I didn't know . . .'

Cee-Cee sensed her nerves; still so young and finding her way, only a few days into this new house, this new life. 'Cee-Cee is just fine.' She gave a small nod.

'We'll be back by eleven, tops. You have our numbers?'

'We have everything we need and we know how to get hold of you if we don't.'

She smiled at the young woman who clearly knew very little about the way of the island; everyone knew everyone else. A request could be made in St David's Head and with no more than a chain of hollering to your relatives that request would be answered in no time from someone up at Royal Naval Dockyard.

'Okay.' Rachel swallowed. 'It's the first time we've left him here and it feels a bit . . .'

'Of course it does. But Oscar will be fine. Don't worry.'

'Okay,' she whispered again. 'I don't really want to go – it's a work thing for James.'

'I am sure you will have a lovely time.'

'Okay. I can do this!' Rachel straightened her shoulders, balled her fists and lifted her chin. 'See you soon! Love you, Oscar! Night night, Mr Bob!' She blew a kiss to the boy and his knitted teddy that nestled in the crook of his neck.

The door closed and Cee-Cee smiled at the little boy.

'Where's Mummy gone?' He looked towards the hallway.

'She'll be back in no time at all, you'll see. Now, where were we?'

'Story,' he reminded, followed by a big, big yawn.

'Oh, you are so smart to remember that!' She clicked her tongue against the roof of her mouth. 'I don't know whether to tell you about the day the whale came or the pirate shipwreck with a cargo full of gold!' Cee-Cee looked down at the little boy whose head had fallen to one side and whose eyes were flickering shut. It was only minutes until he snored like a tiny dormouse: sweet, snuffly and cute as a button.

'Well, little Oscar, you sleep and you dream. And I will sit here and watch you. I will watch you until your mommy and daddy come home. Just like I promised.'

◆ ◆ ◆

She finished watering the tree and considered this.

Maybe I should stop overthinking it. Maybe I should just write as I talk in my heart and head. She liked the idea of this very much. Cee-Cee went back inside the house and sat at the table.

With her pen in her hand she folded back the top sheet of the notepad and she began.

Dear Mr and Mrs Croft, Rachel, James,

I write because sometimes I find that words that get knotted in your throat are smooth and ordered when you put pen to paper. I see your loss. I feel your loss and it takes me back to a time when I did not feel life was worth living. A time when my pain was such that I prayed for the angels to take me under their wing and relieve me from my burden. Of course they did nothing of the sort, their message loud and clear: Who are you, Miss Cecilly Symmons, to think you can command the angels? So I lived a half-life. A quiet life. Until I met Oscar. He didn't care for my sadness. He didn't have time for my reflection, no sir. He ran at me and took my hand and pulled me from the gloom. He made me chase around that house playing games. He brought me joy, that little boy who loved me. He made me love life again! All by loving him. You see, I thought I had been denied the chance to raise a child, but I had not. That chance was given to me at a time in my life when I had no right to expect it. Not that the joy was any less for that. So I thank you both, and I thank you for Oscar, and as God is my witness, if I can hold his hand and ease his path to heaven then that will give my life a meaning greater than I could ever have dreamed. With love to you, amen.

Cee-Cee

TWO

Rachel had had the strangest sensation of someone watching her while she slept; in truth she had rather liked it, taken comfort from it. She was frustrated now that she had woken here in this present. She lay on her side and stared towards the ocean. Three days on and there was still no place she wanted to be. She eyed the tablets on the nightstand, comforted by their very presence. They were a mild sedative prescribed by the young doctor whose name she now knew was Dr Kent, like Clark, but alas he was without any special powers. How she wished this were not the case. How she wished he could make time go backward like the Superman of her youth, flying faster and faster the wrong way around the earth until he stopped it spinning and sent it back a little and then with his grief exhausted, he had been able to swoop down and take his love into his arms and she was present, not gone; restored. Like magic.

How can I do that? How can I make time go backward? I have read books – The Time Traveler's Wife, The Time Machine – are they true? Who knows? Maybe fiction is a cover! Who can I ask? Maybe there are people on this earth who can take me back to that moment when I shouted 'Love you!' from the shower room and then James asked me, 'How about another glass of fizz? It's not going to drink itself,' and I would say no! I would scream no! NO! NO! NO! And I would run to Oscar's cabin and I would sit on the floor in front of the door and I would watch him sleep, watch him move in slumber, never leaving my post and if he stirred, I would say, 'Go back to sleep, my darling, Mummy's right here.' Oh, oh, to have that moment again!

She crept down the stairs in her nightdress and hovered in the hallway. She looked through to the kitchen and stared at James through the open door, feeling her top lip curl in an expression of distaste. He was eating breakfast cereal. Eating! Filling a stomach with fuel for the day ahead. It was alien to her how he could do any such thing, how could he dance to the pulse of life when for her, time was fractured and her needs reduced to simply crying and seeking oblivion. How could he carry on? Did he not care? Or was it simply that he didn't care as much? It had to be that, and she hated him a little for it because if he didn't care as much as she did, wasn't as affected, then she truly was all alone.

'Morning,' he called from the table, she was aware now that he looked straight at her. 'I . . . I didn't know whether to wake you. I came up for a couple of hours, but mainly I sat on the sofa last night.'

She nodded. *I didn't ask.*

'Do you want some coffee, love, or . . . or some toast?' He faltered, his voice soft.

'Do I want some toast?' She stared at him and her body folded. 'I can't eat. I can't.' She shook her head. 'I don't know how you can, to be honest.'

She watched as he slowly placed the spoon on the table and swallowed hard, as if he had a lump in his throat.

'This isn't a competition of grief. This isn't about who hurts the most, who has suffered the most.' He spoke gently.

Me. I can't say it out loud, but that is me. I win! I win this fucking competition because I am destroyed but you – you seem to be functioning. You can exist! I win! I fucking win!

'I know that, James.' She blinked.

'I need to . . . I need to try. I need to.' He broke away in tears, burying his face in his hands as he sobbed noisily, his shoulders shaking.

Slowly she made her way back up the stairs and fell into the bed only recently vacated where she pulled the duvet over her legs, ready for her next bout of oblivion. Her tears slipped from her eyes, tracing a familiar path over her nose and temples, dripping into the already damp pillowslip. Glancing at the clock was her private torture. She tried not to, but it was as if her eyes were drawn to the digital display by something stronger than her will.

◆ ◆ ◆

When she woke she realised she had again slept away most of the day.

Sixty hours. Since I noticed him gone.

Six was a record.

Ten times six, sixty . . . don't think about it. Don't think about it!

As her eyelids, which felt full of grit, grew heavy, she heard the bedroom door creak open. Cee-Cee crept forward and bent low. 'You need to eat something.' Her tone, as ever, quiet, calm and matter-of-fact. Steady.

Rachel shook her head; the thought of eating was repellent.

'I can't. I can't eat.'

'You need to try.'

She watched the woman place a dish of chopped fruit on the nightstand.

'Cee-Cee – I wish . . .' Her voice was a little slurred. 'I wish I could turn back time.'

The woman took a deep breath that was part sigh. 'There isn't a single soul the world over who hasn't thought the very same thing. But truly there ain't no point in wishing; you have to let yourself heal. Sleep and heal.' Cee-Cee walked over to the bed and smoothed the hair from

Rachel's forehead. It was an unusual act of intimacy and warmth and she was grateful for the human contact that gave the smallest lift to her spirits. Rachel reached up and held her arm. 'Can . . . can you hold me, Cee-Cee?'

'Oh, sweet child!' The housekeeper sat on the edge of the bed and held her in her arms, rocking her slowly like she was an infant. Rachel laid her face against her chest and breathed slowly, holding on to her tightly, as if she were a lifeline.

'I can't do it, Cee-Cee. I can't be like this. I need to be out looking,' she whispered, before closing her eyes again.

'Shh. Sleep, child. Sleep.'

In her pre-doze state she thought about the conversation between her and James about four months after they had moved into the house on North Shore Road. Cee-Cee had kind of come with the property, having worked for the previous incumbents for decades. The reference they'd supplied had been more a glowing testimonial of someone they'd clearly held deep in their hearts, rather than a professional recommendation for a member of staff.

Rachel had not only been glad of the help, something she had never had before, but also Cee-Cee's quiet efficiency meant that finding her feet in this new house and new island was a doddle. The woman took care of everything, and she was just wonderful, wonderful with Oscar! When Cee-Cee spoke to him, held him, her whole demeanour changed, as if he lit something within her. At the very sight of him her face broke into a smile, her eyes widened and her hands joined together, as if giving thanks for his very presence.

Of course it was no substitute for having Rachel's mum on speed dial and only a couple of hours away, or being able to call on her friends if she had a question or had run out of Calpol, but listening to Cee-Cee sing to her boy as she bathed him, watching the extreme care and attention with which she pressed his clothes, told him stories and prepared his food – it warmed Rachel's heart and it certainly glad-dened Oscar's.

There was no doubt he loved her.

'Cee-Cee! Cee-Cee!' He would run to her, launching into her arms when she arrived in the morning or when he came out of school.

'Careful now, little Oscar,' Cee-Cee would scold mockingly. 'I am not a young woman any more and you will knock me over one of these fine days and then who is going to fix your breakfast?' This she delivered before kissing his face and holding him close to her, as if relishing the contact.

The two played endless games of hide-and-seek. Oscar liked to hide and Cee-Cee would call out, 'I'm coming to find you!' often without properly applying herself as, with a small wink in Rachel's direction, she went about her business. When she did locate him – behind a curtain, sitting under a cushion or in the bottom of the closet – he would ask, 'How many counts, Cee-Cee? How long did it take for you to find me?' And she would reply, 'Oh, hundreds and it took an hour!' This pretty much satisfied him.

'How old do you think Cee-Cee is?' Rachel asked once, as she flicked through her magazine, sitting on the steamer chair on the bal-cony next to James, who tip-tapped into his laptop. He worked ridicu-lously long hours and when he did finally manage to extricate himself from the office, would then spend a further hour or two working at home. She nagged him occasionally but knew that this was part of the price they paid for this house, this life.

He looked up at her and smiled. 'Well, actually I *know* how old she is, so you guess.'

Rachel considered the housekeeper's wiry frame, smooth, burnished skin and her nippy movement.

'I'm going to say late fifties, but she looks good!' She tilted her head to one side.

James laughed. 'Wrong.'

'Older or younger?' she quizzed.

'Cee-Cee is seventy.' He held her eyeline, waiting for her reaction. She pulled off her sunglasses and squealed her response. 'Seventy? Are you kidding me?'

'I am not.' He sucked his teeth. 'I did a double take when I saw and had to check. It's true; she is seventy.'

'Flipping heck, I want to go to the secret fountain that she drinks from; she looks amazing!'

'That's what island life does for you. Doubt she has a worry in the world,' James surmised.

'I think she's beautiful.' Rachel looked out to sea, picturing the older woman's high cheekbones and deep-set grey eyes, her wide mouth, and beautiful, elegant hands.

'I guess she could be, but good God, it's hard to see past the fact that most of the time she looks so *miserable!*' he shuddered.

'Don't be mean, James.' Nonetheless, she giggled over the top of her Diet Coke.

'I am not! I'm just saying! My grandma used to have a phrase – "a face that could curdle milk" – and I never fully appreciated it until I started to look at Cee-Cee over the breakfast table each morning.' He reached out his hand and ran his fingers up along her smooth, toned calf. 'Do you think she was born that way?'

'No!' she tutted. 'And you are being mean, James, and I don't like it.'

'I'm only joking with you. You know I love Cee-Cee.'

'No one is born sad.'

'Maybe Cee-Cee is the exception,' he whispered.

It was only a minute later that she heard the shuffle in the bedroom behind them and the light tread of a slipper on the tiled floor. She turned to watch their housekeeper move rhythmically across the room with a stiff broom between her palms, swishing it left and right in a hypnotic dance.

A few days later, mid-morning, Oscar was at school in Hamilton and Rachel sat at the dressing table, slathering cream over her neck and face and jutting her chin to look for the re-emergence of the stubborn stray hair that had taken up residence there. Gripping the tweezers – her weapon of choice – in readiness, she clacked the little metal prongs together as a warning. Announcing her intention to the offending stubble, letting it know it would never be given refuge on her face, not while she was still in possession of her faculties. It was like a battle. It was incredible to her how this woody little interloper seemed to spring up in less time than you would think it possible to cultivate.

Cee-Cee arrived to strip the bed linen from the king-sized bed and fold it into the laundry basket. It must be Friday. As was customary, the beds would then be left bare to 'air' until late afternoon, when fresh-scented sheets would be tucked in just so, and the plump feather pillows decked in immaculately pressed pillowslips. Friday-night bedtime was always her favourite, the scent alone enough to make her dizzy with joy.

'Let me help you, Cee-Cee. I'm only being vain. Truth is I don't bother with make-up and stuff half as much as I used to when I lived in England. It's so hot it just slides off my face!'

As was her way, Cee-Cee ignored her, busy with the task. Rachel pulled off the bottom sheet and folded it into the hands of the housekeeper.

'I hope you don't mind me saying, Cee-Cee, but two things: James told me how old you are and I wanted to say that if at any time the job gets too much for you—'

'It's not too much for me,' she fired back. 'But if you have any complaints—'

'No! God, no! You are absolutely amazing,' she interrupted, keen to reassure her. 'I don't know what I'd do without you. I really don't. I can't imagine being here alone; please don't think that's what I was getting at. I was just going to say that I am more than happy to do more, anything you need me to. In fact, I hate my laziness; it's very seductive, doing nothing, and I can't work here, which is fair enough – jobs for Bermudians is right – but please make use of me. I don't want to step on your toes or interfere when it comes to chores. I know you have a particular way of doing things and I don't want to mess that up. Plus, I know you are the custodian of this house, I am just passing through, but I was thinking that maybe you could sit down sometimes and I can get you a nice cup of tea? How would that be?'

Cee-Cee paused, staring at her as if she were talking nonsense.

'And secondly, I just wanted to say that I can't believe you are knocking seventy. You are beautiful. Really beautiful.'

Rachel felt her face colour. Cee-Cee stuffed the linen into the wicker basket and stood with her hands clasped in front of her.

'I heard what Mr Croft said about me looking miserable and sad.'

'Oh.' The comment was unexpected and she felt the spread of shame across her chest and neck. 'He was joking, ignore him. He can be an idiot sometimes.'

She stared at Cee-Cee, who held her gaze, quite unabashed and undeterred by the awkward nature of the topic.

'He spoke the truth. I am sad, sadder than sad. But I was not born this way. In fact, I was always happy. My childhood was wonderful. Wonderful.'

Rachel took a step forward and placed her hand on Cee-Cee's warm, slender arm. 'Oh Cee-Cee! No! Why are you sad? I hope it's not because of us? I would hate that. We absolutely love having you here, love having you in the house – as I have said, I don't know what we'd do without you! And Oscar just adores you. He really does. You and he have a special bond. You know that, don't you?'

The woman ignored the compliment. 'I'm not sad because of you. I'm not sad because of working here. I like working here—'

'Good! That's good,' she interrupted, relieved.

'The fact is my sadness came to me over five decades ago and that's just how it is.' She shrugged. 'I lost my baby boy. He died.'

The topic was so horrible, the announcement so unexpected, so at odds with the shield of privacy under which the woman ordinarily operated, that it rather threw her.

'Oh, Cee-Cee, he did? That is the most awful thing.' It felt awkward to be the recipient of information so very personal when she didn't know the most basic thing about her. These felt like facts she had no right to.

'Yes. Yes, it is. But there it is. That's what happened. He died.' She nodded.

'How old was he?'

'He was seven weeks old.' The woman did nothing to try to stem the fat tears that fell down her cheeks and dripped from her chin. Rachel jumped to her nightstand and grabbed a fistful of soft tissues, balling them into the housekeeper's hand. Cee-Cee blotted at her distress as she cried unabashed in the bedroom.

'I am so sorry to hear that.' Instinct told her to pull the woman into a tight hug, but Cee-Cee had always kept her distance – never with Oscar, but certainly with her and James – and she was acutely aware of crossing a line, embarrassing her. They were different generations from very different worlds.

'I can't begin to imagine what that must have been like.' Again she laid her hand briefly on her arm and shook her head; this was the truth. 'What was his name?' She felt her embarrassment flare; was it okay to ask for this detail? Did discussing him bring relief or merely prolong the agony of the moment? Rachel swallowed, relieved by the slight lift of a smile to the corners of Cee-Cee's mouth. This tiny memory, this one question enough to bring a flicker of joy.

'He was called Willard after his daddy.'

'Willard,' she repeated, trying to picture a baby with sweet, fat cheeks and the beautiful eyes of his mum.

'And he was perfect.' Cee-Cee shrugged, as if that was all that needed to be said; no reason, no disease, no understanding. Rachel saw the pain etched across her brow.

'It must have been a terrible, terrible thing.'

'It *is* a terrible, terrible thing.' Cee-Cee shot her a look, almost instinctual, a sharp lesson that this pain did not diminish, nor did the shock fade and that the image of a baby boy called Willard, forever stuck at seven weeks old, still had the power to reduce this lady, now in her seventies, to tears. 'Lord only knows that's the truth. It is terrible,' she repeated. 'He was fine.' She looked into the middle distance, as if still struggling to accept that this might have happened. 'I fed him, I put on the cotton nightdress my grandma had sewed for him and he was cosy and fine. I put him in his bassinet on my bed and I went to sit on the terrace, trying to catch the breeze coming up from Warwick Long Bay; it was a fearful hot night. And not more than an hour later I went to check on him and he wasn't right. He was cool.' She shivered, rubbing her arms as if remembering the feel of that temperate skin. 'And that's when I got sad. And I am sad, sadder than sad, and I won't ever stop. Not till I see him again in heaven. Because that is what I believe – that when you get to heaven, you get to gaze upon the thing you loved the most.' Again the corners of her mouth lifted in the beginnings of a smile.

Rachel swallowed; the woman's grief was tangible. It spun a cloak that covered them, there in that beautiful room on that bright, sunshine-filled day. The walls were suddenly dark and the corners gloomy because talk of death pervaded them, coating everything they touched. She felt the rise of discomfort in her gut, but she wanted to show Cee-Cee that she cared and was interested. 'And you didn't have any more children?' She was trying to piece the puzzle together, using snippets of the woman's life. The woman who had a hand in each and every intimate aspect of their lives: who counted while Oscar hid, who sang sweet songs as she bathed him, told him stories, washed their clothes, prepared their food. A woman whom Rachel knew so very little about.

Cee-Cee looked up and drew a breath, straightening her shoulders, as if rallying. 'No more children. No more husband.' And there it was again, an admission so stark it cut the air around them. 'Willard would be fifty on June twenty-fourth. Fifty,' she repeated, as if still trying to figure out how this could have happened, how the boy she'd fed and loved was no longer here and how the sneaky thief of time had stolen decades from right under her nose.

Rachel felt a wave of sorrow and wished she knew what to say, what to do. James was so much better than her in situations like this. It was his skill: the ability to work a room, say the right thing, chameleon-like in his attentions with the right gesture, pitch and always, always with something fast, funny or appropriate up his sleeve that could divert any conversation, anyone.

'I expect you want to get on,' she'd whispered.

'I expect I do.' Cee-Cee lifted her arms wide and folded the bulky duvet cover in half and half again, gathering it into a bundle and placing it in the basket.

Now, she felt Cee-Cee's arms slip from her as she stood, vaguely aware of her creeping from the room. Rachel placed her head on the pillow and closed her eyes.

I sleep.

And then I sleep some more.

It's like someone has shut off my awake valve.

It's like having to navigate in a strange city where each narrow road looks the same; there are no landmarks, no hints and no signs. I am driving fast and yet can't see the road. All I know, is that in one direction lies a sheer cliff and in the other, an open meadow and it's only when I reach one that I shall know which is which.

I am terrified.

I am sad – no, I need a word beyond sad . . . I am bereft.

I am desolate.

I am broken.

I am so broken that what I want to do is put my foot hard to the floor and head for the cliff.

Yes, that's what I want.

So why don't I?

Two things.

Cowardice and the fact that no matter how small, how unlikely, there is the tiniest of chances that I will get to hold my boy in my arms once more,

Yes, just for one second of feeling his face next to mine, I would wear this cloak of grief for ten lifetimes . . .

Rachel sat up quickly in the bed. This was how she woke now – alarmed, gasping for breath and with the churn of sickness at the cloudy thought somewhere at the back of her mind that she had to be somewhere or had missed something very important. As if someone had thrown something cold over her. It usually took a second for her to remember the event that had cleaved open her world. And when she did remember, her tears fell, and it was like it was the first time she had heard the news.

Images of Oscar crowded her thoughts, and the sickness in her gut and the feeling that she needed to get to him were almost paralysing.

Sadder than sad.

These words she now fully understood.

Slipping her arms into her dressing gown, she pulled on some cotton socks; her grief had left her with a permanent chill that made her bones ache and kept her skin dappled in goosebumps. Collecting the Tic-Tac box from the dresser, she ran its smooth surface over her cheek, and with it safely ensconced in her palm, made her way along the hallway. Pausing at Oscar's bedroom door, she placed her hand on the white-painted wood and smiled. This was a little trick she played on herself, picturing him on the other side of the door, either snug in his bed with an open book lifted over his face or sitting cross-legged on his rug with his cars spread around him in a traffic jam. By not opening the door, it was easy to imagine and it helped soften the spike of thoughts that threatened to lance her sanity.

Weakened, she gripped the wooden handrail and trod the wide, curved stairs, making her way across the vast double-height hallway, heading toward the kitchen.

The phone on the table rang. She rushed to it, swallowing the optimism that rose in her throat, able to picture nothing but sweet reunion, the moment when she might take her boy in her arms once again!

Where have you been, my love? On a boat? You swam to a boat? You clever thing! But you are home now and I will never, ever let you go . . .

'Hello?'

'Rachel?'

'Mum,' she managed, caring little for the ricochet of disappointment that echoed around the word.

'Oh, my little love, my little girl! Your dad spoke to James a couple of times and I didn't know whether to call straight away or what to do.' She paused. Rachel cried silently. Her mum spoke softly: 'I have sat up for two nights just thinking about you all and praying, something I haven't done for a long while, but, Rachel, I will try anything and everything. I can't get you out of my mind. I thought you might be sleeping or busy, and truth is we are all just in bits; we don't know what to do for the best, and I am so worried about you. My heart is broken.'

She nodded. *And mine . . . shattered into a million pieces and scattered into the deep, deep sea.*

'Is there any news?'

'No. No news,' she whispered from a throat lined with broken glass so every word cut.

'I just can't . . . I just can't imagine . . . my poor little Oscar. He was such a lovely little thing.'

He is such a lovely little thing. Her brain made the adjustment as her mum continued.

'It doesn't seem real, Rachel; it doesn't seem true and I hate that we are so far away; I feel helpless. I went up to the big Tesco to get some bits in and I was all of a daze. I saw Mrs Hicks and she said I looked peaky and I just broke down right there and then. I abandoned my trolley and Dad was waiting in the car and he didn't know what to do. Should we try to come over? Your dad says we can get a loan and Peter said he could help us with the fare.'

She pictured her parents and brother having the chat around the little kitchen table in their house in Yate. Of course if she wanted them there Rachel would pay for flights – if only all problems could be fixed so simply with a quick flourish of her credit card. 'There's no need to come, Mum, thank you, though. There's nothing to do.' Her response, she knew, was neutral, numb. *Nothing to do that will make a difference or help bring Oscar home, otherwise I would be doing it.*

'I don't really understand. What happened? Did he fall in? I hate boats, you know I do, and I hate the sea and this is why . . .' She faltered. 'My mum, your gran, lost her brother at Dunkirk, never got over it. He was weighed down with his kit and whatnot.' She sniffed and Rachel erased the image that formed, unable to cope with a thought like that. 'I can't stop thinking about that little boy, our lovely little boy. I hear his sweet voice on Skype, "Hello, Nana!" he'd always say, so excited to show me something and talking nineteen to the dozen. And I can't believe he's gone.'

'He's not gone,' she spat. 'We don't know what happened and until we do—'

'But, Rachel, James said that there had been a terrible accident and that he'd been killed, drowned—' Her mum broke away, crying.

'James said that?' She felt an incendiary flash in her veins and hung up the phone. Racing into the kitchen, she spied Cee-Cee at the sink. 'Cee-Cee, where is James?'

Cee-Cee turned slowly, her lack of speed in itself an irritation.

'Where's James?' she fired.

'I think in the garage.' The woman blinked and looked as if she had been about to say more.

Rachel dashed out of the back door, along the path and around the house. She yanked open the side door to the triple garage and almost ran to where he stood. There was a second where she registered the look of surprise on his thinned face.

'Rach,' he began.

'How could you? How could you tell my mum the things you did?'

'What things?' He blinked.

'You made it very clear to her that things are . . . final. You gave her no hope!'

'Because I need to be able to tell someone what's going on, and I can't talk to you.'

'That's bullshit!' she shouted. 'You have no right to say that stuff to her, to anyone!'

He opened his mouth as if to speak, but closed it again.

She looked down, noticing for the first time several envelopes on the arm of the chair. He followed her gaze.

'There have been hundreds of emails too, literally hundreds. One very long one from Vicky and Gino. I only skimmed it, but it was very kind. Vicky called, she left you a message, sent you her love.'

She nodded, unable to picture having the conversation with her best friend at home, the girl she had grown up with, the first person after James she had shared news of her pregnancy with.

Guess what? Guess what? She had held the tops of her arms and they had jumped together like a skipping duo.

Clever, clever girl! Vicky had hugged her tightly and kissed her face.

Rachel only saw Vicky when she went home, but they regularly swapped emails and messages. It was one of those cherished relationships where they simply picked up where they had left off. She half sat, half collapsed into the chair and reached for the envelopes. James wiped his face with his palm. 'I was putting them out of sight; I figured you weren't ready. There are others.' He paused as she gathered them to her chest. Most had stamps, a couple had been hand-delivered. Some addressed to Mr and Mrs Croft, others to Oscar's mum and dad. She placed her finger in the small gap under the gummed flap of an envelope and pulled out the pale-blue card with a white dove on the front. Gingerly, she opened the stiff card and read aloud, '*So sorry to hear of your terrible loss. Keeping you in our thoughts and prayers, Mr and Mrs Wentworth.*' She looked at her husband. 'I don't know who they are.'

He shook his head. 'I don't know who most of them are. We've had dozens, from all over the island, all walks of life.'

She handed him the card and felt a flare in her chest. 'How dare they send things like this to us? How dare they? Everyone has given up on him. These seem so final!'

'I think' – he coughed – 'I think it's that everyone is a few steps ahead of you, of us, and that's easy for them because they are not torn apart like we are.'

'Well you need to set them straight! There is still the chance . . .' She paused, losing her thread. 'You need to stand up for him, James!'

'I . . .' He gasped.

'What's the matter with you? We don't know anything, nothing! He might be on a boat, he might, he might . . .' She looked up at the ceiling, trying to find the words.

'He might what?' He spoke through a quivering mouth, battling a fresh wave of tears as he took a step towards her. His words when they came were slow, considered. 'He's not coming back, Rachel. He's gone. He died and the fact that you won't accept it is making me dread every phone call, every knock on the door because when it gets confirmed, when they find . . .' He paused. 'I am so afraid of how you are going to react, how you are going to cope that it is making this living hell even worse, if you can possibly imagine that.' He rubbed his eyes and face and slumped down on the battered armchair that sat by the wall, surrounded by an assortment of cardboard boxes and old tennis rackets, buckets and spades, inflatables, and a mountain of sandals and beach shoes; the detritus of family life. 'I feel like it's okay for you, you only have to worry about you, you have submitted entirely to your grief, but I don't have that luxury. I need to keep things going and I am so, so worried about you.' He looked up.

'You think it's okay for me? Did you really just say that?' Her chest heaved.

'I . . . I didn't mean it like that, I meant—'

'You don't know anything!' she screamed with her fists clenched, white-knuckled, as she shook.

She watched as his face crumpled once again and his head hung down. 'Please, please, Rachel.'

'Don't you "please, Rachel" me! I will not give up on him, I won't! He might be on a boat, he might—'

'No! He is not on a fucking boat! It has been three days and if he was on a boat or had been picked up by a boat or had swum to a boat – if anyone knew anything, they would have come forward! We would know, it would have been picked up by now.' He raised his voice. 'It was an accident. He either fell or jumped, we will never know, but he is gone! He is gone!'

With teeth bared, she lunged for him. James caught her by the wrists as she sank, hollowed by grief and weakened by sadness, falling until her head nestled in his lap. He held her fast, until her limbs stopped thrashing and her breathing steadied. They were silent and still for some minutes, as the distasteful dance came to an end.

'I can't accept it, James. I can't let myself think it might be true. I want to stop every clock. Break every watch. I don't want there to be any more time or any future, not for anyone if there isn't for one him and there isn't one for me.' She whispered the admission. 'It's like the universe has placed two hooks here and here – one through my heart one through my head – so that every breath, every movement, even blinking, hurts and it's exhausting, but necessary because if these hooks are removed . . .' She closed her eyes, tightly. 'They are the only things keeping me upright. Keeping me anchored. Without them I'm nothing, just a puddle of skin and bones melted by grief.'

'I know.' He knotted his fingers in her hair and soothed her scalp. 'I know.'

She continued to talk. 'I can't stand it. I don't know how I am going to get through this. It's too tough, too hard. I don't think I can do it. I don't think I want to do it. I wish I could just disappear.'

'Don't say that! Don't ever say that! You can do it, you have to, and we can, because we have no choice.'

'I . . .' She sat up, resting her arms on his knees, sitting now on the cool floor. 'I blame myself. And I blame you, too.'

James nodded, as if this much he knew and these too were his feelings.

'When I see you sleeping by my side, I detest your peace. I want to shove you awake and shout at you; why . . . why didn't you remind him, "Stay in your room, Oscar! Never go up on deck without us!" Why . . . why didn't you shackle him to the bed, nail up the door, lie across the floor, anything – anything to keep him where he was supposed to be, to keep him safe—' She halted at the sound of his sob.

'I think that too. Why didn't I? Why didn't I?' he cried.

'And why did you get the fucking boat in the first place? Why did you do that?' She sobbed. 'You were just showing off! You knew they could be dangerous!'

'I . . . I thought Oscar would love it. I thought we would love it. I don't . . . I don't know.' He covered his face with his hands. 'I don't know anything any more.'

And again the silent minutes passed, while these latest hot words of destruction pierced their core and neither made further comment on the terrible phrases they sharpened and fired as weapons.

Standing shakily and mentally heading back to the sanctuary of her bed, she looked back at her husband. 'Throw those cards and letters away. All of them. Throw them away! Can you imagine what it would be like for Oscar if he saw them?'

CEE-CEE

Cee-Cee returned the clean china plate back to the cupboard and wiped her hands on the dishcloth. It was a hot night with the kind of heat and thickened air that foreshadowed a storm. Even the bugs were jumpy. Sitting on the bench that ran along the back of Grandma Sally's porch, she looked to her left and pictured her gran rocking in her chair as she fanned her face on a night just like this. Glancing to the right, she smiled at the terrace where her mom and dad had done the same.

She opened up her notepad and took the pen in her hand.

Cee-Cee looked up and thought some more about those early days when she and Oscar were still getting to know each other.

She had closed the book and placed it on the little boy's nightstand. He yawned.

'So what did you learn today at nursery?' She had smiled, tucking the duvet around his shoulders to take the chill from the air conditioning.

'I did drawing.'

'You did drawing? You are an artist! Maybe one day you will have a big exhibition in Hamilton or even New York! Can you imagine that?'

Oscar laughed.

'What did you draw?'

'Umm, I did dinosaurs and a digger and a car with a big snake on it.' He spoke with the slur of fatigue.

'Well, that sounds like a masterpiece, little Oscar, a masterpiece!'

Oscar wriggled on the mattress and placed Mr Bob under his chin, the sign that he was readying for sleep.

'Shall I sing to you? Shall I sing you a hymn, little Oscar?'

He nodded and let his head fall to one side on the pillow.

Cee-Cee took a big breath and closed her eyes.

> 'Gentle Jesus, meek and mild,
> Look upon a little child;
> Pity my simplicity,
> Suffer me to come to Thee.
>
> Lamb of God, I look to Thee;
> Thou shalt my Example be;
> Thou art gentle, meek, and mild;
> Thou wast once a little child . . .'

She'd looked up as Rachel pushed open the door. 'Cee-Cee, I heard you singing, and you have the most beautiful voice!'

Cee-Cee shrugged, as the woman leaned over her son.

'Ah, I was coming to say goodnight. He looks so tiny when he's asleep.'

'He does.'

'We are just going to have a drink, Cee-Cee – by the pool. James has invited Mr and Mrs Williams from next door over.'

'I know them.'

'Well, you are more than welcome to come and join us.'

Why would I want to do that? Mrs Williams is as haughty as she is thin.

'No, thank you, but I will sit with Oscar for a bit and then I'll go home.'

'Okay, well, night night and if you change your mind you know where we are.'

'Goodnight.' Cee-Cee waited for the click of the door in the door-frame then sat back in the wicker chair with her hands folded neatly in her lap.

'Mr and Mrs Williams?' she whispered. 'I think I will pass.' She chuckled.

She looked now at the notepad, open on her lap. 'What to write to you?' She looked up, hoping that some God-given inspiration might fall into her lap. 'Maybe I could tell you some of my stories. It might help. It could be a good thing that you know a little about the island where Oscar will always live. Ah, Oscar . . .' She paused and looked up over the garden wall and down towards the beach. 'I do know that when I was hurting real bad, back when . . . stories would have helped, distracted me.' Cee-Cee smiled.

Rachel, sweet girl,

I have been thinking about what to write to you and wanted to start by telling you this: everyone I have ever loved and everyone I have ever lost are still with me. Every day, all around. I see them, I feel them and I remember them. They are not gone, not truly, and I know that is scant comfort to you right now, but I hope in time . . .

I think, no, I hope that writing will be an easier way to get all the things I want to say — things that seem locked in my mouth — flowing from my pen and into your hands. I have not written letters for some time and it might be wise to warn you that my thoughts and those I choose to voice are whatever comes to me and for that I make no apology, as I know no other way. I see your pain and I recognise it as my own. I know that things are hard for you right now, and that you would rather not face each new dawn. I also know you will not believe me when I tell you that this will not always be the case, but it's true. Things get easier, they do, as the months and years pass by, you will see.

Time heals. Time heals.

Someone said that to me once and Lord knows I wanted to punch him! It felt like an insult, like I didn't know my own mind! But he was right. He was. It does. And maybe at my time of grief I didn't know my own mind.

Despite our being together through this hardest and saddest of events, you still know so very little about me. I would like to put that right. I will try and distract you with my stories. I will try to show you that you are not alone in your sadness and that this little island is a wonderful place, a place where my history lives and yours too, because it's where Oscar now lives.

I think a lot about heaven. I think it was Mark Twain who said, 'You can go to heaven if you want, I'd rather stay in Bermuda!' I used to fret over this sometimes in my more restless hours. Suppose this was as good as it got? Suppose my little island, shaped like a fishhook in the middle of the Atlantic Ocean with its myriad of hidden bays and secret coves, edged with full and ancient palms, the icing-sugar sand and crystal-clear blue water, is the most beautiful place in the whole of creation? You see, I had banked on there being a place so breathtaking, so perfect, that when the Lord sent one of his messengers to take me under his wing on my final journey, I would see such splendour that I would weep! My concern was what it might feel like if, when I peek out from beneath those fine angel wings, my thoughts were, 'Hmph, not as pretty as where I've come from! Ain't a patch on Warwick Long Bay with a stiff breeze knocking up the foam against the rocks and the sun warming your skin as you lie on that soft, pink sand . . .'

But I guess that whenever I arrive at wherever it is I am going, I shall just have to be polite and say that heaven is indeed the most beautiful thing I have ever seen! He'll know though, the Lord. He'll know cos I never could tell a lie. Nearly seventy-five years on this earth and my lack of guile and my trusting nature have been both my blessing and my curse. If I could have my time again, I would surely learn how to twist the truth a little, honey up the words that sit on my honest tongue, and have a bigger voice to fight for what is rightfully mine. I am damn sure if I had, I might have kept me a husband.

I got it from my Grandma Sally, she couldn't lie either, but Lord she had ten times my courage. As far as we all know, she spoke nothing but the truth in her ninety-four years alive! 'Offend or please,' she'd mutter, as if neither were of any consequence or interest to her. My grandma's honesty was the reason my mom cried on her wedding day, and why my daddy refused to come in the house if she was visiting — and she used to visit a lot. On account of the fact that she lived next door, which was just as well for me, as my bedroom was in Grandma Sally's house. This arrangement was partly out of necessity, with my mommy's house being short on space, and partly because I was good company for my grandma; by all accounts I kept her young.

'Him?' She had, according to the story, pointed at my daddy when my mom brought him home, and near enough popped with rage. 'Of all the boys on this island, some with brains in their heads and strength in their boots, you pick him?' My mom didn't so much as twitch. Instead, she placed her hand on my daddy's arm and didn't look back. Her choice was made!

But I am racing ahead with my stories when you still don't know some of the basics. Let me fill in the gaps for you, my dear.

My name, as you know, is Cee-Cee Symmons. My mom (despite any protestations from her mom!) married Mr Symmons and she was, before marriage, a Tucker; this was my Grandma Sally's married name. Cee-Cee is short for Cecilly. I don't think I have ever been called Cecilly — well, maybe once or twice in church or way back at school when a new teacher didn't know the convention that just because you had a name written in a register didn't mean that was the name you were called.

I am neither the only nor best example of this.

My best friend Eliza-Jane Clara May Brown was, and still is to my knowledge, called Clara, on account of there already being an Eliza in the form. Thomas Ivor Newton was commonly known as Newton Junior — his daddy who ran the hardware store on Front Street was Big Newton, and Moses Temperate Mills was, and always has been, called Buddy, no matter that he now has a fancy job in government. He might walk every day with his head held high and neat creases down the front of his shorts, as he strides into the fancy building in Parliament Street, but he is still Buddy to those of us who have known him longest.

I don't know why we called him that.

So, what else to tell you?

Or, more specifically, what to tell you first?

I was always skinny, not too tall, but stronger than any man has ever given me credit for, both physically and mentally.

I have lived on Bermuda my whole life.

And I have never left her shores. Not once. I have never been on a plane, nor a ship.

This island — she is part of me and I am part of her and that's just how it is; can't imagine anything different.

Despite what you might assume, I never longed for bright city lights or hustle and bustle. I was always more than content to wake each day and breathe in great lungfuls of the fine sea air that swept through the open window, blowing away the worries of the night-time and bringing with it the promise of something new.

I have listened to tales of my family and can give you ten, maybe twenty examples of folk who had that itch; adventurers who left the island and spent the rest of their lives trying to figure out a way to get back to her. Some managed it, not all. Some now lie in rich earth or dusty soil the world over, nothing more than bones and dust. And this tells me all I need to know: why go in the first place?

For me personally, I am sure that if there is anything in the whole wide world as good as diving into the cool, frothy Atlantic Ocean on a hot day when the cotton dress clings to your back like a second skin and the road home lifts under the gaze of the sun, then I am yet to hear about it.

As a girl, I all but lived in that ocean. That same ocean that I know you despise was like a mother to me. It didn't matter that the water might be swirling and fierce, so much so that you couldn't see the eels, wrasses and blue angels sniffing around, waitin' in the depths to graze your ankles and send a scream from your lungs that would fill the hot, still air. No sir, when your body, aching from chores, got dipped in that cool, cool water, it was as if you could breathe for the first time that day. It was like being baptised all over again in that sweet water that is as good as any I've ever seen in the holy font at St Anne's Church, Southampton Parish.

It was my favourite thing: to lie on my back in that water and stare at the big sky, watching the Bermuda longtails circle overhead, as the water lapped my ears and made the whole world echo. I didn't know about desire or any man-made, grown-up carryings on — they were not part of my world.

Not yet.

I have always been just one woman, doing my best, struggling with all the good Lord put about my shoulders and placed in my hands, but as the saying goes, and as Pastor Raymond was always keen to remind us, 'He never gives you more than you are able to handle.' I'm not sure that this has always felt true, but I have to believe it is true.

My momma always said, 'All any of us has is our story. The other stuff ain't of no 'portance.'

And I can now see that she was right.

What else to tell you, Rachel?

I'm thinking . . .

I guess I should say that being the housekeeper in your home with that perfect view of the ocean has made me very happy, not only because of the view, but because of you and James and Oscar. I won't ever forget the day you all arrived. Oh! That little boy! He was my darling! My joy! And he crept into my heart where I was more than happy for him to lodge. I never had the chance of a whole brood of grandchildren and great-grandchildren, but Oscar filled that gap for me. He was a total wonder to me. I remember how he liked to keep me busy! Stories before bedtime and any spare moment during the day we'd play hide-and-seek. God only knows that boy had a love of it. I spent an age roaming the rooms and looking behind curtains. I now wonder who was fooling who, as I skirted by his tiny feet sticking out from under the duvet or ignored his giggle from behind the wardrobe door, saying, 'Now where on earth could he be?' I sit here now on my porch, laughing to recall the pantomime!

His loss has made me think a great deal about my own life, my own sadness and in some strange but comforting way it has helped me let go of certain things that sat in my mind like a pebble in a shoe.

Funny, isn't it, how we think our opinions, our expressions of distaste or approval, are so important? Until something truly big happens in your life and you look back at everything that has gone before and see it for what it is: insignificant. I know you will understand this more than most. And I am quite sure that when I slip away from this world, I will look back at its big, green, open spaces and its deep-blue, life-giving oceans and I will see just how insignificant! We are no more than tiny, tiny specks, nothing more.

I have never been one for big-headed carrying on; didn't think I was the cat's whiskers like some I could mention. Miss Eliza-Jane Clara May Brown . . .

Not that I will mind when I do slip away, not at all. I don't fear it, Rachel. I remember Grandma Sally sitting me down on this very veranda and telling me this: 'In Bermuda there are three steps between heaven and hell. Each step is more than a mile wide. On the bottom step sit those with an excess of money and an excess of time. These folk have the furthest to climb and you can spot them as they have clean fingernails and good shoes. On the top step sit those with a dearth of money and a dearth of time; these folks bear the calluses from a wooden tool held tightly against their palm and have sandals on their feet, but their journey will be swift, as reward for all they have endured. And on the middle step sit those that have meat once a week and enough money in their pocket for a little rum when the fancy takes them. These folk that sit on the middle step spend their time judging them that sit above and below.'

I looked up at my grandma's round, shiny face and asked, 'Which step will I be sat on?' I waited, eager to hear how far I had to climb.

She took my grubby fingers inside her warm, dry palm and kissed my forehead, 'You are going straight to heaven, girl, and when you get there I'll be waiting.'

And truth is, I kind of like the idea of that. I like it a lot.

Cee-Cee looked up at the rumble of thunder overhead.

Well, the evening is marching on and there is a storm coming in for sure.

I like to remember Oscar hiding from me, happy, excited and both of us knowing I could find him any old time but playing along anyhow. He was a smart little boy, ain't no question.

Cee-Cee

THREE

It was eight weeks to the day.

One thousand three hundred and forty-four hours.

One thousand three hundred and thirty-eight hours over the record.

The fact no longer made her sick or sent her hysterical, instead it simply provided another layer of numbness, the words forming a barrier like one of those preserving jellies – aspic and such – to glide over her thoughts, cementing the horror in its latest form. Layer upon layer of fresh imagery that was too uncomfortable to contemplate; smothering the very essence of her, until it was buried, nothing more than a tiny, unreachable kernel where a seed of happiness and rationality lay.

Throughout the night, with the moon casting pools of silvery light on to their marital bed, she would look across at James with a mixture of envy, revulsion and deep sadness, and wonder how sleep like that was even possible for him. It gave an unpleasant tension to her muscles and a sour lick of distaste to her spit. Once or twice in the early hours he tried to reach for her hand; she would then hold her breath and roll slowly out of reach, unable, or more accurately unwilling, to give or receive comfort when everything felt so very raw. She could barely remember what it was like to fall asleep and wake with her leg cast over his hip, skin to skin. This was just another way in which she found it almost impossible to recognise him as the man she so loved, the man whose contact she had craved. The realisation saddened her less than it should. Her nights, by contrast, were busy with thoughts, memories, guilt and recrimination jostling to be heard. A jumble of images crowded her brain – recollections both loud and detailed. Sleep came pawing as dawn broke and seemed to fall deepest prior to the alarm that shook her husband from slumber.

James did as he always had: swung his legs and sat on the side of the bed, checking his phone, stretching his back and rubbing his hair and face. It would have been hard for her to explain the rage that swirled in her gut and the hostility that danced on her tongue.

How dare you! How dare you go through life as if it was any other day! Are you not aware? Are you healed?

Instead she said nothing and closed her eyes tightly, feeling the ache in her eyeballs as she tried to keep them closed, and the hot burn of his fingertips on her shoulder as he left the room.

'Shh, go back to sleep, my love. Just sleep . . .'

Rachel rarely left the bedroom balcony. She was without the energy or inclination to do so. Shunning all normal conventions like washing, cleaning her teeth or brushing her hair – these tasks relegated to another lifetime when cleanliness and so much else was part of a 'normal' routine. Instead, she sat, day after day, in her crumpled pyjamas, her long hair wound into a greasy knot, ignoring the unpleasant dairy-like odour of herself and cradling her Tic-Tac box full of sand as she stared at the ocean in a constant vigil, calling to her boy.

Her eyes darted to each crest of white, every flicker of movement, any boat travelling a little quicker than the last, as if it might be carrying an urgent cargo.

Mayday! Mayday! We have on board a small child picked up from an unseen sandbar! A boy, no less, plucked from a sargassum mat. A miracle! Everyone listen! Oscar is coming home!

She liked to picture the headlines and smiled at the thought of the photograph that would accompany it: her kissing her boy on the face as she held him tight.

Cee-Cee moved quietly and slowly, as if her demeanour had shrunk to fit the mood of the house, depositing glasses of water or cups of chamomile tea on the nearest surface, running a sponge over the pristine bathroom and placing a tall vase of freshly cut agapanthus on the dressing table. Rachel could do no more than offer a whispered 'thank you', comforted by her presence and yet unable to meet her gaze, eyes fixed on the horizon. The tea would cool until an oily film sat on its darkened surface; the water would gather dust particles and the flowers wilted. Not that she noticed. She didn't notice much other than what happened out at sea.

Shifting her legs on the wooden stool that sat in front of her chair, she became aware of her husband standing in the doorway behind her. She pulled her soft, cotton shawl around her narrow shoulders.

'Rachel?'

'Mmmn?'

He walked forward and stood by the glass wall of the balcony, looking out across the ocean, joining her on her quest, whilst addressing her over his shoulder.

She looked at the back of his head, his body inside the crisply laundered white shirt. The shape of him now changed, shoulders bowed, weight-loss rendering him diminished, slight even. The back of his dark hair peppered with grey that she hadn't noticed before. He had returned to work a few weeks ago, which she found to be extraordinary. How he could entertain something so normal, familiar, routine and irrelevant when their lives had been irrevocably shattered was beyond her.

'You are going back to work?' she had asked with barely disguised shock.

'I have to, Rach. I don't want to, trust me.'

Trust you? Trust you? You couldn't keep him from leaving the cabin! You bought that boat! You told me it was safe!

'. . . but I have to. I can't lose my job as well.'

He had told her that it was necessary and that whilst the words of condolence were sincerely offered by his peers, they were accompanied by nervous enquiries as to the state of projects and events for which he was responsible. He had to keep working, couldn't let that aspect of his life unwind too. Watching him fasten his tie each day and reach for his car keys was mystifying when it was all she could do to keep her eyes open – not that she managed it all the time, still giving in to bouts of fitful sleep. He reminded her of the violin player on the *Titanic*, fiddling as the ship sank and all around gasped their last.

'Is this how it is going to be?' he asked flatly, pulling her from her thoughts.

'What do you mean?' She watched him grip the rails, his knuckles white.

'Are you' – she saw the almost imperceptible shake of his head and heard the sharp intake of breath – 'are you going to stay up here, hiding away?'

She placed her hand over her mouth, embarrassed by the small laugh that had escaped.

Where else would I be? What else is there to do?

'I am not hiding away, but there is nowhere else for me to be. I can see everything I need to from here.'

'It's hiding.'

'Hiding?' she repeated, staring up at him, as she pictured Oscar running into Cee-Cee's arms. *How many counts was that? How long did you look for?*

'Yes, Rachel.' Her husband's tone now a little more impatient, with an undercurrent of irritation for which she had no time, none at all. If he of all people did not understand this limbo in which she existed . . .

He turned to face her. 'I mean, is this it? You, sat up here, staring blankly out towards the ocean, muttering to yourself, and me excluded, pushed away. Nervous. Skulking downstairs, wondering whether to come up and check on you, whether it's okay to even speak to you.'

'I don't even . . .' And then the words fogged and she lost the point she had been about to make.

'Do you want me by your side? Is it possible we can talk? Or is it better to leave you alone? I am at a loss and I feel like a stranger in my own home and it feels horrible. I am grieving too and it's made doubly hard by you isolating yourself and excluding me.'

'You don't need to come check on me.' She swallowed.

'Is that it?'

Go away and leave me alone! Leave me alone! Leave me alone!

She stared at him, uncertain if she had screamed this aloud or only in her mind.

'Well, your silence answers some of my questions at least.'

Mentally his words and any deeper meaning were dismissed; she simply didn't have the energy.

She shook her head at him and pointed towards the deep blue. 'Can you imagine what it would be like if Oscar appeared in the water, waving or calling, and I only had a second to hold him in my sights, to pinpoint him, to let him know that I am right here and that we will come and get him? Can you imagine if I *missed* that second?' She finished with a nasal snort of derision – how could he not get that?

'This is how you spend your days.' It was more a lament than a statement of fact. 'No wonder you are so very tired, my love.' He reached for her hand and kissed her knuckles before restoring her cotton shawl, which had slipped down. He left her alone to her lookout.

Days later, how many she did not know and it did not matter, she must have fallen asleep, as she was aware of Cee-Cee standing by the side of the bed. 'You have visitors; they were insistent. Would you like me to send them up or send them away?'

'Visitors?' she repeated, sitting up and rubbing her eyes in a half-wakened state. There had been many callers – people from local churches, from James's office, neighbours – all eventually dismissed by Cee-Cee, as Rachel was without the desire or energy to face anyone.

Cee-Cee bent low. 'It's some of the moms from Oscar's school.'

'From school? Oh! Oh, Cee-Cee! Oh God! I have to see them!'

Her heart beat quickly, and as she swung her legs over the side of the mattress, she felt light-headed at the possibilities; maybe one of his school friends *had* come with a boat and taken him for a play date! Maybe they got stranded and their radio broke! Maybe they had only just managed to get back! She jumped up from the bed, shoving her arms into her dressing gown and tying it around her narrow waist, as she raced down the wide sweep of staircase, her bare feet glancing from the edge of each step, fleet of foot like a child on Christmas morning.

She cast her eyes over the three women standing in the hallway. She had never noticed before how they all looked remarkably similar with high, glossy, blonde ponytails; weighty diamond rings on their third fingers; Tiffany bangles that slid down on to the backs of their hands; neat, loose, gold, rectangle-faced watches; white sneakers; tanned legs; and shiny, manicured nails. She could not imagine ever going to so much trouble over something as incidental as her appearance, not when there were things far, far more important to occupy her thoughts. But of course she had. A lifetime ago.

Swallowing the wave of nausea that leaped in her gut, she gripped the bannister, pausing on the bottom step as she pictured sitting on the top floor of Brown and Co. on Front Street where the bookshop and café with the best view in town resided. A chilled fruit smoothie in her hand, Rachel had laughed as she and these women sat with a clutch of stiffened cardboard shopping bags around their feet, filled with baubles, fluff and frippery – stuff . . . She remembered making a call to Cee-Cee: 'Would you mind just picking him up?' She had lifted her shoulders and widened her mouth, narrowing her eyes in mock contrition for the amusement of these women. 'You are a star, Cee-Cee! I shan't be too long, but the girls and I are just catching up.'

'Rachel!' Alison, Hank's mother, stepped forward. With arms out-stretched, she pulled her from the step into a hug. Rachel felt the quake in the woman's limbs and stood reluctantly inside the loose embrace with her arms hanging down. She felt the pat of Rita's hand on her back – her son Finlay was in Oscar's class – and Fiona, Daisy's mum, stood with a desperate expression, shaking her head and whimpering a little, a tissue clutched in her palm.

'Oh Rachel!' Fiona sighed. 'How are you?'

She shuffled back, freeing herself from their grasp, wondering if it would ever be possible to answer that question. The three stood in front of her forming a little trio of bobbing heads. Rachel was surprised by the swirl of feeling that stirred in her gut. These were the women with whom she had shared lunch, drunk wine, played sport, shopped, consoled, hugged and complimented. These women were her friends, and yet their very presence sent a lightning bolt of jealousy and hatred through her very being. She clamped her teeth together to stop from voicing all that gathered on her tongue.

It's not their fault. It's not their fault. It's not their fault.

This mantra she repeated in the hope that it might prevent her from firing hurtful, poison-laden verbal arrows into their mouths and down their throats.

Why do you all look so sad? So concerned? You have no idea what this is like, so don't pretend you do. You have your children. You will collect them from school today, from a room where there is an empty desk. You will grab their coat and PE bag from a hook next to a redundant peg and you will write out party invites, recounting on your fingers because you can't figure how twenty-eight has become twenty-seven. Then, with a momentary start, you will remember Oscar. But your thoughts of him will be fleeting, and more so as time goes on. But for me? It will never end. I don't wish your children any harm. But a small part of me hates that you get to tuck your babies into their beds tonight and I do not.

'We have called before,' Alison began. 'We know there are no words, but we wanted you to know that we are thinking of you. We all are. It's all we can think about, all we can talk about. Everyone sends you their love. There have been prayers at St Ada's – all the kids are devastated. Hank, you can imagine . . .' Alison paused for breath.

Rachel took a step back. 'Did . . . did anyone pick him up?'

'Hank?' Alison questioned and looked at her watch. 'It's not time yet, sweetie, they don't finish until three thirty.' She watched as Alison and Rita exchanged a knowing look.

Rachel shook her head. 'No, not Hank, Oscar.'

'I don't . . .' Fiona knitted her brows in confusion. 'I don't follow.'

'Did anyone take a boat out on the day he went missing? Did any-one want to take him for a play date and come and get him?'

The women looked from one to another, their mouths flapping, lost for words. Rachel continued, 'I think they might have. They might have moored alongside *Liberté* and taken him from the deck and they might have got lost or shipwrecked and maybe their radio stopped working, and I wondered if that was why you were here, to give me the details so that I can collect him, and I won't be angry, I promise! No one will be in trouble. I will just be so pleased to have' – her voice faltered and remerged thin and high-pitched – 'to have my little boy back!' She sank down and felt a pair of hands on her shoulders.

Cee-Cee, who had come down the stairs, now stood behind her. A sentinel. She placed her hands on her shoulders while talking over her head to the women who cried and reached for each other's hands. 'Mrs Croft is very grateful for your enquiries. May I see you out now?'

Rachel watched as the women walked slowly across the grand hallway, glancing back with stricken faces, shepherded by the housekeeper
right out of the front door. Cee-Cee closed the door and looked back
at her.

'I thought,' Rachel began. 'I thought . . .'

Cee-Cee nodded. 'I know, my sweet. I know.' The housekeeper took
a seat next to her on the bottom step and wrapped her arms around her,
holding her close while Rachel cried silently.

'That can't be it, Cee-Cee, it can't be! He has to come back to me.
I miss him so much and it hurts. It's hurting me!' She placed one hand
on her heart and the other on her stomach lest there be any doubt as
to where the pain lurked.

'You have been cut; you have had something wrenched from you
and it will hurt. It does hurt. I know it.'

'Make it stop, Cee-Cee! Please! Please make it stop!' She fell forward
until her head rested on the woman's lap.

'Shh . . .' Cee-Cee cooed. 'Shh . . . Just breathe. Breathe.' She
smoothed the hair away from her face.

A few minutes later Rachel had calmed a little.

'Why don't you go back to bed? Shall I make you some tea and
bring it up to you?'

Rachel nodded and slowly made her way back up the stairs. Each
step required effort, as if her feet were made of lead and the stairs were
a mountain. As she passed Oscar's room she hesitated and reached out
for the handle. Twisting it slowly, she turned and pushed the door open.
Scanning the room, it was instantly evident that her son was not in it,
and this was less of a surprise than she might have imagined. The bed
was beautifully made and his toys were, as ever, boxed or tidied by his
devoted Cee-Cee.

On his desk was a flat Lego board studded with half-built creations,
free-form sculptures and towers awaiting his embellishment. His lidded
Batman cup, perfect for night-time sips, was in situ on his nightstand.

His trainers, school shoes and football boots were lined up by the wall next to his wardrobe. Rachel inhaled the scent of him that lingered here strongly. His hooded towel with his name embroidered on the back was slung on a hook on the back of his door, and his bookshelf, crammed with stories, looked a little forlorn, abandoned. She sat on the end of his bed and let herself slip sideways until her head was on his pillow; she inhaled the scent of him and it was intoxicating. There was a lump underneath her head. Reaching up, she felt around, until her fingers touched upon something . . . Mr Bob!

'Oh my God! Oh my God! Cee-Cee! Cee-Cee!' she screamed as she hurtled once again down the stairs, this time with a newfound energy. 'You need to call Mackenzie! Call him right now! And James too. They have to come here right now! This is important!' She held Mr Bob to her chest. The raggedy, knitted ted whose arms and legs had gone rather floppy over the years and who had one eye that had become unpicked.

'Oh, Cee-Cee! This is incredible!' She bounded into the kitchen, while Cee-Cee abandoned the tea-making and quietly, with a look of embarrassment, made the calls.

A mere thirty minutes later James, shortly followed by Mackenzie and his colleague in a police car, pulled into the drive and almost ran into the house, their pace and expectant expressions matching her urgency.

Rachel bounced on the spot with fists clenched, eagerness spilling from her as the newly arrived trio congregated in the kitchen.

'Are you okay, darling?' James looked at her with a concerned expression. She couldn't wait to share her discovery, knowing it would change the face of everything!

'James, Mackenzie, I have something wonderful to tell you!' She took a deep breath, hardly able to hide the grin that split her face. 'Oscar has been here. Oscar has been in the house, and this means he is alive and he is somewhere, but not out there!' She pointed to the wall beyond which lay the Atlantic Ocean. 'I knew it! I told you! He has been home, he was in his bedroom, he . . . he must have snuck in or someone snuck him in and we have to find him, but the good news is, we can find him, we can, because he's not in the sea!'

She tried to figure James's expression, as he blinked at her and took a step forward. 'Why do you say that, Rach, what has made you think that?' The soft, placatory tone to his questioning irritated her beyond belief; she had wanted him to be as elated as her.

She beamed, knowing she was about to produce the proof. 'I found this!' Reaching inside her dressing-gown pocket, she pulled out Mr Bob, holding him aloft with both hands for all to see. James looked a little pale and Mackenzie stared at the floor.

'Mr Bob! His ted! He can only sleep with him on his pillow and I just found him *under* the pillow on his bed, hidden. Oscar must have brought him home and put him there! So now we just have to find him!' She placed Mr Bob over her nose and smiling mouth, twisting her body back and forth with joy, like a child with a gift, as she inhaled the imprint of her son.

James shook his head. 'No, Rachel, Oscar hasn't been here.' Again that softened rasp that made anger ball in her gut. Was he not listening to her?

'So how do you explain this?' She shook the knitted doll in her husband's face.

He glanced at Mackenzie, who looked away, and she again got the distinct and uncomfortable feeling that the two were conspiring. 'I didn't want to tell you, but I forgot to pack Mr Bob for our trip.' He paused. 'When I put Oscar to bed on the boat that night, we couldn't find Mr Bob and Oscar got . . . He got a bit upset and so I sat with him for a minute or two and then he seemed to fall asleep anyway; he was tired.' He pinched the bridge of his nose, seemingly exhausted by having to recollect that last night, those last moments.

'You forgot him?' She was aware of her harsh accusatory tone.

'Yes.'

'But why didn't you say that to me?' She stared at him, trying to catch up and deal with the latest blow to further sever the strands of hope that were trailing thinner and sparser with every day that passed.

'I didn't want you to know,' James began, his voice breaking. 'I didn't want you to know that Oscar's last night was spent without the thing that brought him comfort. Didn't want that to be the thing that drags you from sleep in the early hours, like it does me.'

I have seen you sleep . . . I have watched you . . .

The exertion of events and the crushing disappointment of facts now revealed left her feeling weakened. Rachel leaned back against the countertop. 'Sorry, Mackenzie, I thought . . .'

'It's not a problem.' The man gave the briefest of smiles and adjusted his hat. 'I wanted to come and talk to you anyway, Mrs Croft, and now is as good a time as any.'

James instinctively walked to his wife's side.

Mackenzie pulled his shoulders back, as if hoping that a professional stance might aid this most difficult of tasks. 'It has been eight weeks; I am sure I don't need to tell you that.' He ran the tip of his tongue over his top lip. 'Whilst we will keep the file open, I wanted to confirm to you and I suppose ask you to prepare yourselves for the possibility that we may never recover your son's body.'

She stared at the man, unsure what she was supposed to do and say in response to that information. She heard the wall clock ticking overly loud in her ears. James remained still by her side. She saw him nod in her peripheral vision; he had clearly already considered this.

'The ocean can be a fearsome opponent and her depths are wide and far-reaching; sometimes people just disappear into her.' Mackenzie paused and blinked, what else was there to say? 'But you have my numbers; please call any time. And if anything else comes to light, if there are any developments, I will of course be in touch.'

'Sorry for today.' James spoke on her behalf and again she felt powerless. *I thought, I really thought . . .*

'Don't be.' The policeman held up his hand, as if directing traffic. 'As I said, I had to come and speak to you anyway. Far from easy, I know, but I do think it is important that you set your expectations.'

Rachel watched the policeman leave before making her way back upstairs to the balcony to continue her watch, this time with Mr Bob in one hand and her Tic-Tac box in the other.

Sixteen weeks. Sixteen weeks. Two thousand six hundred and eighty-eight hours . . . Two thousand six hundred and eighty-two hours past the record.

It was a rainy day, the first in a long time, and Rachel deliberated over what to wear, settling on a waterproof walking jacket, a hat James had used for fishing and a thick beach towel to cover her legs. Fat droplets of rain splashed on the balcony floor and made her view out over the ocean hazy at best. Her lack of vision frustrated her. The warm water ran in a tiny tributary from her scalp to chin, falling into the quickly sodden towel that felt quite uncomfortable against her chilled skin. She heard the door creak open and Cee-Cee appeared, the water gathering in her curly hair like tiny sparkles of glass. 'You should come in, child. You will catch a cold.'

Rachel shook her head and continued to stare ahead. 'What if today is the day, Cee-Cee? What if I see something? I can't miss it. I can't.'

Cee-Cee walked forward and closed the top of her jacket under her chin. She gave her soft, crinkle-eyed smile. Rachel barely acknowledged the sound of the door closing again, thankful that Cee-Cee didn't try to cajole or push any further. She liked how it gave reason and acceptance to her task.

Any break in the clouds allowed her to see parts, but not all of the sea and something quite remarkable happened. It was as she focused on the small areas of blue turned green in the mist of the downpour that her brain somersaulted through possibilities previously unconsidered.

This new thought process gave her a shot of energy and excitement. It was with an almost manic desperation that she ran from the terrace, into the house and down the stairs, skidding on the tiled floor in her wet socks.

'Cee-Cee?'

She turned from the kitchen sink.

'Goodness, I didn't hear you come in. You made me jump. Are you okay?'

Rachel offered no apology; there was something far more pressing on her mind. 'More than okay! But I can't find my laptop, and I need it. Did James take it?' She pulled off the fishing hat and slipped her arms from the waterproof jacket, bundling them and putting them on the kitchen table.

'No, it's in the study, I'll get it for you.' Cee-Cee shook her hands into the sink and wiped them on the blue-and-white checked dishcloth tucked into the waistband of her skirt.

Rachel sat at the table, poised, as she rubbed the excess of water from her hair and face. Cee-Cee returned and placed the machine in front of her.

'Thank you, Cee-Cee.' She smiled, placing her hand on the woman's arm. Cee-Cee patted her fingers.

'I feel . . .' She tried to explain the bubble of joy in her gut.

'You feel what?' the housekeeper asked, softly.

'I feel excited! Really excited!' She bounced in the chair and decided to ignore the pained expression on the woman's face.

'We need to keep steady.' Cee-Cee spoke calmly. 'We need to keep steady and we need to breathe slowly.'

Rachel watched her head for the sink and gingerly opened up the computer, letting her fingers caress the keys that knew well the touch of her son as he scoured Nickelodeon and the Disney Channel in search of his beloved cartoons. She hesitated as the search-engine page sprang to life and she typed the word 'Kelpie' into the Google bar. Running her finger over the text, she read aloud: '*Shape-shifting water spirit inhabiting the lochs and pools of Scotland. It has been described as a horse, but is able to adopt human form.*' She leaned closer to the screen and, squinting, she read on: '*Narratives about the kelpie also serve a practical purpose in keeping children away from dangerous stretches of water.*'

She sat back and considered this, before typing 'Mermaids', and again reading aloud: '*Mermaids are sometimes associated with perilous events such as floods, storms, shipwrecks and drownings.*' She felt the breath stutter in her throat and swallowed, leaning in again. '*In other folk traditions they can be benevolent or beneficent, bestowing boons or falling in love with humans.*'

Cee-Cee walked behind her; Rachel turned in the chair. 'Can you imagine anyone or anything not falling in love with Oscar if they met him?'

The housekeeper smiled. 'Well, as the Lord is my judge, I can say that it was certainly that way with me.'

Rachel noted the tremble to the woman's bottom lip. 'That's what I am talking about, Cee-Cee. This is why I am so excited!'

◆ ◆ ◆

James was a little late home.

It was a whistling sunset with the tree frogs out in force, providing the Bermudian night music that had so enchanted them when they first arrived, but now was simply part of the background. Tonight, however, it was as if she heard it afresh.

Cee-Cee had left a chicken curry in the pot on the oven, the cushions were plumped, floors swept and steamed and the lamps were switched on. The atmosphere was one of peace. Thankfully the rain had stopped and, as ever, the island seemed to glow in the aftermath of the downpour. Leaves were shiny, roads and buildings washed free of dust and the air smelled damp, earthy and full of promise that things might bloom.

'Hey.' His smile was hesitant but genuine. He looked around the room and she guessed he was trying to gauge the reason why she had left the refuge of the bedroom and balcony and was seated in the kitchen for the first time in as long as either of them could remember.

'That rain was really something today.'

'Yes. I got drenched,' she added.

'Woodlands Road has flooded again and apparently there has been some water damage in St George's.'

She nodded, trying to keep interest, but bursting with all the things she wanted to tell him.

'How are you doing?' he asked with caution, placing his backpack on the floor and slowly rolling up his shirtsleeves.

'I'm good,' she answered truthfully. 'Really good!'

'Really?' He walked towards her, his relief palpable and his tone cautious. 'That is wonderful news.'

'Cee-Cee left you a curry.'

'That's great. Are you hungry?' She was aware that they had not sat and eaten together since that night on the boat, the night before…

Rachel shook her head and tucked the wisps of her long hair behind her ears, as she sat up straight. 'Sit down, James.'

He sat.

'I need you to listen to me. Listen very carefully.'

'Okay.' He smiled at her.

'I was sitting in the rain earlier and I saw something in the ocean and it got me thinking.'

'Right.' His smile faltered a little and he bit his bottom lip.

'There are things in this world that we do not understand.' She gesticulated with her hands, as if this might help enforce the point.

His eyes scanned her face. 'Yep, I guess there are.'

She watched him knit his fingers and place his hands in his lap.

'In olden times, people thought the earth was flat. They thought if they sailed far enough they would fall off the edge!' she continued, with a slight smile playing about her lips. 'But now we know that's not true, we laugh at the idea.'

He nodded, trying to follow. She sensed his unease.

Get to the point, Rachel!

'What I am saying, or trying to say, is that there are things we don't understand right now that one day might seem very ordinary to us. And we should not discount those things.'

'I'm not sure I am following.' He scratched his scalp.

She threw her head back and laughed. 'Okay, things like kelpies, merpeople and giant sea turtles that can carry a person for hundreds and hundreds of miles across the ocean! Underwater cities! Atlantis! Air pockets inside ships where lost fishermen can live! There are legends and stories that persist and have persisted for hundreds of years! Now, don't you think that's interesting? I mean, if these things were to be discounted, then I think they would have been by now; but they are not. Stories keep cropping up all over the world – tales from fisherman who *see* things, experience things, and they know the ocean and all its secrets like no others.' She sat forward, her words bubbling from her on a river of excitement. 'There was this guy in Peru I read about who was lost overboard from a ship and his crew searched and searched until reluctantly they gave up; they had to go back to shore and tell his wife and family that he was lost! Can you imagine? They even had a funeral! A funeral, James!' she stated, wide-eyed. 'But then months later, he walked up a beach unscathed and he told them he had been living in an underwater cave, carried there by a giant sea turtle!' She watched his mouth twist, but he stayed quiet. It was her cue to continue. 'If anything had happened to Oscar, I would feel it.' She held her chest. 'I would. I am sure of it, James! But I don't, I don't. Instead, I believe he is being cared for by something we don't understand!' She cocked her head to one side and leaned towards him. 'That's what I think.' She laid her hands flat on the table, as if in conclusion.

There was a moment or two of silence while both allowed her suggestions to permeate. This was followed by his sudden and surprising gasp of sadness that seemed to start in his throat, as that was where he placed his hand, as if struggling for breath.

His apparent distress took a little of the shine from her discovery; she had hoped that he might be as excited as her at all the possibilities.

'Do you *know* what a kelpie is?' she pushed, convinced that if she could make him understand, as she did, his sadness would be replaced with hope.

James shifted back in his seat and held her gaze. 'There's no such thing,' he whispered, squeezing his nose with his thumb and forefinger.

'But, James, there are many tales of kelpies who can take on human form and—'

'There is no such thing, Rachel,' he interrupted, speaking a little louder, as he shook his head. 'I wish there were . . .'

'But, James, I have spent the day reading about—'

'No!' he yelled. 'No! There is no such fucking thing! This has to stop! *You* have to stop or we are both going to sink under the weight of it! I am stretched so thin I think I might break!'

'This is not about you!' she countered. 'It's about the fact that our little boy might be out there somewhere.'

'No!' He stood and slammed the chair to the floor, kicking the table leg so hard it shifted from its position. He put his fingers in his hair, pacing, as he spoke. 'No! That is not true, that is not the case. Oscar died. He died! He drowned, Rachel. He jumped off the boat or slipped from the boat or hit his head or whatever and he drowned and that is it!' His voice cracked. 'And as well as missing him, hurting for how he was lost, I am also going nuts tiptoeing around you because you are so fragile! And I don't know what you are going to come up with next.'

She felt herself shrink in the chair, fear and a loss of reason lapping at her heels. 'I . . . I can't help it, I . . .' she began.

'I know, I know you can't.' He seemed to calm a little, as if this was what was required to make the progress he so desperately craved. 'But I am so lonely, working so hard through my exhaustion and the truth is' – he drew breath preparing himself to utter the words that he knew would cut, as surely as drawing a dagger from its sheath – 'I can't look at you. I don't want to look at you. I'm able to distract myself with one million small things during the busy day, but the very second I step back through the door, just the sight of you drags me back to that moment with you staring at me from the cockpit of the boat, and me with two mugs of coffee in my hands with absolutely no idea how everything, everything was about to turn to dust! My whole life and everything I thought I could rely on slipped through my fingers in a matter of minutes! I will never forget the expression on your face. I see it all the time and I can't stand it and I can't stand that it is you, my Rachel, who I feel this way about.'

Your Rachel has gone. She left on that boat with Oscar.

She stared at him, taking in every comment, laying it down as law in her heart and noticing that, despite the intense nature of his words, she felt very little.

James carried on talking. 'And you are lost in a world of kelpies and fucking mermaids and I can't help myself, let alone help you! These conversations, these obsessions, they divert your grief but don't help you heal, and watching you, listening to you – it feels like losing Oscar again, every single day!'

'I do lose him every day! Every day!' she shouted.

'But, Rachel, you need to try, try really hard to move forward, to look up and see the world.' James held the countertop.

'HE WAS MY WORLD!' she screamed.

James whipped around. 'I think we both know that's not true and I guess that's the problem. You were busy on the island, you built walls of gin, tennis and having lunch with your girlfriends – and you lived within those walls; often you didn't see him when you had the chance because you were out with the girls, shopping or hanging out at Brown and Co., and now those walls have fallen and you are left with nothing at all! You have nothing to say because the world you created has gone and you are aflame with guilt that stops you seeing clearly.'

She felt her body fold, as she sank to the tabletop, as if the hooks that held her up had finally been removed.

I wish I could go back, I wish I could go back and be a better mum, a different mum . . .

'I loved him! He is my little boy and I love him, James!'

He stood with his hand at his throat, eyes ablaze, panting, until he calmed a little.

'Oh my God! My God, Rachel, I'm sorry. I'm sorry. I know you loved him, I know you did,' he croaked, pushing his thumbs against his eyes.

'And I thought I had time,' she whispered. 'I thought I had time.'

'We both did.'

She heard him give in to the tears that had been building, not that she made any attempt to comfort him. She couldn't; her mind was entirely occupied with an earlier thought, which was loud, invasive and provided a single note of clarity.

Your Rachel has gone. She left on that boat with Oscar.

Sitting up, she dried her eyes on her sleeve, as an idea formed. A brilliant idea. The answer.

'Are you working tomorrow, James?' she asked with an unexpected lightness to her enquiry.

'No, it's Saturday.' He sniffed. 'I'll be home.'

'Can we . . . can we do something together?' She asked slowly, holding his gaze, flattered by the wide smile that now broke across his face.

His words when they came coasted on something that sounded a lot like relief. 'Yes, of course we can. Anything, we can do anything you want to Rach, together.' He laughed through his tears.

Rachel hadn't slept. Not that this was anything new, but what was new was how she spent the longest hours waiting for dawn. She let the cool, cotton sheets caress her skin and got lost in memories of carrying Oscar, of giving birth. The moment her parents laid eyes on him for the first time, her dad looking at his tiny feet and declaring with certainty that he could play for Rovers. Welcome, happy thoughts.

At mid-morning on the bright, sunny Saturday, Rachel shrugged off her pyjamas and showered, both of which were unusual for her of late. She slipped into her cut-off jeans and a T-shirt and sat on the balcony off the bedroom, letting herself get lost in the churn of the ocean, drawn as powerfully as ever to the dip and swell of the water, watching boats come and go from the dock and always, always looking out to the horizon, as the sun dappled its surface with sea diamonds.

She sat for some while enjoying the quiet and in deep contemplation, until she stood calmly and kissed Mr Bob before placing him on James's pillow. Then she wiped her eyes and made her way down to the kitchen.

'James?' she called with a sense of urgency, wary that he might have changed his mind about an outing.

'What's wrong?' He looked up from his laptop.

'Nothing's wrong, but . . . but I'm ready now, ready for us to go out together.'

He closed the computer and stood, smiling. 'Where do you want to go?' His tone was curious and at the same time she could see his concern for her latest whim. 'I mean, I don't mind, we can go anywhere. It'll be good to get out of the house together, get some fresh air, walk a bit.'

She stared at her husband and spoke with hesitation. 'I want . . . I want you to take us out on the boat. I think we should go out on *Liberté*.' She watched the colour drain from his face as he double blinked.

He shook his head. 'We haven't . . .' He paused. 'I don't know what to say. Do you think that's a good idea?'

'I do!' She smiled her enthusiasm. 'I really do, James! I wasn't ready before, but now I am. I want to go out on the boat and I think it will make me feel close to Oscar, make *us* feel close to Oscar,' she enthused. 'I think it might help, I really do. I have been on the terrace going over everything in my head and something struck me last night while we were talking. I keep thinking of the last time we felt happy when we woke on the boat – in those minutes, those glorious minutes before . . . when everything was good, when we were wonderful!'

'We were wonderful,' he whispered, his expression one of sadness.

'I think we should go out on *Liberté* and clear our heads! What do you think?'

'I . . .' He was seemingly at a loss for words. 'Truthfully? I don't know what to think. I feel nervous.'

She took a step closer and held his arm. 'I do too, but that's okay, James. I have spent so many hours staring at the ocean and what I want to do is be *on* the ocean. Please! Please!'

He rubbed his palm over his face, looking concerned. 'I haven't taken her out since . . .'

'I know, I know. But that's why it's a good thing to do. Together. Please, James! For me?' she implored, squeezing his arm and staring at him with a look of desperation.

'Okay.' He nodded, his response measured. 'Okay.'

As the car drove along, hugging the coast road that took them around to Spanish Point, Rachel felt the swell of anticipation in her gut. It took all her strength not to turn and look at the back seat, which would confirm that Oscar was not sitting there, humming away to himself, as he did in her mind.

'Thank you, James, for doing this.'

'I have to be honest, Rachel, I'm still not sure it's the best idea.' He glanced over at her.

'I think it is.' She leaned towards him. 'I realised that all I want, all I have ever wanted, is to be close to Oscar, and I can be by being on the boat – the last place he was – and by being on the water.'

'I'll go with it, Rachel, but if at any time you feel it's too much; if you change your mind or you just want to come home, then just say the word.'

'I will.'

She looked across at the man she had married, Oscar's dad, and she felt a wave of affection for all that they had shared.

'Just because I am lost, it doesn't mean that somewhere in my mind there isn't a perfect picture of the three of us. I think about us in Richmond.' She smiled. 'I think about our wedding day and I think about the day he was born and the look on your face when they handed him to you, all wrapped up, like I had given you the world.'

'You did, Rach, you did give me the world.'

'I did.'

They drove the rest of the way in silence, both smiling and with a feeling of quiet contentment, but for very different reasons.

Rachel walked behind her husband on the dock, inevitably thinking of the last time she had done so with Oscar running ahead. *Be careful, darling!* she had shouted after him.

Liberté had been cared for by Leonard and his crew, who had kept her clean and her engine primed. She felt a punch of nausea as she looked at the deck and the porthole on the side, the window into the cabin in which her boy had laid his head for the last time.

Night night, Mummy!

Love you!

'Are you okay?' James asked rather sternly, his way when trying to control his anxiety.

She nodded.

'Don't forget what I said, we can go home at any time; even making it down here is a huge step forward, Rach.'

'I know. And I'm fine,' she lied.

Rachel took a deep breath and gripped the narrow stanchion, placing her foot on the deck with trepidation. She had forgotten how the movement of the boat was quite unlike any other and closed her eyes briefly. The feeling underfoot was enough to take her back to that last day, the events of which now played in her head like a speeded-up showreel, ending with her on the floor of the police boat with the weighted blanket about her shoulders pushing her down, down until Dr Kent gripped her arm on the dock at Spanish Point, where he stood waiting with his needle poised.

She helped cast off the rope from the mooring and pulled up the fenders as they left the marina, as if it were any other sailing trip.

James called back to her, 'Are you okay?'

She gave the double thumbs-up, making her way across the gangway, only briefly glancing at the stairs that led down to the galley.

Rach, Oscar! Coffee's ready!

She reached the white vinyl cushions with the navy piping and sank down on the foredeck. With a genuine rush of excitement in her chest she stared ahead at the wide expanse of ocean dotted with rocky out-crops, sandbars, coral reefs and narrow archipelago clusters that made navigating the route to Bermuda's shores so hazardous. James hit the throttle and they motored out.

Rachel rested now on her elbows with her feet planted in front of her and tilted her head back, letting the sun and fine sea spray coat her, connecting her to the ocean.

'I'm coming, baby! Mummy's coming, Oscar!' she whispered into the wind as it whipped her hair around her face.

Liberté picked up speed. Twenty minutes later they reached deep water and James slowed the vessel, anchoring up. He came to join her on the foredeck and sat down by her side. They let the sun warm their skin.

'I think you were right. This is difficult, but it also feels quite wonderful.'

'It does.' She agreed. 'There is something about the gentle rocking of a boat. I have always thought so.'

'There is.' He yawned. 'I'm exhausted,' James confessed. 'I am always exhausted, but it's been one hell of a day. Who am I kidding? It's been one hell of a week, month, year . . .'

'It has. Go to sleep, James,' she cooed, reaching out and smoothing his hair from his handsome face, savouring the feel of his skin beneath her fingertips; once so familiar, it now felt like something brand new. He raised his hand and touched her fingers with an expression of pure sorrow, almost as if the sweet longing for what they had once shared flared in his mind, as it did hers. She watched the furrows on his brow disappear under her gentle touch.

'I don't like to nap and leave you here with no one to talk to.' As he spoke, his face fell to one side. Sleep began to claim him.

'I'll be right by your side.' She leaned forward and kissed his cheek, an act once so commonplace, but today it was quite distinct. It was the sweet, sweet kiss of goodbye.

Rachel sat up straight. She pictured her parents probably in their little breakfast nook in Yate and she sent them thoughts.

I love you both, I do, and I want to thank you. Thank you for always being there for me. I know you will understand. I know that you cannot envisage a life without Peter and me and that is the life I face – one without my boy – and it's not a life I want. And not a life I choose. She took a deep breath and felt nothing but a beautiful sense of calm. *And you, Vicky, my best, best friend, be strong and grab all that life throws at you. You will watch Francisco grow into a wonderful little man, just like his dad, and know that I have always treasured you. Always.*

This was it; the conclusion to this terrible chapter and with it an end to the suffering, the pain, the insomnia, the desperation.

Rachel felt a sense of peace and a flicker of something close to euphoria.

She had figured it out.

She watched as James lay back and before too long the twitch of his limbs stilled and his chest rose and fell with the deep, deep breathing of sleep.

Rachel knew time was of the essence. She stood slowly and would have found it hard to describe the serenity in which she found herself bathed, body and soul. It was a new and welcome peace. There was no fear. There was no hesitation; just a sense of calm resignation that had been missing from her life for so long. It gave her clarity and for that she was grateful. She trod softly to the back of the boat and took two, then three steps to the edge, and as quietly as she could, she lifted first one foot over the guardrail and then the other. Glancing quickly at the foredeck to check that her husband hadn't stirred, she took a deep breath and looked forward.

Rachel Croft jumped.

The water was colder than she would have anticipated and certainly than she remembered. She plummeted down beneath the surface, dropping until she reached a point where her body hovered and her natural instinct was to kick her feet, pull with her arms and go back to the top. But this instinct, she knew, was one to fight against. The water was a little foamy around her point of entry, and she instantly lost her bearings.

Not that it mattered.

Nothing mattered now.

With her hair floating all around, she opened her eyes and, bar the sting of salt, was able to see quite clearly. She felt the air that had filled her lungs start to run out and she turned in the water, with her head down, preparing to dive deeper to take one

Final.

Big.

Breath.

Her chest started to burn and she fought to control the rise of panic in her body, which despite her mind's steely intention had yet to catch up. Rachel floated in a star formation beneath the water. She hovered in the sea, waiting for the moment when her body would do what had come naturally to her since the moment she had been born: take a breath. But this breath would be her last, making her one with the ocean that had claimed her boy.

The desire to breathe was strong and getting stronger.

Two things happened simultaneously. As Rachel opened her mouth to let water stream into her lungs, she saw a flicker of light in the distance. Her eyes narrowed and widened, and there, almost within touching distance, she saw Oscar! It was him! Oscar!

Her heart lifted and her spirit soared with joy.

She saw his face, his beautiful, beautiful face.

He looked directly at her and he smiled his cheeky grin. She took in his little straight nose, dotted with freckles, just as she remembered it. His fair hair sat around his head like a halo and as he turned in the water to dive deeper, Oscar looked back over his shoulder and waved.

Rachel used the last of her strength to lift her hand and waved back at her boy, who was spirited away beyond her gaze.

As deep as the ocean, Oscar, and as high as the sky. I am with you and I will always love you. Always.

◆　◆　◆

A sharp, violent yank pulled her upward, a force so strong that she had no option in her weakened and disorientated state but to go with it. Her head broke the surface and she was aware of James yelling, 'No! Don't you fucking dare! Don't you dare! Don't you do that to me, Rachel! No fucking way! No way! Stay with me, you fucking stay with me!' he screamed in her face, crying, dragging her through the water, pulling her hair and anchoring her head to him under the chin, as he kicked backward towards the hull of *Liberté*.

She began to cough, a brutal cough that drew water from her lungs, leaving her retching and hacking until she had cleared her airways and was left gasping for breath. James hung on to the ladder at the back of the boat and caught his breath, crying, as she clung to him. 'I saw him, James!' she struggled to speak through her tears. 'I saw him! I saw him. And he looked . . . He looked happy!' She sobbed, as she bobbed in the cool Atlantic. 'I saw him! I saw him!'

James wrapped his free arm around her and held her close as they both concentrated on breathing between bouts of sobbing.

'He's not here any more, Rachel. He is gone! He died! He is dead . . . He's dead and you need to let him go! I can't stand it any more! He is dead! And you need to let him go. He is not in a cave or with a kelpie; he is not coming back, not ever! Please. Please,' he shouted before the next bout of tears robbed him of the means to speak. The two bereft parents clung to each other in the ocean, wet clothes now weighing heavily on their skin.

'I know,' she whimpered. 'I know! I know! I know! I know!' she cried loudly, with her head tipped back in the water, shrieking for the whole world to hear as she howled at the big blue sky. She screamed and raged until she thought her lungs might burst.

Finally, righting herself, she placed her hands on her husband's face and fixed him with her stare. 'I have always known! He died, James! He died, didn't he? My little boy. Oscar. He died. He's dead. He's dead. I know it, he's dead and he's not coming home! He's not ever coming home . . .'

Rachel and James sat quietly on the foredeck with the duvet cast over their legs, until their clothes and bodies dried in the failing embers of the sun and they succumbed to stupor, quite exhausted by the events of the day. She took a deep breath and closed her stinging eyes.

'Thank you for coming after me.' Her voice was a husky rasp through a throat sore from screams and sea water.

'I'll always come after you, Rachel, always. That's a given.'

They watched the sun begin to sink.

'Did you . . . did you want to die?' he asked with a catch to his voice.

'I think I did at that moment,' she confessed, and it was a hard admission to make.

'And what about at this moment? Or in a moment tomorrow or the day after?'

Rachel shook her head. 'I can't lie, James, over the last few months I have always felt it was an option if things got too much for me to handle – a last-resort option, but an option nevertheless. But I have never planned it or truly considered how until this afternoon. I might have mentioned it vaguely to Cee-Cee but she just got angry, dismissive, and I get why.'

'Because she loves you?'

She shook her head. 'No, because she understands that it's selfish and it causes ripples that are far, far reaching. We know this.'

'Yes.' He sighed.

'And she told me that things get better.'

'Do you believe her?'

'I don't know. I want to.' She picked at the edge of her T-shirt.

'Me too.' He looked out over the horizon. 'I can't live like this, Rach. I can't do it any more. I know I can't make you happy and I don't know how to help you. I don't even know how to help myself.'

'I know.'

Their conversation was calm, rational; gone was the whiff of hysteria that had book-ended all their exchanges for the last few weeks.

James continued. 'I don't know what the answer is. I try to think of it, but I keep going around and around in circles and every possible idea leads me back to that moment when we realised he had gone, and the pain is real and fresh every single time.'

She sat up and wrapped her arms around her raised knees. It was as if the fog lifted and she had clarity of sight and mind that had been missing for some time.

'I can't go through that again, what you did today . . .' He sighed.

'I can't either. I need to break the cycle for us both.' She nodded. 'I need to leave, James. I need to get away from Bermuda. I am unravelling. I have bad thoughts about everything.'

She watched his mouth fall open, as if in shock, and he took a second to compose himself. 'I thought you were going to suggest we go to counselling or, or have a break or something, but you are going to leave me, leave Bermuda?' His tone was incredulous, eyes narrowed and a catch to his throat.

'I need to leave everything. I need to leave *this*!' She threw her arm around in an arc. 'I don't want to be wandering around with a face that could curdle milk in my seventies still wondering, still watching the bloody sea! I can't do it! I need to figure out how to be . . . how to be without him.'

'And without me,' he whispered.

She looked at him, wanting for words.

It would only be later that she reflected on the fact that bar voicing his surprise, he had offered no real resistance, made no suggestion to the contrary. He hadn't fought for her. This only added weight to her decision; it was what they both needed. Time apart to think clearly, to shake off the wearying shackles of grief that bound them to this place and to that point in time, when she had popped the kettle on the hob and casually wandered the boat, looking for her boy.

Rachel stood on the balcony and looked out over the ocean. Cee-Cee stepped from the bedroom and stood by her side. 'The taxi will be here in half an hour.'

'Thank you, Cee-Cee. I am really going to miss you.'

'As God is my witness, I will do my best to care for Mr Croft. So try not to worry. I will keep you in my prayers.'

'Thank you. I can't quite believe that I won't be seeing you both every day, but James and I are so broken, Cee-Cee, misshapen and I think if I stay here I might lose my mind.' It was a stark admission that she wasn't sure she had voiced out loud.

'I understand. More than you know.'

'Did you ever feel like you might lose your reason?' She turned to look at the woman who had outwardly kept this ship running when they had come aground.

'Yes.' She gave a single nod. 'And then one day, like you, I realised that I needed to navigate this new life. Start over. You need to find a way, like I did. Mine is not a life I would have chosen, but it's my life and that's all there is to it.' She folded her hands together. 'And I do believe that my time, my sadness, is part of a bigger plan – God's plan – and therefore I am not meant to always understand it.'

Rachel gave a wry sideways smile. Oh, for the comfort of believing in heaven and hell; how much would that faith ease her burden? She gathered her thoughts.

'Truth be known, I have started to feel angry. I had everything, everything. My James and my baby boy. That was all I needed, all I could ever need.' She considered this. 'And this new world of grief, this changed existence, was given to me in a split second and I didn't ask for it!' She shook her head. 'I'm angry at the world, Cee-Cee.' She swallowed the emotion that threatened. 'It doesn't matter how many times I play it over in my head; I can't understand how it's all gone, in just the blink of an eye. And I struggle with the fact that there is absolutely nothing I can do, because that world with my James and my boy – it doesn't exist any more.'

Cee-Cee lifted her chin and looked Rachel in the eye. 'That is about the sum of it. Yes.'

'You said once that things will get better. Does it hurt any less?' She watched Cee-Cee swallow as she reached out and ran her fingers over her cheek. Rachel welcomed her touch.

'Things will get better, child, but no. No, it does not hurt any less.' The woman spoke flatly. 'I wish I could tell you otherwise. I wish I knew how to construct a lie that might sweeten your sleep, but I don't know how.'

Rachel felt the crush of disappointment underpinned by a melodious note of thanks at the fact that Cee-Cee hadn't felt the need to feed her a false cliché. She also felt some kind of relief that this tie to Oscar, this wearying yoke of grief she carried was not going to ease, as anything less, whilst it would be a more pleasant way to live, might dilute the strength of feeling she had for him and that would never do. Her pain kept her grief sharp, kept him in focus.

'So what happens from here onwards?' She hardly dared ask. 'How do you go on?'

Cee-Cee shrugged and drew breath, drawing her cardigan around her form.

'The fog of grief never lifts.' She shook her head. 'Never. But you find a way to travel through it, see beyond it, almost. There are times – most days, if not every day – when something stops me in my tracks and knocks the breath from my lungs and it's all I can do not to topple over. That still happens, even now, and I know it always will, but it's not raw, not physically painful like it used to be. I have got used to it and therefore know how to manage it. It is like a large chunk of me is missing and I had to adapt and figure out how to exist without it. I have somehow learned to forge a path forward. But I can't lie: my boy still sits behind my eyelids and lies curled in the palm of my hand.'

Rachel closed her fingers; this she understood.

Cee-Cee looked out to the horizon. 'And with each year that passes, the small details have faded almost in response to how hard I try to remember them and that is a new, fresh pain all of its own.'

'Torture.' Rachel offered up the word. 'I know what you mean. I can only think about Oscar's hair when he was a baby. It slipped through my fingers like silk, too insubstantial to grip, like something otherworldly: silky, thin, fairy-like. And its colour! Not one colour at all, but light brown with streaks of pure gold and pale yellow. All the colours of an autumn palette captured in those fine strands. This is what I do now. I remember him piece by piece, like the curator of something rare and fading, who needs to catalogue each tiny element, preserving it in memory. And it's a race against time. I'm fearful I might . . . I might forget one tiny dimple above the knuckle of his toddler hand, or the slight lift to the outside arch of his right brow. And to forget these details? Not to have him preserved in my memory, complete, recreated in every single detail? Oh my God! That thought, that very idea is so horrific because that would be the beginning. The beginning of the end of forgetting every single bit of him and that would kill me. It would kill me.'

'Yes, torture,' Cee-Cee agreed. 'But there is one irrefutable fact and that is that life does go on. It goes on for the world Oscar was part of and it goes on for you.'

Rachel looked at the woman whose words were a balm of sorts. 'I . . . I am not always sure I want my life to go on.' She thought of James yanking her from the water.

'Hmph.' Cee-Cee made a noise. 'It is not about what you want or even what you need, it is about how it is. You are not the first and you won't be the last and all you can do is make it part of your story and as I said, try to navigate your way through the fog.'

I know I won't be the first or last, but I can't believe anyone has ever felt this depth of sorrow and survived. I hope I have your strength, Cee-Cee. She looked down.

'You feel unique, and of course the way you hurt is just that, but let me tell you that while you mourn your boy, I give nothing but thanks for him. He was a shining light, helping me on my journey. He brought me pure joy! An old woman, a stranger, and yet he gave me more happiness than I had any right to expect.'

Rachel smiled at the thought of this; she pictured Oscar laughing, as he jumped into the pool, landing on his inflatable shark with precision, gripping with his arms and legs. A rare feat topped and tailed by many big-splash failures.

Look, Mummy! Look! Watch me do it again!

'Yes, he was pure joy. You know, Cee-Cee, I wish over and over that I had stayed awake that night or risen earlier on that morning.'

'You think I haven't wished every minute of every day that I had watched Willard closely in the hour that I lost him?' Cee-Cee interrupted, sharply. 'Of course I have! But I can't change a thing and neither can you. I loved little Oscar. I loved him! I never got to tell my stories to Willard, I was denied the chance, but I got to tell them to Oscar – it was important! Because after we are gone, what is left if not our stories? And they have gone with him! And my heart . . . my heart weeps for my boy and my little Oscar, who gave me that second chance.'

Rachel fell into the arms of her housekeeper and the two stood locked in an embrace.

'Safe travels, sweet girl. Safe travels,' Cee-Cee whispered, as their hearts beat in unison to a rhythm that only mothers who have grieved for their children could know – and would not in a thousand lifetimes wish upon any other.

It had somehow felt easier not to say a long, drawn-out goodbye to James – easier and cowardly, yes, but it was he who had set the tone when he kissed her on the cheek in a platonic farewell and left early that morning for the office so she could pack and leave without his presence.

'How long do you think you might be gone?' he had asked, lingering in the doorway, unable to look her in the eye.

'I don't know,' she answered truthfully. 'Just until I figure things out.'

'Right.' He tapped the doorframe with his wedding ring and just like that, he was gone.

As her plane took off from L. F. Wade International Airport, Rachel pressed her face to the window, pleased that the craft lilted to the right, dipping as it turned and giving her a clear view of the wide expanse of ocean. At this height, she could make out the dark shadows of reefs and sandbars, the clusters of shipwrecks and the fade of turquoise to darker blue, as the water stretched on and on towards the horizon. She closed her eyes for a second and spoke to her boy.

I am always with you, Oscar. Always by your side . . .

The plane began to right itself, course set. She glanced down at the towering white lighthouse at Gibbs Hill; they had enjoyed many a supper in its shadow, sitting on the cliff edge with the sun sinking and a perfect view of Jew's Bay with Heron Bay beyond.

Rachel delved into her handbag and shook a little pill from the brown plastic bottle that Dr Kent had prescribed. Her slumber was deep, instant and welcome, far better than sitting awake and counting down the three thousand four hundred-odd miles, each one taking her further and further away from the island that held her husband and her son.

CEE-CEE

'Safe travels, sweet girl. Safe travels.'

The taxi pulled out of the driveway and instantly the big old house on North Shore Road felt different. She closed the front door and walked past the sitting room, picturing Oscar fresh from his bath, running around the room, trying to evade her grip.

'You need to let me dry your hair!' Cee-Cee brandished the towel as the little boy jumped behind her on the sofa and then back down to the rug, darting this way and that around the room in his pyjamas like a tiddler in a bucket trying to escape capture.

'Oscar! You can laugh and run around as much as you like, but you are not going to sleep with wet hair, it will do you no good!'

Reluctantly he sat down hard on the pouffe and leaned back against her. Cee-Cee gently cradled his head in the fluffy white towel and soaked up the residue of water that ran in tiny rivulets down his slender neck. When she had finished, she raked at his parting with her fingertips, styling his soft, straw-coloured hair into something flat and neat.

'You'll do.' She kissed his head and he stood, running now around the edge of the rug.

'Upstairs, Oscar, it's bedtime.'

'I'll race you!' he had called, and she chuckled.

'I'll race you with my seventy-year-old knees!' She laughed.

By the time she got to his room, he was under the duvet with just his head poking out and Mr Bob by his side.

'Cee-Cee?'

'Yes?'

'Hank says when his wobbly tooth came out, he got ten dollars from the tooth fairy!'

Five-year-old Oscar pulled and prodded his teeth determinedly and huffed in disappointment to find that they were stuck fast.

'Ten dollars! That is a king's fortune.' She smiled. 'Maybe I should put my teeth under the pillow and pay off the mortgage!'

'Pay off the mortgage?' He looked at her quizzically.

'I don't have a mortgage, but it's an expression.' She laughed again. 'Don't you go worrying about your teeth, and don't go wishing your life away! One day you will blink and you will be very, very old like me!'

'You're not very, very old!'

'Try telling that to my aching bones.' She smiled. 'Being old is a privilege, Oscar, of that I am sure. It gives me time to reflect. It's like when we walk up the hill to go to the supermarket and we need to take a breather, so we park on the wall or bench and sit and watch the world pass by for a moment or two while everything settles.'

The little boy nodded.

Oscar pulled Mr Bob into the crook of his neck, as ever only half listening. It was getting close to his sleepy time. His mum and dad were having dinner at the Reefs and Cee-Cee would sleep right here in the chair until they returned. Keeping watch.

Cee-Cee smiled at the memory and ran a cool glass of water, which she took to the kitchen table, before lifting the notepad from her bag, along with her pen.

Sweet Girl,

I have just waved you goodbye and my heart aches with all I am trying to keep inside it. I shall miss you! Oh, how I shall miss you! And how I will miss the family that I came to love, now just one: James. My heart aches for him too. I feel part of this family and I hope it is okay for me to say that, it's the truth. I see Oscar everywhere I look and now you, only recently gone, will linger in the quiet corners of rooms and in the shadows of the hallways where laughter used to live. I will add you to the list of the many people in my life that made an impact — those who taught me things that now live on in my consciousness; single moments that made me laugh, made me cry. Not always big things, either. I think about a woman wearing lemon-coloured gloves and a white pillbox hat, who I bumped into outside Trimminghams on Front Street, when I was no more than a girl. She was carrying a fistful of brown paper bags with ribbon handles containing Lord knows what, but they looked fancy. I was young and had been rushing and we banged against each other, all elbows and ribs, a-clattering on the hot pavement. With clothes and pride askew, we both knelt to the floor to gather what had been dropped and apologised profusely, equally keen I would say to bring our encounter to an end. As I turned away, still half in tune with the voice of the woman whose lemon gloves I greatly admired, I heard her mutter to her friend, 'Did you see those killer cheekbones? Lucky girl!' Now I have to confess that the shape and prominence of your cheekbones is not a learned skill nor something you can do a dang thing about, but I took the compliment nonetheless and my heart swelled a little. Little did that lady in the lemon-coloured gloves know that on that day when my confidence was low and my spirit beyond fragile, these few words gave me the shot in the arm needed to go and do and say what I had to. She, of course, would never know, but it was a lesson to me. Kind words or a compliment can heal, just like mean words can cut.

Yes, I remember her even now.

Cee-Cee looked around the kitchen and glanced at the clock, wondering if she might take Rachel up a cup of tea, before remembering that she had left.

'Don't be stupid, Cee-Cee.' She closed her eyes. 'May the Lord keep you safe, and may his angels guard you while you fly.' She turned her attention back to her letter.

I also think a lot about my best friend Eliza-Jane Clara May Brown. Oh, Clara and I have history! I don't rightly know if our lives were so interwoven because we were best friends or we were best friends because our lives were so interwoven. Even here, even now, that question is no clearer to me. Clara was as fine a friend as I could ever have had — at least, that was what I believed, but I only had sight of half of the deck of cards, as my daddy might have said.

Clara loved being in our house — by our house I mean Grandma Sally's house, where I might have told you I slept, with my mommy and daddy in the house next door. I loved to sleep with my gran in her two rooms. Her sons, my uncles, worked up at The Royal Naval Dockyard in Sandys Parish and slept in the rough accommodation provided, no more than bunks and a bucket by all accounts. But there weren't nothing rough about Grandma Sally's house. It was painted in the prettiest shade of lilac, with the traditional white limestone-blocked roof that like all the other roofs on the island, looked like the upside-down hull of a boat. The inverted steps just the right shape to resist hurricanes and the clever design meant water flowed over it and was collected with ease. Clara always dithered at the end of Grandma Sally's path, making a great show about whether she should come in or go home. I think she liked me to plead with her, it made her feel wanted, and who can't relate to that? She'd stand there running her palm over the small hibiscus bush that had sprouted, drawn like a buzzing bee to them vibrant pink blooms. I can see her now, holding those delicate, silk-like petals and then swiping them under her broad nose, inhaling the remnants of that lingering perfume like it was smelling salts. I heard her, time and again, stating with certainty, 'When I'm older, I'm going to live in a big old house with hibiscus plants all around the edge, so I can wander into my garden and pick a bloom whenever I feel like it!'

I naturally added this, her utmost desire, to my daily prayer, which was primarily a celestial shopping list for all the things I figured those around me might need or want. The Almighty God must have been listening, because to my knowledge, Clara got one of the prettiest houses in the whole of Warwick Parish and a man who could afford it on account of his promotion at the ferry company.

Clara had been the youngest of five, and she lived further along in Pembroke Parish, towards Hamilton, just off Marsh Folly Road, backatown, near the stinking dump. That's where she lived in one room of a wooden construction with meagre proportions with her momma, Eula. It was sad, but true that Momma Eula showed Clara more impatience than love. Grandma Sally said that Eula had figured her child-rearing days were over and having waved off her last teen on the path of self-governance, was looking forward to enjoying her twilight years with her feet up and a strong pipe in her hand as the sun set.

The appearance of Clara, all ten pounds of her, exactly nine months after a brief, but by all accounts, delightful evening spent at the Swizzle Inn in the company of a Ghanaian gentleman stopping over on our island on his way to New York, was a little unexpected and most unwelcome. Not to mention a scandal. I figure these things shaped my friend in ways we did not yet know. Not that I gave a hoot about her beginnings — not then, and not now. I only mention it because it popped into my head and as I said, my thoughts and those I choose to voice are whatever comes to me and for that I make no apology.

It was while we dithered on the path one night having spent the afternoon at the beach that Grandma Sally came outside. 'Good evening, girls,' she called from the porch, with her hands on her broad hips. 'Who would like a bowl of my green split-pea and ham soup?'

How we smiled, our mouths watering at the very suggestion.

Momma Eula would just have to wait.

I can picture Grandma Sally now, ladling the thick broth into two white enamel bowls with a blue-painted edge, and setting them on the little table on a white embroidered tablecloth. Now, I don't want you to go thinking that my family were anything high and mighty, we were no wealthier than the next and carried humility about us like a comfortable yoke, but my grandma had a certain refinement about her, picked up from working in some of the finest houses on the island. Once, she was called to work up at Government House, where she got to pass canapés around while the governor himself hosted dignitaries from London, England. Yes! England. The governor's name was Admiral Sir Ralph Leatham and he thanked her in person for helping the evening go smoothly. She told me she spent the whole time in awe of the jewellery worn by the ladies – brilliant diamonds and gold chains with rubies and sapphires so plentiful she wondered if they had found treasure in a wreck on our own shores. She concluded that even the plainest woman with a pinched nose, thin, bloodless lips and a pointy chin could be made to look pretty with the addition of these baubles. My daddy, overhearing, pointed out that no matter how many jewels anyone hung from their person or their clothes, it was 'portant to remember that we all shit through the same hole. God forgive my coarseness, Rachel, but that is what he said.

And he was right.

All those years waiting at tables and helping at events and soirées, meant Grandma Sally knew a thing or two about being a host and keeping a home. She was never to be seen without her hair fastened inside a white, floppy, linen hat and her feet stuffed inside white leather shoes that were at least half a size too small, causing her instep to bunch up like a trotter and sit in a rounded lump that pushed against the stiff sides of those shoes.

Her most prized possessions were three things: a delicate green, glass-shaded lamp with pale glass fronds that hung like a fringe all around it and, once the kerosene wick was lit, bathed the room in its amber glow. A bamboo card table, worn and stained the colour of strong tea through age and sea air, and a dainty blue-china, hand-painted cup and saucer with a fluted edge picked out in pure gold! A generous home-owner for whom she had worked had gifted her all of these things. It delighted Grandma Sally that these objects, deemed good enough to grace the parlour of the fashionable Madam Jean-Laurent Laroche from Paris, France, now sat inside her humble little house in Warwick Parish. The beautiful trinkets and hints of finery, no matter how patched, with which my grandma surrounded herself were proof of how far she had come. She always reminded me that it was a mere slip in the hand of time, not much more than one hundred years previous that her great-great-grandma had toiled in slavery, living outside with no shelter and no need of a pretty lamp or tablecloth. I kept that knowledge close to my heart and it shaped me every day.

It still does.

So there we were, enjoying our soup, when Grandma Sally walked to the closet in the corner and opened the door. 'I've got something to show you.' She pulled out a swatch of stunning white organza fabric covered in a raised pattern of cherries that sat in bunches of twos with the relief of foliage behind. It was something quite beautiful. 'Oh, it's so lovely!' Clara clapped her hands together. 'Is it for the dance?' she asked. My grandma nodded and I concentrated on my soup, feeling a flash of guilt to be the owner of something so showy and so very beautiful. I was never that kind of girl. 'I shall make a very long skirt with a petticoat underneath and a nipped in *little waist with a contrast sash. I've given it a lot of thought,' Grandma Sally explained. I didn't want to boast, but my stomach swelled with excitement — either that or I was full of hot soup. 'And what about you, Miss Clara, what are you planning on wearing?' Grandma asked, and Clara sat up straight and said, 'Actually, I don't think I shall be going this year; I may have other plans.' And I will never forget what came next: 'Oh well, that is a shame,' muttered Grandma Sally. 'What in the Lord's name am I going to do with this?' From inside the cupboard, she drew out a second swatch of the exact same fabric but in a delicate shade of pale pink; it was equally as beautiful! 'I was fixing on making you the same dress in this, but if you have other plans...' Grandma Sally shook her head and made to return the fabric to the cupboard.*

'Grandma Sally, bring me that fabric! Of course I'm going now!' Clara boomed, and wrapped the piece around her head, delighted.

Yes, we were sisters in every sense. Although sisters I now know should look out for one another, help and support each other. And there weren't nothing sisterly about what she did to me in my time of need, my time of distress.

Nothing at all.

Cee-Cee sat up straight at the sound of the front door opening. She must have fallen into a doze.

'Well, look at that. Time got carried away with me.'

'Are you okay, Cee-Cee? You're sitting in the dark.' James spoke softly, as he switched on the kitchen light.

'Well, I didn't realise the time!' She stood, embarrassed, and walked to the stove.

'I don't want any supper, Cee-Cee. But thank you. I'm not hungry. Not tonight.'

'There is cheese in the fridge if you get peckish later.'

He nodded. 'Did . . . did she get away okay?'

'Taxi picked her up fine.' She saw the look of sadness in his eyes.

'I miss her already. In fact' – he shook his head and looked out of the window – 'I have missed her for a long time now.'

'What is meant to, comes back to you.'

'I hope so.' He gave her a brief smile and coughed to mask his emotion. 'Let me drop you home.'

'No, I like a walk at this time of night.' She walked to the table and folded her notebook and pen back inside her bag.

'It's starting to get quite dark, Cee-Cee.'

She smiled at him. 'James, I know every inch of these roads with my eyes closed. I have been walking them for more than seventy years. Now get some rest.' She nodded at him and made her way across the vast hallway where her footsteps echoed in the quiet.

FOUR

It was hard for Rachel not to think about the last time she had been in England. Two years ago they had come home for Christmas. Oscar had been beyond excited; Hank had told him quite casually one breaktime that when he had gone to *his* grandmother's for Christmas, it had snowed. In the week before they left, Oscar could barely sleep for the excited planning of all he would do during the snow-filled vacation in his mind.

'I am going to build a big snowman and go sledging and we can have a snowball fight!'

She hadn't the heart to tell him that Hank's grandma lived just outside of Breckenridge, Colorado, where at this time of year snow, and lots of it, was almost guaranteed. The same, however, could not be said of a 1970s housing estate in a Bristol suburb where the best they could hope for was a smattering of frost, which quickly turned to grey sludge under the wheels of vehicles. Rachel figured it better to let him dream and plan, hoping that the distraction of all the attention from his UK relatives, an abundance of chocolate figures on the Christmas tree, and Treacle the cat to play with might be enough to divert him from the rather disappointingly mild winter that was forecast.

'You can help me, Dad,' he had enthused. 'And I'm going to get the sledge and go from the top of a hill and I might take off and fly across

Bristol! Like they do in *The Snowman*, and I'm going to get some snow and put it in the freezer and I'm going to bring it back to Bermuda and give it to you, Cee-Cee!'

Cee-Cee had clutched her chest in excitement. 'I have never seen snow in real life! Thank you, Oscar, that would be wonderful! I shall look forward to it.'

'I've never seen snow in real life either!' Oscar piped up.

She and James had laughed, sipping their gin and tonics and looking at each other over his head in the middle seat on the plane, wondering how they would manage not only Oscar's snow expectations, but now Cee-Cee's too!

The memory was as vivid as it was painful and now, here alone, the sight of her dad in the arrivals hall brought a lump to her throat. While all around them joyful reunions rang out in the form of squeals, howls, whoops and laughter, the two stood sedate and quiet, hugging each other tightly with something akin to relief.

'It's all right, my babber. It's all right.' He spoke the affectionate term into her hair and she closed her eyes, ignoring the background noise and squashing her face against his coat. She wished she were still a little girl, when these words spoken with certainty by her daddy could fix just about anything.

Despite the blue sky of this October day, Rachel was cold. Her dad glanced at her shivering form as she folded into herself on the front seat and cranked the heating up in his Ford Mondeo. She hadn't the heart to tell him that her chill went all the way down to her bones.

'Your mum packed snacks.' He nodded towards the back seat before restoring his gaze to the slow lane of the M4. 'There's a box of ham sandwiches and a flask of tea and some fruitcake if you are hungry.'

'I'm not, Dad, thanks.'

'You've lost weight. You look thin.'

She nodded. This she knew.

'We've got your room all ready. Mum changed the bed linen and Peter took all the cardboard boxes of his junk and put them in his garage. Mind you, about time. I think some of it was his old university files and things. I've wanted it gone for a long time; cluttering up your old room like that.'

'Thank you.'

'Do you want to nap? I can recline the seat.'

She shook her head. 'No, I'm fine, Dad. I slept on the plane.'

With relief they settled under a blanket of silence for some minutes. Rachel used the time to stare at the wide embankment of the three-lane motorway, where full trees provided a roadside canopy, hinting at the lush farmland that lay beyond. This one impressive thoroughfare reminded her of how narrow Bermuda was, with its three tapering main roads that defined boundaries, and the high walls and narrow lanes that were claustrophobic at times when the traffic was heavy. She held her hands out, flexing her fingers to catch the steady stream of hot air that came from the dashboard. Rachel thought her dad looked older, paler, greyer and she felt a spike of guilt at the fact that she had mentally disregarded her parents' grief in light of her own. She recalled James saying something similar about his mum and dad. Her in-laws, always a little aloof, preoccupied with their own busy lives, had written apparently and offered to come over.

A quick glance at the clock told her it was nearly midday here. James would be having his breakfast. This one small fact already made her feel so very far away from him, not only in miles, but in time too. It was another indicator of how their lives were becoming even further out of sync.

'It is lovely to see you, babber, despite everything. We have been' – he swallowed – 'we've been so worried and so sad of course.'

She nodded.

Her dad continued. 'I can't believe it.' He shook his head. 'None of us can.' There was the unmistakable sound of tears in his voice. 'Such a lovely, lively little lad.'

Rachel looked out of the window and read the sign:

Reading Services 3 Miles
Chieveley Services 24 Miles
Membury Services 43 Miles
Leigh Delamere Services 83 Miles

She then stared at the lorry in front, which had a large loaf of sliced white bread on it – anything, anything to distract her thoughts and dilute her dad's words. He seemed to take her lead and once his breathing had found its normal rhythm and his distress abated, they drove on without further discussion.

And that suited her just fine.

On previous trips, she usually felt her excitement mount as the car pulled on to the A432. There was something about seeing place names familiar to her youth – 'Chipping Sodbury', 'Wickwar', 'Iron Acton' – each one with a picture and an event associated with it in her mind: eighteenth birthday parties, twenty-firsts, Bonfire Nights. Her tummy would bunch with fondness at the sight of houses where school friends had once lived, the Horseshoe pub, where she had taken many an illicit sip from her teenage years onward, and the petrol station where she had worked on countless weekends in order to save money for holidays and festivals – including one fantastic summer trip to Ibiza, where she would meet a boy called James Croft who would promise her the whole wide world . . .

But not today; today there was no joy in being 'home', no nostalgic flutter at the thought of belonging to a place that carried her history in its very soil. It was disappointing, but not wholly surprising, that the feeling here was the same as it had been in Bermuda: a sensation like she was floating, belonged nowhere; lost in time and caught between the pincers of grief that refused to loosen their hold no matter where the house or time zone in which she lay her head.

As her dad ratcheted up the handbrake and unclipped his seatbelt, her mum came rushing down the path in her slippers, her dark, short hair revealing a strip of grey root at the scalp. Her tears fell and she held a red dishcloth up to her face.

'Oh my God! Oh, Rachel!' She pulled open the passenger door and without waiting for her to get out, slumped against her inside the car, holding her in a fixed position and howling her tears. 'I can't believe it. I can't!' she sobbed. 'That poor little mite. I can't stop thinking about him and I just wanted you home where I can look after you. That's all I wanted and here you are.'

Her mum was near hysterical and Rachel felt the pain she expressed mirrored in her own gut, twisted and inflamed with all it tried to contain.

Eventually her mum straightened, her eyes puffy and her mouth slack. Rachel climbed from the car and jammed her fingers into her jeans pockets; her hands still cold in this chilly climate, a good twenty degrees cooler than Bermuda and without the humidity to which she had become accustomed.

'Come in; Dad'll bring your bag.' She linked her arm through her daughter's and led her through the front door.

Treacle, the ginger tom, stood as if waiting for her in the hallway. She noted the age that had crept over his handsome face and bent to stroke him as he sidled against her legs. Oscar had been so in love with Treacle, scooping him up and burying his face in his soft fur. *Come on, Treacle!* he would call, slapping his leg, hoping to call him to heel like a puppy.

Each time Rachel stepped inside the house in which she had grown up, she was slightly taken aback by how small it was. Not in a sneering way, but more that it fascinated her. The perception of her youth was that there had been plenty of space inside the three-bedroomed, semi-detached modern dwelling for her and her parents, her brother, all of their friends, their fat cat, a guinea pig or two and even visiting relatives from far and wide. And yet now as she stood in the narrow hallway, she realised that the entire downstairs would fit inside the kitchen-cum-dining room of their house on the North Shore Road. She wondered what Cee-Cee would make of the thick-flocked wallpaper, swirly-patterned wool carpets, toasty radiators, the abundance of cushions and the clutter of ornaments, all harbouring dust. She had been inside Cee-Cee's cottage once; it was cosy, but without so many of the elements that made a British home. The walls were painted stone, the floors cool ships' timbers, and the fireplace was blackened on either side where woodsmoke cast its shadows as it danced up the chimney.

She could hardly bear to look in the neat sitting room where pictures of Oscar at a variety of ages graced the mantelpiece and the top of the television set, along with those of his two cousins – her brother's kids, Hayden and Nate.

'What can I get you, darling, a cup of tea?'

'Yes, thank you, Mum.' She didn't really want a cup of tea but knew that the distraction for them both would be most welcome.

'The police still not found anything?' her mum asked in such a matter-of-fact way as she filled the kettle that it caught her a little off guard.

'Not yet,' she whispered.

Maybe never and maybe that's better . . .

'Peter said he'd come over when you are a bit more settled; I said I'd let him know, poor mite. He and Julie have been proper cut up over the whole thing. It's made them really tighten their grip on Hayden and Nate, but I told them an accident is an accident, nothing more, nothing less.'

Rachel bit the inside of her cheek.

Poor Peter and Julie. Yes, it must be tough, sitting at home with their two kids while my heart and soul are shattered.

Again she felt guilt at the flash of hatred she felt towards these people, her own kin, on whom she would not wish ill for anything in the world! And yet . . . and yet this feeling was almost instinctual.

She looked at the spot on the wall where the photograph of her, James and Oscar on board *Liberté,* tanned and smiling used to live, pinned there for more years than she could remember, along with a couple of postcards. She noticed the picture was missing.

'And how's poor James doing?' Her mum shook her head. 'I hate to think of him on his own.'

Rachel leaned on the countertop, taking the hint that her mum was less than impressed with how she had left him in Bermuda. It didn't matter whether she was three or in her thirties, to be censored by her parents caused the rise of guilt in her throat just the same and it didn't taste pleasant. 'I think we both needed a bit of space, Mum.' It was an understatement, a hint of the truth that she felt they might destroy each other had she stayed.

'And I said to your dad, all that money, that lovely life, and it just shows nothing is foolproof; no amount of wealth can save you from heartache. Life can be so cruel.' She poured hot water on the tea bag in the mug.

Rachel felt the punch of her mum's words, softened by the knowledge that they came from a place without malice, a loose tongue and a stream of thought that babbled without regard for where those words, no matter how sharp, might land.

'And talking of your dad, he's driving me bloody crazy. Won't talk about his feelings and gets upset at me for crying all the time. But I can't help it, Rach, honest to God I can't. I don't know how to stop my tears. And if I mention what's happened, he leaves the room.' She grabbed the kitchen roll and tore a square, balling it into her eyes, as if to prove the point. 'He comes in from work, has his tea and goes walking. Walking!

Says it clears his head. I think his head'd be better cleared if he stayed here and talked it out, but no.' She sighed. 'That's what he does each night, puts on the work boots he's taken off not an hour since and treads the same route by all accounts. He goes out round Engine Common and up to Rangeworthy and then across and back down the Jubilee Way. Peter says it's about seven miles, give or take. Every night. Seven miles! Can you imagine? He'll be needing new boots by Christmas at this rate. New knees by the summer.'

'Do you mind if I go and lie down, Mum?'

'Of course not, babber. Here's your tea.' She handed her a green-and-brown paisley-printed mug that had lined the shelf for more years than either of them could remember. Rachel held it and felt the echo in her palm of countless warm drinks taken morning, noon and night. This one little cup and tea; constants in celebration, commiseration and now in mourning. 'If you need anything just shout and I'll cook us all a lovely tea for later.'

'Thank you.'

'Oh!' her mum shouted, wiping her hands on her skirt. 'I nearly forgot! This arrived for you day before yesterday.'

Rachel watched her walk to the shelf over the radiator in the hall-way and grab a brown envelope that was propped against the wall. She knew even from this distance that it was Cee-Cee's handwriting on the envelope that lay in her mum's palm. She felt the corner of her mouth lift in a smile. It was strange to see this thing here in her childhood home, flown from Bermuda, all the way over the Atlantic Ocean. Her two worlds colliding at a time when she least expected it.

'Look' – her mum flipped it over – 'this was written on the back: "*Please keep for Mrs Rachel Croft, many thanks*",' she read aloud.

'It's from Cee-Cee.'

'Your housekeeper?'

'Yes.' *My housekeeper and my friend.*

'It must have raced you here!' her mum offered brightly.

'She sent it ahead.' *So it would be waiting for me.*

Rachel held the letter to her chest. As she trod the stairs, she saw Oscar marching up ahead of her two years earlier. 'I can touch the walls on both sides, Mum!' he called out, fascinated by the narrow walkway and the small square of landing at the top. He loved it here: neat, compact, cosy.

Her bedroom was as she remembered it, minus the cardboard boxes full of Peter's junk that he preferred to keep at their parents' house rather than clutter up his own pristine new-build, less than a mile away.

She stood by the window with a view over the square back garden and tore open the envelope.

Rachel, sweet girl,

I have been thinking about what to write to you and wanted to start by telling you this; everyone I have ever loved and everyone I have ever lost are still with me. Every day, all around. I see them, I feel them and I remember them. They are not gone, not truly, and I know that is scant comfort to you right now, but I hope in time . . .

Rachel paused and swallowed the sob that built in her chest. She wanted nothing more than to see and feel her son around her every day, but to do so without the pain and ache of longing that accompanied every thought of him now. She scanned the rest of the words; some paragraphs brought her small comfort.

. . . I see your pain and I recognise it as my own. I know that things are hard for you right now, and that you would rather not face each new dawn. I also know you will not believe me when I tell you that this will not always be the case, but it's

true. Things get easier, they do. As the months and years pass by, you will see.

Time heals. Time heals.

Her dad knocked on the door as he entered. 'Here's your case, love. Have you been crying?' He wheeled it to the end of the bed.

'Yes. I got a letter from Cee-Cee. She is lovely and what she says always makes me think and I don't always want to think. Sometimes I want to switch off.'

'I understand that. Are you going to have a doze?'

'I think I might. I'm always tired.'

'That's just your body's way of coping, shutting down to conserve the little reserves you have left. Listen to it, Rach, sleeping is the best thing.'

'Thank you, Dad.'

'Your mum, she . . .' He looked up at the ceiling and drew breath.

'I know.' She gave him a small smile.

'What's that?' He nodded at the Tic-Tac box in her hand.

'It's sand and shells that I found in my pocket. On the day . . .' She paused. 'From where we lost him.'

He nodded and headed for the doorway. 'She's right about one thing, though – my walking has kind of taken over. It keeps me from thinking and wears me out sufficiently so I can sleep. Come with me, if you like.'

'I might.' She crossed to the single bed of her childhood, the one where Oscar had slept while she and James were relegated to the blow-up bed not a foot away on the floor. She lay down in the dip in the middle of the mattress and pulled the duvet over her shoulder, taking instant comfort from the familiar view of the floral wall and the dressing table at which she had spent hours curling her hair, curling her friend Vicky's hair and practising her make-up – trying to make herself pretty, trying to land a handsome boy like James Croft. A small part of her yearned for that simpler time when someone like James Croft was an idea and she did not know that pain like this was possible.

And it just shows, nothing is foolproof; no amount of wealth can save you from heartache . . .

'I was only a lad.' Her dad spoke and she jumped, having almost forgotten he was there. 'But I remember very clearly when my dad died and my mum shut down completely, like a robot with an off button, and it was scary. But she came back to us. It took a while, but she came back.' He spoke softly, her lovely dad.

'Thank you, Dad, and thank you for picking me up.'

'Always. Whenever and wherever, that's my job.'

'And it was my job to keep Oscar safe.' Her voice broke at this rare, unfiltered admission.

'You can't think like that.' He walked back into the room and sat on the side of the mattress. 'You can't!'

'I can't help it, Dad. I am so, so sad.'

'And it breaks my heart, poppet. It takes time. My mum had us little ones and so she had to battle on, even though she was a widow, but she did it, she came out the other side and you will too. I know it, but you have to trust time. Be patient.'

'But that's just it, Dad; when a wife loses her husband she's a widow, but I've lost my boy, I'm not a widow, so am I still a mum? What's the word for someone like me?'

She watched the sadness steal his smile. 'You are and always will be Oscar's mum. Always.' He spoke through trembling lips. 'And he was very lucky to have a mum like you, just like you were very lucky to have a boy like him.'

'Do you think . . .' She swallowed. 'Do you think I was a good mum?' she asked softly of the man whose judgment she trusted, watching his expression for clues as James's words rang around her head in a dull chant: *You built walls of gin, tennis and having lunch with your girlfriends – and you lived within those walls, often you didn't see him when you had the chance . . .*

'Oh, Rachel.' He gave a tortured smile, clearly trying to keep his distress at bay. 'That is the one thing you can take great comfort from. Oscar adored you, as you did him. That was obvious to anyone who saw you together.'

'I keep thinking about all the times I didn't spend time with him when I could have. I keep thinking, what if—'

'Don't do that. Don't.' He was emphatic. 'Those what-ifs can only lead to a very dark place.'

'I'm already in a very dark place,' she whimpered.

'I know.' He squeezed her shoulder beneath the duvet.

Her mum called from the bottom of the stairs, 'Brian, leave her be, she wants to rest!'

He stood and winked at her. 'Coming, Jean.'

Yate was, compared to Bermuda, grey. It did, however, suit her mind-set. The featureless tarmac paths, pale-brick walls, soulless cul-de-sacs and standard roads all leading to remarkably similar pale-brick housing estates, none of it required any thought or contemplation. Bermuda was by contrast a wonderful, wonderful assault on your senses, where music blared from open-topped cars, mopeds carrying tourists buzzed like bees, seeking quiet spots on secret beaches or cool drinks in the shade. The blue, blue tinge to the air made everything look different, and the sun cast a golden, lucky glow over everything it touched. It made jewels and water sparkle, teeth whiter, smiles wider and the future rosy – or so she had believed.

Here, quietly walking the pavements with her dad of a dreary, driz-zle-coated evening, wrapped in a coat and scarf, there were no distrac-tions of sea diamonds, no shards of sunlight to cast interesting shadows on the dullest of walls. No fronds of green fern to tickle your face and shins as you meandered, no wildflowers to grab your attention and ignite your interest, no bends in the narrow road with picture-postcard views waiting to take your breath away around every corner. No nods from strangers, certainly no waves from strangers, and not that many smiles.

She thought of Johnny 'Mr Happy' Barnes who stood each and every day at the Crow Lane roundabout wearing his straw hat, waving to commuters and tourists alike who were making their way into Hamilton, and telling people that he loved them. It made you feel good. Here in Yate, everyone seemed a little busy, a little preoccupied, and that too suited her just fine. She wondered what Johnny Barnes would make of it here.

The first time she accompanied her dad on his seven-mile hike, it had felt like a chore. Reluctantly, she had given in to his coaxing and stepped out into the cool, damp evening. Plodding with one foot in front of the other she was wary of slowing his established pace. Yet rather than speeding up, tiredness pulled at her muscles, which were out of practice and more used to sitting coiled on a wooden steamer chair with a light blanket over them, as she stared at the vast expanse of the Atlantic Ocean.

Her dad was right: the physical tiredness did help her sleep for a while, a couple of hours at most. But as was now routine, and paying no heed to the change in time zone, at three a.m. she was wide awake, staring out of the double-glazed window at the inky-toned night sky, crying violently until she thought her lungs might burst, and fighting to catch her breath with the pain of longing deep in her chest. At these times, she sent love and messages out across the ether to Oscar, not knowing where or when they might reach him.

She and James had spoken a couple of times since she'd arrived nearly a week ago. Their polite enquiries were punctuated with long, silent pauses when all that she was too afraid to say jumped into her mouth to be swallowed with the thick, acrid spit of cowardice. After every call she replaced the receiver with a very real sense of frustration, tinged with relief.

◆ ◆ ◆

Peter came to visit on her third day home.

'Here he is!' She had almost forgotten the thrill with which her mum announced his arrival, and she had almost forgotten how very irritating she found it to see her so flustered and delighted by his lanky presence. He loped into the kitchen, his face pinched, a wool scarf at his neck, despite the rather clement day, and his hug weak.

'Cup of tea, darling?'

'Please.' He, like her, knew the routine by now and took a chair opposite Rachel in the cramped breakfast nook, where Treacle had taken up one of the four seats and a combined salt-and-pepper rack and nap-kin-holder with a picture of Cala d'Or, Mallorca on the front, took pride of place at the end of the table. It was a souvenir from their first trip aboard, back in the days when her mum, too, had wanted to chase the sun. This was before her sense of adventure had been overwhelmed, eventually losing the battle to all that frightened her about travelling: the weather, the food, the flying . . . It had always pissed Rachel off that her mum was so content to remain within these four square walls. Now, however, she saw the sense in staying put. Safe.

'I was going to write, but I didn't know what to say.' Peter gave the mealy-mouthed excuse and she thought of the dozens of letters and cards that James had secreted away in the garage – she had quite forgotten about them until that moment. None, she now knew, were from her brother.

'That's okay, lovey. It is hard, and no one knows what to say.'

Rachel stared at her mum, who had issued the apology that wasn't hers to give, and Peter's face, smiling, too easily placated by her hollow words.

'So, how's James doing?' he asked, tapping the tabletop lightly with his fingertips. She considered picking up the wooden table mat and slamming it on to his hand to make it stop.

'Erm' – she swallowed – 'not good.'

'Here you go.' Their mum placed the mug of tea in front of him and returned to the sink to find the next chore.

'And how are you?' He slurped.

'Pretty rubbish actually.'

'What happened, exactly?' he asked with a casual air that shocked and distressed her in equal measure, as he blew over the surface of his tea with pursed lips, sending little ripples out over the surface. She thought of the water, the calm sea into which she'd plunged. *Oscar! Oscaaaar!* Calling until her throat was raw.

Where to begin?

She looked down. 'I don't know exactly and that's one of the hardest things.' She hoped that might be the end of his enquiry, but no.

'Okay, so not exactly, but what happened?'

Rachel sat up straight. 'We had gone for a three-day trip on the boat, and on the first morning out we couldn't find Oscar.' She swiped the tears that fell at the memory of the moment.

Rach, Oscar! Coffee's ready . . . Do you want me to bring it up?

'Jesus.' Peter ran his hand over his face. 'And what, he'd just jumped in?'

Rachel sat back and shook her head. 'Like I said, I don't know.'

'Well, what did the police say?'

'They don't know either.'

'I couldn't stand that, the not knowing, and I suppose until they find a body, it could be anything.' He exhaled and took a sip of his tea.

'I wonder if he hit his head and slipped in or just went for a swim and got into difficulty.' He let this hang.

Rachel felt the bile rise in her throat.

'Julie works with a woman whose sister lost a child. Terrible thing. She ended up in her local equivalent of Barrow Gurney.' He gave the name of the mental-health facility that they had mocked and taunted each other with as children, swapping invented horror stories; everyone at school had insensitively and ignorantly done it. 'But hers wasn't an accident or anything,' Peter continued. 'The kid was born with a heart defect, no one knew and they went to watch him on sports day and' – he made a kind of clicking noise with his mouth, and demonstrated falling horizontally with his long fingers – 'he keeled over and was gone. Just like that; only twelve. Julie still worries about that now, with Hayden and Nate, especially on sports day, but I've told her it's very unlikely.'

Rachel had the forethought to plunge her head beneath the table; she closed her eyes and could smell and feel the orange bucket that she had pressed to her chest and held in her hands.

'Jesus Christ!' she heard Peter yell, as she vomited in the space under the table where once she had hidden from him in a game of hide-and-seek, a long, long time ago.

It was not long after Peter had left, and her mum had swabbed the floor with a wet mop and a liberal dash of disinfectant, that she decided to call James. She lay on the bed with Mr Bob at her neck and was relieved that he answered instantly, not giving her time to panic or back out.

'How are you?' she asked.

'I'm at work, so . . .' he answered, with the code that she knew well: *I can't talk; people are around me; to be discussed . . .*

'Do you want me to call back?'

'No, no, I'm just going outside.'

She pictured him making his way through the plush offices and heard the change in background noise as he came to stand on Pitts Bay Road with its lush green lawn, huge palms, only a hop, skip and a jump from the water's edge and the Fairmont Hamilton Princess Hotel, where he and his team were regulars for lunch and drinks and were on first-name terms with the maître d'. She looked up out of the window, over the neighbour's roof at the grey sky of the late afternoon and thought how odd it was how the climate so quickly became normal. She knew James would be in a short-sleeved shirt and she shivered.

'How are you?' He returned the question.

'I don't know. The same.'

'Yep,' he conceded, matching the sentiment. 'I saw Mackenzie outside Lindos.' She tried to picture the two men bumping into each other at the supermarket, a setting so informal for a topic so terrible. James continued, 'Still nothing.'

She nodded, realising she had been holding her breath. She ran Mr Bob over her cheek.

'It goes without saying, Rachel, there is money in our joint account for whatever you need or whatever makes things easier for you. You know that.'

His customary kindness caused her tears to prick.

'Thank you, James.'

There was an uncomfortable silence. James coughed to clear his throat and as before, she felt the weight of the awkward pause. How could they talk about the weather, traffic, what they'd had for supper, the news, the house, his job – all the things that used to fill their conversations – because there was a big, black hole in the middle of their world and everything normal, and everything that had gone before had tumbled into it.

It was as if she were trying and failing to find something in common with a stranger after all topics had been exhausted. It was hard to believe this was the man she'd slept with and whose arms she had fallen into. The man who had proposed to her one Christmas Eve with tears in his eyes and who had held her hand as she bore their beautiful son into the world. She pictured the two of them one crazy night when Oscar was small and in the care of Cee-Cee, leaving after dinner at the Reefs and heading home. They had stopped at Warwick Long Bay and run down to the water, turning right and walking in the moonlight until they reached Jobson's Cove. It was her favourite spot on the whole island.

Laughing, they'd shed their shoes and clothes, abandoning their belongings in a neat pile and wearing nothing but underwear, they'd held hands, squealing at the naughtiness of it all as they ran down the gentle shelving of soft sand and into the warm water of the secluded narrow bay. The high rocks either side provided shelter and the moon lit the water around them like something otherworldly. They'd swum and thrashed, splashing each other and coming together to hold each other tight, kissing in the gentle ripple of the tide and lying back in the surf without a care in the world.

'I sometimes think I am too lucky,' she'd confessed, flipping over and treading water.

'What do you mean?' James laughed.

She'd swum over and wrapped her arms around him, kissing his face and holding him tight. The feel of his skin against hers in the water was exquisite.

'My life,' she began. 'I'm just an ordinary girl from Yate and look at me! I live here in paradise with you, my beautiful man, and our boy and our house, and we eat dinner at the Reefs and everything we have and all that we do and' – she'd swallowed the tears that rose in her throat – 'I feel too lucky; like I don't deserve it and I worry that it can't last because it's too perfect.'

James had reached up and taken her face inside his palms. 'But that's just it, Rach – you are the most extraordinary girl I have ever met.'

He'd laughed. 'You are my mate as well as my wife, and you are the best mum. Don't you worry, this life is just going to get better and better.'

'Are you still there?' His question down the line shook her from her memory.

'Yes. I'm still here.'

'How are your parents?'

She took a deep breath. 'Oh, you know the same. Peter was here asking me questions about Oscar and I was sick under the table.'

'Ignore him. Peter is and always will be a fucking knob.'

Rachel's reaction was instant and unplanned.

She laughed.

It was a proper giggle that escaped through lips that had become conditioned to tears. She gasped and placed her hand over her mouth as the sweet taste of laughter was now replaced by the bitter tang of distress. How dare she laugh? How dare she feel even a flicker of happiness after Oscar . . .

'I have to go,' she offered curtly. She ended the call abruptly and gave in to the tears that helped restore the status quo: familiar, all-consuming and comforting because of it.

CEE-CEE

On the way to the linen closet with an armful of freshly laundered towels, Cee-Cee peeped in on Oscar's room and of course it was just as she had left it. She blew in a kiss to land on his bed and quietly closed the bedroom door, thinking of the first time she had gone inside after that dreadful, dreadful phone call.

With a tremble to her lip and a twist to her heart, she had reached down to pick up the stray bricks of Lego that littered the rug, before sorting them into matching shapes and placing them in the correct boxes on the desk. A fiddly job. Next, she turned the flat Lego board so it sat at a right angle to the wall, as neat as she could make it, running her fingers over the half-built towers and buildings that he had started. She picked up and dusted the lidded Batman cup and placed it back on his nightstand. Next, she paired and lined up his trainers, school shoes and football boots, placing them by the wall next to his wardrobe. His hooded towel with his name embroidered on the back was given a shake and hung on the hook on the back of his door and she ran the duster over his bookshelf. Lifting the duvet, she let it fall and then with the palm of her hand, smoothed it into shape, before lifting the pillows to arrange them just so. It was then that she saw Mr Bob – abandoned on the mattress; it looked like he had slipped down beneath the headboard. She wondered how Oscar had managed to sleep without him by his side.

Cee-Cee reached down and pulled the knitted ted from his hiding place. Lifting Mr Bob to her face she inhaled the scent of him, the little boy she loved. Without warning her legs folded beneath her and she collapsed on to the floor. Sitting on the rug with her knees raised and her back resting on his bed, she let out the deep, loud howl that had been building in her chest since she had taken the phone call nearly an hour ago.

'Noooooooooooo! No! No! Please almighty God, no! Not this. Not this. Not this! Not him. No! No! No! I beg you, hear my prayer, hear me, Lord, please!' She closed her eyes in prayer and with Mr Bob at her chest she sobbed, hot, thick tears drawn from deep inside. Her heart felt like it might break. 'My boy. My boys . . . my baby and my little Oscar. Too much. It's too much!' She howled and she rocked; it was as if she could feel Willard's tiny form in her arms and Oscar's hand inside hers. She screwed her eyes shut and tried to picture the words in her Bible that might offer solace when she needed them the most.

And just like that, at the memory of the day, Cee-Cee was crying. She placed the towels in a neat stack in the linen closet and walked through the master bedroom out on to the balcony. She took a seat in the wooden steamer chair that had been Rachel's refuge and stared out at the big, blue sea.

FIVE

Rachel turned carefully beneath the duvet, trying not to disturb Treacle, who had taken to sleeping illegally on the end of her bed. Far from complaining, she liked the feel of him close by, the weight of him against her legs. It was not only comforting, but it made her feel less lonely; he was the perfect companion who asked no questions and didn't fuss when she cried.

In the throes of sleep she often, out of habit, reached for James, stretching her fingers, expecting to feel his warm skin beneath her touch. The realisation that he was thousands of miles away was a jar to her senses, and recalling the reasons why even worse.

It was early, the grey morning skies a gloomy contrast to the light-filled starts to the day on her island home. She lay in the mattress dip and listened to the sound of her dad in the bathroom through the thin wall, the flush of the loo and the sound of shower spray hitting the plastic base of the bath. His shift at the washing-machine factory started at seven and this had been his routine for as long as she could remember.

She thought about the four bathrooms in the house in Bermuda, three of them rarely ventured into. Now, huddled in this little bed, she marvelled at how they had lived as a family, growing up with just one loo and one shower, never questioning it, thankful for all they did have. Life in their big house on North Shore Road had quickly become the norm and she had to admit it was lovely not to have to plan your ablutions around somebody else's body clock and not to have to stand with your legs crossed in desperation when you came in from school and your brother took all the time in the world behind the locked door while you banged on it and shouted fit to burst.

She lay on her side and held Mr Bob under her chin with the Tic-Tac box flat in her palm.

I wonder how you are feeling today, James? I wonder when this pain in my chest will go away? I wonder when I will feel happy to wake up instead of disappointed? I wonder if I ever will? Where do you rest, my Oscar? Where do you sleep, my baby? Rachel whispered, thankful for the wave of slumber that swept her thoughts from under her and rocked her back to sleep.

The sharp knock on the door woke her. She must have slept in.

'Rachel?' her mum called as she came into the room. 'Julie's popped over! Shall we give you a minute to get yourself together? Good. See you downstairs in a mo, then; bring down any laundry and open the window. I'll go and pop the kettle on.'

She sat up and rubbed her eyes, trying to sort the complex burble of information issued too quickly by her mum. Julie was here, that much she knew, that and she had to get up.

Her sister-in-law sat at the table in the breakfast nook, nursing a cup of tea. Her lank, mousy hair fell over her face and her glasses sat low on her sharp nose, her expression as ever one of disdain. It wasn't Julie's fault; it was just her default resting face, as if something or someone had cheated her – the world had let her down again and she expected nothing less. Julie thought most things were unfair: other people's successes, other people's luck, other people's lives. Rachel could hear her nasal sigh: 'They're getting another new car! It's not fair . . .' The noise she associated with her was a downcast sigh. James had nicknamed her 'the optimism hoover'. It used to make her laugh.

'Cup of tea, love.' Her mum deposited the mug in front of her as she took a seat.

'Thank you. Hi, Julie.'

'Rachel.'

Her sister-in-law visibly coloured and toyed with her phone before turning to her mother-in-law, who now had her head in the fridge.

'Did I tell you I got a lovely shoulder of lamb from Artingstall's in Chipping Sodbury? I went over for a walk with my sister and it was half price so I grabbed it and have put it in the freezer; thought we'd have a roast on Brian's birthday weekend.'

'Oh smashing, love, good idea. I'll do spuds and a pud.'

Rachel looked from one to the other and was struck not only by the way her brother's wife seemed to be morphing into her mother-in-law, but also how Julie appeared to be ignoring her.

She wished she had stayed upstairs and eyed the door, wondering how quickly she could make her excuses and leave, and whether anyone embroiled in the birthday-lamb discussion would even notice.

Her mum closed the fridge and came over to the table. Julie budged up and Jean took a seat next to her. She reached over and squeezed Rachel's hand.

'Julie said she was nervous about seeing you, didn't know what to say. I told her it was okay to feel that way.'

Rachel nodded, embarrassed at how her mum spoke for the grown woman, just as she had for Peter. She could picture her brother and his wife having a domestic and her mum chipping in with, 'Come on now you two, play nicely together!'

Julie continued to look downward and Rachel wasn't sure if she was expected to offer solace and help grease her sister-in-law's verbal path or whether the convention was to sit it out and hope she found her tongue. Both felt like a bloody imposition and her pulse raced.

'It's okay, Julie, we can talk about it; it helps,' her mum cooed.

Helps who exactly? Rachel wondered, but rather than give vent to all that bubbled inside, she kept quiet, reminding herself that there was no perfect response.

'So how you doing, then?' Julie asked quietly with an air of reluctance, reminding her of when Oscar had to be coaxed into offering thanks for an unwanted gift, eyes down, fingers fidgeting, feet pointing towards the door.

It didn't go unnoticed that everyone asked her this, and her embarrassment at a lack of suitable response hadn't lessened.

'I don't know, really.'

While still the best she could manage, it was a thin response that satisfied no one, but that was too bad. She simply didn't have the words and was actually glad of that, certain that to verbalise the depth of hell into which she had plummeted and the fierce, brutalising grief that dogged her every waking moment would only sour the thoughts and live in the memory of all who had to hear it. Even she in her altered mental state knew that that was unfair.

'I can't imagine.' Julie shook her head.

Lucky, lucky you.

'We have had a terrible time trying to explain it to Hayden and Nate. Just terrible.' Julie tutted and seemed to find her voice. Her mum joined in with a sigh, borrowed from Julie no doubt, and a nod, as if confirmation were needed. It was an annoying symphonic duet, lacking empathy and understanding, and was more than Rachel could stand. She took a sip of her tea, preparing for what might come next.

'I mean, they weren't that close, the kids, were they, really? Not with you all being so far away, and I think they found him a bit boisterous when he did come over, but they were cousins at the end of the day. I was up sleepless, thinking what to say and how to say it. It's been terrible.'

Rachel stared at her and felt her jaw muscles clench.

Yes, terrible. So you've said . . .

She wondered simultaneously how Julie had been able to make the whole horrific event about her and whether she was aware that to use even the mildest negative association towards her son made her want to grab the Mallorcan cruet-and-napkin holder and smash it over her head.

'How *are* the boys?' She pictured her nephews: ten-year-old Hayden and eight-year-old Nate. Sweet kids, playful and pleasant.

'They're fine. At my mum's. It's an inset day.' Julie slurped her tea. 'So a day off school.'

'Julie thought it best not to bring them over in case it was too much for you,' her mum explained.

'There's no need to hide them away,' she whispered, part of her having to admit that to see small children, especially boys, was still very, very tough and it seemed that when outside of the house that was all she saw – boys of Oscar's age, Oscar's build . . .

Her mum nodded and reached for a napkin, crying without warning, and this in turn was a trigger for her own tears. It was a reminder that each of them was grieving and there was no right or wrong way. Rachel slipped guiltily from the table and trod the stairs with Treacle hot on her heels. She quietly closed the bedroom door and climbed under the duvet.

Boisterous, loud, inquisitive, funny and wonderful; you were all this and more. My lovely boy . . .

Rachel and her dad continued to walk of an evening, largely in silence, bar the odd observation on the weather or some other exchanged tidbit about their day. Their route was unchanged, out round Engine Common and up to Rangeworthy and then across and back down the Jubilee Way. Her pace better now, she walked along the rain-soaked tarmac without thought or consideration of the conditions, the cool blast of air in the shadow of night often the best part of her day. Their path was lit by the bright lamp posts that would have been out of place on Bermuda's streets, where many areas were dark, thick with undergrowth and the song of the tree frog, which were sometimes picked out in the glow from cosy house lamps flooding out over the palm trees, giant ferns and twisty lanes.

As they neared home, with her trainers quickening at the prospect of the warm bath that awaited her, they saw Mrs Donaldson coming in the opposite direction. Their neighbour pulled her aging retriever, Rusty, to heel.

'I thought it was you!' the woman called, her tone jolly and excited, telling Rachel that she couldn't possibly know. Her pulse raced and her mouth went dry at what might come next. She looked behind her at the straight line of pavement and realised there was nowhere to run and nowhere to hide.

'Evening, Margery.' Brian stepped slightly ahead of his daughter, instinctual in the way he tried to shield her, and her heart flexed because of it.

'Hello, Brian, Rachel, well, how lovely to see you, dear! Goodness me, you have lost weight; you need some of your mum's home cooking. Please tell me you are not trying to lose weight; you are positively skinny!'

'I'm not dieting.' Her stomach sinking, she bent to pet Rusty, avoiding the woman's gaze.

'It is so lovely to see you! I didn't know you were coming over. How long are you staying?'

'I'm not sure.' She swallowed at the unsatisfactory truth.

'You didn't pick the best weather – been grim, hasn't it? You could at least have brought some of that sunshine with you! Mind you, we are off to Lanzarote in three months. Can't wait – bit of sun, glass of sangria, just the thought of it gets me through the long nights. We are going with some friends from the bowling club. Ray's not that keen, but I've told him you can't spend your life in front of the telly.'

Rachel raised a false smile.

'Oh, but it must be lovely for Jean having you here. I thought I hadn't seen her out and about; that explains it. I know she misses you all so much. It's not the same when your kids are far away. I'm lucky, mine are only over in Thornbury and the buses are quite good, but even so I wish they were right next door! I can only imagine how hard it must be for her. I bet she's spoiling Oscar rotten! I remember the last time you all came over and she was feeding him chocolate for breakfast!' She chuckled.

Brian gave a small laugh at the memory and she too pictured him sitting on the sofa with a chocolate-smeared mouth. 'What have you had for your breakfast, Oscar?' she had asked with mock disapproval. 'Not chocolate!' he answered, 'I had . . .' He put his finger in his mouth and thought hard. 'What did you tell me to say I had had, Nanny? I can't remember!'

'He must be getting big! How old is he now?' Margery pulled her from the memory and she was grateful. Her heart thudded and she felt the pulse in her throat.

I don't know what to say to you . . . I don't know what to do . . . If I tell you, you will tell other people, share this awful, awful news that will itch under your skin and burn an image in your mind until you pass it on and they will pass it on with the same need and then eventually the whole world will know . . . and that will make it real. I like it when people don't know. I like it that you picture us all at home, in the sunshine, together and not dismantled.

Rachel had known this day would come, and somewhere in the back of her mind she might even have rehearsed words that would sufficiently satisfy the enquirer without causing distress to her or them. But right here, right now on the pavement, standing opposite Mrs Donaldson, with Rusty sniffing at her calf, she was damned if she could remember what those words might be. She heard her dad take a sharp breath and this she understood; it was the pain of recollection, the horror of the facts and the latest reminder of where they were in this stage of grief.

She tried for diversion. 'I am here on my own, actually.'

Mrs Donaldson was not in the mood for diversion. 'Oh no! What a shame. Not that it's not lovely to see you, of course, but I know how much Jean misses that little boy. How old is he now?'

'He was seven last birthday,' she offered quietly.

We had a bouncy castle in the garden. James tried to organise games like musical chairs for the sugar-fuelled crew, but they scattered like mice, preferring to run around, and so he gave up and nursed a beer on the diving board. Cee-Cee strung up bunting and balloons in the trees and Oscar and Hank both dressed as Spider-Man and fired Nerf guns at their classmates. A sponge bullet hit Daisy and she cried and Oscar gave her a special Spidey hug by way of apology and let her fire back at him. She took aim and missed. He gave her three goes, she got him in the end, right on the chest, and peace was restored. He went to bed exhausted, but happy . . .

'Good lord, time flies! Seven! I still picture him as a toddler.'

'Actually, Margery, we have had some terrible news.' Her dad swallowed.

'Oh no, is Jean okay?' The woman clutched the front of her coat and Rachel saw then that this would be a reasonable assumption – her mum being older and a bit overweight was the first thought that might occur . . . whereas the very last would be anything to do with the healthy, vibrant, beautiful seven-year-old boy who had his whole life ahead of him.

'Something awful happened' – he paused – 'and Oscar passed away very suddenly. It was an accident. At sea.'

She looked up at her dad, thankful that he had found the courage to speak the very difficult words, succinct and formal. She stored them away, noting at the back of her mind that they did not provoke the same jolt of anger as when James had said similar. Her dad did nothing to halt the tears that fell down his ruddy cheeks.

Mrs Donaldson opened her mouth and reached out to Rachel; she gripped her arm tightly. Rusty seemed to sense the change in the air and almost cowered next to her. 'Rachel! Oh my goodness! Oh no! I don't know what to say.' She shook her head. 'I am so, so sorry. He brought so much joy. Goodness me.'

Rachel nodded, touched.

'What can I do? How can I . . . how can I help?'

'You can't,' she whispered. 'But thank you.'

Now at a much slower pace, they made their way home. The weight of the conversation with Mrs Donaldson about their shoulders made the last mile tough. She looked back at the woman and her dog. They hadn't moved, but stood near the lamp post, as if newly reminded of how quickly a life can change and wary of taking a step in the wrong direction. This she understood. This was what her life was like now, no longer confident that every step was going to fall on solid ground. It meant she navigated her way with trepidation, wary of the fall.

Forgoing her bath, Rachel eschewed her mum's offer of cocoa and carried her aching bones to bed.

As she lay there her phone rang. It was James.

'Hi,' she whispered.

There was a pause, 'I was just . . . just thinking about you. Are you okay?'

She cried noisily and he matched her tear for tear across the miles, their distress a duet that erased the distance between them. No matter how far apart, they were still two parents who had created one heart that no longer beat.

'James!' she managed.

'I know. I know . . .'

They sobbed until he broke the rhythm, 'I . . . I need to go, Rach. I am in the line at the bank and people are looking at me and I need to get home . . .'

She let her distress wash over her, cradling the phone to her. She could hear the murmur of her parents' conversation, talking at a lowered pitch in the kitchen. Her dad was probably filling her in on their encounter with Mrs Donaldson. Rachel clung to Mr Bob and rubbed the smooth Tic-Tac box on her cheek. She pictured her dressing-gown pockets full of wet sand on that day; it played in her head like a home movie, over and over and over. Mrs Donaldson had looked shocked, bewildered, and this too she understood. It was still a shock to her that Oscar would forever be seven, missing his arrival into double figures and so much more: starting big school, university, his first girlfriend or rather his first proper girlfriend – one he didn't fire a Nerf-gun pellet at. She pictured Daisy and Hank and all of his classmates who would go on to do all the things denied to him because of one moment of inattention, one casual wander too far.

She considered, as she often did, that one second where he would have been airborne and things could have been so different, that one second when she had a glorious opportunity to turn this life-destroying event into nothing more than a 'that was close' moment. She pictured grabbing him, pulling him back on to the deck, smiling and kissing his freckled face whilst chastising him, relief pouring from grateful lungs and a heart full of thanks. If only she had not in that moment been sleeping, having sex, laughing with James as they sought pleasure with the door locked. Inattentive. Distracted. Responsible.

Rachel heard the doorbell and waited with her head lifted slightly from the pillow to hear her mum's familiar sing-song greeting. The doorbell rang again. With no small measure of reluctance, she flung the duvet back and grabbed her dressing gown, pushing her arms into it and fastening it around her waist without haste, hoping that by the time she opened the part-glazed front door, the caller would have given up and gone, saving them both the pain of interaction. No such luck. She could make out the blonde top of a head through the small glass pane and hoped it wasn't Julie. Her sister-in-law was more than she could cope with today. Any day.

But it wasn't Julie.

With her slumbering, red-haired, eight-month-old in her arms, it was her best friend Victoria, whose parents lived further along the street and with whom she had walked to school and shared her formative years, until the lure of a life with her beloved James Croft took Rachel far, far away.

The two women stared at each other and there was a moment when neither spoke. They exchanged a look of pure sorrow as understanding flowed between them like a current. Friends and mothers.

'My mum told me you were home. I didn't know you were coming back or I would have been straight over. I wrote, I called and I have not stopped thinking about you for a single second.' Vicky breathed. 'Can you hold him while I go and grab his baby bag?' Without further discussion or hesitation, as was her way, Vicky placed the sleeping Francisco in her arms and dashed back up the path. Her friend would never know what this gesture meant. She thought of Julie and Peter, who kept her nephews away, building the drama, stoking the fear, and yet here was Vicky, not only unafraid to broach the subject, but trusting her, one mother to another, to hold her most precious thing.

Rachel turned and caught sight of herself holding the boy in the hallway mirror. She pictured standing in the exact same spot, holding Oscar at a similar age. It was the most beautiful, sweet torment imaginable. She had forgotten the exact feel and weight of a sleeping child in her arms. Dozing with abandon, entirely trusting, as his little head lolled against her shoulder. Lowering her face, she inhaled the distinct scent of his toddler's scalp and fought not to crumble under the memory that surged in her veins. Vicky returned with a large, padded bag of baby paraphernalia, which she hitched up on her shoulder before taking her friend in her arms, enveloping her and her child.

'Rachel! Oh, Rach. My mum told me when it happened. She bumped into Brian. I can't believe it. I just can't.' Vicky placed her fingers on the side of Rachel's face, as they cried. 'I would give anything for you not to be going through this. It is so cruel and must make the world seem like a wicked place.'

'It does.' Rachel let her lips graze Francisco's head in a kiss.

'I loved Oscar. I loved him; he was just like you: so funny and feisty and smart. I can't imagine a world without him in it. I can't believe that Francisco won't get to know him. I used to picture that all the time, the two of them hanging out. It doesn't seem possible.' Vicky shook her head, and far from finding the conversation distressing, Rachel was strangely comforted by her friend's ability to speak about him with such ease. It was again something no one else had quite managed, herself included. Even her mum framed each reference to her son with the stutter of nerves and a swallow of unease.

Vicky held her arm. 'I don't know how to take this pain away from you, but I will do anything. What you are going through is the last thing in the world I wanted for you, my lovely mate. And I know that there are no words so I won't try to find them. Let's just go and sit on the floor of the front room like we used to.' She turned right with confidence, into the small, square lounge where they had whiled away many an hour, lying on their tummies on the rug, watching episodes of *Friends* and *Big Brother*, dipping into a shared bowl of popcorn.

Rachel hiccupped her tears and cradled the little boy to her chest.

'Let's pop him on the sofa.' Vicky dumped her baby bag on the floor and removed a couple of cushions and Rachel lowered him gently until he lay, arms wide, still sound asleep. Vicky fetched his knitted blanket and tucked it around his sturdy legs and fat little feet clad in red-and-navy striped socks. She used the cushions she had removed to build a little wall along the edge, hemming him in so he wouldn't fall.

They sat on the rug with their backs against the sofa, Francisco sleeping behind them. 'Did Oscar snore like an old man?' Vicky asked.

'Not really, it was more a sweet snuffle.'

'This is weird for me, Rach. I have known you nearly my whole life and yet I don't know what to say right now. I'm not equipped, so if I mess up just let me know.'

'You're doing fine.' She spoke earnestly.

'I think it's best if we have a sign.'

'What kind of sign?'

'If I say or do something wrong or that makes you feel uncomfortable or if you just want me to shut up, then we should have a sign or a word that means I know instantly and we don't have to discuss it, we can just change tack.'

'Okay.'

They both looked towards the window. Vicky spoke first: 'What about a word like "peaches and cream"? You would only have to say that and I would know to change the subject or the scenery.'

'That's three words,' Rachel pointed out.

'Well, this is why you got two A levels and I could only manage a diploma in art.'

Rachel smiled warmly at her friend, only realising now in her company just how much she had missed her. A rush of tears, matched by Vicky's, instantly followed this flicker of happiness. They sat crying and holding hands for some while.

'I like the idea of a code. "Peaches and cream" is good,' she managed eventually.

Vicky blew her nose on a tissue and rubbed her eyes; she took a deep breath and exhaled, as if readying herself. 'How's James doing – stupid question, I know. I just really want you to talk about James so I can gauge how you're feeling about everything.'

Rachel swallowed. 'He is broken, like me, but going to work every day and has sort of created the illusion of normal to a degree. We talk once a week or so and it's awkward and comforting at the same time. He called the other night and he was in the bank and we just sobbed and strangely that made me feel better, more connected to him. But sometimes I feel so angry with him I want to shriek, and others I miss his arms around me. I am very confused.'

'Of course you are.'

'I can't seem to help it. I keep thinking if only we hadn't got that bloody boat . . .' She let this trail. 'Cee-Cee, our housekeeper, is around. And she's great.' She disliked how this sounded – as if she had handed the baton of this very important role in her husband's hour of need to Cee-Cee. She disliked even more the element of truth in it.

'I suppose he has no choice if he has to work; he can probably only function by creating that illusion.' Vicky, as ever, offered a caring, balanced view. This was just one of the things that Rachel most loved about her.

'Yes. I understand that. But it was hard being with him. Too hard. We couldn't talk easily and when we did it escalated into a fight in an instant, flared into us saying the most hurtful things before we had time to think about it. It was like everything he said to me and everything I said to him was a match to kindling. We both needed space.'

'I guess you are both too hurt to think straight.'

'We are, but I could never have imagined a situation where we would think that the solution was to be apart; never.' She closed her eyes briefly and pictured dancing together on their wedding day. *How quickly can we get rid of all these guests?* he had whispered into her ear as he held her close . . . 'I guess the point is there is absolutely nothing about my life right now that I could have imagined.' She looked around the small living room. 'James and I are fragments of ourselves and none of this has a rule book. It's like we are floating, broken.'

'Because you are, honey.' Vicky squeezed her hand. 'You are.'

Rachel nodded. 'Yep.'

'Can you talk about what happened or is that peaches and cream?'

'I can talk about it a bit,' she whispered. 'We'd taken the boat out and I woke up happy, I remember that much, and it was the last time I felt happy. And I don't think I will ever feel happiness again. Not that I mind – I don't. I kind of want to feel this sad as it keeps me tied to Oscar and what's happened and I don't want to forget a second of him, don't want it to dilute. Does that make any sense?'

'Not to me,' Vicky answered with typical candour. 'I think I would have to keep looking forward just to keep going, but you have a unique and terrible outlook and only you know what will get you through this. There is no right or wrong. Only what's right for you.'

'I left the cabin and Oscar was not on the boat. He'd . . . he'd just gone.' She felt the prick of pain in her chest, remembered jumping into the ocean in her pyjamas, screaming, crying and calling out to him, *Oscar! Oscar!* and she could hear James in the water on the other side of the boat, screaming louder than she had ever heard . . .

'And I know I should be there for James; I know we should be there for each other, but . . .'

'But what?' Vicky coaxed.

Rachel looked at her friend, preparing to speak the thought that had lain dormant on her tongue since that moment when she looked up at him on the police boat. 'I blame him to a degree.' She let this sink in. 'And he blames me and we are both right to do that.'

'No, no, it was an accident, Rach.'

'I know, but we'd had a bit too much to drink and when we woke up in the morning, instead of going instantly to find Oscar and make his breakfast' – she took a deep breath – 'we had sex and lay there look-ing at our phones for a bit. Can you imagine?' She folded her arms over her raised knees and gave in to the tears that fell. 'I looked at a news article about *The Real Housewives of New York*, just some irrelevant gos-sip and I sat there reading that, instead of . . .'

Vicky twisted her body to face her. 'Rachel, we have all done that and worse and it is right that you mourn your boy, that beautiful boy.'

She broke away, as her voice cracked. 'And I don't know how you recover, I really don't. But waking up and checking your phone is just normal life. God, I have left the back door unlocked with Francisco asleep in his pram in front of it, and then felt a wave of relief that no one sauntered in and took him. I have left candles burning on the mantelpiece, forgetting to blow them out, and only noticed in the morning, thankful the bloody house didn't burn down. I've jumped amber lights in a rush and not got T-boned by a lorry. I have even had a glass of plonk or two and it was only when I went upstairs that I realised Gino and I hadn't switched on the baby monitor and Francisco was screaming so hard he'd been sick. There isn't a parent in the land who hasn't done this shit. But I was lucky.'

'I wasn't lucky,' she whispered.

'I know. But you can't beat yourself up. You can't.'

'James said that I wasn't the best mum, that my social life was more important.'

'Well, that's not true!' Vicky cut in. 'You were a great mum.'

You *were* a great mum. Not *are* a great mum. That's over. Done.

'I think about all the things I could have done differently throughout his whole life, but also because we don't know when he left his room. It's possible, isn't it, that had I got straight up and gone into him, he might have still been in bed and I would have woken him and he'd still be here?' She let her head drop to her chest. 'I mean, just because we couldn't see him, couldn't find him, doesn't mean he wasn't still close, and by the time the police got there with proper search crews and equipment he had gone too far, just disappeared. I keep thinking over and over that if only we had looked differently, or harder, or sooner! I don't know.' She rubbed her temples. 'But the thought that I should have done something differently – I never stop thinking about it.'

'Oh, Rach. Yes, it's all possible, but you can't change it. You have to try to let those thoughts go.'

'It's hard.'

Vicky sidled closer to her friend across the rug and held her once again in her arms. She kissed her forehead. 'I know it is, my love. I know.'

This was how they sat for a minute or two.

'Shall I brush your hair?' Vicky dug into the baby bag and pulled out her Denman brush.

Rachel bumped forward and Vicky sat behind her, brushing her hair with long strokes that eased the throb of her scalp and took her away for a moment or two.

'I have always loved to brush your hair. It's incredible, so long and shiny. Beautiful.'

Rachel closed her eyes, not in the mood for any kind of compliment.

'What's it like being home?' Vicky asked.

She thought about the crappy interactions with Julie and Peter. 'I think it's always hard to go home under any circumstances, let alone now I am so messed up. Peter and Julie drive me crackers, and Mum means well, you know.' She shrugged.

'I love your mum and dad, you know I do, but you can't stay here in Yate – you'll go mad.'

'I'm already mad.' She picked at her thumbnail, ripping it with her teeth.

'Madder, then. How long are you thinking of staying in the UK?'

'I don't know.'

Maybe a little while longer, maybe forever, I can't think too far ahead . . .

'You need to come to where I am so I can look after you. And you need to be near life, not sat here looking at the four walls. I don't think it's healthy for you. And where we are in Bishopston is good for that. It's bustling. You can come and stay with us for as long as you want. You know that. We have a spare room and it's just waiting for you.'

'I don't need looking after.'

Vicky laughed. 'Actually, you do. And it wouldn't be the first time. Do you remember when we left the Mandrake that time and you said the exact same thing?'

Rachel pictured the nightclub that had been a favoured haunt of their youth.

Vicky mimicked her voice: '"I don't need looking after, Vicks!" God, you were adamant, and the next thing I knew you'd jumped on that bloke's mountain bike and nicked it; he called the police and we were all chasing you down to the Watershed and the shit was hitting the fan and they were all screaming at me, as if it was my fault, and by the time we all got down there, you had crashed into the fountain and wet yourself.'

'Oh, Vick!' She leaned back and placed her head on her friend's lap. 'That feels like a lifetime ago. I can't remember feeling anything other than like this. I miss him so much. It hurts.'

'I know, my babber, I know.'

'And I wasn't joking; I am mad.' She paused to choose the right phrase. 'I only half believe that he is not coming home again. I used to think he might be being cared for by mermaids or something similar in an underwater city.' She looked up to see the look of sadness cross her friend's brow. 'And then I thought he was on a giant sea turtle, surfing the waves and whooping and hollering! Having the time of his life, as he gallivanted far, far out at sea.'

Vicky gave in to a kind of strange, strangled sob.

'I told you I was mad.'

'Not mad, darling, just broken, grieving.'

At that moment Francisco woke with something like a giggle and kicked his arms and legs, unfazed by the strange environment, and his happy gurgle changed the atmosphere in an instant.

'Hello, darling! Hello, you!' Vicky cooed, as she scooped him up and grabbed his bottle. 'Here, Rach, give him this while I sort his nappy out; he'll need his bum changing.'

Rachel sat back against the sofa and held the little boy in her arms, watching as he guzzled his drink with both hands on his bottle. She had quite forgotten the total preoccupation with which they did this, fixed on nothing other than drinking and filling that tum. It was lovely to see.

If I had this time again, Oscar, I would never let you out of my sight. Not for one single second, I would not play tennis or go shopping, not ever. I would be a better mum. I would hold you close to me and never, ever let you go . . .

CEE-CEE

With James at work, Cee-Cee sat ensconced on the balcony. She was still adjusting to the new quietness of the house. After Oscar, Rachel had dictated the rhythm of the place. In the past weeks prior to her leaving, a slow gentle pulse of grief had crept from under the bedroom door and bounced from the walls of the hallway, tumbling down the stairs, filling each room with the saddest of echoes. Cee-Cee had spent many minutes hovering outside closed doors with an ear pressed to the cool wood, wondering if the mistress of the house slept or was in need. Rachel's calls of distress, often made in a semi-wakened state, would send a jolt of alarm through Cee-Cee's body no matter where she was or what chore occupied her. And whilst Cee-Cee wished nothing but peace for her, she realised she missed the noise of her, having found it comforting, occupying. Now she faced not only a familiar loneliness, which she thought she had outrun, but also the deafening quiet. It was a hard thing to describe, but her heart carried a new ache at the fact that James and Rachel Croft were apart. She felt a little like the conduit needed to keep communication flowing where she was able. Her prayers were that they would find a way back to each other, believing that this was where true healing lay.

Cee-Cee looked out over the shoreline and noted the salt-bleached twigs and seaweed washed up on the tide; she thought of Grandma Sally, gently scolding her and Clara, as they trod the path to home.

'Good Lord above, child, what is this in your hair?' She reached out with nimble fingers and removed a large sprig of sea grass, dropping it on the floor and wiping her hands down her starched, white pinafore. 'You two been rolling around in the surf again?'

She smiled at the memory. 'We were always in that water!' She chuckled gently and opened her notepad, raising her pen,

Dearest Rachel,

I wonder if you heed my prayers, which I send out to try and help you settle in the darkest of moments. It is still a shock to my soul when I think of all that has happened, particularly now you have gone and I do not have the distraction or joy of your company. It feels like punishment. Seven years old! I don't think I will ever make sense of it, but as Pastor Daniel says, maybe I am not meant to make sense of it; although I confess that in my saddened state it has been hard to take comfort from that.

The breath stuttered in her throat and she placed a hand on her chest, until the threat of further tears had passed. She did this, cried alone, when James wasn't present, wary of allowing her grief to become part of the burden of the house.

I will continue to tell my stories to you as a way not only to remember happier times, but also as a way to distract my mind from the pain of grief which seems to have quite taken me over, even more so since you left the island. I would like to tell you all about the big dance. Happy times. Goodness me, there was so much excitement over the dresses we were going to wear! And I remember, as the big day loomed closer, Clara and I were plain crazy with giddiness.

I went outside to wave Clara goodbye one evening after dance practice and Albert Romsey called at me from over the street, 'Hey, you!' I wasn't strictly allowed to talk to boys, but it was only Albert Romsey. I had sat next to him at Sunday school since I was three years of age and his momma knew my momma – in fact they might have been cousins somewhere down the line. I figured he didn't count. Clara turned her head, 'What do you want, pea brain?' She was always fearless! Albert Romsey, who was one of Willard's cronies, visibly shrank back against the wall. 'I... I need to give you this,' he stammered, as he stood there holding out a folded piece of white paper in his shaking hand. I took it out of pity for the poor stuttering fool and Clara and I laughed. Seemed our giddiness wasn't confined to thoughts of the dance.

Albert ran away faster than a monster hog fish off St Catherine's Beach who has seen the glint of a spear in the water. I unfolded that single, crumpled sheet and read the words, scrawled with the stub of a pencil in a hand that had yet to develop decent penmanship, then shoved it into my dress front pocket. 'Are you kidding me? What does it say?' Clara yelled. Well, I tried to keep my reply casual even though my heart beat fit to burst right through my ribs.

'It's only Willard goofing around.'

'Goofing around how? Urgh, Willard Templeton!' She spat like his name was poison and pulled a face, sticking out her pink tongue in disgust like she had found a rock skink in her stew. I watched, more than a little perplexed, as she made her way up along the road on her way home. Standing at the gate, I heard her disgruntled mutterings float back to me on the sweet, hibiscus-scented breeze, coming up from the scrubland and over the South Road. Truth was, I was glad she had gone.

I kissed Grandma Sally goodnight, washed up and said my prayers, going through my list of wants for everybody I loved, before crawling under the heavy, embroidered Portuguese shawl that was my top blanket. I fingered the piece of paper that lay beneath the flat cushion on which I lay my head. Not that I needed to read it again; the words were etched in my mind:

I very much look forward to seeing you at the dance. Willard.

That was it, nothing more.

I could tell he was trying for polite and formal and that alone tore at my heartstrings. Sweet Willard with patches sewn on his britches and leatherless toes on his brother's old shoes, which had to be at least two sizes too big.

In truth, it would be hard for me to tell you, and do justice to, just how much that scrawled note containing no more than twelve words meant to me. But it meant a whole lot. Of all the girls in our class and of all the girls at our church, Willard Templeton had picked me. And to my knowledge, I had never been picked for anything before by anyone. I liked the way it felt.

So, there we go, Rachel — that was the start of it. Waiting and thinking about all the possibilities and I marvel that something so small as a greasy ol' scrap of paper could start a course of events that would change my life in so many ways. But it did. Not that I realised it at the time.

Anyway, not much point in trying to over-figure it.

Not now, anyhow.

What would be the point of that?

The dance became my every waking thought; I went through my lessons and chores in a daze! Now, I had never been that enamoured with clothes, never really given them more thought than was necessary. That was until I stepped into the dress that Grandma Sally had made me. I know I shouldn't go boasting, but I felt like . . . it's hard for me to know the words for just how I felt; I felt like . . . I felt like someone else — yes, that was it. I felt like the kind of person who could do just about anything she put her mind to. The kind of person a certain boy might choose to send a note to, over and above all the other girls he knew.

I very much liked the way the long petticoat and overskirt swished around my ankles and I liked running my hand over the little bunches of embroidered cherries that sat proudly on that delicate skirt of white organza. Even my daddy looked up from his seat on the porch and nodded with a smile that split his face and my mom, she said I looked like something out of Paris — not sure how she'd know on account of the fact that she rarely left our parish of Warwick, even moaning if she had to travel all the way up to St George, and she had never, to my

161

knowledge, left the shores of her beloved Bermuda, but I took it for the compliment it was intended anyhow.

Clara, too, looked fine and I noted she had a slick of coral-coloured lipstick.

There was so much I was excited about: the band, the decorations, the dancing, of course, and seeing Willard. Willard who I must confess managed to sneak his face into my other thoughts; Willard who had passed me a greasy note via Albert Romsey. In truth, I felt summoned, expected, and it wasn't a bad feeling, no sir. I guess it was the beginning of starting to feel desired, and may the Lord strike me down if I am wrong, but I do not believe there is a soul living who does not wish for that.

Clara and I arrived and were mightily impressed by the way the old wooden hall had been transformed into something real snazzy. Lights had been wound around the trunks of trees, paper bunting was strung across the ceiling in ten different colours, and streamers hung at the windows, blowing in the wind. We made straight for the large tureen of fruit cup that was dished out into paper cups with a glass ladle.

It was Clara who got asked first, by Thomas Outerbridge. There was nothing fancy about his asking; his actions, like him, were large, confident and without a hint of self-awareness. He more or less walked over, as if he might be going to ask directions or if we had seen someone, but instead of talking, he reached out and took Clara by the hand, pulling her into the middle of the dance floor.

The band upped the tempo and I can tell you with certainty that you would have thought it was her and Thomas Outerbridge who had been twirling around on Grandma Sally's floor practising, having shifted that dusty rug and the sofa! They were perfect, in time and in sync, as if they were made for each other. Clara smiled like I hadn't seen before, a different smile — like she had a secret — and I felt a leap of joy in my gut for her, my best friend who had gone rather quiet if you can believe that! Thomas was a big-boned boy and she slipped in and out of his arms like a waif and I could tell that she liked it very much. I watched how her dress flitted this way and that and thought I must tell Grandma Sally how the fabric moved to the tune of them horns and strings.

And it was while I watched my friend dance, laughing with joy and swept up in the moment, that Willard Templeton appeared by my side. I had been looking for him and even figured he might have changed his mind about attending, so to see him there made my breath stop for a second and I felt a little dizzy because of it. He reached for my hand. Oh, Rachel dear! I feared my heart might leap from my chest or at the very least that folk would hear it beating! Willard had lost some of his bluster and he walked me to the middle of the crowd where we swayed from side to side with our arms locked together. Now, I don't want to paint you a false picture; Willard was a boy with a reputation. I had heard folks mention him in the same sentence as many a girl from Sandys to St George and every parish in between. I studied him, this boy with the bad name, and looked up at his smooth skin that had yet to feel the scrape of a razor, his hair, cut neat, and the slight fray to the point of his right shirt collar which made my heart wilt. I didn't know it at the time, but as I moved against him and heard his voice whisper softly in my ear, 'You look mighty pretty,' I began to fall in love. Whatever I knew or thought I knew went right out of the window. I was convinced that we were unique and that things would be different for us. He was fascinating to me, every bit of him: his skin, voice and the curve under his chin, a place where I wanted to lay my head and kiss the space above his heart. We danced slow and long, and on my honour, I am convinced even now that I would never have needed another thing if that were how I could have spent my days. Hand in hand with Willard and with the slow music filling my head and the twinkle of lights all around and the bright array of bunting.

I have never forgotten a single detail of it: that special night when my spirits and hope were lifted higher than I knew possible; when it felt like the whole wide world was at my feet and I was anything but ordinary.

It was nearly ten o'clock when the music came to an end, the big overhead strip lights were switched on suddenly and we blinked and leaped apart. Chaperones started clapping in corners for people to leave sharply so that Mr Whittaker could sweep the hall and his team of volunteers could rip down the bunting. That was when Willard looked at me — not in a regular way, but in a way that told me that the night might be coming to an end, but this was just the beginning; like we shared a secret. It was a look full of promise and I won't ever forget it. That feeling! Oh, Rachel! There was no feeling like it on earth. Cross my heart that it was the best feeling anywhere! Do you know this feeling? I am sure you do.

Clara and I walked home followed by a big, full moon that lit our way, chattering like we hadn't seen each other for a month.

As we had predicted, Grandma Sally was sitting out on the veranda waiting to hear all about it. We sat on the step and gabbled some more with our beautiful long skirts gathered into our laps, loath to remove them and step into dull old nightclothes. We wanted to prolong the magic. Grandma Sally wanted to know all about the decorations, the music and of course what the other girls were wearing. I could hold my head high and tell her with no word of a lie that we were the best-dressed. 'We were princesses,' Clara surmised, and I smiled at her with something like a gut full of hope in my stomach, not only filled with thoughts of Willard Templeton and how he had looked at me, but also because she was right: we were princesses. I didn't know at the time that this was not enough for Clara. She wanted to be queen . . .

SIX

Rachel made her way downstairs for the family dinner with a feeling of dread in her stomach. 'There's another letter for you, love. I've popped it on the shelf in the hallway. It's the same as before from Gee-Gee. I recognised the stamp and the writing.'

'Cee-Cee!' It irritated her that her mum could so easily misname this wonderful woman who had helped her get through the darkest days of her life.

'Did you have a nice time with Vicky?' her mum asked as she lifted the saucepan full of peas from the hob and tipped them into the slightly misshapen plastic colander over the sink, filling the space with a plume of pea-scented steam.

Rachel nodded, not quite sure if it was a *nice* time; she felt no inclination, however, to try to describe how her capacity for happiness had been all but destroyed; every encounter, every event now filtered through the sediment of grief that removed any potential joy from it. It had been good to see her friend and a lot of what she'd said made sense.

'Did she have her little one with her?' Julie asked a little sheepishly, having decided it was still too much for Rachel to have to deal with her nephews and therefore leaving them with her parents every time she came over. Rather than take comfort from their absence, Rachel actually felt it was some sort of punishment and it hurt more than she cared to admit.

'Yes, he slept most of the time. He's a lovely baby.' She watched the way her brother looked down and swallowed the awkward lump in his throat.

'Vicky said she thought I should maybe get out of Yate and go and stay with her for a bit.' She spoke her thoughts aloud.

'Really?' Peter snapped.

Rachel looked at him, unsure where this tone had come from or why.

'Yes, really. She has a spare room and she thought—'

'Oh, well that's nice,' Peter interrupted. 'After all Mum and Dad have done for you.'

'Peter!' her mum called with a slight tut from the sink, her tone the same one she had been using since he was a small child. Rachel felt her pulse quicken; she had forgotten how snipey he could be, how spoiled he sounded and how much she detested it.

'No, I'm sorry, Mum.' He looked at his wife and jutted his weak chin, and she wondered if this display was as much about showing off in front of the gormless Julie as it was about his petty, misplaced jealousy. The irony wasn't lost on her. Yes, she had a life in a warm climate, but he had his wife by his side and his two kids to tuck up in their beds in a matter of hours. She would, of course, have swapped the house, the pool and the view of the sea for what he had in less than a heartbeat.

Peter continued, 'I mean, I know you've had it rough, Rachel, but you're doing what you always do: pitching up here and disrupting everything – it's typical. I know you're going through shit, but just be aware of what this means to Mum and Dad and to all of us. And now, after they have made room in their lives for you, you're talking about upping sticks and going to stay with Vicky!' He shook his head like a disappointed teacher.

'I don't have to *make* room in my life for her or you; you *are* my life!' Her mum spoke with more than a hint of emotion.

Rachel smiled at her.

'Well, I knew you'd defend her!' Changing position, he kicked the supporting leg of the table and it juddered. Rachel stood, the little appetite she might have been able to summon now gone entirely.

'You might think you know what I am going through, Peter, but you don't.' She pulled her sweatshirt sleeves over her hands to hide their trembling. 'And I am glad, because I would never want another person, let alone my own brother, to feel this way, ever. But if you were to find yourself lost or sadder than sad, I really hope that I would be kind to you, because it's a fine balance for me right now between keeping calm and managing to wake up each day, and fucking losing it!' She shouted the latter and her breath came in short bursts; her nostrils flared and her eyes darted around the table. She was certain that had her mother put water glasses at each place, as they did at home, she would have grabbed each one and hurled them against the wall. Even imagining the act brought her some small sense of release.

'I don't think there is any need to talk to Peter like that.' Julie spoke through a mealy mouth and placed her hand on her husband's thigh.

'Please shut the fuck up, Julie!' she fired.

'Don't talk to Julie like that!' Peter banged the table.

'Come on, poppet, it's our walk time.' Her dad's voice came from behind her. She looked over her shoulder and he was already in his jacket with her waterproof in his big hand.

'Oh, Brian, really? I am just dishing up tea!' her mum whined, as she spooned cooling peas on to five plates set on the countertop. The equal measuring out of the fiddly green vegetable was seemingly more important than the tornado of disquiet that hurtled around the breakfast nook.

'It'll keep.' He gave a single nod in conclusion.

◆ ◆ ◆

They walked the first mile or so in silence and Rachel felt her muscles unknot and her heartbeat settle.

'She means well. Your mum.'

Rachel nodded, deciding not to comment on how she found it beyond infuriating the way the woman disgorged all that sat in her head, the muddled soup of emotion that flowed without filter or discrimination, seemingly oblivious of the storm brewing around her.

'I know and I'm sorry, Dad. I didn't want to argue with Peter, I don't have the strength. And I shouldn't have sworn at Julie. And it's so unfair on you and Mum. I'm sorry.'

'Peter is . . .' He spoke without lifting his eyes from the pavement. 'Peter is a complex lad. I think he feels a little trapped by life, and so to see a free bird like you flying high has always been a little hard for him to swallow. Not that I am justifying his behaviour or condoning it, but I hope it might help explain it.'

'God, Dad, we have invited him and Julie over numerous times, offered tickets, and James tries calling him every time he's over here to see if he fancies a beer, or if he's got tickets for the football, but he has always sniffed away our efforts to get closer.'

'I know, and as I said, he's a complex fellow, but not a bad one, not really. He just needs to cut his mother's apron strings and the ones that now tether him to Julie.'

'I get it.' And she did.

'And for the record, I think Vicky is right. You do need to get out of Yate. It's no good being holed up in your old room day in and day out with only Treacle for company. You need to be with your friends.'

'Are you asking me to leave?' she asked with the wobble of rejection on her lower lip, the prospect almost more than she could handle.

Brian stopped walking and turned to face her; he reached out and gripped her shoulders with his hands where the working man's ring of grime sat under his fingernails. He held her gaze. She was further distressed by the glint of tears in her dad's eyes. 'If I could have a wish, it would be to see your face every single day of my life over that break-fast table.' He swallowed. 'Or it would be to turn the clock back to when you were small and you would wait for me on the wall to come home from work, waving like crazy when you saw me come around the corner. Rachel, I want you by my side. You are my little girl! My little girl . . .' He paused and gathered himself. 'And because I love you so much I only want what is best for you, and right now what I think is best is being somewhere where you are not surrounded by memories that drag you down and people who don't necessarily know what to do or say for the best. That's what being a parent is all about: loving you no matter how far away you are.'

She took a step forward and rested her head on her dad's heavy work coat that smelled of petrol and glue. And this was how they stood under the glow of a street lamp. She closed her eyes and thought of her one wish, and that too involved turning back time.

Rachel stamped her feet on the welcome mat and unzipped her jacket, thankful that Peter and Julie had left. She picked up the letter from the back of the shelf and took it up the stairs, carrying it like a fragile thing. The letters were something she treasured – a link between the world she had left, but where her heart remained, and here, where she was hiding out. She lay on the bed and opened it, getting lost in Cee-Cee's tales of Clara and descriptions of another time.

> *. . . Yes, we were sisters in every other sense. Although sisters I now know should look out for one another, help and support each other. And there weren't nothing sisterly about what she did to me in my time of need, my time of distress.*
>
> *Nothing at all.*

Rachel reread the letter, particularly the final paragraph, and she thought of Vicky, her lovely mate, best friend, her sister in every other sense, who knew exactly what was best in her time of need.

James didn't answer his mobile, so she tried the home phone. It was Saturday; she wasn't sure if he had resumed his old routine and was playing tennis with one of his pals. This thought left her feeling torn. It caused a ripple of misplaced anger to flare in her veins at the fact that his life could go on without her, without Oscar. And yet at the same time she felt a flicker of happiness that he was not sitting alone at home, abandoned by her.

It was Cee-Cee who answered the call. Rachel pictured her in the kitchen and felt a jolt of nostalgia for the woman and the room in which she stood. It was the first time she had felt anything close to this since leaving a couple of months ago. She smiled to be in contact with the woman who she now, through her letters, knew better than ever. The woman who had been so very excited about the dance, for which her Grandma Sally, living in the cottage that was now Cee-Cee's home, made her and her friend Clara the most exquisite dresses.

'Cee-Cee, it's me, Rachel.'

'Well, it is certainly wonderful to hear your voice.'

'Cee-Cee, I can't tell you how much I love your letters!'

'Well, I am certainly glad of that.'

She picked up the note of embarrassment in the woman's tone. 'It takes me back to Bermuda and I know the roads you talk about, the beaches you mention, and it's like I am there and it feels wonderful, because I am there in that time, before . . .'

'Then I shall carry on putting pen to paper, Rachel.'

'That would make me very happy.' She paused. 'You asked me in your letter if I knew that feeling when you meet someone and you feel full of promise and excitement for everything that lies ahead.' She pictured the first time she and James kissed, the way her heart leaped, and she knew . . . 'I do know that feeling – I did.'

'I knew it.'

Rachel could tell she was smiling and this in itself gave her a feeling of promise, of hope.

'I keep you in my thoughts and my prayers, child.' Her voice was thick with emotion.

'Thank you.' She noted the way Cee-Cee did not ask how she was – that much-used question that seemed to be the opener for every conversation and one she was no better at answering now than she had been at the very beginning. Cee-Cee's words all that time ago came to her now: *I am sad; sadder than sad and I won't ever stop . . .* It was without doubt because the housekeeper understood this life lived bereft.

'And how are things there, Cee-Cee?'

'I have no news, really; nothing changes. I am keeping things just so.'

Rachel pictured Oscar's room, dust-free and neat as a pin, and her heart flexed with gratitude.

'I am glad you are with your parents, and I hope you are finding peace.' Cee-Cee's warm, rich tones were as calm and soothing as ever.

Rachel noted she didn't use the word happy because Cee-Cee knew that happy was a stretch too far, peace was the very best she could hope for.

'Not yet,' she said honestly, 'but I can see that peace might lie ahead and so I guess that is progress of sorts. When I was in Bermuda I could only see a dark abyss. It was all I could do not to fall into it; in fact, there was a time when I wanted to.'

I jumped, Cee-Cee! I jumped and I wanted to end it all! And sometimes I crave the peace I felt when I had decided to go and join my boy . . .

'That passes. It does.'

There was a beat or two of quiet when, across the oceans, the two women were connected by all that they didn't say. Rachel felt energy in the silence. She closed her eyes briefly and pictured her housekeeper in the vast home that had grown so small and become a prison. The grand façade on the North Shore Road that housed rooms where sadness and regret ran down the walls and pooled on the floor. She pictured Cee-Cee, busy day and night with that mop, but no amount of cleaning could wipe away the scent of despair.

Cee-Cee broke the quiet, speaking slowly. 'Being with family and those you love. That is where you will find peace.'

Rachel thought of her mum and her dad, of Peter and Julie, of Vicky and little Francisco and she thought of James . . . her James.

'These people who love you and whom you love, these people who share your blood and live in your heart; it is with them that you will learn how to move forward. They are the keeper of your stories and the custodian of your memories.'

Rachel nodded, feeling the all too familiar slip of tears down her throat and along her cheeks.

'Your family, your kin, that's all you have; it's all we have. Those in the present and those gone before, we all share the same things and we are bound. Understand that it's in the life-defining moments, when a scream leaps from your throat, be it in joy or fear, and your hands reach out to grasp the wisps of reassurance that float in the ether – strands from a fine gossamer cloak woven of memories and stories – yes, it is in *that* single moment when your eyes and those of your ancestors are aligned, *that* is when you are touching your history, your people, your heritage. That's when lessons can be learned. And whether they are living or whether they have passed on, it doesn't matter, not in time. We are and we will always be together. That is how you move forward, Rachel.'

'Thank you. Thank you, Cee-Cee,' she managed, quite overcome by the woman's eloquence, wisdom and the beauty of her advice. It was one thing to have read it in her letters, but quite another to hear it whispered down the line person to person.

'Let me go and find James. I think he is in the garage. Do you want to hold on or shall I ask him to call you back?'

'Yes, ask him to call me back, and thank you again, Cee-Cee. Take care.'

'May God bless you and keep you safe.'

The woman's blessing had the unexpected effect of making her cry harder. Rachel *wanted* to be kept safe from the harm that threatened to take her sanity or urged her to find somewhere high up and jump. She pictured Oscar again and the way he had waved at her from beneath the water, happy. He had looked happy . . .

James called back within minutes. His tone was flat and she sensed she was disturbing his peace. It felt horrible and jarred even more in comparison to the way in which Cee-Cee had comforted her so.

'Have you heard from Mackenzie?' she asked with her heart in her mouth.

'No. But I don't expect to. He said they'd only contact us now if they had news.'

She let this permeate. And felt a small sense of relief that there was no news, that nothing had been . . . found.

'I just wanted to let you know that I'm thinking of going to stay with Vicky for a bit in Bishopston. I think it might be better for me than being cooped up with Mum and Dad.' She stole her dad's phrase.

James gave a wry laugh. 'I thought you were going to say you were thinking of coming home.'

'Do you think I should?' She waited, torn, reading what she could into the pause and aware of an icy dread in her stomach that he was going to ask her to go back to that house where she would constantly be within sight of that big, big sea where Oscar lived now. And similarly dreading that he would *not* ask her to go back, as if her absence, like injured skin, had healed over, leaving no place for her there. She cradled the Tic-Tac box in her palm.

'Honestly? I don't know,' he began. 'Part of me wishes you were here, but then I think about those months with you sitting upstairs and it was hard, Rachel, it still is hard. And then that day on the boat, when you—' He broke away. 'I think about that a lot. It could have ended very differently and you didn't think what it would be like for me? And I wonder how you could have done something like that.'

'I wasn't myself.' *I'm still not myself . . .*

'I know it's difficult for you, of course, but I don't want you to come home.' He paused, as if to let this sink in, and her gut twisted. Despite knowing it was the truth and at some level understanding why, she felt her hand slip a little further away from that of the man who used to rush home from the office at lunch, just to spend a little time with her. James continued, 'I know how horrible that sounds. I had a knot in my gut, so afraid of doing or saying the wrong thing, and that's gone now. It's like I have one less thing to worry about, if that makes any sense.'

She was thankful for his frankness, no matter how much it hurt.

'I love you,' he whispered, choked. 'You know I do, but I don't know how we go forward from here. I can't picture it.'

'I can't picture it either,' she confessed.

They were quiet for a moment, letting this sink in. It was James who spoke first. 'It's the worst thing, not being able to see ahead when I thought I had life sussed – more than sussed. I held this image in my mind for so long of our future, working hard for that time, always thinking ahead to Oscar at ten, then Oscar as a teenager, always think-ing of and planning for the things we would be able to do when he reached those milestones: playing cricket, skiing, or just him and me sitting on Elbow Beach, sharing a beer. And you and I like bookends to his life, happy bookends, all dependent on each other, and now . . .' He let this hang for a moment. 'Now there is a big hole in that future because he's gone and you are not here and I know I have to paint a different picture, create a new future. But I don't feel like I can; all I want to do is sit and wish I could go back to what I had. It's tough.' She heard the unmistakable sound of emotion in his voice and knew his words were a mirror to her own lamentations of loss. 'The thought terrifies me, Rach, and makes me feel so sad, but I don't know how else to survive. It almost feels better not to think about what I have lost, but to try and find a new, different path.'

'You don't mean forget him?' she squeaked.

'No! God, no! Not ever, ever.' He cried openly now. 'Of course not! But sometimes it's less painful if I don't think about him, don't try to figure when he went or how. It kills me.'

She nodded down the phone and reached for Mr Bob, who she placed under her chin. This she understood because it killed her too.

Gino lifted her bag from the boot of the taxi.

'Are you sure you don't mind putting me up for a bit?' She knew it was one thing to receive an invitation from her friend, but that didn't mean her husband was on board. She hated the idea of imposing.

'Rachel, you are welcome to stay for as long as you want, you know that.' Gino walked up the path to the open front door. 'But there are rules,' he yelled over his shoulder. 'You do not touch my *Star Wars* models or agree with Vick that we need to declutter the study, by which she means throw away my motorbike magazines, and you are never, ever to mention that blue football team that your dad favours while you are under my roof.'

'Rovers?' she asked with genuine innocence.

'That, my friend, is strike one! We are a Bristol City house; red is the colour and I can't have you mentioning the "R" word in front of Francisco. Kids are easily influenced.'

She nodded. 'Got it.'

As she stepped inside the warm hallway of the Victorian terrace on Egerton Road, Vicky came hurtling down the stairs.

'Here she is!' She wrapped her friend in a warm hug. 'I've just put him down for a nap. This means we have uninterrupted coffee time for thirty whole minutes! Sorry, I'm being bossy. Do you want to unpack or get coffee?'

Rachel smiled at her friend who had always been bossy; this awareness of it, however, was new. 'Coffee sounds good.'

Gino parked her suitcase at the bottom of the stairs and walked over, planting a kiss on her cheek and crushing her in a hug. 'I was so sorry to hear what happened, Rachel. I feel for you and James.' Whether subconsciously or not he placed his fingertips over his heart.

'Thank you.' She had always liked the Italian's wonderful nature, open with his emotions, affectionate and desperately loyal to his family.

Vicky and Gino's house was lovely: homey and warm, with stripped, waxed floorboards dotted with rugs, a cast-iron fireplace in the sitting room and bookshelves in the alcoves either side of the chimney breast stuffed with books, family photographs in mismatched frames and the odd relic from their time travelling – a brass Shiva; a brightly coloured, miniature thangka painting; and a set of Japanese prayer beads carved from cherry wood and hanging from a hook. The sofas were square, deep and soft, covered in creased linen the colour of string, and peppered with boldly coloured, embroidered cushions.

The kitchen had the same relaxed air with old pine, butchers-block countertops, and a windowsill crammed full of herbs in a collection of earthenware pots. A shabby green dresser lined one wall, home to an eclectic assortment of serving dishes, plates and pottery mugs, some with handles missing, now stuffed with pens or paintbrushes. The walls were painted ochre and Gino's beloved copper cookware hung from a cast-iron rack above the oven. A knife block sat by the hob. Gino always said that on the outside he might have been a systems engineer, working up the road at British Aerospace Engineering, but on the inside, he was a chef. The centrepiece to the spacious, glass-roofed addition was the eight-foot refectory table, crowded at one end with piles of clean laundry, a stack of magazines and a large, crowded bowl of fruit. Rachel was glad her friend hadn't felt the need to make her home pristine; it made her feel more welcome.

She thought about the clean, cool lines of the villa in Bermuda and wondered how entering that made people feel: the acres of cold tiling, the white walls and crisp, painted edges. She wasn't sure it was a true representation of her and couldn't be classed as homey, but she supposed it was rather more impressive. Small wonder they were all happier on the cosy boat. And just like that she pictured jumping from the side of *Liberté* trying to see through the curtain of hair that fell over her eyes, as she bobbed and dived in the water, as fear set in her bones.

'You all right, honey?' Vicky stared at her. 'You look pale.'

'I'm okay,' she managed, her voice small.

'Why don't you two go out for coffee?' Gino suggested, as he unstacked the dishwasher. 'It's a bright, blue day!'

'Yes! Great idea. There's a fab café around the corner, just five minutes up the Gloucester Road.'

Vicky grabbed her coat and the two women walked up Egerton Road arm in arm along the uneven pavement. 'I love living here.' Her friend beamed. 'I like being able to walk up and grab a pint of milk if I run out and I like the fact that there is life all around me and I can take Francisco out for nice walks and we are both interested in what's going on. He seems to like the big red buses, and who can blame him?' She laughed. 'And there are so many great little shops and always someone to say hello to. I think I might have felt a bit isolated anywhere else, giving up work and staying at home.'

Rachel nodded. 'When I first got to Bermuda, I was really torn. We kind of had it all – the house, beach on our doorstep, the lifestyle. But I was lonely and I couldn't see the point of living somewhere so wonderful. I didn't have anyone to share it with. I mean, it was nice to have Cee-Cee around but we weren't what you would call friends, although since Oscar . . .' She swallowed. 'I guess it has brought down all barriers, as it does when someone sees you stripped bare with your soul and your heart exposed.'

Vicky squeezed her arm.

Rachel continued, 'I found it hard not having Mum or you to call on. And we had made good friends when we lived in Richmond. It was a bit of a shock to the system.'

'I bet. So how did you make friends?'

'Through James's work mainly. I met a lot of other ex-pat wives, British and American, and they were all friendly enough and then I started taking Oscar to kindergarten and the mums there became my friends too.'

'But you didn't love any of them as much as you love me,' Vicky asserted. 'The role of best friend was never vacant.'

'Of course not. Never.' She looked at her friend and spoke the truth. They shared a childhood and history, and they loved each other.

'Have you spoken to James?'

Rachel nodded. 'It's so confusing. Part of me wants to speak to him, misses him, and another part wants to keep far, far away and have no contact at all. I can feel what we had slipping away.' She held her friend's eyeline; this was a tough confession to make.

'Don't say that. You guys are going through so much, I am sure that after some time apart you will be able to find a way to go forward.'

She shook her head. 'I love him, Vick—'

'I know you do and he loves you. That's always been obvious,' Vicky interrupted.

'But something has happened to us; something other than losing Oscar, or more accurately because of losing Oscar.' She swallowed. 'It's hard to explain, but it feels like someone has snipped all the threads that held us together as a couple, and I can almost tell you the moment it happened: when we were at sea, while they were still searching. I looked over at him and something had changed. I felt it in my gut. I had only ever looked at him with love, lust even.' She paused, thinking about that morning when they woke, climbing on top of him. 'But I stared at him and felt a flash of something that was a lot like hatred.'

'Oh, honey.' Vicky's tone dripped with sadness.

'It's true. I haven't said that to anyone.' She looked at her friend, knowing she would keep her confidence, as she always had. 'And there are two things that I can't shake from my mind.' She took a breath. 'It's what we touched on at my mum's. I keep thinking that we were having sex while Oscar . . . while Oscar might have been struggling or afraid; he needed me! And kind of linked to that is that I know I will never have sex with James again. I don't want to. I couldn't. I couldn't stand to lie next to him let alone touch him. And that is the beginning of the end, isn't it?'

'Yes. It can be.' Vicky nodded. 'But maybe that's only how you feel right now.'

'No, Vick. It's how I feel and how I have felt since that moment and I have this knowledge that this is how it will be. I resent him, I blame him.' She ran her fingers through her hair. 'It's hard to justify or explain. I *know* deep down it's not his fault, but I can't help it! He was the reason we had the boat. He was the reason I wasn't out of the cabin, why I wasn't up earlier.' She shook her head. 'And the craziest thing of all is that it was me who initiated sex that morning, me who delayed us and yet . . .' She shrugged. 'It's like everything we had before – the whole ten years leading up to that morning – has shrunk to nothing, and every single thought and feeling I have towards James is *from* that morning, and I can't move past it.'

'What's the other thing?' Vicky asked. 'You said there were two things you couldn't shake?'

Rachel swallowed. 'It sounds stupid, but I keep thinking about this one night, a month or so before that day; James was late home and I ate with Oscar. I cooked spaghetti and he was fidgety, playing with his supper, but not eating it. I was impatient, he was making a mess and I snapped at him and told him to eat nicely. He asked me if he could have some ice cream instead and I shouted. I was tired and I yelled, "This isn't a restaurant, Oscar, you don't get to reject your main course and go straight for pudding! If you don't eat your pasta you don't get ice cream, it's that simple!" And he cried and I sent him upstairs and then he fell asleep.' She bit her bottom lip. 'I can't stop thinking about that night, the fact that he might have gone to sleep hungry, and what would the harm have been in letting him have a bowl of bloody ice cream?' She rubbed her hand over her face. 'I didn't know we were on a timer, didn't know how little time I had left and I wish . . . I wish I hadn't shouted at him and I wish I had taken him up a bowl of ice cream.'

Vicky nodded with a look of pure anguish.

'You know, Rach, you said you were worried that you had been a bad mum and that has bothered me. You weren't; I saw it first-hand. You were attentive and interested and patient, you loved him.' Her voice cracked. 'Christ, we all get tired, we all snap! But even now, after he's gone, you are thinking about the tiniest detail, worrying over his bowl of ice cream and the fact that he might have been sad, hungry. Do you think those are the actions of a bad mum? Of course not! You knew him. You loved him and you were a bloody good mum.'

Rachel stared at the road ahead, quite unable to express just how much the words of this woman, whose opinion she valued, helped ease the guilt from her shoulders, scratching at the miserable surface of self-doubt and recrimination and allowing a flash of pride to peek through.

The two walked on in silence, each digesting the futility of her worry and noting how these small things could become big things simply by a twist on the dial of fate.

The café, oddly named 'rewer', was great. The lighting was low and the walls covered with a variety of pictures and ornate gilt mouldings with aged mirrors and numerous dark-framed, Edwardian floral images that looked like the etchings from a botanist's catalogue. The tables were honey-coloured, gnarled and pitted wood with jam jars on them full of cutlery, next to other jam jars with sprigs of wildflowers in them, and the chairs were mismatched. A long, dark-wood bar ran down one side of the room and glass shelves were fixed to the exposed brickwork on the wall behind an elaborate, shiny coffee machine.

The two staff she saw – a man and a chic, older woman with dark-grey hair wound on top of her head in a loose bun – both wore denim, with industrial-looking aprons with leather detailing.

'Hi there.' The woman smiled and pointed at the rather clunky-looking, leather-topped iron stools positioned along the bar and then to a collection of smaller, empty tables at the back. 'Where do you fancy?'

'I think the back today.' Vicky made her way through the café with the confidence of a regular patron. Rachel followed in her wake.

'Apart from travelling over here, which is a blur, and walking with my dad, which I don't think counts, this is the first time I have properly been out.'

'You are doing great.' Vicky reached across the tabletop and squeezed her hand.

'No little one today?' The man appeared by the side of the table. He had a close-cropped dark beard, and hair that was too long so he had to keep pushing it behind his ears.

The question had made Rachel's heart leap; for a split second she had thought he was addressing her and felt the usual surge of panic at how she might respond.

'No. He's with his dad. We officially have half an hour of grown-up time.'

'Quite right too.' He smiled. 'Right, let me guess' – he pointed at Vicky – 'soy latte with hazelnut shot and a slice of carrot cake?'

'Yes, thank you.'

He turned to Rachel. 'And for you?'

'Erm, is there a menu?'

'Only in my head, so what would you like first, drinks or specials?'

'I don't want anything to eat – drinks.'

'Hot or cold?' he fired.

She felt a flicker of irritation and glanced at the door, considering bolting. 'A coffee, please, I'll just take a coffee.'

'Latte? Americano? Cappuccino? Regular? Large?'

'Why don't you just print it on a menu?' She was curious.

The man leaned towards the table and lowered his tone. 'Standard answer, we think it builds a relationship between customer and staff. Look at us' – he touched his chest and then pointed at her – 'here we are chatting! All ice broken, so it clearly works, but unofficially' – he leaned further in – 'we have so few items on the menu that I think it might lose us customers.'

'Why do you have so few items?' Vicky asked quizzically.

'Because there is only my mum and me out here and my dad in the kitchen, and he can make four or five things really well and she can only remember four or five things really well and I am only good at ordering stock for four or five things really well.'

'Okay, then.' Vicky linked her fingers, resting them on the tabletop. 'Now we know.'

'I'll take a black coffee, please,' Rachel said, keen for him to leave them alone.

'Coming right up.' He rushed to the back of the bar.

'I am right, you know.' Vicky held her eyeline. 'I don't think there is a person on the planet who hasn't lost someone and felt guilt or remorse over one small word, one insignificant incident or one missed opportunity. You need to not fixate on the ice-cream thing.'

Rachel wished it were as easy as letting the thought go.

Vicky continued, 'When my nan was ill a couple of years back, I went to sit with her every day, just for an hour or so after work. She was in St Peter's Hospice and sometimes she just slept; I don't know if she knew I was there all of the time.'

'Yes, I remember when she was ill. It was one of the many times I wished I was closer to you.'

'I worked late one night and called Gino to say I was exhausted and he suggested I go straight home; he knew it was a lot – juggling work hours and sitting with Nan into the evening. So I did. I went home, had a bath and fell into bed. My mum called in the morning to say my nan had passed away that night. And I know it's different because Ivy was old and she'd had a long life and it wasn't a tragedy.'

Rachel felt grateful that Vicky knew the difference, validating her own terrible sense of injustice.

'But it was still awful for me because I loved her.'

'Of course.' Rachel pictured the cantankerous old Bristolian lady who used to moan at them when they had their music too loud or stomped on the floorboards as they learned a dance routine in Vicky's bedroom. She thought Ivy had always been very old.

'My point is that I have never thought about the hours and hours I spent by her bedside, the thousands of cups of tea I made her over the years or the lovely moments we shared . . . I only think about that one night and how I let her down; one night that was my chance to say goodbye!'

Rachel looked at her friend and understood her point, but took no comfort from it.

'It's true, Rach, no matter where or when or who we lose, we all have those things that beat us up from the inside out.'

'One soy latte with a hazelnut shot and one black Americano and one large slice of carrot cake with two forks, just in case you change your mind.' The man unloaded the round tray and was gone again.

'He's chirpy today.' Vicky nodded after him, as she sipped the froth from her drink.

'What does "rewer" mean?'

'I have no idea, ask him.'

Rachel shook her head; she wasn't curious or bothered enough to do that.

'What will happen, Rach, if they don't find Oscar?' Vicky's words, albeit softly spoken, were still a sharp knife to Rachel's breast. 'Will you have a service or some kind of funeral? And would that be here or in Bermuda, do you think?'

'P . . . peaches and cream,' she managed. 'Peaches and cream.'

CEE-CEE

Oh Rachel,

It was some treat to speak to you the other day on the phone. I am filled with joy that my stories bring you back to Bermuda. I feel a connection to you as if we were kin. To see your pain raw and exposed takes me right back to certain days and nights of my youth. Once or twice when you had fallen asleep while I was working, I came and sat with you and watched you sleep. You would stir, cry and I would whisper, 'Go back to sleep, go to sleep, child . . .' And in truth it brought me peace to watch your face lose its tight angles and your brow smooth in slumber. I knew from my own heartache that there was nothing I could do, apart from offer words of solace where I could and keep the house and everything in it as neat and tidy as it could be.

I know that I would have liked someone to do the same for me in my hour of desperation. Ah, but you don't know how I reached that point, do you? I should explain.

It all started immediately after the dance. The author of my much-famed note and I, we didn't make a formal plan, and as my daddy liked to remind me there wasn't much permission asked, but Willard Templeton used to crop up like a bad penny. A penny I was always delighted to find! I remember him sitting in the pew opposite mine at church and loitering in the street near Grandma Sally's and thinking it curious that he often had business within feet of where I lived. I didn't dare hope that the reason for his proximity might be anything other than coincidence, I didn't dare! But now, of course, I know it was. And truth is, had I known for sure, I fear I might have burst with joy. He then started to do a thousand little things to let me know that, even though we hadn't discussed any details as such, we were progressing. And it made me happy. Happier than happy!

One evening after school Clara and I caught the bus down to Horseshoe Bay and as was our habit, we raced through the pine woods, along the path and across the soft sand into the sea. Now, as I might have mentioned, I was always a good swimmer, making headway, pulling against the current, but kicking strong. It came natural to me. I'd look over my shoulder and see Clara shrieking fit to burst, 'Cee-Cee! Help me! I'm gonna drown!' as she crawled about on all fours with a clump of sticky seaweed on her head, hanging down like a sea witch's fringe.

Clara never quite made it out to the calm and it was the same spectacle every time: her being tossed around in the foam and yelling so loudly that folks would stop their bikes and get off to see what the hollering was in aid of. I was always the timid one and I have always thought that as a pair we probably put out the right level of noise into the world. It was just one of a million ways that we compensated for and complemented each other.

It was the most wonderful time of day when the sun started to dip, and the world took on that majestic pink hue – the colour of a conch's lip – and shadows crept from the soldier-straight pines out over the sand. Clara and I lay at the water's edge, bobbing on the salty crest, letting the shallow sea drag us out and push us in.

Friday night was always the best time of the whole week. No school the next day and apart from church on Sunday and a whole heap of chores, our time was pretty much our own. Clara stood and raised her dress to show me her cotton panties, full of sand and hanging down like a baby's diaper at the back. 'I've got half the seabed in here!' Lord, she waddled like a cowboy along the beach with the white cotton fabric stretching down her thighs and filled with wet sand! 'Help me, Cee-Cee!' she hollered, as she tried to shake it out right there and then. I could only laugh and clutch at my stomach; laughing so hard I could hardly take a breath and feared I might pee.

And the next time I opened my eyes, she had gone a little quiet and Albert Romsey was walking up the beach with Willard, my bad penny, by his side. I felt my heart go boom-boom at the sight of him and sat up straight with my shoulders back. Grandma Sally told me if there were two things a man wanted in his future wife it was the ability to make a decent Bermuda fish chowder and good posture. I couldn't yet make decent chowder, but my posture was better than most. And yes, I was, after no more than one measly dance and a couple of brief exchanges, thinking along these lines. Clara slunk back to where I sat and dropped down by my side. Our dresses clung to our wet forms and I guess my underwear might have been a little insubstantial. The boys stood by our side and the four of us looked out towards the horizon as the sun sank, almost in reverence and with the same hush we adopted when Pastor Raymond was preaching and it felt like he was speaking directly to us.

I saw Willard glance at me more than once and I watched his gaze lower to my chest. His eyes widened and I felt his longing. At the same time, I could feel the swell of something in my stomach that matched his expression and felt a lot like laughing, but on the inside. Now, I had never been proud of my body, never fully realised that these swells and bumps covered in skin had any function other than supporting all the soft and important bits that God created. This was something of an awakening and I liked the way it felt. I liked it very much. Six years before when, walking the railway track near Baker's Hill, Moses Furbert had said, 'That ain't no bosom much worth considerin'' when I'd let him peek down my frock and he let me look inside his shorts. We'd laughed then, at the absurdity of the fascination, deciding silently and I suspect mutually that the world of bodies and bits and pieces, and the mystery of what went where, could wait until we was much older. And it occurred to me right there and then on Horseshoe Bay, with every inch of my being aware of the proximity between me and Willard, that much older had indeed arrived.

And I guess this was the essence of all that pulled me towards and bound me to the boy with the reputation, the boy with an eye for the girls and a name that people spoke with a sneer. It was a powerful force, a physical thing that to this day I cannot *entirely explain, but I say without shame and in front of the Lord who might be listening: it was physical and wonderful and something like magic.*

The four of us walked home together, keeping to the raised inside bank along South Road. Willard hung back and I did too and, like it was the most natural thing in the world, he reached for my hand. I won't ever and could never forget the way it felt to have my palm safe and warm against his. I could have walked a thousand miles. I was light as air and happy as a white-eyed vireo chirping day and night. But if I was surrounded by sunshine, Clara was the opposite; mired in a dark, brooding cloud, the likes I had never seen before. She went quiet, surly even, her shoulders sloped downward and her mouth set thin.

This was the beginning.

This was the first sign I had that she was going to change or maybe it was me that was changing. It doesn't matter which, not now.

It didn't happen overnight, but it might as well have. It was more than sulking; it was like Clara had decided that there wasn't enough of me to go round and that if I chose Willard then I couldn't have her too. I tried to reason, tried to coax, I believe Grandma Sally even tried scolding her over it. Until one day I realised that there was no amount of apologising or pleading that could change things. And when I stopped pleading, stopped fretting over how to fix it, that was when Eliza-Jane Clara May Brown, my Clara, my best friend in the whole of creation for more years than not, more or less disappeared from my life. Just plain cut me off like I had never existed. How could a person do that? I often wonder. What lurks inside them that makes them think that is in any way okay? Why do they think they are so superior that they can?

My questioning changes nothing — not then, not now. She holed up like a land hermit crab and retreated to that two-room shack where Momma Eula shouted at her for nothing much. My heart missed her. My arms missed her. Grandma Sally missed her — we all did. It shocked me. My world was much, much quieter. It was like some kind of grief to me; at least that was how I would have described it until real grief came along and then I realised how little I had ever cared about anything. Clara May included.

But I am getting ahead of myself, as I am wont to do, dear Rachel.

So Willard and I fell in love. I loved him. I truly loved him, longed for him, wanted to see him and, Lord forgive me, touch him too. He became everything. We married quietly in St Anne's Church, Southampton Parish, when I was just seventeen years of age, and it was more than perfect. My daddy walked me up the aisle with a rare look of pride, my mommy cried throughout my vows and Grandma Sally wore her favoured white linen hat, but fixed fresh white oleander and purple Bermudiana to the band. They stood out to me, vivid and bright and beautiful, just like Grandma Sally herself, and truth is, if I picture that day, which I do from time to time, the first thing I see is those beautiful, colourful blooms the sight of which gladdened my heart.

On the day itself, and on the days either side, Willard looked a little sheepish, his actions a little unsure, his voice quiet, and he had specks of nervous sweat on his top lip and spittle in the corners, but I didn't mind none. I didn't want no loudmouth. What I wanted was to be Mrs Willard Templeton — and I was!

I remember the first night we spent together at Grandma Sally's, lying as man and wife, giggling silently and happily while Grandma Sally sat on the terrace in her rocking chair and a big moon filled the sky and pulled the tide high just for us. I woke up the next day and I felt different because I wasn't just little Cee-Cee Symmons; I was Mrs Cee-Cee Templeton, wife of Willard, and that was really something. The thin, gold band on my left hand gave me something I had never had before: status. I was a married woman! I also believed it gave me security, because the way we loved each other had surely never been felt before by any two people on God's sweet earth. It was something of an obsession, powerful and all-consuming. I felt such joy. In fact, I was filled with happiness without the need for food or socialising; all I wanted was to feel Willard's skin next to mine and to hear his soft voice whispering a thousand promises into my ear. I still hear them sometimes, those promises, dotted with words like forever . . . future . . . children . . . prosper . . . together. These words might have been easy spoken and warmly received, but they were all lies. But how was I to know that? I do believe that if anyone had told me so, I would have laughed them out of town. Oh Rachel, dear, I was many things, but mainly I was naïve . . .

SEVEN

Eight weeks had passed since she'd moved into Vicky and Gino's, and Rachel noticed that, physically at least, she had started to make a slow creep towards recovery. Her sleep pattern was more regular and the sour taste of sadness and guilt had faded a little from her tongue. Her limbs were no longer stiff with anxiety, her back muscles marginally less knotted, and the churning of her stomach, which robbed her of her appetite, somewhat eased, meaning that morsels of food no longer turned to ash in her mouth. All of which was welcome, but still each feeling and every thought was wrapped and sealed in the paper of grief, as if she had no right to move on from this catastrophe. Moreover, she found herself questioning whether she really wanted to. Her mind still coasted on the whims of her loss; dreams and wakefulness were confused, with the prevailing image being of Oscar on the back of his giant turtle. She also found that moments of potential happiness – like holding a sleeping Francisco in her arms, sipping from a mug of hot tea on a cold day or sauntering along Ladies Mile in Clifton, beneath the russet-tinged leaves – could be hijacked by memories of Oscar so clear, or thoughts so potent that she was instantly reduced to the desperate woman weighted down by a grey blanket on the damp bottom of a boat, trying to catch her breath and wishing to sleep for eternity.

She and James spoke with regularity, and the distance between them allowed for more honest conversation. If anything, it felt a little easier to talk openly without having to sit opposite him. His face and tortured expression mirroring her own only heightened her sadness, whereas the voice and ear on the end of the phone offered an anonymity that meant thoughts and words could be frank.

'I hurt so bad.'

'Me too.'

'I am lonely – even when I'm with people, I am lonely.'

'Me too. I am lonely.'

'I am angry. So angry. Why? Why us? What had our boy ever done to deserve to have his future taken away?'

'I know. I know. I am angry too.'

'I still don't believe it. I still can't accept it.'

'When are you coming home?'

'I don't know. Do you want me to come home?'

'I don't know.'

Their phrases were interchangeable and mutual tears now the finale to nearly each and every call.

Whilst Vicky and Gino went out of their way to make her welcome, she was becoming ever more aware of the confined communal areas and how the family adapted their lives to make space for her, which was something she didn't want. Even their kindly efforts at inclusion made her feel like a burden. The idea made her shiver. She tried to picture James being as accommodating to someone taking over the spare room of the flat in Richmond where space had been at a premium, and could envisage him whispering questions of 'How much longer?' into her ear before sleep.

Plus, it wasn't only her that had taken up residence in their lovely family home in Bishopston; no, she had brought with her the sweeping cloak of sadness that dusted the floor where she walked, trailed behind her up the stairs and stained the furniture on which she sat. And that felt most unfair. The last thing she wanted to do was outstay her welcome, despite Vicky's assertions that this was impossible. The big question for her was what to do next, whether to find her own place to live, go into a hotel, book a flight back to Bermuda, or maybe it would be best if she headed back to her mum and dad's for a bit. Trying to sort her thoughts on the topic, weighing up the pros and cons of all options left her feeling exhausted and more muddled. She had tried and failed to get a steer from James, but he was as confused as she, and if anything this only heightened her sense of limbo. It was as unpleasant as it was unsettling.

As was often the case, today was proving to be a tough one.

Rachel had woken in the early hours to the sound of Francisco crying. In her semi-sleeping state she had thought it was Oscar who was calling and had felt her heart leap and her senses jolt in her need to get to him. She then sat up and couldn't figure out where James was; maybe he had gone to fetch the baby? She stared at the empty pillow as her mind caught up, sifting the facts from her dream. She laid her hand on the space where James used to lie in a house far away, where they would take turns fetching a child who no longer made this or any other noise. She tried, but could not imagine, Oscar quiet. Rachel fell back against the pillows, feeling the heft of grief that crushed her chest. Closing her eyes, she heard a voice whispering a memory. 'Go back to sleep, go to sleep, child. You will find peace . . .' and lulled by this soothing murmur, she did just that.

◆ ◆ ◆

With Vicky at her mother-and-baby swim session in Horfield, Rachel decided to venture to rewers alone. The walk was a welcome distraction and she liked the fresh air, and the coffee was far better than anything she could whip up. Plus, she liked to get out from under Gino's feet on the days he worked from home, returning with a fancy cake or wrapped sandwich, part of her campaign of thanking the couple who had thrown her this wonderful lifeline.

The place was half full and the owner, he of the close-cropped beard and chirpy nature, whom they now knew was called Glen, smiled and gave a small wave.

'Where's your friend and the little man?' he called out.

'They've gone swimming.' She unwound her scarf and took a seat at the bar.

'Cor, rather them than me, it's bloody freezing today!' He rubbed his arms.

'Indoors, of course, and very warm by all accounts.' She thought of taking Oscar to swim on the beach in the hot sun and their daily dips in the pool.

Look, Mummy! Look! Watch me do it again!

'What can I get you? Usual?'

'Sorry?' She blinked.

'I was asking if you wanted a drink, your usual maybe?'

'Please.' Rachel felt a surge of warmth that felt a lot like belonging. It felt good to have a 'usual'.

She sat facing the window and watched the traffic passing by on the Gloucester Road. It was strange how she felt able to hide here in this bustling, crowded environment and yet in the quiet of her Bermuda home, even when alone, she had felt exposed, judged.

You are wrong, James – that was so unfair! He was my world! He was! And I was a good mum. Vicky said so.

On a small island she knew there would be no escaping her son's peers, who lived close, shopped close, swam close. She dreaded the idea of bumping into them with their parents as she pushed the trolley around Lindos. And worse still having to witness the awkward coughs and nervous greetings from the mums like Alison, Rita and Fiona, who would grip their kids' hands extra tightly, as if she were an unpleasant reminder of how quickly it was possible to lose all that was precious. As if her very bad luck might be contagious.

Bermuda was also, like any small place where people lived cheek by jowl, an island where the rumour mill often went into overdrive. She could well imagine the school community and the friends they had made through James's work, whispering comments between sips of wine or shouting thoughts between tennis shots: *Where was she exactly when he fell in? Is it true she was drunk? How could you not lock the hatch? I am always so careful on our boat . . . I mean, I shouldn't say this, but I do think it was neglectful.*

'Here we go, black Americano.' He placed the mug on the counter and drew her from her thoughts.

'Thank you, Glen.'

'No worries. It's Rachel, right?'

'Yes.' She nodded and took a sip of the restorative, warm, smoky liquid. 'I wanted to ask you, what does "rewer" mean? I've been wondering since Vicky first brought me here.'

'Ah.' She watched him pause and pull out a damp cloth with which to clean his countertop, as he shook his head ruefully. 'I lost my B.'

'I'm sorry?'

'It's "rewer" because I lost my B. It should be "Brewer". But the B fell off.'

'How did it fall off?'

'Actually, I don't think it did. I suspect it was nicked, as there was no sign of it anywhere, excuse the pun. Students, probably – they nick all sorts.'

'Why don't you get another B?' She took another sip.

'Two things: Bs are more expensive than you might think, fitting them even more so, and secondly, we are now known as "rewers" – we even have a listing in the *Good Coffee Bristol Guide* – and it feels like tempting fate or a change too far to add that B.'

'And it's a talking point, I guess.'

'Well, we're talking about it!' Glen smiled at her.

She nodded and looked down, not wanting to chat any further, but happy to have her curiosity settled.

'Rachel, if you don't mind me saying . . .' He hesitated and licked his bottom lip, seeming to weigh up whether to continue or not. She braced herself for what might come next. 'You seem . . . you have always seemed . . .'

She stared at him. *I have seemed what?*

'You seem very sad,' he levelled, his face colouring as he struggled to get the words out.

It was the first time a relative stranger had voiced what most must have observed and it surprised and comforted her in equal measure. She thought of James's observation of Cee-Cee – what was it he had said?

My grandma used to have a phrase, a face that could curdle milk.

She felt a flash of unease that she and her husband had dared to be so insensitive to a woman still in mourning, a woman on a personal journey that they could not have begun to understand. Until now.

'Well, I guess that is because I *am* very sad,' she managed. *Sadder than sad . . .*

He held her eyeline for a second or two before speaking. 'I guess it's true, isn't it?'

'What?' she asked.

'That everyone has a story.' He nodded and turned back to his cleaning chore, and she was thankful and warmed by the fact that he had left it at that.

◆ ◆ ◆

In her quest to give Gino and Vicky space, and to take advantage of being so close to her mum and dad, she decided to go and have supper at her parents' house. Her mum squeezed her tightly in a welcome hug, and from his chair in front of the television her dad gave his subtle wink over the top of *The Gazette*.

'There's a letter for you, love.' Her mum pointed to the envelope in its usual spot. Rachel picked it up and popped it in her bag to read later.

They took their places at the kitchen table and her mum ladled healthy portions of shepherd's pie and boiled, diced, mixed vegetables on to the plates.

'Would you like a glass of Shloer? We've got some left over from last Christmas,' her mum asked eagerly.

'No. Thanks, though, Mum.'

'We have really missed you, haven't we, Brian?'

'Yep.' He nodded. 'It's not the same walking in silence on my own when I could be walking in silence with you.'

She smiled at her lovely dad.

'It's been strange knowing you are in Bristol not Bermuda and yet not seeing you,' her mum summarised.

'I think everything is a bit strange at the moment,' she suggested.

'Are you warm enough at Vicky's? Do you want to take an extra duvet?'

'No, I'm good, Mum, plenty warm enough.' Her mum had always believed that every house apart from her own was chilly and unwelcoming.

'Well, there's one in the airing cupboard if you change your mind. You look a little bit better, I would say – got a bit of colour in your cheeks at long last, hasn't she, Brian?'

Her dad nodded, concentrating on getting the right meat, mash and veg ratio on to his fork.

'Are you sleeping better, love?' her mum asked with a worried expression.

'A bit.'

'That's good. And have you spoken to James?'

'Yes.' She felt a bolt of longing fire through her, remembering how she liked to have him close by when they were visiting her parents, dissecting the interaction later, laughing at their shared insights.

'I do worry about him. I want to give him a big hug. I feel bad that we are all here together and he's stuck out there with strangers, no family. His mum and dad are useless I know.'

Rachel was reminded of Cee-Cee's words: *These people who love you and whom you love, these people who share your blood and live in your heart; it is with them that you will learn how to move forward.* At that particular moment, she felt bad.

'So what did he have to say?' Her mum spoke now with a mouthful of food.

'Not much, truth be told. We kind of go around in circles.' She sighed, looking out into the garden, trying to think how best to describe the practical, succinct exchanges peppered with expressions of their loss and mutual sadness, which now constituted their chats. It was a million miles away from the endless phone chatter of their courtship, where they would burble for hours, whispering into the receiver, curling the wire around their fingers, talking about anything and everything, laughing and laughing and laughing with no subject off-limits no matter how frivolous. It had never been choresome or awkward – quite the opposite. 'We kind of ask briefly how the other one is doing and there is a long pause, as if we are both wondering whether to say all that we need to, and we cry together and then we hang up. And immediately after I feel a little bit better, but completely exhausted and I am sure it's the same for him.'

'That breaks my heart. He's a good man and he's your husband! You need to talk properly. Support each other.'

'I know that, Mum. And I can't explain how hard it is.' She wished her mum would stop her commentary, knowing she couldn't satisfy her many questions.

'No, you can't. I think whatever Dad and I have had to face it has made us stronger, hasn't it, Brian?'

He looked at her and before he had the chance to respond, Jean continued, 'I think it's the same with Peter and Julie; things are sent to test us and it *should* make you stronger,' she offered definitively.

There are lots of things that should be but are not. I should not be here. I should be living my life in Bermuda. My son should not have disappeared from the side of our boat. My heart should not be broken.

Rachel set her fork on the side of the plate. 'I would have said the same about us. But with all due respect, nothing that you and dad or Peter and Julie have had to go through is anything like what we have experienced. Nothing at all.'

'Well, it's a shame.'

She stared at her mum and then at the mountain of food on the plate in front of her, wondering what the smallest polite amount was she could eat.

'Yes' – she swallowed – 'it is a shame. I am quite full, actually, Mum, I—'

Without warning her mother let out a wail, a loud, all-consuming bellow that was distressing and shocking all at once.

'Jean!' Her dad jumped up and rushed to her side of the table. 'What is it, love?'

'I can't . . .' she began, her head shaking, her fingers balled into white-knuckled fists. Sadness and anger robbed her of the ability to speak.

'Mum?' She reached out and held her hand across the breakfast nook.

'Oh Rachel, Rachel!'

'Don't cry. Please don't cry! What is it?' she asked, as her dad palmed circles on his wife's back over her cardigan. Rachel pushed a floral paper napkin into her hands. Jean grabbed it and blew her nose.

'I'm sorry. I am. I can't help it.' She sniffed.

'What's wrong, Mum?' she coaxed.

'I have *missed* you,' her mum began, speaking so quickly that Rachel had to really listen. 'I have missed you for years! I tried being happy for you, pleased that you were living that wonderful life in the sunshine, and I told everyone how great it was to know you and James and the babber were doing things we could only dream of. But the truth of it is, I have hated every single moment of having my girl and my grandson out of reach!' Her tears fell again. 'And when the call came in that Oscar had gone . . .'

Rachel watched her face collapse again in tears.

'I felt as if someone had ripped my heart out!' she shouted through gritted teeth with the napkin scrunched in her hand. 'And I know I don't always get it right, I know because I don't know what to say. All I can think of is to make sandwiches and cook supper and wrap up slices of fruit cake in case you get hungry and to put the boiler on so you can have a hot bath because I don't know how to make it better, Rachel! I don't know how to fix it! And James – I love him! *We* love him, and I can't stand that he is all on his own hurting just as much as we are but without anyone to make it better! It's not fair!' She smacked the table with her free hand and she and her dad jumped. 'And I try and keep it all in. I do. I keep it all in and I try and keep all the plates spinning for you and Peter and Julie – the bloody waste of space that she is – and everything else. And you go walking, Brian – well, good for you! And I sit here alone and bake another bloody cake just so that I am *doing* something and I can't stand it any more! I can't stand it! I can't stand it!'

Rachel felt her pulse race, ill-equipped to handle her mum's outburst and taken aback by the ferocity of her words. The whole encounter left her with a new-found compassion for the woman who was mourning too.

'It's okay, Jean. It's okay. I love you. I love you.' Her dad closed his eyes and reached for her. And she saw her mum's shoulders relax a little, remembering in that moment what it felt like to have someone to fall into who could make things feel better. It fired a bolt of loneliness through her very core.

Her dad pulled his wife into his arms and held her fast, and Rachel knew that these people who lived in each other's hearts would indeed help each other heal. The sight of them locked together made her miss her husband more than she could express.

Rachel watched from the sidelines, an interloper, intruding on a moment of tenderness between these two people she knew she had taken for granted. She had heard her mum's roar and understood now just how much she was hurting too and, like her, like Cee-Cee, like all of them, was doing her very best to get through each and every day.

Rachel kissed her mum goodbye softly at the end of the evening with a new, unspoken understanding.

'I love you, Mum.'

'I love you too, my little girl.'

Her dad glanced at her as they drove along the M32; he had jumped at the chance to give her a lift home.

'Are you okay?'

'Yes, Dad.'

'That had been building in your mum for quite some time, I'd say.' He kept his eyes on the road.

'I know, and I think she might feel better for it.'

'Yep.'

'I can see that it's hard for her to understand how it is for James and me now. It's hard for me too and I do feel guilty that he is there without family, but, Dad, we were killing each other.' She bit her lip.

He nodded. 'Only you and James know what it's like and only you and James know where you are heading.'

'That's just it, Dad. I don't think either of us knows where we are heading, but the more time goes on, I can't see us heading there together. And it should make me sad, but it can't. It's like I don't have any sadness left for that.'

'And that is between the two of you, no one else. But I would say this: you had a good marriage, you were friends and maybe this is a stage of your grief, but you will come out of the other side feeling different.'

'Maybe,' she conceded, running her thumb over the Tic-Tac box full of sand that sat in her coat pocket. 'I am thinking about what to do right now, Dad. I don't know whether to get a flat or go to a hotel.'

'Things not working out at Vicky's?'

'No, things are lovely. She and Gino are great.' She looked out of the window at the big Ikea sign and pictured trawling the aisles, looking for bedding and lamps, starting over . . . Even the thought of it made her feel tired. 'I just don't want to encroach on their space, and it's hard to be a relaxed little family when you have a guest, I know that. But if I leave there, it forces me to make a decision about what I do next and that is scary. If I take a flat it gives my life here a sense of permanency, and if I go into a hotel that suggests it's a stepping-stone towards going back to Bermuda, and I don't think I want that.'

'You need to talk to James. Properly talk to him.'

'Yes.' She nodded. 'I know.' She heard her husband's words now, crystal clear in her mind: *I can't look at you, I don't want to look at you . . . I'm able to distract myself with one million small things, but just the sight of you and I am dragged back to that moment and I can't stand it . . .*

After he dropped her off at Vicky's, she waved her dad goodbye and, using the key they had given her, Rachel let herself into the house in

Egerton Road, stopping short in the hallway at the sound of laughter drifting from under the closed door to the sitting room. She hung up her coat and transferred the Tic-Tac box to her sweatshirt pocket before knocking lightly with her knuckles as she opened the door.

'Hey, Rach! Come in! How were your mum and dad?' Vicky asked, swinging her legs to the floor from where they had rested on her husband's lap, like a babysitting teen who had been caught unawares with her boyfriend by the earlier-than-anticipated arrival of the parents. She noticed the almost imperceptible flex of Gino's jaw and felt that she was imposing, ruining the moment, and this she understood.

'They're fine, the same. You know.'

'Yes, I do.' Vicky laughed. 'God love them.'

'Would you like a glass of wine?' Gino reached for the bottle that nestled on the floor by his feet.

'No, I'm good. Early night for me.' She was sure there was a flicker of relief on his face. 'I am thinking about what to do next,' she began. 'You guys have been wonderful to me and I have loved staying here—'

'Uh-oh, this sounds like goodbye.' Vicky pulled a sad face. 'We love having you here!'

'And I love being here, but I can't stay indefinitely, and I don't want to, so I'm thinking what to do next, but just thought I should let you know that I'm either going to get a flat—'

'Yes, get a flat close by! That'd be so great; then I can see you whenever I want and you can look after Francisco and it'd be so cool.' Her friend bounced on the sofa.

Rachel nodded. 'Or I might go back to Bermuda. I need to speak to James.'

'Of course.' Vicky calmed a bit, her wine-filled enthusiasm brought under control by this reminder of her life. 'I do love you, Rach.'

'I love you too.' Slowly she backed out of the room and made her way up the stairs.

She lay on the bed and read Cee-Cee's letter, quite lost in the build-up to her wedding and saddened by Clara's behaviour.

... It didn't happen overnight, but it might as well have. It was more than sulking; it was like Clara had decided that there wasn't enough of me to go round and that if I chose Willard then I couldn't have her too.

'That's so sad, jealousy.' She spoke aloud as she called her husband. Nerves fluttered in her stomach in anticipation of the conversation she knew they had to have. Looking at the time on her phone, she worked out that it would be four in the afternoon; he'd be in the office.

'Hi, Rachel.'

'Can you talk?' she asked, more wary than she should have been when talking to her own husband and her tone threaded with nerves at the topic she was about to launch.

'Yes, sure. I'm in the car actually, so good timing. Just been back to the house. Cee-Cee was taken ill and so I shot back and have just dropped her at home. She was insisting on walking – you know what she's like. I had to more or less bundle her into the front seat.'

'Oh no, what's wrong with her?' She sat up, concerned.

'Not sure, but she didn't look great. She was a bit breathless and looked clammy. She said there was a sickness bug going around and a friend of hers from church had been ill, so probably that. I told her not to worry about coming in, of course, and to call if she needed anything. I know she won't, so I will pop in tomorrow on my way home to see how she's doing.'

'Good idea, can you take some soup and some flowers?' She pictured Cee-Cee in her neat cottage.

I will write back to you Cee-Cee – I will write you a long letter. She felt guilty for not yet having replied to her mail.

'Will do.'

'Do you think it'd be okay if I called her? Just to check in?'

'Yes, I think she'd like that. God, it's hot today.' He sighed.

She tried to remember the feel of the heat and humidity. The way her hair would hang limply about her face, make-up slid from her cheeks, and to step from the air-conditioned car or house into the out-doors would make her instantly sweat. It was strange how having lived on the island for so many years, it had taken only a few days back in Blighty for her to get used to wearing jerseys and sitting in front of the fire in bed socks, and for her to forget exactly how it felt to wake in the soft, blue light of a sun-drenched day where the warmth soothed her muscles and softened her mood.

'It's night-time here and quite chilly.'

'Sounds lovely. Do you remember how cold our old flat used to get?'

She heard the smile in his voice as she too pictured their home in Richmond not far from the river, with its high ceilings, stripped wooden floors and pointless low radiators that pumped out heat that would whoosh out of the rattly, drafty windows or up to the space below the roof.

'Yes. I remember the alarm clock going off each morning and nearly crying because I didn't want to go and use the bathroom; the floor used to feel like ice under my bare feet.' She scrunched her sock-covered toes in recollection.

They were both silent for a second, as if each trying to reconcile how much they had unravelled since those heady days of young love in a new marriage when everything and anything felt possible.

'How are you today?' he asked. The loaded question was no longer the first thing they asked, and that in itself was progress. They both now knew enough to recognise that it was a day-by-day process, and that any improvement could be hacked away as quickly as it was gained.

'I'm thinking about what to do next. I'm considering moving out of Vicky and Gino's, not that they don't make me welcome and they haven't asked or anything, but I want to give them back their privacy in their own space. You know.'

'Yes.'

'I don't know what to do, James. I have thought about moving to a hotel, but that just feels a bit like putting off a decision. Or I could take a flat here . . . or I could come back to Bermuda.'

'They are all options,' he agreed. She noted he did not, as anyone with the desire might have done, urge her to come home.

'I can't imagine being there.' Rachel spoke aloud her thoughts.

'I can't lie, I feel particularly nervous about seeing you.'

She was glad of his candour. 'I feel the same.'

'Do you . . . do you miss me at all?' he asked. His voice sounded a little strangled.

She held Mr Bob to her chest and answered as best she could. 'I miss everything about our old life and I wish' – she closed her eyes – 'I wish I could turn the clock back to when things were normal, before.'

'Of course.'

'But the new us, the us with our hearts shredded and with the memory of what happened so crisp in our minds' – she looked at Mr Bob – 'I feel like I don't want any part of it and putting distance between where it happened and me has helped in some way.'

'I know.' His voice was low. 'It's a difficult thing, but I was talking to Max at work about it and I suggested that it's like a phenomenon: when you are grieving, to add another person who is also grieving *more* than doubles that grief. It turns it into something overwhelming, something even more unbearable. A tsunami.'

'Yes, it does.' She paused. 'I think I will take a flat, for six months maybe.'

'Yes.' His confirmation was the push she needed to take the step.

It felt like a door closing.

'Give my love to Cee-Cee and don't forget, soup and flowers.'

'I won't. And you take care, Rachel.'

She held the phone to her face, aware of another fine strand of connection being severed between them. She slipped down on to the pillows and thought about her mum's outburst earlier.

I try and keep it all in. I do. I keep it all in and I try and keep all the plates spinning . . . and I sit here alone and bake another bloody cake just so that I am doing something and I can't stand it any more! I can't stand it! I can't stand it!

Rachel looked up at the chimney pots outlined against the inky blue, star-filled sky. It was true; all of them were trying their very best just to get through each and every day.

CEE-CEE

'Hello?' Cee-Cee blinked as she flicked on the lamp, pulled the Portuguese shawl up over her shoulders and gripped the phone to her face as she sat up in the bed.

'Cee-Cee? It's Rachel. James told me you weren't feeling too well and I'm worried about you, so thought I would give you a call.'

'Well, that's wonderful.' She felt her heart flutter a little; this was exciting and yet a little invasive. The one thing that stood out to Cee-Cee was that if this girl was worried about her, even a little bit, it showed her grief had shifted from the all-consuming sadness that meant there were no spare thoughts for anything other than her loss. Rachel might not know it, but this was progress.

Cee-Cee realised that she now felt a little self-conscious to be in direct contact with the woman who knew some of the most intimate aspects of her life. She found it easy to write, cathartic even, but this was different. Plus, it was very, very late, almost eleven p.m. 'I am better now – completely fine! Just a bug. No need for anyone to worry.'

'I am very glad to hear it.' Rachel laughed. 'I've told James to come over with soup for you tomorrow.'

'Well, I don't need soup! And I don't need him going out of his way.' Cee-Cee felt the pull in her gut of anxiety; she did not want the Crofts to think she was incapable of performing her duties.

'I think he just wants to take care of you. And if I were there . . .'

Cee-Cee was surprised by the swell of emotion in her throat.

'It's nice to hear your voice, Cee-Cee. It's late and I couldn't sleep.'

'What is the time in England?'

'It's just before three a.m.'

'Goodness, child! You should be sleeping!'

'I can't. My head is too busy. I picked up your latest letter from my mum's. I can't tell you how much I love your stories. They transport me back to that time and it's wonderful. I have just read all about your wedding.'

Cee-Cee beamed. 'Ah, yes, my wedding. And you know, Rachel, to be able to share my story is something very comforting.'

There is no one else . . . Willard gone . . . Oscar gone . . .

'Comforting. Yes,' Rachel agreed. 'And I appreciate your advice because you know how I feel, you know what it's like. Most people don't. And of course, I love that you loved Oscar.'

'Oh, I did! I did! I can't lie to you, my heart is damaged. I miss that little English boy.'

'I know, and he was so lucky to have someone like you in his life.' Cee-Cee caught the catch in Rachel's voice.

It was me who was the lucky one.

There was a moment or two of silence until Cee-Cee spoke.

'Will this call be costing you a fortune?'

Rachel sniffed. 'No! No! It costs nothing as long as I call after a certain time; I got a deal with Three.'

'Oh, right.' Cee-Cee had no idea who or what that was.

'Cee-Cee, can I ask you what happened after your wedding?'

'Oh, it's a long story.'

'I have a large cup of tea and I am quite comfortable sitting on my bed.'

Cee-Cee moved up the bed and rested her back on the headboard. She took a deep breath and felt her spirits soar in anticipation of telling this woman, still a stranger in so many ways, the details of her life.

'Well, I think in particular about one hot, hot August day. Apart from the heat it was nothing but an ordinary day, at least it was until I received a letter – more accurately a note – pushed into the mailbox and without signature.

'The paper was unremarkable, faintly lined and torn jaggedly from a notebook. It wasn't written in fancy ink pen, but a plain old ballpoint. The second note that had been surreptitiously cast in my direction, and whilst of a very different nature, it had just as much of an impact as the first.'

'What did it say?' Rachel prompted.

Cee-Cee smiled at her interest. 'Well, I can see the words now, scrawled off the lines, and if the contents of the note hadn't been enough to send fire into my veins, then this poor line-discipline was in itself more than enough to cause a flicker of irritation. It was no more than four lines that said: "*Willard has broken your trust. He is not faithful. And he is brazen in the execution of his sin, committed at his place of work.*" And it was signed: "*A friend*".'

She heard Rachel gasp. 'Huh, no!'

'Yes!' Cee-Cee was happy to hear Rachel so engaged and her obvious shock bonded the two closer, they became allies. She felt that this was a good distraction for the girl, as well as a joy for her to have someone to tell her story to. 'And I don't mind telling you that I fell backward on the veranda, sinking down into Grandma Sally's chair. The breath left my lungs and I was hot, so hot, I could feel the warm beads of sweat running down my face.

'Willard, my husband of eighteen months was carrying on with someone.'

'Cee-Cee, that is awful. Just heartbreaking – how did you know it was true?' Rachel asked.

Cee-Cee, touched by the girl's sympathy, pictured herself as a bright newly-wed whose dreams were fading like the bloom on her dried bouquet.

'I just knew it. I felt it. And as God is my witness, I am ashamed to say that all I could think of was: why hadn't I been able to keep him happy? Why wasn't I enough? How had that joyous bubble in which we had existed come to burst already? And more important, what would happen now?

'As I sit here tonight, I wish I could reach down to my nineteen-year-old self and say, "It's nothing to do with you, Cee-Cee Templeton! It is all him! Feeling blue and down in the dumps is like howling at the wind and rain while a storm rages – ain't nothing you could have done to prevent it!" Not that it would have hurt any less.

'Grandma Sally came outside, alerted by my crying, and asked what the matter was. Now, apart from the goings-on in our marital bed and the strength of devotion I felt to the man I was married to, I had never had a secret from Grandma Sally, and without hesitation I handed her the note. Well, she read it and read it again and she gave a tight-mouthed little shake of the head and said, "You need to put on your best dress and you need to go and see him at his place of work. You need to face it head-on." She might have been right, but as I stood at the pale stone bus shelter in my best dress, a pale-blue cotton frock with a white tie belt, only usually worn for church and Cup Match weekends, I felt my nerve fade and my legs turn to jelly. I looked at the bend in the road and wondered if it might be possible to make out I hadn't seen the note, to keep quiet about the whole thing and hope that Willard might settle down and that Grandma Sally might not raise the subject and that my faith in him might heal.

'It was a lot of hopes. Too many.

'I decided to leave it to fate. I would count to ten and if the bus hadn't shown up by then, I would leave, walk home in the heat, have an iced tea and think things over; but if it came before I got to ten, then I would go into town and go and see Willard at the Hamilton Ferry Port where he worked, and I would have it out, face to face.

'I started to count. One . . . two . . . three . . . four . . . five . . . and it was as I was about to take a breath and mentally reach for six that the single-decker bus appeared. So there it was, fate had decided.

'It wasn't too busy and I took up a seat at the very front, as was my God-given right to do, and sat with my back straight, all the way along South Road and along into Front Street. I jumped off a stop or two early to give me a chance to compose myself. And I walked briskly, nodding hello to the people I knew, and there were many, some like Mrs De Souza calling out, asking after Grandma Sally, and I lifted my hand and shouted back, "She's good!" – knowing that if I stopped and chatted, I just might never get away or, worse, lose my nerve. My stomach churned at the thought of the conversation I was about to have with the man I loved, and my heart raced in preparation for what I might see. After all, the note had been very clear: "Brazen in the execution of his sin, committed at his place of work."

'I tried not to think about my daddy working along in Pitts Bay Road, not five minutes from where I walked, for fear of giving in to my cowardice and running right into his arms and telling him all my woes.

'I wasn't concentrating much on my surroundings, but was thinking of how I might address Willard and how, no matter what, I had to remain confident and dignified; *this* above all else.

'It was as I walked past Trimminghams that I clashed with a woman not much older than me, wearing lemon-coloured gloves and a white pillbox hat. After I had apologised and accepted hers in return, I heard her mutter to her friend, "Did you see those killer cheekbones? Lucky girl!" and as I might have mentioned, it was these few words gave me the shot in the arm needed to go and do and say what I had to.

'I spied my husband before he saw me. He was leaning back on the metal handrail with one foot in its shiny, brown, company-issue loafer, raised and resting on the metal grill of the fence that stopped folk who queued for the ferry tumbling into the dock while their noses were in their newspapers. There was a girl stood by his side. I can confirm she was indeed wearing cherry-coloured lipstick, as well as a fancy red-and-white frock with a neat, starched collar. She had one of those bodies that went in and out in all the right places, with a tiny waist and a bosom that needed a whole lot more upholstery than my thin vest could ever have provided. I thought she looked pretty, but I couldn't hate her for it. It sure as hellfire wasn't her that had stood next to me in St Anne's Church, Southampton Parish, and taken them vows!

'I watched Willard talk to her with his head cocked to one side, so he had to look at her through his lashes, and I saw the slight smile on his face and I remembered the many sweet nothings that had passed his lips while he spoke to me in the exact same way. And truly it felt like a dagger to my heart.

'I walked over slowly, paying little heed to the policeman who stood in his British uniform on his little raised island at the intersection, blowing a whistle and directing the traffic – horses and carts, buses and suchlike – with his straightened arms and bendy elbows. Willard threw his head back to laugh at something that young Miss Bosoms had said, and it was as he lowered his gaze that the laugh stopped and his eyes widened and just for a second he looked a little afraid and I was glad. I told myself, "Don't you let him mess with you, Cee-Cee! You have killer cheekbones!" I must be stupid, Lord knows, because at the sight of that look of fright I felt sorry for Willard. He was my dear heart and to cause him even the slightest of harm or worry did not sit well with me.

'I was some kind of fool.'

'You were in love, Cee-Cee: a fool in love!'

'Yes, that I was, Rachel, dear. A fool in love.'

EIGHT

Rachel spread the property paper out on the tabletop, holding her coffee in one hand as she perused the flats for rent, running her finger up and down the columns. Vicky rocked the pushchair back and forth in an effort to calm Francisco, who wailed loudly. There were some pretty one-bedroom places off the Gloucester Road and at rates that were affordable. She knew she and James had savings that would more than cover the costs, and it was only going to be a temporary measure while she figured out what to do next, but this was still a new direction for her and felt very different from when they spent money together as a married couple with a common goal and one earning pot. This felt very different indeed.

'Bless him, is it wind?' Glen's mother, Sandra, asked, as she whipped by with a plate of bacon and eggs resting in her palms.

'Don't think so, he might be teething, but I can't see anything,' Vicky answered. Her breathing grew faster and her cheeks reddened as her agitation increased. 'I think I'll take him outside.' She looked at the handful of other patrons, wary of disturbing their peace.

'No, don't be daft; it's raining! Give him here!' Sandra, having deposited the plate, tucked the dishcloth into the leather loop that hung from her funky apron. Francisco almost instantly calmed and rested his head on her shoulder.

'Ah, love him! This takes me right back!' Sandra jostled on the spot, patting his narrow back and smiling. Rachel swallowed the tears that surged; she could still feel the imprint of that little bundle in her arms.

It's a boy! Congratulations! . . . Oh my God, Rach, we did it! We did it! Look at him!

'Avocado and poached egg on toast!' came the call from the kitchen, as Keith placed the food at the pass.

'Glen! Order up for table five, but I've got my hands full!' Sandra called across to the bar where her son made coffee; clearly she had no intention of handing back the baby and getting on with her job.

'Oh, Sandra, give him to me.' Vicky stepped forward.

'No, love, I'm having the time of my life!'

'Avocado and poached egg on toast!' The call this time was louder and sharper.

Rachel scooted away from the table and walked to the back.

'I'll take it. Table five?'

'Yes, and come straight back for the soup.' The grumpy-faced Keith tutted.

She wasn't sure if he was joking, having expected at least a small nod of thanks. Glen smiled at her from the coffee bar as she placed the plate on the table and pointed to the jam jar full of cutlery. 'Soup won't be a sec.'

'Can I get some ketchup?' the girl with the avocado called after her. Rachel bit her lip, wanting to ask who in their right mind would put ketchup on avocado? She got to the bar as Glen pulled a bottle from under the counter and slid it over to her, whilst taking payment from one customer who was leaving and monitoring the progress of a coffee spewing from the complex machine for another. With the ketchup deposited, Glen's grumpy dad called, 'Soup!'

She rushed past Vicky and Sandra, who laughed quietly as she collected the bowl and chunk of soda bread and took it to the table.

Sandra sat in the seat she had vacated as another customer grabbed her arm. 'Where's the loo?'

'Oh, at the back, on the left. Mind the step as you go in!'

'Excuse me, but can I get more toast?' a man at the bar called.

'Of course.' She nodded and went off to ask Keith for the order.

Things settled after the mid-morning brunch rush and Rachel went back to the table where Francisco now slept soundly and Vicky laughed, looking quite at home.

'You are a doll. Thank you.' Sandra smiled at her, careful not to move and disturb the slumbering infant on her shoulder.

'Yes, thank you for that,' Glen chimed. 'Don't suppose you want a job?'

'A job?' She wrinkled her brow.

'Yes. Doing what you have done this morning, but we give you money in exchange for your services!' He laughed.

'I know how a job works.' She looked at her friend, seeking support. What she got was something quite different.

'You should definitely take the job. We would probably get a discount on carrot cake and that alone is worth it. Plus, I now know where I can get free babysitting. I might never leave.'

'Trouble is I don't know how long I'm going to be here.' She looked down at the floor, feeling torn.

To take a job made things seem permanent, but she had to admit the idea of earning her own money and doing so in a place in which she liked to spend time was quite appealing. She remembered the day she left her job in digital marketing, a senior role she reluctantly relinquished when she was eight-and-a-half-months pregnant and her boss, Irene, was worried about her waters breaking on the new carpet.

'You'll be back in the saddle before you know it!' Irene had boomed and Rachel had believed her, unable to imagine choosing to stay at home and look after her baby full-time, thinking it would be a matter of balancing her career and motherhood. But one look at Oscar and stay at home she had, and she had loved it, every second.

'Long enough to rent a flat by the look of things.' Sandra drew her from her thoughts, eyeing the paper, still spread on the tabletop.

'Have you worked in a café before?' Glen asked, his brawny arms folded across his chest.

'Yes, but not for a long time – while I was at uni.'

'And what did you do after uni, what was your last job?'

She looked at Vicky, wondering how her morning coffee had turned into a work-experience session and now this informal interview.

'I worked for a train company, before moving abroad.'

'Oh well, customer service is customer service, isn't that right, Glen?' Sandra chirped.

'Yep.' He nodded. 'You'd get your own apron.' He twirled around, modelling the thing that he considered might be the enticement she needed.

Rachel raised a small smile. She and Vicky exchanged a look and neither divulged the fact that Rachel had ended up as head of digital marketing before giving it up to become a mum, Oscar's mum. Employment laws meant it wasn't possible for her, as a non-permanent resident, to work in Bermuda. Her plan had always been to re-establish her career when they came back to the UK, whenever that might be. Running around a café with plates of toast could not have been further from her mind. It felt a bit like starting again.

She heard Cee-Cee's words loud and clear: *And then one day, like you, I realised that I needed to navigate this new life. Start over. You need to find a way, like I did.*

She looked at Glen's hopeful expression. 'I'll think about it.'

◆ ◆ ◆

'So this is the sitting room, it's bright and sunny.' The estate agent stood back and let her walk into the room on the first floor. He was right; it was bright and sunny and with a glorious view along the street of chimney pots – it would do just fine. And though it was a far, far cry from the view out over the horizon on North Shore Road, she liked the neat galley kitchen that looked on to the sitting room, the big bedroom and the Victorian-styled bathroom.

'I think I'll take it.' She made the decision there and then. The main advantage too was that it was mere minutes from Vicky and Gino's – a safety blanket of sorts.

'I don't think you'll regret it; it's a cracking flat and will be nice once you've made it your own, brought all your furniture and your bits and bobs in.'

Rachel looked from the grey matte walls and white skirting boards, cast-iron fireplace and empty bookshelves to the letting agent. 'Furniture,' she muttered, as if realising for the first time that all she had in the UK was a bag of clothes, a rather ratty stuffed toy and a small Tic-Tac box full of sand.

When the day of the move came, her mum and dad insisted on donating a mattress that had lived under the bed in Peter's old room for some time. It would do. It was after all only for six months and then she would either be heading back to Bermuda or seeking something more permanent. She tried not to think too far ahead, ridiculously hoping that a solution would present itself and save her the anguish of making the difficult decision about what came next. The result was this half measure, a sparse flat dotted with her meagre possessions – limbo. It did, however, feel quite pleasing to hang her clothes in a wardrobe without worrying that she was encroaching on someone else's living space. She declined the offer of donated pictures and a TV, not wanting to make it too homey or established, not wanting to get too attached and also at some level quite liking the austerity, the hint of discomfort that kept in her a place of mourning and suffering. It helped to keep her ache for Oscar alive.

As she finished arranging the bouquet of lilies, a gift from Vicky and Gino, into a glass vase, also gifted by her friend, her phone rang. She popped the vase on the windowsill in the bedroom, the blooms instantly brightening the place.

'Hi, James.' There was a split second when she forgot their estrangement and, concentrating on the flowers in the window, answered the call with her usual joy at seeing his number pop up, just as she had done thousands of times. In the past they had been quick calls from him to share something funny he had seen or to ask what was for supper or if she wanted to attend a function they'd been invited to or to see how Oscar was. She gathered herself just in time, reeling in her note of enthusiasm for her next question: 'How is Cee-Cee doing?'

'Well, she's back at work and as you can imagine doesn't want any fuss.'

'I *can* imagine. I spoke to her on the phone; we had a lovely long chat.'

'Yes, she said; I think it made her day. I'd say she's a bit slower than usual. I left for work the other morning and she'd arrived early, and as I was leaving I saw her asleep on the sofa, so I put a blanket on her and drew the curtains.'

'You are a good man, James.' This she meant.

'Of course she didn't mention it when I next saw her and clearly doesn't want it mentioned.'

She pictured the quiet, industrious lady with the upright stance and sense of pride.

'So,' he began, 'I got your email with your new address and stuff. You went for it, found the flat.' His tone was neither congratulatory nor disapproving, but rather neutral, which to her mind was more damning, indicating his lack of passion either way.

'Yes. It's small, but fine and handy for where I need to be. I've kind of been offered a job. Which I think I might take.'

'A job?' She heard a note of disapproval. 'What job?'

Rachel felt awkward discussing it; it had been one of the hardest things about living in Bermuda, her inability to work, and having taken a break to look after Oscar before they left the UK, it had always irked her how any career aspirations had been put on hold while James worked hard and soared ever higher. Not that she would have given up one day of being a stay-at-home mum, recognising it as the privilege it was. But she had always felt a little torn once Oscar had started school, Cee-Cee had come into their lives and her time was her own to be spent idling. *And I missed out, I know I did; all the days I chose not to collect him from school, time wasted when I could have been with him – my own private torture.*

'It's working in a café. I think it might be good for me to do something now that I can. It gets me back in the habit of working, plus it means I won't be raiding our account. I want to pay my own way,' she whispered.

'So a new home and a job, that's quite a move forward, Rach. I'm pleased for you.'

His words felt like a new distancing between them and she was surprised by the twist of regret in her gut.

'Well, it feels right for now, that's all, and I've taken the lease for six months so I can regroup after that and take stock.'

'Six months?' he questioned. 'That can feel like a lifetime.'

She knew he referred to the fact that it was a little over eight months since they had lost Oscar. 'Yes,' she agreed. 'And yet at the same time a blink of an eye.'

'Yep. I don't go into his room. I can't bear to, but I suppose we should talk about his things.'

'There is nothing to talk about,' she answered in a clipped tone, feeling the grip of helplessness at the fact that if he decided to disturb

Oscar's room, or God forbid get rid of any of his belongings, there was very little she could physically do about it, being so far away.

'Okay. Okay, Rach.'

She changed the topic. 'I know you said that working hard was a good distraction for you, stopped you thinking.'

'That's true.' He sighed. 'I am almost on autopilot during the day, and if I can climb into bed exhausted then there's a good chance I might get some sleep; otherwise I lie awake listening to the sea and thinking, overthinking.'

Rachel closed her eyes and could hear the sound of the sea lapping the boat on the morning she had woken on that bright, beautiful, terrible, life-changing day, and just like that her tears manifested themselves and she was again lost to a tidal wave of sorrow. 'I have to go, James . . . I'm sorry. I have come over really sad.'

'That's okay, happens to me all the time. I understand.'

She nodded, knowing that he might be the only other person in the whole wide world who did.

'Speak soon, James,' she mumbled before ending the call and sinking down on to the duvet-covered mattress that sat in a corner of the bedroom of her rented flat.

It was the second day of her new job at rewer – it made her smile now every time she walked through the door and she spied the spot from where someone had stolen Glen's B. James had been right: she had fallen on to her mattress the night before with a welcome ache to her legs and a tiredness that helped switch off her brain. It was a rare treat to fall into such a deep sleep without the need of a tablet or the torture of watching the clock creep slowly towards dawn, pleading for the release of slumber.

Prowse

She arrived early and donned her apron. Glen came out of the storeroom adjacent to the kitchen. 'Morning, Rachel – so you came back?'

'You sound surprised.' She smiled at him.

'I guess I thought it was about fifty–fifty. My dad thought eighty–twenty, and not in your favour.'

'What about your mum?'

'She was one hundred per cent – reckons she can spot staying power, commitment.'

Rachel tied her apron around her waist. There was something about putting on the uniform of the place that gave her a sense of belonging.

'Well, I'm glad you did. And we got you this.' He pulled a white envelope from his apron pocket and handed it to her in a rather theatrical pose.

'Oh.' She was a little taken aback and for a moment had to ask herself if she had forgotten her own birthday. Her brain was such a muddle nothing would have surprised her. It was however, a welcome-to-your-new-home card, with a picture of a slug crawling towards a snail shell and grinning widely. Glen, Sandra and Keith had all signed it.

'Thank you. That's really kind.' She was touched and folded the card into the wide front pocket, removing the Tic-Tac box so she could lay it safely at the bottom.

'What's that?' He nodded at the small square container that she handled with such care.

'It's . . .' She looked at it, trying to think how best to describe just what this little plastic box meant to her, but realised that there were no such words. 'It's just something I like to carry around and keep close to me.' She replaced the box and straightened, avoiding eye contact and hoping he didn't probe further. 'So, what's first today?' She twisted her long hair into a bun.

'Tables could do with a good wipe over, and if you check the salt and pepper and clean up the ketchup bottles that'll be a good start.'

'On it.' Rachel made her way to the kitchen, happy to still keep her secret sadness close to her chest. It was no one's business but hers.

◆ ◆ ◆

After five weeks, Rachel fell into a steady routine. It amazed and petrified her how, when fully occupied, she had on occasion let Oscar slip from her mind for a moment or two, and when realisation dawned, she would flee to the bathroom and sob, repeating over and over, *I am sorry, Oscar. I love you, my darling boy. I am with you, always.*

Her calls with James grew less and less frequent until once every ten days or so it was almost a surprise to see his name on her phone screen. At these times she would rub her thumb over the gold band that sat neatly on the third finger of her left hand, a reminder of vows spoken with conviction in a flower-filled chapel under a blue June sky, unable to have foreseen a situation when all that they had and all that they planned could go up in smoke quicker than she could strike a match.

Her favourite days were when Vicky came into the café with Francisco and sometimes with Gino too. There was something wonderfully social about handing her friends cake and hot tea and chatting to them when the crowds dispersed. She liked how Glen joined in too. He and his mum had always been inclusive; grumpy Keith, however, who apparently had only given her a twenty per cent chance of holding down the job, was another matter entirely.

It was the end of another long day. Sandra and Keith had finished up and she now mopped the wooden floor of the café as Glen totted up the day's banking at the bar, counting coins into piles before tipping them into small, fiddly plastic bags of single denomination in a rounded number.

'Would you like a coffee, Rachel?'

'Oh, yes, I really would, that'd be lovely. Thank you.' She looked forward to the restorative caffeine that would fuel her walk home via the supermarket where she would pick up a granary loaf and some fruit. She pulled out one of the bar stools and watched as Glen pressed buttons and banged the grill of the space-age-looking machine that created the best coffee in Bristol. And one she had yet to master. She and Sandra had shared a moment over how protective Glen was of the contraption.

'It's been a busy day, thank you for your hard work.' He spoke over his shoulder.

'No worries. It's good for me.' She made the remark off the cuff.

'Good for you how?' He grabbed the small jug of milk from the countertop fridge propped against the back wall and topped up her mug.

'Thank you.' She took the coffee into her palms and sipped it. 'Lovely.'

'I was asking how is it good for you to be so busy?' he pushed.

Rachel considered her answer. 'I guess when I am really busy it stops me from dwelling on things, keeps my head occupied.'

Glen grabbed a stool and pulled it up on the other side of the bar. The two sat facing each other with the cool countertop beneath their forearms.

'You need to keep your head occupied?'

She nodded and stared at the foamy head of her drink.

'What, as a distraction?'

'Uh-huh.'

'So come on, Rachel, what's your story?'

She shrugged. 'What's *your* story?' she fired back, figuring if she could deflect the enquiry it would at worst give her time to think of a suitable response and at best make him forget that he had asked. She had yet had to say out loud what had happened to her, why she was in Bristol, and it was something she dreaded – exposing her sadness to relative strangers.

Glen took a deep breath. 'Well, I was, until this time last year, engaged to be married, but a fortnight before the big day, with invites sent, dress bought and honeymoon booked, it finished.' He chopped his hand on the counter. 'That was it, over.'

'Oh, Glen, I am so sorry. That's not good. I bet she will regret it.' Glen was nice-looking, funny and kind, and she tried to picture the girl who had broken his heart, wondering what bit of him his fiancée didn't like.

'Why would you assume it was her that ended it? Charming!' He looked at her quizzically.

'Oh, was it not? I don't know why! Maybe the way you said it, with a real sense of heartbreak.'

He gave a short snort of laughter. 'I'm only teasing you; it was heartbreaking, and it was me who called a halt. Not that that makes any difference at all; hurting someone was, I found out, just as hard as getting hurt. My main regret is that I didn't find the courage to say anything sooner, when I first had the inkling and before things went too far.'

'When did you first have the inkling?' She was curious.

'I think the moment we started talking about marriage and I felt more cornered than overjoyed. You're married, right?' He nodded towards her left hand.

She nodded. 'I didn't feel like that.' She pictured driving from her parents' house to the church in a shiny, flashy car with her hand resting inside her dad's on the wide, leather seat with nothing but the flutter of joy in her stomach. 'I was just excited and happy to be getting married, so I guess that was a red flag for you.'

'Yes. The thing is, I don't believe that either of us was that happy, not properly happy. Carly – her name is Carly – was preoccupied with the wedding plans and used to talk about the day a lot; each and every tiny detail, from table decorations to sugared bloody almonds in a net as favours, but never about us or what was important. I had this feeling that it was the big event that was propping us up and I sensed that once the wedding was out of the way, neither of us would be satisfied with our everyday lives. The mundane wasn't enough for her, she was always planning the next big thing, whether we could afford it or not, and I couldn't see me keeping up. Truth is, I didn't want to. I pictured us standing in the aftermath of the reception and wondering what to do next, whilst juggling the ever-increasing credit-card balance, and that's not right, is it?' He yawned; the day's work seemed to be catching up with him.

'No, it's not.'

'I think you have to be happy in the now; that's all we've got, really. That said, I chickened out for months.' He gave a wry laugh. 'It was hard to start the conversation about ending things while she was squealing over a bit of taffeta or on the phone to her mates about the hen weekend. You get the idea.' He slapped his thigh.

'So what was the thing that forced your hand, made you speak up?'

Glen ran his palm over his dark beard. 'She was getting more and more frustrated with me. She kept saying that I didn't know the right thing to do, didn't know instinctively how to make her happy, and the irony is that she was wrong. I *did* know instinctively what the right thing to do was; I was just finding it hard to pluck up the courage to do it. But that phrase rang in my head – the fact that I didn't know how to make her happy struck the bell of awareness. So I sat her down—'

'Here?' Rachel tried to picture them.

'No! Not here. I was working as a graphic designer in London. This' – he looked around the café – 'is my plan B.'

'Shame someone stole it,' she quipped.

'Yes!' He laughed. 'But this is what I always wanted to do deep down and I figured that as I'd found the courage to end my relationship,

I should also jack in my flourishing corporate career and come back to Bristol and open a coffee shop and kitchen, right around the corner from where I grew up!'

'You really went for it.'

'I did. Several friends and my parents all thought I was having some kind of breakdown. I mean, end my engagement, yes, but give up my fancy car for this? They thought I must be crazy. But they hadn't seen my coffee machine!'

She smiled. 'And what do you think now, a year on?'

'I think it's harder work than I realised, but I know it was the right decision. I wake up happy. I like my days, I like every day, and I can't remember feeling like that before. It's what we were talking about earlier, about being happy in the now.'

'I get that.' She took a glug of her coffee.

'So come on, Rachel Croft, that's me laid bare, now it's your turn. What's your story?'

She shifted in her seat and tried to think how to begin. Her words were slowly delivered, paced, allowing her to keep control of the rise of sadness in her chest. It was time for her to face her fear and say it out loud. All of it.

'I am married, yes, but not living with my husband; he is abroad.'

'Abroad where?' He sat forward.

'Bermuda.'

'Bermuda? Who lives in Bermuda? That's like paradise! Is it in the Caribbean? I've seen pictures of it but can't picture it on a map.'

Rachel envisioned the little fishhook-shaped island in the middle of the Atlantic Ocean, twenty-one miles in length and only one across in places, dotted with palm-fringed coves and verdant, twisty lanes that all held special places in her heart.

'Lots of people think that, but it's not in the Caribbean; it's in the North Atlantic and it's a group of islands – five main ones and hundreds of little ones. And it is paradise, or at least it can be.'

'So you were living there too?' he asked, wide-eyed, interested.

'Yes.' She nodded.

'Near the beach?'

'Yes.' *With a view of the big, deep, blue ocean . . .*

'And just to get this straight, you gave up living in paradise for a flat off the Gloucester Road and to come and work in my coffee shop?'

'Yes.'

'Now why on earth would anyone do that?' He chuckled.

'Because I needed to be somewhere different,' she began, reaching into her apron and running her fingers over her Tic-Tac box. 'Something . . . something bad happened,' she almost whispered. This was new territory, bringing up the subject that lived at the front of her mind day and night. It was terrifying.

Glen reached over and grabbed a handful of paper napkins, pushing them across the countertop towards her, his expression one of concern. She hadn't realised she was crying; it had become as natural and as unremarkable to her as breathing.

'Thank you.' She folded one and pushed it under her lower lashes, watching her tears form rounded, mascara-tinged blobs on the paper, before continuing. 'We had a son, I have a son, I had a son . . .' Rachel shook her head, hating the confusion on her tongue. 'And we lost him.'

'You lost him?' he asked softly.

'He disappeared at sea. From our boat. I woke up one morning and I couldn't find him.'

'Oh my God! He died?' Glen asked with a visible lump to his throat, and his eyes crinkled in the understanding of sadness.

'Yes.' She took a great gulp of air. 'He died.'

It was a strange thing; these words, this fact that she had carried around in her gut like a boulder floated from her mouth with ease, and once it had gone, she felt lighter because of it.

'How old was he, is he?' He clearly picked up on her confusion and sensitivity.

'Seven.'

'Seven . . .' He repeated the small number that made the tale that much more horrific. 'What's his name?' he asked softly.

'Oscar.' She mouthed the word that used to fly from her mouth a hundred times a day.

Oscar! We are leaving in five minutes! Oscar! Your breakfast is ready! Oscar! Come and say goodbye to Cee-Cee! Oscar! Please take your Lego off the stairs before someone trips up on it!

And now it was a name archived in her memory, a word with no use in the present because she didn't need to call him any more, didn't need to speak to him any more. To say it out loud, to introduce him to Glen felt like a wonderful reminder of the little person she had grown and lost. She again saw him astride the giant turtle, tanned and with sea spray sitting around him like a halo.

'Oscar.' He nodded. 'I can't imagine what it must be like.'

'It's a living hell.' She looked him in the eye, speaking without guile.

'I bet.' He held her gaze.

'It's the worst kind of torture and it doesn't go away. My grief is relentless and exhausting and it hurts physically and mentally. I am so broken that frankly, Glen, I am amazed that I am still alive, still functioning.' She found it surprisingly easy to be this bold with the stranger, knowing that if she were to be this blunt with her parents, James, or even Vicky, they would worry, intervene, rally around, and what she needed was exactly what she got from Glen: the acceptance of her words without judgment or suggestion.

It was liberating.

'And your husband is still in Bermuda?'

'Yes.'

'That must be tough on you both.'

'It is, but we are' – she looked up to the ceiling – 'we are pretty broken and that's a sadness all in itself. He's a good man, a really good man, but we are . . .' She took a breath. 'We are bent out of shape.'

She heard James's words, whispered, choked: *I love you; you know I do, but I don't know how we go forward from here. I can't picture it.*

'I am sorry for what you've been through, Rachel, you and your husband. It's horrible.'

'It is horrible.' She could only agree.

The two sat quietly, letting the enormity of her story, freely told in the heat of the moment, settle over them like dust.

It was Glen who broke the silence, speaking in no more than a hush.

'Has it lessened in any way, even a little?' She noted the way his eyebrows lifted in hope.

Rachel considered this. 'It hasn't lessened, but it has changed.' She looked out on to the street, at all the people sauntering by on their way home or heading out for supper. She tried to think of how best to phrase it. 'It's not the raw, uncontrollable grief that it was at the beginning, and actually that whole time feels like a bit of a blur. I remember the feeling but not the detail, if that makes any sense.'

'It does.' He nodded.

'And now . . . now it's like if you've ever trapped a nerve in your back or when your eyesight goes. It is the same every day, painful or a struggle, but you adapt, learn to live with it. The pain I feel has become normal, part of me, part of how I live now. I am not as shocked as I was by what has happened. I accept it, but I still don't think it's real.' She blew her nose. It was hard to explain.

'Well, I think you are amazing to be coping in any way at all. Thank you for telling me. I know there is nothing I can say that will make it better or take away your sadness, but if ever you want to talk to someone or you need a diversion, then let me know and I will do my best to try to make you feel less sad.'

Rachel looked at him in the half-light. 'Thank you, Glen.' She dabbed again at her eyes and took her empty coffee mug to the kitchen; it was time she thought about heading home.

We are pretty broken, aren't we, James? She spoke to him in her mind, wondering if her thoughts would float across the water.

CEE-CEE

'Good morning, James.' She placed his coffee on the tabletop and went to the oven to retrieve the two plump croissants that had been warming there.

'Morning, Cee-Cee. How're you feeling today?'

'Good.' She knew her tone was stern but didn't want there to be any doubt over her ability to work. She placed the croissants in front of him.

'Thank you, Cee-Cee, I can get my own breakfast, but I love that you do it for me; it's a real treat.'

'I like doing it.' She spoke the truth. 'Oscar loved his breakfast. It was his favourite meal of the day! He would lead me a merry dance. "Bacon! Ketchup! More bread!" We used to laugh every morning.'

'I would hear you two chuckling as I came down the stairs.'

She watched him pause and swallow, knowing it was important to talk about Oscar, remembering how when she had lost Willard the way his very existence became a secret, a thing too dreadful to mention, had hurt her as much as his passing.

'I think, Cee-Cee, about all those little things that now we have lost him have become big things. I nearly broke down the other day in Lindos looking at his cereal on the shelf.'

She busied herself at the sink, not wanting to witness his distress, giving them both a bit of privacy.

'I can only imagine what it's like for Rachel at those moments,' he continued. 'At least I get to picture him here and I can still see his things and it helps a bit.'

'You miss her.'

He nodded.

'Maybe it's easier for her not to have to see them. You know I lost my little one?'

'Yes.' He kept his voice low. 'Rachel did tell me.'

She nodded that she had expected as much and that it was fine. 'I couldn't stay away from his clothes or his bassinet. Eventually, my grandma swept the place of all trace of him. It helped at first, but then became a great sadness and I think I would have liked to have kept his things around me.'

'It's hard, Cee-Cee, isn't it? I still can't go into Oscar's room without collapsing, and yet at the same time I want to be near his things. I want to remember.'

'Of course you do, James.'

'Rachel is living in a small flat with a mattress on the floor. I understand her need to pare her life down, to help her concentrate on the one thing that occupies her thoughts and to try and come to terms with everything, but I think she is punishing herself.'

'I understand that too.' She turned towards him. 'I think it's a normal part of loss – the guilt.'

'Oh, I have plenty of that too!' He gave a dry smile.

'He was a happy, happy boy, always remember that.'

James looked up at her and this time did nothing to stem the wave of sadness that came over him. 'Yes, yes he was. A happy boy. I don't know how to be happy without Rachel, without Oscar.'

This admission, made in tears, was testament to how previous boundaries had been erased in the wake of Oscar's death, and with it came a closeness, a new sense of kinship for all who found themselves at the centre of this tragedy. Without forethought, Cee-Cee walked over to the table and wrapped the young man in a hug and it was far from embarrassing; it was in fact quite lovely to be able to help a person in their moment of need. It felt like the greatest thing to do. She closed her eyes and thought of her baby's daddy, who she doubted had ever reflected on the loss of his boy, or her for that matter, in this way. James was a good man. She had the feeling that the future might just be bright for these two young people whom she loved, and took faith from her belief; what was meant to come back to you, did.

'I miss him. I miss her.' His voice was muffled through his tears.

'I know,' she cooed. 'I know.'

Cee-Cee changed the bed linen and ran her mop over the floors before sitting down at the kitchen table with her pad and pen.

Oh Rachel,

I have thought all morning about what to write, what to leave out, but I think I should tell it as it is. It has been a very sad day so far. James was upset at the breakfast table, missing you and Oscar, and it has had such an impact on me. Even now, on occasion, the memory of my own pain comes at me in a wave so fresh, so new and shocking that it's enough to take my breath away and bring me to my knees. But it's thankfully rare. I prefer now to treasure the time before I lost my son. And this will be how it is for you! You will think about Oscar and your reaction will be to smile and not to cry, and how wonderful will that be? It is what he deserves! As for me? Yes, I try to think of those hours, days and weeks and the wonder of it. Not that it was an easy time for me, not at all.

I guessed before I knew for certain that I was with child.

I kept the secret like a fragile thing captured in my cupped hands, a thing with wings that might take flight at any moment. The only person I might have shared it with was Clara, but she had been missing from my life, self-exiled, since I took up with Willard. But to be carrying a baby? Oh! I had never known such joy! I believed this child would not only be the sweetest gift I could ever have wished for, a purpose in my life, but I also figured it would be the thing that brought Willard back to my door and into my bed. It was as the Bible said: 'Her children rise up and call her blessed; her husband also, and he praises her.'

And this, too, I believed: that who I was and what I was would change in Willard's eyes when I became a mother. I recalled the way my daddy had glanced at my mom when he didn't know I was looking, his expression close to reverence and brimming with love, and I prayed and prayed that I would see that same look in the eyes of my husband when he looked at me. And I thought that maybe carrying a child might be the thing that made it happen.

I thought this was how it would turn out, but the good Lord had other plans for my life and for me. Willard seemed more shocked than delighted by the news that I was confined with child. I don't know why — it was surely as plain as day that we were leaving the fate of my body in the hands of God, making no moves to interfere with His infinite plan and nature itself. I think he stayed home for a day or two; by that I mean he came home from work at the end of the day and I ladled him supper into a bowl and was pleased as punch to see him. In truth, I was moved to believe that this was the start of a change in him and the very thought filled me with hope. The air felt different. Food tasted good and I slept better than I had in an age with Willard by my side on that feather mattress at the back of Grandma Sally's house.

My sadness was all the more when he started pacing, scratching his head and stumbling over his words, his eyes looking anywhere but at me in the way that he did when he was fixing to lie. I knew the signs. I'd had enough practice in our short marriage. And I think the day he up and headed off to town with a spring in his step was harder for me than at any other time because unlike every other time I had hoped, no believed, that things were going to be different, and it was the disappointment that was hardest for me to swallow. I cried, Lord, I did! Sitting and howling on the veranda as a storm cracked overhead, sending its bruised clouds and driving rain down to match my misery. It was disappointment that buckled me, certainly, but also I now think a whole heap of hormones swirling around inside me, which found release in those angry tears. Grandma Sally said very little on the subject, as was her way when she knew there were no words that were going to be able to change a thing.

I think I can say without pride that I liked the way I looked pregnant. Even my daddy commented on my bloom. I wasn't afraid of the stretch of skin over my stomach; I wasn't afraid of much — more excited than scared. And the birth was not too bad, not too bad at all.

Grandma Sally mopped my face and talked sternly to me and it was in a beautiful haze of achievement that they placed

my boy against my breast. Willard Junior had arrived in the
world and he was . . . he was beautiful! The most beautiful
thing I had ever seen and he was mine. All mine. I held him
in my arms and he stole my heart and my future. It really
was that simple. My boy, only seven pounds two ounces and
yet hitting my planet like a meteor of far greater proportions,
disintegrating the world as I knew it and rebuilding it in his
image.

And that was how it was. His face sat behind my eyelids with
every blink and his welfare and his joy were the reasoning
behind every decision I made. I swear he was the best distraction and waste of time ever created. And he was doing fine,
getting stronger every day, and whatever his future held, I
was sure it was going to be something wonderful — how could
it not?

We sent word to Willard and he came by a whole forty-eight
hours after our little one had made his entrance into the
world. He said he had waited to give me a chance to settle
down, but I could tell by the scent of rum on his breath and
the bleary-eyed fumbling with which he reached for the boy
that the truth was he had just been sidetracked. 'What's he
called?' he asked. 'Willard Junior,' I replied. The man cried
and I didn't have the heart nor the inclination to explain I had
named him so not out of respect, but so that the boy might
have some link to the man I sensed would be more absent than
not. And even though I didn't labour under any illusion, and
I knew rightly where my priorities now lay, I still felt a flicker
of happiness at the sight of my husband cradling his firstborn
son in his arms. More than a flicker. I cannot lie to you, Rachel.
It was a happiness that filled me up.

I guess it's still strange now that in my whole seventy-five years on earth, of all the things I have done and seen, it was during these seven weeks of being Willard's mommy that I felt the most complete. The most happy. I had everything I had ever wanted — no, I had more than I had ever wanted. I got into a routine and my every waking moment revolved around my little boy. I didn't care too much about Willard Senior. I stopped counting the days of his absence and I was entirely content with my baby. And what a baby he was! Tiny fingers and toes, the sweetest fat cheeks and big, big liquid brown eyes that looked into your very soul.

I loved him.

I love him.

It gets no easier to tell you what came next.

I have rarely spoken of it.

It's like taking the lid off a jar with all the miseries of the world packed tightly inside, and that is a fearful thing to do.

But I think I owe you the details and I think it's about time. Bear with me, dear child, sweet girl. I will go and have some tea and I will return to this letter.

Here I am.

Willard Junior was seven weeks and three days old. It was the end of a perfect day. Grandma Sally had held him in her rocker and my daddy sang to him as he fell asleep, beautiful hymns in his deep, rich voice that spoke directly to your soul. Willard had fed well and I laid him in the wicker bassinet that sat on one side of my bed. I left the windows open on both sides of the room to cool him down. The weather was fierce; it was just before Cup Match and there was the usual excitement in the air. I could hear the fast drumbeat of the Gombey musicians practising higher up in the parish and my feet tapped along in time. I went to sit on the terrace hoping to catch a breeze and I sat out for a while, not too long.

I went back inside to check on Willard Junior and maybe fetch a glass of iced tea.

I peered into the bassinet and I noticed that his tiny face seemed to have slipped from its anchors slightly on one side and his right arm and leg looked like they dangled, as if a little disjointed. I picked him up gently and noticed that his limbs had gone strangely stiff. His eyes had rolled back in his head, his beautiful, big, brown eyes, meaning I could only see the bottom of his iris and the white orb beneath. I have never been so scared, so panicked. His face was contorted, his mouth twisted, and from the corner of his tiny, perfect, rosebud lips dribbled white, foamy spit that spilled over his cheek, which had taken on a bluish tinge.

I was struck silent, trying with all my might to summon a voice, a noise, but everything was stuck in my throat by a plug of fear. I won't ever forget how that felt.

Helpless.

Each second felt like an hour.

'Oh, my Lord!' I managed to scream eventually. I did. I screamed loud enough for the whole of Warwick Parish to hear and some have mentioned it to me since.

'Call an ambulance!' I yelled. 'Call an ambulance! Help me! Get help!' I have never felt so terrified in my whole life before or after. I whipped off his cotton, embroidered nightie and he lay in my arms in his napkin, and I kissed him and I sobbed, sending prayers up to heaven and hoping I could somehow make him better.

That I could somehow turn back time.

But I could not.

I prayed for a miracle.

But no one was listening to me, Rachel, not on that day.

My little baby, Willard Junior, not eight weeks on the planet, had left me.

Gone under the wings of a blessed angel, taken from me in all but body. I won't ever, can't ever forget the moment I lifted him from his cot and his little arms hung down and I knew . . .

Willard Senior didn't come by.

I had to take him alone and say goodbye in a little room where he lay on a tin-topped table with a brown luggage tag tied around his narrow ankle, the kind you might put on a suitcase or a package, and that bothered me.

It still bothers me.

I don't remember much after that.

I slipped away from my mind and I lay down on that feather bed at the back of Grandma Sally's with one hand resting in that bassinet, as if my baby still slept soundly. I knew as long as I didn't look into it I would be all right.

Grandma Sally told me that on the day we lost him, all the hibiscus turned from red to white, as if weeping away their colour for the loss of him.

I think about that a lot too.

There were a lot of visitors and there was a lot of talk.

Clara never came. I thought she might.

I heard the rumours spoken behind my back in church and I heard the whisperings of those sat behind me on the bus. Some said they thought I had sour milk or other some such nasty nonsense. I never paid no heed to that. I couldn't pay much heed to anything other than my pain, my loss.

And that was that.

I carried on, somehow. A husk. I was sadder than sad with the joy gone from every bit of my life. I worked in houses, I worked in factories, I worked in hotels, earning my crust, toiling without too many thoughts other than paying the bills.

And the wheels of life kept turning.

I lost my mommy.

I lost my daddy.

And then I lost my Grandma Sally, but God forgive me when I say, while those deaths were sad, they were nothing compared to losing Willard Junior.

He was my life, you see.

And then, one bright day, most unexpectedly, your beautiful family arrived from England. I was a little nervous and I remember James being so polite, shaking my hand, and then you walked in, so young and so beautiful with kindness written on your face, wary of doing and saying the wrong thing. And this in itself made me smile and made me like you even more because it was as if you hadn't realised that it was your house and you could do and say whatever you wanted!

God and his holy messengers work in mysterious ways, of that I am sure, and as you know on the day little Oscar came into my life, well, that was one I won't ever forget. With his fair hair, blue eyes and cheeky smile, I had never seen a child like it! And oh! He near as anything stole my heart and I let him.

I let him in, Rachel, I did. He made me happy!

That darned hide-and-seek! 'How many counts did you do, Cee-Cee? How long were you looking?' And I will never forget the feeling of his little arms around my neck and getting to bathe him and cook his supper and wash and press his clothes ... It gave me more happiness than I ever thought possible and for that I will forever, forever feel blessed.

He was my second chance!

Who would have thought? In my seventies, I got another shot at happiness from your little English boy.

This has been a hard letter for me to write, Rachel, and I am sure it will be a very hard letter to read.

I send it in love to you, sweet, beautiful girl.

Cee-Cee x

NINE

Rachel stepped out of her front door and waved to her neighbours of four months. It was a shared student house of six, as far as she could make out. Certain names she heard regularly – Josh, Olly and Jasper – although other faces seemed to come and go, often girls holding high heels in their hands, tiptoeing barefoot along the path of a morning. This sight of their lives laid bare, evidence of parties, empty bottles on the pathway, discarded pizza boxes on top of the bin and music drifting from beneath sash windows cracked open just a little, all took her back to when she first met James and life had been good. Interestingly for her, it was these times she held in her mind as the heydays, and not the opulent fine dining and fast cars that came later with his success. The student crew were always polite, smiley, and why not? They were young, living in this incredible city without too much to trouble them other than the odd assignment and what appeared to be a very healthy social life. She felt the familiar pang of regret that Oscar would not get to do this. *Forever seven, my little boy . . .*

Today, three of the boys sat smoking on the front step in jeans and sweatshirts and beanies; she wouldn't mind betting they were coming in late rather than having woken early. With legs stretched out in front of them, they soaked up the rays of morning sun that managed to sneak past the high chimney pots and into their front yard. They had their tunes turned up. Rather than take offence at how they hijacked the quiet of this chilly morning, she liked the sights and sounds of life around her.

'Morning,' one of them called. As she looked up to respond, her eyes shot to the back of the hallway of the house through the open front door.

'Oh my God!' she called out. The boys stared at her and one sat forward and removed his sunglasses.

'Are you okay?' he asked a little nervously. Ignoring him, she locked her front door, shoved the key in her bag and marched determinedly up their path.

It was fortuitous that Vicky and Francisco were in situ when she arrived at work for her late shift. Francisco, newly walking, beamed, clearly pleased as punch with his new skill as he teetered from chair to chair. *Quite right too.* She smiled. It really was some achievement.

Last week she had stood watching him wobble like a drunk, and Sandra, en route to the kitchen with a tray loaded with dirty plates, had winked at her. 'Don't tell me you're feeling broody?' Rachel had not known how to answer; instead she gave a small nod and concentrated on wiping down the tables. She had in truth been thinking of Oscar's first steps, recalling how she and James knelt at either end of their lounge of the flat in Richmond, hoping the soft carpet would cushion his inevitable fall. They had cooed and coaxed with their arms spread wide, encouraging their boy to go it alone, whooping with euphoria when he managed one, then two steps unaided. As Sandra laughed, Rachel had looked over at Glen and smiled, grateful that he had kept her confidence, Sandra displaying no sign that she knew her story.

Using her hip now to push open the front door, she rushed in and stood, waiting to be noticed.

'What the . . .?' Glen came out from behind the coffee bar and Sandra bent double, laughing, as she stared at Rachel, who stood with her back to the window.

'Keith! Come and look at this, will you!' Sandra hollered to her husband, who duly walked from the kitchen, wiping his hands on a dishcloth.

'Where on earth did you get that, girl?' he asked, with a rare and genuine smile.

'The boys who live opposite me. It was hanging on the back wall of their hallway!'

Glen shook his head and stepped closer.

'Yours, I believe.' She smiled and handed him the large B that the students had apparently stolen for a bet on a night out a little over a year ago whilst under the influence. 'It was in the house opposite mine; the boys were a little sheepish when I asked how they came by it.'

'The little sods!' Vicky joined in.

'Yep, and I told them as much. Not that it is excusable, but they have agreed to give out flyers for the café at strategic points along the road for at least three Saturdays, for free.'

Glen looked at the large acrylic B that he could barely handle. 'I never thought I'd see you again!' He kissed the top of it. 'The big question is, do we reinstate it and change our name, or do we hang it in the bathroom in homage to our original name?'

'I think we need to vote.' Rachel spoke up.

'Yes, good idea.' Glen popped the letter on the floor and clapped. 'All those in favour of returning to "Brewer" – put your hand up now.'

Everyone looked from one to another but no one raised their hand.

'In that case, it's unanimous – we place this fella in the loo and will be thankful for his safe return.'

Rachel felt the bloom of something a bit like pleasure in her gut, the sensation pulled from a memory of a time before, when she had the capacity for feeling this way. It felt strange, but welcome. It had been a long time since she had allowed the flames of happiness to flicker inside her. Vicky caught her eye and smiled at her, giving her a small nod.

◆   ◆   ◆

It was at the end of a long day that Rachel took a seat at Vicky and Gino's kitchen table.

'So tell me again.' Gino chuckled, shaking his head as he stirred the pasta sauce with a wooden spoon and sipped red wine with his free hand.

'The students opposite Rach's flat had nicked the B!' Vicky explained.

'And they handed it over without a fuss?' He laughed. 'Standards are definitely slipping. In my day there would have been talk of a ransom!'

'Ransom?' Rachel narrowed her gaze. 'They are lucky they didn't get into trouble. Anyway, they didn't have much choice about handing it over: I marched in, straight past them and went very schoolmarm on them.'

Gino turned to look at her. 'You know, Rachel, it sounds like you have got a bit of your spark back, and that's a good thing. Anyway, I'm just going to check on Francisco.'

'You mean check the football scores, don't you?' Vicky tutted.

'I don't know what you mean! Is there football on tonight? Who knew?' Gino held his arms aloft in protest and grabbed his wine before sneaking from the kitchen.

Vicky refreshed her glass. 'He's right. You do seem to be a bit more' – she exhaled, looking for the word – 'I don't know . . . a bit more awake, engaged.'

Rachel considered this and sipped her wine. 'I guess so. It's an odd thing; usually when you feel this bad you want to reach a point when you feel better, but I can't say I wholly welcome the change. I mean, I am sleeping better and I have had days where moments of sunshine peek into the gloom, and it feels nice in that instant, but rather than feel really good about it, I actually feel guilty that the fog is lifting and worried about what that means if my heart hurts a little less.' She paused. 'I mean, what kind of mother am I if I can shake this off? Even a little bit. As it is, if I don't think about him for an hour or so, I cuddle Mr Bob to feel close to him and I throw a kind of prayer out into the universe with my little Tic-Tac box full of sand between my palms.' She didn't feel stupid sharing this with her friend, who knew her back to front and inside out. 'I don't know if I want to feel better, Vicky. Not really. I think I want to spend my life missing him and keeping him here.' She touched her heart.

'But, Rach, it doesn't have to be either/or. You can love and miss him every second of every day for the rest of your life, of course! But you can still move on. That's just life and you can't stop it.'

'No, sadly.'

There was a moment of quiet while the two exchanged a knowing look. Vicky put down her wine and sat up straight.

'Don't say that,' Vicky spat. 'Don't you ever say that!'

Rachel hated the glint of tears in her friend's eyes. 'I'm sorry, Vick, I didn't mean it. Not really. I am okay now – getting better, I think – but there was a moment back there . . .'

'A moment when? What happened?' her friend asked with a look of pure anguish.

Rachel looked down and let her words tumble out on a carpet woven of shame and sadness. 'I . . . I asked James to take me out on the boat and . . .'

'And what?' Vicky whispered.

'I tried to join Oscar.' She was unable to keep the tremor from her voice.

'Oh my God! Babber!' Vicky laid her hand on her arm.

Rachel looked around the kitchen at the wonderful paraphernalia of family life, someone else's family, and felt alone, despite the physical reassurance from her friend.

'I can't stand to think of it,' Vicky said.

'Me neither,' Rachel confessed. 'I was at my lowest point and I didn't know how to carry on without him; I didn't want to. James jumped in and pulled me out of the water—'

'Bless him.'

'Yes. It's partly the reason why we are where we are – he said as much. I mean, not that we weren't totally on the cliff edge, we were, but he said to me: "How could you do that to me, Rach?" And I tried to explain that it wasn't really me, I mean it was, but it was me with every thought fogged, muddled.' She closed her eyes, threw her head back and took a deep breath, recalling the burn in her lungs when she was wanting for air. 'Cee-Cee has this belief system that I envy.' She smiled, thinking of the woman. 'She thinks she will see those she has lost again in heaven.'

Vicky reached across and held her friend's hand. 'Who knows, my darling. Who knows. And if ever you feel like that again, if ever you think that checking out is an option or a possibility, promise that you will call me.'

'I will.'

'Promise me!'

'I promise.'

The two friends exhaled and sat quietly, letting the words permeate.

They both looked towards the door as Gino yelled from the sitting room, 'Come on, you reds! Get in!' Vicky laughed and Rachel joined in. It broke the tension and they sat up straight, smiling, as if trying to steer the evening into happier waters.

'Glen's nice.' Vicky sighed into her wine.

'Yes, he's great. It's a good place to work and I'm grateful that he gave me the job. I know it's kept me sane. Well, nearly.'

'Do you think if you were more . . .' Vicky faltered.

Rachel stared at her. 'More what?'

'I don't know, I was thinking that maybe down the line a bit . . .' Again she hesitated.

'Spit it out, Vick!'

'Okay. Glen kind of hinted to me that he might quite like to take you out for a drink – a *drink* drink. Like a date. I told him you were way off that.'

Rachel stood hurriedly and sought out her bag and coat with her eyes. 'I have to go.'

'No! No, you don't!' her friend implored.

'I do. I want to go home.' She pushed in the chair and pulled her hair from her collar.

'Don't be like that! I was only saying . . .'

'Yes, I know what you are saying and it makes me feel sick and angry and I can't fully explain why, but it means that Glen and even you don't know what it's like to feel this way.' She swallowed. 'Because if you did, you would not ever think, you wouldn't dare to suggest . . .' Rachel felt the surge of tears. 'I am only just hanging on, Vicky. Literally, hanging on by my fingertips – I am still on that cliff edge! Clawing each day to stay anchored to this world. There is no room for anything or anyone other than missing Oscar, and if there was' – she drew breath – 'if there was an inch of space for something or someone, I would fill it with James.' Her tears turned to sobs that robbed her of speech and contorted her face. 'I would,' she cried. 'I would fill it with my James.'

Vicky rushed around the table and took her friend in her arms. 'I am sorry. I am so sorry. I didn't mean anything by it. It was just chat. I wouldn't hurt you for the world.'

Rachel shook her head against her shoulder; it wasn't Vicky's fault. She didn't understand, had no clue what this felt like and she so loved her best friend that she was glad she did not.

Rachel considered the rather subdued supper they had eaten after the change in mood the night before. She walked into the café with a new and uncomfortable awkwardness, aware that Glen and Vicky had discussed her and conscious of his intentions. She felt sick at the idea that she might have given him any reason to think their relationship was anything other than friends and tried to recall the exact nature of their conversation when they had shared secrets over coffee. It meant she now had her guard up, and this in itself made her more than a little uncomfortable.

'Any more Miss Marple activity to report? Not located Shergar, have you, on your way in this morning?' Glen chuckled from the coffee bar, still happy to have his missing letter returned.

'No.' She hated the curt nature of her response, aware of how off she sounded, but not sure of where the happy medium lay between being friendly and giving off the wrong signal.

'Oh. Okay, then.' Glen made a clicking noise with the side of his mouth and turned his attention to the women at a side table who had waved that they were ready to order.

Rachel cleaned the shelves at the back of the coffee bar, removing the jars of coffee beans, stacks of mugs, the box of filter papers and all the other natty accoutrements that gave the place its vintage edge: old coffee tins, a battered tin sign depicting a 1950s diner, and three old caddies in rusted green metal with ill-fitting lids. As she bent forward to swipe the damp, bleach-soaked cloth over the back shelf she heard a clatter and without pausing to think she stepped back, crushing the Tic-Tac box beneath her foot and scattering sand and tiny shells over the stripped wooden floor.

'No! Oh please, no!' she shouted.

'Rachel!' Glen dropped his order pad and rushed over as several customers abandoned their food, drink and conversations, looking over with necks craned to see what might be the cause of such an unearthly yell. Keith came running from the kitchen with the first-aid kit in his hand and Sandra looked on, deathly pale.

'Has she hurt herself?' she asked with one hand at her chest.

'It's okay, Mum. I've got it.' Glen signalled with his eyes to carry on.

'Oh no, no!' Rachel wept as she knelt on the hard floor and tried to scoop what she could into her hands. She stared in dismay at her cupped palm, in which sat a mixture of sand, fluff, shards of plastic, coffee grinds all bound with licks of milk and scraps of dirty napkin 'No . . .' she whimpered, unable to articulate the swirl of emotions and refusing to believe what had happened in a single, careless moment.

'It's okay, Rachel.' Glen spoke soothingly and laid a hand on her shoulder.

'It's not okay!' She shook her head and wiped her nose on her sleeve as she sat back against the wall on the other side of the bar. 'It's not okay. Nothing is okay.'

'Can . . . can I get you anything?' he asked with an air of reticence, placing his hand in his apron pocket, which she had inadvertently shrugged off.

'No.' She looked up at him briefly. 'I just need to sit here for a bit and work out how to stand up.'

'Okay.' He spoke softly. 'Well, you take your time. We don't need that, Dad, but thanks.' She heard him dismiss his father and whisper something to his mum. Not that she cared, only able to concentrate on the gritty, contaminated contents in her hand.

As she sat hidden behind the coffee bar, listening to the hum of conversation reigniting all around her, she felt as if she were floating, looking down on the heap of a woman sat on the floor of a coffee shop, miles and miles away from where this sand had been gathered; miles and miles away from where her little boy rested. And she saw this was her life, adrift in a sea of people where lives carried on and she tried to move among them, broken and bent out of shape. Again, loneliness washed over her.

Her phone rang in her pocket. She was surprised to see it was James on the line. It was eleven a.m., making it six o'clock in the morning in Bermuda. Her heart thudded and she suspected that for him to call so early it would be nothing good. She pictured Mackenzie knocking on the door in his neatly pressed shirt and straightened cap. *Mr Croft . . .*

'James? What is it? What's happening?' She clutched the phone to her face, cursing the tears that fell.

'It's okay, Rach, don't cry.'

She felt an instant relief. 'James, I . . . I broke my Tic-Tac box. I trod on it and it's gone everywhere and the contents are all mixed up and—' She broke off.

'Shh . . . It doesn't matter. It doesn't matter.'

'It matters to me,' she squeaked.

'I know.' He sighed. 'I know.'

There was a hush while she listened to him breathing, remembering how she had scooped the soft wet sand from the pockets of her dressing gown and how it had felt so vitally important to preserve it.

'It's early there.' She sniffed. 'Is everything all right?'

'Not really, and now I've heard you are upset, I'm not sure if I should call back later.'

'No. James,' she cut in, 'whatever it is, please tell me now. I couldn't spend a day waiting and wondering – that would make anything you have to tell me infinitely worse.' She coughed and sat up straight, pushing her feet down on to the floor, trying to steel herself, as she closed her eyes.

What have they found? Tell me now! What have they found?

'I understand.' He took a breath. 'The thing is, Rach, I have just had a rather distressing call from one of Cee-Cee's neighbours.'

'Cee-Cee's neighbours?' She swallowed, still thinking the news might be related to Oscar and trying to piece together how.

'Yes. It's really sad, but Cee-Cee passed away last night. Her neighbour saw her front door had been left open, which was unusual, and so went in to check and she was in bed, asleep and had gone. The woman said she looked peaceful and the church and her cousins are dealing with everything.'

'Oh,' she said with a strange sense of relief and such sadness. She still lived with the dread of them finding proof that Oscar was gone. Some people, Vicky included, had suggested that the retrieval of skin and bone would give her some kind of closure. She felt quite the opposite, knowing that the discovery of anything physical would provide her with a million fresh images that would keep her awake in the middle of the night and was highly likely to take her back to square one of grief. She remembered all too well how it had felt on that terrible day when she lay on the bottom of the police boat and Dr Kent met her on the dock and slipped a needle under her skin, trying to contain her rising hysteria.

'Poor Cee-Cee. Poor Cee-Cee.' She pictured the kindly woman who had cared for them through good and bad. She thought about the long, long letters written to her in love, making Rachel the custodian of her stories.

'Yes,' James croaked, and she realised that the housekeeper had been one of the only constants in his life of late too, now gone.

She felt a flash of guilt that he was alone. 'She loved Oscar. She really did.'

'Yes,' James agreed. 'And he loved her.'

'He did,' she managed. 'He used to run her ragged, I am sure, but she said he gave her new life, energy.'

James gave a snort of laughter. 'They were friends.'

'Yes. They were friends, that's true; age didn't come into it.'

'She was my friend too, actually, Rach.' She heard the emotion in his voice and felt a bolt of guilt fire through her at the fact that their housekeeper had had to take care of James when she had been unable to, followed by a wave of love and gratitude for Cee-Cee who had been happy to do just that.

'Mine too. I shall miss her. I shall really miss her. I liked knowing she was there. I liked getting the letters she wrote to me, and her advice has helped me more than she ever knew. She knew sadness, James, like us, but she believed it was part of a bigger plan that she was not meant to understand. She told me she didn't fear death; she believed she would get to see the people she had loved and lost, her Grandma Sally and her baby Willard.'

And Oscar . . .

'I think that's nice.'

'Yes, it is.' She sighed. 'Can you let me know when the funeral is?'

'Oh, of course.' She heard his sharp intake of breath. 'I honestly didn't think you'd come back, but I am really glad that you are. That's great, Rachel, really great. It'll be good to see you. And I think it's about time. There are things that are much easier to say face to face than over the phone. And as I say, it's time.'

'I . . .' she stammered, without the heart or confidence to tell him that in fact she had only been enquiring so she could send flowers and hadn't considered flying back to Bermuda, not until he had suggested it.

Rachel finished the call and found the strength had returned to her legs. Looking at the mess all over the floor she knew it would be impossible to sort. She ran her fingers through it and pictured Oscar waving to her through the water. She stood slowly and popped her head up above the bar.

'Glen, is it okay if I nip out for a bit?' She acknowledged the fascinated nudges and stares of some of the customers.

'Of course! You take your time.' He smiled. Kind and lovely Glen. Rachel grabbed her bag from the back and walked slowly down the street, thinking about her dear friend Cee-Cee and wondering if she had got her wish, if she really was reunited with those she loved right now. The thought made her smile.

Vicky answered the front door with Francisco on her hip. 'Well, this is a nice surprise! Are you okay, honey? I'm so glad you've come.

I've been thinking about our chat last night; I couldn't sleep. The last thing in the world I would want to do is upset you. You know that. I wouldn't offend you for the world. It was wine and it was supposed to cheer you up; it all went wrong.'

'I do know that. It's okay.'

'You look pale,' Vicky added, studying her face.

She nodded. 'I'm having a bit of a day.'

'Blimey, it's only just gone eleven! Come in, come in!'

Vicky walked into the little study and handed her son to Gino. 'I'm working, Vick! Or trying to!' He tutted, still managing to kiss the face of his son, now plonked on his lap. 'Hi, Rach.'

'Hi.' She waved.

'I know, Gino, but I just need five minutes with Rach. Thank you! I love you! I love you!' She blew a kiss and closed the door before he had time to further protest. 'Cup of tea?'

'No, thanks.' Rachel shook her head and sat at the kitchen table. Vicky sat opposite, mirroring their positions of the previous evening.

'So, what's up? Why is today such a write-off?'

Rachel ran her hands over her face and planted her elbows on the tabletop. 'Cee-Cee, our lovely housekeeper who used to look after Oscar, passed away last night.'

'Oh no! That's sad. How old was she?'

The question by comparison confirmed the absolute horror of her son's passing. *Seven . . . he was just seven . . .*

'She was well into her seventies, but very young in mind and body; a dynamo. She was lovely. Quiet. Oscar loved her; they had a wonderful connection and that's really hard for me. There aren't that many people who knew him like she did and now she's gone too. She wrote me the loveliest letters, written from the heart. I love her story – she knew tragedy, but it made her wise, made her kind.'

'I am sorry for you. I know how fond you all were of her.' Vicky sighed.

'We really were. Plus, I might have just told James that I would go back to Bermuda.'

'For good?' her friend asked, wide-eyed.

'I don't think so. I don't know!' She ran her hands through her hair. 'I feel so confused. I'm scared about going back – worried that I might fall into that dark hole where I couldn't see a future.'

Vicky stared at her and she knew they both thought about her confession, and the fact that she had jumped into the water with only one aim.

'But I do want to be there for Cee-Cee's funeral, and I need to talk to James. He said we need to discuss things and I can't deny that. He's right; it will all be much easier face to face. I think he might want to talk about next steps.'

'Like divorce?' Vicky asked softly.

'I guess so. I don't know. Things are in limbo and that's hard for us both. I owe him that conversation.'

'How do you feel about that – the possibility of formally ending things?'

Rachel considered just that and answered, as truthfully as she was able, 'I feel sick, anxious. He's my husband and I am his wife and it's always been him, and the thought of losing him – completely losing him – as well as Oscar feels like more than I can cope with. But how things are right now . . . It's not fair on him and maybe it's what we both need to move forward. I don't know, Vicks. As I say, I'm confused. And having to face my future? I don't know if I'm ready. Maybe this limbo suits me a bit, stops me having to figure everything out.'

'Well, I can't say I won't miss you, but I think he's right. There are things that need sorting out. It's not healthy just to let things drift.'

'God, Vick, there is so much unhealthy about my life right now, so much that needs addressing.'

'So take the plunge. Dive in!'

The moment the words left her friend's mouth, Rachel saw herself leaping from the side of the boat and her face crumpled.

'Oh God, Rachel! I didn't think! I am such an idiot!' Vicky banged the table.

'It's not your fault, and I wish . . . I wish that simple words didn't send me into a spin like they do. It's exhausting.'

Vicky squeezed her arm.

'And it has been a really shit day. Just before I heard about Cee-Cee, I trod on my little Tic-Tac box with sand in it, you know the one?'

'I do,' Vicky whispered.

'It went everywhere all over the floor and was mixed up with gunk.' She sobbed, picturing it again and realising just what she had lost.

'Oh no! I'm sorry. I know how much you treasured it.'

'I did, and I feel crap for not taking better care of it,' she admitted. *I can't take care of anything; I lose everything that is precious to me . . .*

Vicky stepped forward and scooped her friend into a close hug. 'You are right; you are certainly having a bit of a day. I love you, Rach. It'll all be okay.'

'I know.' She closed her eyes. 'I love you too.'

Rachel washed her face and made her way back to the café. It was just as the lunchtime rush was starting and in truth she was glad of the distraction. She spent the best part of two hours ferrying full plates and then empty plates to and from the kitchen, where Keith laboured over a hot stove and Sandra kept the atmosphere light with her soft voice and unabashed singing. During the early-afternoon lull she caught up with Glen at the bar.

'I'm sorry about this morning, freaking out like that in front of customers and then running off for an hour.'

'That's okay, I shall dock your wages accordingly.'

'Of course.'

'I'm joking, Rachel. You gotta do what you gotta do; I get that.' He smiled at her and she got the distinct feeling he referred to more than just her emotional outburst and surprise absence.

She nodded at him. 'I might need to go to Bermuda.'

'Oh, okay.' He placed his hands on his hips. 'When were you thinking?'

'Maybe next week.'

'Oh, gosh, right! Nothing like a bit of notice.' He sucked air through his teeth.

'Our friend passed away, and—'

'No need to explain. As I said, you gotta do what you gotta do.' He took a breath. 'Will you be coming back, do you think?'

She noticed the slight nervous warble to his voice. 'I don't know,' she answered truthfully. 'I need to talk to James and make a plan, but the thought is scary. It feels like moving on, and I have been avoiding that for a while now. I am stuck, Glen, and James is too, and that's not fair, I know. I wish I could give you a definitive answer, because that would mean decisions have been made, but I can't.'

Glen looked down at the floor. 'I will do my best to keep your position open, but if we get busy then . . .'

'Yes, I expected that.' She smiled at him briefly. 'I'm sorry to be so vague, but I'd rather not say one thing and do another; that's not my style.'

'And I appreciate that.' He coughed and walked over to the coffee bar.

TEN

Rachel's parents insisted on driving her to the airport, and in truth she was glad of the opportunity to spend time in their company. She sat on the back seat like a child while her mum chatted, handed out mint humbugs and tutted at the poor level of driving skill of just about every other road user. This despite being a non-driver herself, a fact that no doubt encouraged her dad to wink at Rachel surreptitiously in the rear-view mirror. Her mum also acted as impromptu navigator, reading aloud the very large motorway signs informing them how far away they were from their destination along with the junction number for good measure. She also gave a regular and uninvited update on what speed her husband was travelling at, accompanied by either a pat on the thigh or a tut for good or bad performance.

'Ooh, before I forget, this arrived for you, lovey.' Rachel watched her mum reach into her handbag and pull out a brown envelope. She took it and smiled at the familiar slant of Cee-Cee's handwriting.

'It arrived yesterday, obviously sent before she . . .' Her mum trailed off, embarrassed and still awkward on the topic of death.

Rachel nodded and put the letter in her pocket, deciding to read it later without distraction. Her mum continued to chat.

'Peter would have come over to say goodbye before you set off, but he's been very busy with work and the boys, and Julie's dad had a turn last week so she's been up and down to Stroud. Poor love.'

Rachel gave a nod, not wanting to discuss her useless brother with her mum, knowing that not only would it fail to change anything about his behaviour, but also aware that if she spoke her mind it might cause her mum upset. Neither, she knew, had the energy or the appetite for that, especially since her mum had given in to the storm that brewed inside her all those months ago. Rachel now understood more than ever that each of them had their own way of coping, and who was to say who was right? It was, as Cee-Cee had once told her, all about getting through each day and not trying to look too much further ahead.

'So how long are you going for, exactly?' Her mum twisted around and spoke through the gap between the front seats.

She was now no better at fielding the question no matter who asked it. 'I don't know, Mum. It depends on a lot of things.'

Depends on how it feels being back, what it's like with James, the state of my marriage and how I cope . . .

'Well, if you want picking up from the airport when you come home, just let us know and Dad'll come down, won't you, Brian?'

'Of course. She knows that.' He spoke plainly and she recalled the words he had spoken to her on one of their seven-mile walks of an evening: *If I could have a wish, it would be to see your face every single day of my life over that breakfast table or it would be to turn the clock back to when you were small.* She took in her dad's broad shoulders on which she knew she could always lean.

'You did seem *very* distressed about your housekeeper. I didn't realise you were that close.' Her mum's tone suggested that her level of upset over Cee-Cee's passing might be inappropriate or misplaced.

Rachel pictured her with her arms spread wide and Oscar running into them. *Can I have bacon and pancakes, Cee-Cee?*

You, my darling, can have whatever you want.

'Calling her our housekeeper doesn't really do her justice. She looked after Oscar; she looked after all of us. And she has been there for James when I wasn't able. She was a massive part of our life in Bermuda, and the worst part is, I don't know if I truly thanked her properly. I hope she knows how much we all loved her.'

'I'm sure she did,' her dad offered.

Rachel thought about the way Cee-Cee had confided in her: *I'm not sad because of you . . . I lost my baby. He died.*

I wish I'd had the courage to wrap you in a hug, Cee-Cee. I wish I'd held you tight and not felt so awkward, just like you did me when I needed it most. She cast the words out into the ether.

'And what did they say at work about you up and leaving with so little notice?' Rachel again noted the tone of disapproval in her mother's question and her choice of critical words.

'They were very understanding and said they would try to keep my job open.' She thought of Glen. 'But at the end of the day, Mum, I gotta do what I gotta do.'

'Hmph, I suppose so.' Jean adjusted her hands in her lap. 'And you've just left that flat?'

'Yes, there's only a little over a month left on the tenancy, so I told the agent I'd let him know in a week or two if I want to re-let it or if he should start showing prospective tenants around.'

'And you've left all your stuff there?'

Rachel gave a small laugh. 'Well, if by "all my stuff" you mean Peter's old mattress, a vase, a laundry basket, two mugs, a plate, some cutlery and a kettle, then yes, I have left all my stuff.'

'Well, I never did.' Her mum sighed. 'And what about James, how does he feel about you coming back after all this time? Is he excited?'

Rachel wished she would stop with the questions, but this was quickly followed by a spike of guilt at the fact that she was again waving goodbye to her parents without a firm date for when she would be returning, or indeed if she were returning at all. She knew it was hard for them. *I missed you, Rachel, each and every single day!* And this alone was enough of a reminder for her to remain patient. 'I expect he is nervous like me, Mum. A lot has changed and I think he will be on edge, but I'm sure it'll be fine once we've seen each other. I don't really know. I am trying not to think about it too much.'

'It'll all come good, babber, one way or another.'

'I hope so, Dad.' She sank down on the back seat and tried to imagine walking back into that house that she hadn't seen for all of these months. Her stomach churned at the thought of it.

Her dad pulled up at the drop-off outside the departure terminal and she hugged him warmly.

'You know we are here, don't you?'

'Yes, always, Dad. And thank you.'

Her mum cried and Rachel matched her tear for tear, not only at the prospect of not seeing her parents for a while, but also at what she might find on that little fishhook-shaped island in the North Atlantic that she had once so loved.

With Mr Bob secreted in her pocket, Rachel stowed her hand luggage and sat back in the chair to undertake a journey that she had done so many times before, but always with either Oscar, James, or both sat by her side.

The plane rose higher and higher, and she knew this time the journey felt different because everything was different. She remembered very little about the flight from Bermuda back to the UK, taken at the height of her grief. On autopilot, she had tried not to think too far ahead, looking at her feet and literally concentrating on taking step after step after step, until she fell into the arms of her dad. She thought back to that time, when she existed in a fog, realising that she had come a very long way, now able to spend whole hours in the day without dissolving into tears; she even managed to keep down a job. And she had found the courage to travel back to the place that held such dark memories. This was progress.

Rachel reached into her pocket and pulled out Cee-Cee's letter. It felt somehow appropriate to be reading these words while the plane sped through the clouds, somewhere close to Cee-Cee's heaven.

Dear Rachel,

I find myself in deep, deep thought.

It's a strange thing, but unlike some, I never expected happiness.

I wished for it, longed for it even, but never felt that it was something I had any right to.

My daddy was the same. I remember my mom saying he 'planned for the worst, expected the least and anything over and above that was considered a blessing.'

He smiled and hid for a living.

And I guess I followed in his footsteps.

While my mom worked shifts inside, cleaning the communal areas, he stood outside of the grand Fairmont Hamilton Princess Hotel on Pitts Bay Road.

Rachel paused from her reading and pictured the hotel, which she and James frequented, a little link to Cee-Cee's heritage that she had been unaware of.

Day in and day out, rain or shine, he opened the grand door made of thick glass and wood, tipping his top hat, smiling at all who wafted by him either entering or leaving the five-star hotel.

I figured his surly demeanour at home was because he had used up all the smiles he had for that day on the pale, pretty guests who shimmied in and out of his doorway. But now I think it was just because he was plain exhausted. I visited him once, secretly, and stood staring from the other side of the street, hidden behind a cast-iron lamp post. Watching as my daddy, the man before whom I cowered and whose rare complimentary words dropped into my lap like shiny diamonds for me to gather up and save for rainy days, stooped low to open cab doors, head bowed. I watched as gaggles of chattering women looked the other way, as he hefted the door to and fro, leaving nothing for him — no 'thank you' or smile of good grace other than the cloud of expensive scent that hovered under his nose, a scent so rich with exotic promise, luxury and wealth that the very bouquet could sometimes reduce him to tears.

I watched my daddy's hand shift stealthily to his thigh and rub, once, twice as with almost imperceptible timing he flexed the foot of the same leg. He had a bad hip, an injury sustained in the war effort when he slipped on rocks up at the Dockyard and smashed his bones. I knew that no amount of fancy livery sitting on his shoulders or high sheen to his shoes could compensate for the fact that he had wanted to be a somebody. A somebody who could walk confidently into the lobby of that very building and would be gracious enough to offer thanks, as an equal, to the man who held the door. A man who might take lunch there and know the name of the maître d'.

My daddy taught me a lot. Not only in what he said, but in what he didn't say. I have his quietness, but not his bitterness. I learned that bitterness lies in your very centre and, like a pit in a plum pudding, can taint the whole thing. Forgiveness is better, sweeter.

You see, I too had plans. Not big plans or grand plans, but if I had dared to peek into my future or tried to imagine what lay ahead, I saw me baking for a family, caring for a family. I pictured warm arms around my shoulders at night and I saw my grandchildren sitting in their finery in the pew in front of mine in St Anne's Church, Southampton Parish, where I could keep an eye on them whilst listening to their sweet songs of praise.

Yes, my dreams were all about family, my family. And I hope I do not overstep the mark when I say that I pray that this is what lies ahead for you, Rachel. I wish for you to find again the joy you had in being Oscar's mommy.

Rachel again paused and took a sharp breath, it was simply too painful a thing to consider.

But for me it was not to be.

Life, Clara, Willard Senior and the Lord Jesus had other plans for me.

When the grief of losing my boy settled a little and the God Almighty took away some of my upset, I didn't want anything nasty in my core. I figured I had enough to deal with without heaping anger and resentment for the state of my world on top of it. I was mindful of that pit in the plum pudding.

I think it was Albert Romsey who broke the news to me — yes, it was him who told me what many already knew and others surely suspected. All, that was, except me, who was preoccupied with my own troubles. I do remember laughing quite heartily as Albert spoke, and that laugh was as much a surprise to me as it was to him. Not that anything about his words on that day was in the least bit funny, no. I think it must have been nerves that got the better of me.

But I do remember as clear as day leaving church and blinking as my eyes adjusted to the bright, blue day, in contrast to the dark interior of St Anne's. I shook Pastor Raymond's hand and loitered on the dusty path of the graveyard, waiting for Grandma Sally, who liked to talk and hang back in the aisle. She always saw our days of worship as something very social.

Albert strolled over in a fashion that did nothing to suggest urgency, and I thought he was going to enquire how I was doing or talk about the weather. On reflection, I am glad he spoke the words directly to my face. I figured two gut punching notes were more than most had to deal with, and truly I don't know how I would have handled a third.

Instead of chatting about the topics mentioned above and with his tone as bold and plain, he said, 'I guess you already know that Willard lives with Clara, backatown.' It was then that I laughed before cupping my hand over my nose and mouth. 'My Clara?' And it was only after that I realised what I had said — not 'my Willard?' I knew she was the greater loss, the one whose betrayal hurt me more because she was my best friend, and what kind of best friend, indeed what kind of friend, would hold me in such low regard as to go after the only man I loved? That still mystifies me and hurts me in equal measure. As for Willard? He was just a dumb thing, led around — too stupid to know when he had it good and too stupid to know what he had lost. But Clara? I thought she was better. And the very thought of her doing that to me, it still cuts me to the core.

You know, strangely, the knowledge that Clara and Willard lived in sin together only a mile or so away from where I laid my head on my pillow each and every night was hard to bear at first, but with my head and heart full of thoughts of Willard Junior, it quickly faded to the background of my mind, where it sat for many years.

I stayed about as far away from them both as I could. I saw Momma Eula a couple of times strolling up in St George around the harbour and we were pleasant to each other. But neither of us uttered the word that had been our glue for so many years. 'Clara.' Both of us, I would say, were relieved when we had made comment on the weather and I had agreed to pass on my very best wishes to Grandma Sally and we were able to part and carry on with our day. Looking back, I suppose Momma Eula might have had a slight shiver to her eye, as if shamed by the goings-on on her very doorstep, and I must confess to thinking she should have a shiver in her eye, because if it was me that had chosen to live in such a way within sight of my mommy's house then she would surely beat me with the yard broom all the way down the street until I saw sense. But

I had heard it said that Momma Eula never did know much about right and wrong.

I remember like it was yesterday the day I saw Willard Senior again. It was only a glance at first, one tiny sighting of a familiar shape and colour that told me he was close. I felt him before I saw him; as those of us who have ever loved will testify, it can be the way with someone whose heart has known your own.

I was walking around the Flatts Inlet when I spied him ahead of me on the path. I watched how he raised his hand and flicked his head towards a man fixing a fishing net on the shoreline. A gesture of greeting unique to him, part nod, part tilt of the chin, equally welcoming and dismissive; it was one his tricks. No matter that it had been over two years since the breath had caught in my throat and my heart danced an unusual rhythm; it was as if that time had been erased. Things I had quite forgotten were suddenly prevalent. I was once again engulfed in the heady scent of his aroma that seemed to dance back under my nose, carried on the shifting breeze. I remembered in that moment what it had felt like to be in love and to be loved, at a time when desire was wrapped in innocence and manifested in our desperate kissing wherever and whenever possible. The Lord knows I knew such contentment under the heavy, embroidered Portuguese shawl on the bed in Grandma Sally's back bedroom and I lived with the promise of a rosy future. So close I could almost touch it. That future shone like an orb, always slightly out of reach, for me, at least.

I stood still on that path like prey unsure whether it had been spotted, hoping that if I stayed still enough, no one would notice me. Him included. I didn't dare breathe. I looked down at my scruffy pinafore and cursed that I had not put on better clothes or combed my hair, not that I would have done either for him, no sir, it was all about me. As if alerted by my change in rhythm, a disturbance in the air around him, he turned and I saw his big brown eyes, which held more than a glint of fear, and Lord forgive me, but I was glad.

He walked quickly towards me and I looked left and right to see where I might run to, but I was hemmed in on both sides by boats and buildings. There was nowhere for me to go. I made my hands into fists and with my arms straight I kept them by my side, trying to still their shake. He stood not a foot from me, skinnier than I remembered and with the corner of his front tooth now chipped and gone. But otherwise he looked the same.

When he spoke, his words were a shock, softly delivered, and yet they hit me like an axe to the heart. Just three words. 'Did he suffer?'

And without having to enquire, I knew who he spoke about and I got the feeling that not only had that question been sitting on his tongue for a good while, but that this thought might be bothersome to him, and in truth, yet again, I was glad. I didn't forgive him, not one tiny inch, but it made me feel like someone else cared about my baby boy, and it made me feel like I was not going through it all alone, and both of these things were, at the time, mightily welcome.

'I don't think so,' I answered as truthfully as I knew how, trying to rid my mind of my son's stiff little limbs and that foamy spit at the side of his perfect lips.

'Willard Junior, named after his daddy.' He spoke with more pride than he had any right to express. 'Time will heal. Time will heal.' He held my gaze and swallowed, and then it was like he couldn't stand to look into my eyes any longer and he looked down at his feet. 'He was a fine baby,' he whispered with a twist of emotion on his lying mouth.

Not that he lied then.

And try as I might and as much as I wanted to be brave, I could not stop my hot tears that sprang.

He spoke only the holy truth.

My baby boy was fine!

Oh Rachel, as God is my witness.

He really was.

And strangely, Willard was right. Time did heal, a little, enough for me to carry on, just...

Rachel folded the letter and placed it back in her pocket. She cried for the sadness her friend had endured and she cried for the loss of her. She thought of Willard Senior and wondered at his pain, she then immediately thought of James, who she would be seeing very soon.

◆ ◆ ◆

It was a little under eight hours later that Rachel found herself in the line at passport control, snaking slowly through the arrivals of L. F.

Wade International Airport. She had forgotten exactly what the high level of humidity felt like and also the fact that the air conditioning here was not the most effective. Sweat pooled on her back and chest. She felt the jump of impatience in her gut, knowing her husband was on the other side of the wall. And at this thought her stomach flipped, sending a bloom of nausea through her core. She was nervous. Hemmed in by tourists fanning their faces with their passports, she listened to the excited burble of anxious holidaymakers, the noise sat over their heads in a cloud of chatter.

She remembered her first time on the island and how she and James had driven in near silence with Oscar on the back seat, taken aback, stunned and on edge until they arrived at their new home and that glorious moment they stepped out on to the terrace off their bedroom. *Didn't I promise you paradise?* he whispered in her ear, as Oscar ran around. *Fearless.*

Having grabbed her case from the carousel, she walked through the double doors and out on to the main concourse. She saw James instantly, programmed to recognise the shape of him in any crowd. The man she was married to looked a little different in real life from the person who lived in her mind. He was smaller and looked older. His muscles had shrunk, his skin a little greyer, looser, his stature diminished, no doubt by grief, and she suspected that, like her, he no longer had any interest in anything as superfluous as his appearance. He was in his jeans and a pale-blue shirt; a belt cinched in his waist and his cheeks were drawn. He needed a haircut. Her stomach rolled at the sight of his face, so familiar – the face she had loved for so much of her life. The father of her child.

There you are . . .

They both walked forward, meeting somewhere in the middle, and instantly they assumed the position that was as natural to them as breathing. James placed his arms around her shoulders and she looped hers around his lower back, resting her head on his chest. This was how they had danced their first dance at their wedding reception, encircled by the smiling faces of all the people who loved them. This was also how they loved, hugging at the start and end of the working day, and this was how they had grieved when James held her and lied, telling her everything was going to be okay.

She inhaled the scent of him and took comfort from it, and he used a single finger to draw her fringe from her face, as he often did.

'Here you are.'

'Yes,' she whispered. 'Here I am.'

The car made steady progress on the almost-empty roads and they were at ease with each other, comfortable. She had forgotten the freedom of movement on the island where traffic was tightly controlled and you were more likely to encounter mopeds than anything else. It was very different from the congestion of Bristol, where traffic sat nose to tail to travel no more than a few miles – the busy city where cyclists ducked and weaved in and out of buses and cars whose drivers honked their tinny horns in frustration. Pretty soon they were on the Causeway, a wide sweep of road with the pale ocean reaching out on either side with sparkling white yachts moored and bobbing on the swell, and before she knew it they were skirting Flatts Village.

'God, James, I'd forgotten how beautiful it is. How blue.' Rachel felt confused. Flames of joy leaped in her gut at being back in this most magical of settings, but then the memory of her life here in those last months swept away the joy, leaving something closer to horror in its place.

'How're your mum and dad?'

'The same. You know.' She looked at him and he smiled.

'And your brother?'

'Still a knob.' She liked the way his mouth lifted as she used his phrase to echo her own sentiments.

'I figured as much.'

'Poor Cee-Cee. I am sad about her; so sad.'

She realised that her friend had been right when she recalled the loss of her parents and others she loved: *While those deaths were sad, they were nothing compared to losing Willard Junior. He was my life, you see . . .*

I understand this, Cee-Cee. I do.

James sighed. 'Yes. I miss her. I wasn't expecting it and I had very much got used to her being around.'

She spoke softly. 'And the funeral is in three days?'

'Yes. At St Anne's.'

'Do they know why she died?'

'I think just old age, no one has said anything else.'

'That's a nice way to go, I think. To fall asleep in your own bed.'

She swallowed, inevitably thinking of their boy who was denied that chance; the punch of grief to her chest was just as powerful now as it had always been. Again she blinked away the uninvited images that crowded her mind, preferring instead to see her boy leaping from the diving board into the pool with a smile on his face and his nose peppered with freckles.

'She was good to us and she has been wonderful to me these last few months. She'd leave me notes and supper and if I didn't eat it, I'd get another note the next day, but that one a little more stern about my need to eat.'

'I am grateful to her.' She felt awkward, as if these words were somehow an admission of her dereliction of their marriage, hinting at the regret she felt at having abandoned him. Not that she wouldn't do the exact same again; her choice to go away had come from a place far beyond reason. 'She loved us,' Rachel surmised, 'and she loved Oscar.'

There, she had done it. She had said his name, broken the glass wall of anticipation as they waited to see who would do it and how.

'She did.' He swallowed. 'I used to talk to her about him and it helped.'

'I still find it hard to talk about him most of the time.' It was a difficult, shameful admission.

'I don't so much. Cee-Cee said something – she said that if we stop talking about him, stop using his name, then not only will others not learn about him and think of him, but if no one says their name, that's when someone really dies. It made me think.'

'I'll try harder to do that,' she offered sincerely, knowing that to talk about him freely would be hard, but to let him disappear, unmentioned altogether? That would be far, far worse.

'You don't have to try, Rach; you don't have to force anything. You just need to keep healing, one day at a time, and I bet you will find one day that you can talk about him openly and remark on things without it cutting you so deeply. It might actually make you feel happy to remember him and not sad.'

She nodded, not sure if this would ever be the case, but recognising the cruel irony that all aspects of her beautiful boy were overshadowed by the way he was lost. Terrible, terrible minutes, but mere minutes nonetheless, that had come to define seven whole years of life.

The car pulled up at the gates of the house on North Shore Road and Rachel felt a wave of familiarity and warmth at the sight of the place she had lived with her family. The pool and gardens were magnificent when seen through eyes that had been absent for some time and were now more used to surveying the grey damp pavements of a crowded city.

James grabbed her case and pushed open the front door. She was quite taken aback, having forgotten the vast proportions of the house. She pictured the narrow hallway of her parents' little house in Yate, and how to pass each other you had to breathe in and skim the wall. She was also struck by how quiet it was, cool despite the heat of the day, and strangely empty without Oscar's yells in play or the hum of his favoured cartoons providing the background noise to their lives. And now there was no Cee-Cee opening and closing doors, humming a hymn or singing loudly when she thought no one could hear.

A house of ghosts.

'I'll take your bag up.'

She noted the swallow to his throat and realised that there was the awkward matter of where she would sleep. It was as sad as it was jarring that they, as a married couple, had reached this point where it could not be assumed that she would take up her space in their marital bed.

'Thank you.' She held his eyeline. 'I could never have imagined feeling this way with you.'

'What way?' He hovered on the wide bottom stair, gripping the curve of the bannister with his free hand.

Rachel shrugged and folded her arms across her chest. 'Like I'm meeting someone I don't know very well, like going to stay with a distant relative and nervous about being around. Worried that we might not have anything to say to each other. Whether it's okay to make a coffee, kick off my shoes; worried about where I might sleep.'

She saw his crestfallen expression and the way his whole body seemed to fold. He took a step back and abandoned the suitcase.

'Please don't feel that way.' He reached for her and pulled her into his chest once more. 'Please, Rachel. You are all I have left and the thought that you feel that way is just about more than I can stand. This is your home and you are my wife!' His voice caught in his throat.

'I can't help it.' Her voice was muffled against his chest. She felt the desperation in his grip and it threatened to overwhelm her. It was a hard thing to accept, but she realised that in the months in which she had been gone, she had got used to being without him.

'I know.' He kissed her scalp. 'And we *are* strange. Everything is strange.'

'I still feel like I am only just hanging on,' she began, hoping he might understand that she was still so fragile, messed up. 'In some ways I'm a lot better than I was, but it's not that I am healed; it's just that I am better at blending in with what other people expect. I'm better at hiding my hurt.'

She felt him nod his understanding.

'Come upstairs with me,' he whispered. Her body stiffened and he clearly felt it. 'I . . . I just want to hold you and I just want you to hold me.'

He reached for her hand and led her up the stairs. They walked slowly, both instinctively pausing as they passed Oscar's bedroom.

'Can I look inside?' She bit her lip, scared.

'Of course you can.' Again he looked hurt that she felt the need to ask.

He went ahead and opened the door. Rachel stepped inside and was pleased to see that everything was exactly how she had left it, how Oscar had left it. Cee-Cee had kept it clean, tidy and aired, and again she threw her thanks out into the universe. She walked to the chest of drawers and opened up the third drawer from the bottom where all his pyjamas were folded neatly and sat side by side, awaiting a warm little body that would languish in them on the sofa, with hair mussed from sleep, kicking his bare feet and eating cereal by the handful. She placed her hand inside and let her fingertips caress the soft cotton that had known the feel of his skin.

'I miss him,' she managed through her tears.

It was the sound of James's gulping sob that caused her to turn. Rachel reached out without too much planning or forethought, and the couple tumbled on to their son's bed, where they held each other fast, as if the feel of the other were the thing that might help them breathe as they cried. They stayed huddled together on the narrow space where their boy had lain. Rachel pictured Oscar pulling the duvet over his chin as she or Cee-Cee read him stories, tucked him in and soothed him after a bad dream. They lay entwined until sleep claimed them.

When she woke in Oscar's room on Oscar's bed, her limbs felt leaden. She had slept deeper and more soundly than she had in months and it took a while for her to fully come to. With a sense of confusion she felt the shape of her husband against her. Awkwardness fired through her as he stirred into wakefulness.

'I still think sometimes he will come home. I still wait for someone to wake me up and tell me it was all a horrible dream.' She spoke aloud without thinking.

James's lack of comment left her feeling hollow. Embarrassment fuelled the anger that surged inside her; she had wanted him to agree with her, to make her feel like she wasn't being ridiculous. His silence had quite the opposite effect.

Sliding her legs from under his, she trod the hallway and walked into their bedroom, and it was as if she had never been away. Her tissue box and tube of hand cream sat by her bedside lamp on the nightstand and her bathrobe hung on the hook on the back of the door. She ran her finger over the counterpane, laundered by Cee-Cee, and again felt the lack of her presence.

Time had stood still here, and this was a source of further confusion. She felt happy that her presence had lingered here in the house where Oscar had lived, but also a little deflated, because if time had stood still, had she really moved on at all?

Rachel unlocked the balcony door and stepped out on to the patio that had been her refuge and her prison after Oscar had gone missing. She stood by the glass wall on the far end and ran her hands along the rail, staring out over the wide expanse of blue. And it was as if time had been erased. She let her eyes dart hungrily from the white crest of waves to the dip and roll of the water with its myriad shadows, each movement in her mind offering up a hundred possibilities. It was like madness, a fixation. And it instantly and powerfully drew her in. She walked backward until her calves felt the steamer chair and sank down on to the cushions, and that was where she sat with her elbows on her knees and her eyes trained on the horizon, watching and praying for the impossible.

Where are you, my little boy? Where did you go? The questions that she had managed to bury for so many months came flying back into her mind, and this alone made her question whether it had been wise to return.

She heard James's soft tread, as he watched her from the doorway. 'Rachel?'

'Yes?' she asked without turning her head.

'Are you . . . are you going to stay up here?'

'Yes.' She nodded and shifted in the seat until she felt more comfortable. 'Just for a little bit.'

'I'll go and get some drinks.'

'Sure.'

James returned and sat in the chair next to her. He handed her a Diet Coke.

'When you were away, I used to sit here and talk to you as if you were sat right there next to me.'

'Did I answer you?' She took a sip.

'No, Rach, I'm not crazy!'

They both laughed, settling back in the chairs, and in that second they broke through the crust of grief, and the hands of the people they were before reached up through the darkness. A happy reminder that they lurked, waiting.

'I have quite liked being by myself. The little flat is empty, soulless really, but it's quiet and sort of cocoons me and that's what it's been like for me, hidden away hoping to transform.' She spoke openly and was glad of the chance to do so.

'Transform into what?' He took a glug of beer from his bottle.

'I'm not sure.' She gave it some thought. 'I know I can't go back to the person I was. I know too much hurt for that to be possible.'

'Yep.'

'I guess I want to transform into someone who knows how to navigate their life through the fog of grief. Cee-Cee told me that.'

James leaned over and clinked his bottle against her cold can of pop. 'To Cee-Cee!'

'To Cee-Cee,' she echoed, and they both drank.

'Are you transformed yet?' he asked, sincerely.

'Not yet.' She kept her voice small. 'Not yet.'

It hadn't been so odd after all. She had simply, when night fell, showered and climbed between the sheets, as she had done thousands of times before. It had been nice to lie next to James once more as tiredness crept over her, company at this the loneliest of hours, reminding her of a time when the world had been less topsy-turvy and how she liked being part of a couple. It had always felt like the two of them against the world – that was, until the world turned on them and took away their happy.

They lay in the darkness, side by side, and listened to the tree-frog symphony, which she had quite forgotten.

'I bumped into Alison in Lindos. I told her about Cee-Cee and that you were coming home.'

Rachel pictured the woman who had stood in her hallway with other mums from school and her face reddened at the memory of that day when her mind had surfed on the chaos of loss.

'She sent you her love and said that she would love to see you. She's called a couple of times, as has Daisy's mum. I knew you probably wouldn't want to see her or anyone, but I am passing it on anyway.'

She noted the ease with which he used the word 'home' and felt a flicker of concern that he might not fully understand that this might only be a visit. 'Home' might actually be the place where she owned nothing more than a mattress on the floor of a rented flat and a job in a coffee shop.

'Was Hank with her?' She almost dared not ask, only able to picture the boy, her son's best friend, laughing with Oscar in the pool or the two of them, chuckling with milk moustaches, snaffling cookies from the plate in the kitchen.

'Yes. He's getting tall, I thought.' James sounded wistful.

She reached under the cover and found his hand, knitting her fingers with his, taking comfort from the warmth of his palm as she tried not to get weighed down with thoughts of how Oscar would forever be a little over four feet tall. In every sense, Hank and the rest of his peers would outgrow him.

'She wrote you a lovely letter too; I put it with all the others in the garage. There are lots of them, Rach.'

'You kept them?'

Throw them away! All of them!

'I did.' He released her hand and leaned up on his side with his head propped up. 'I only glanced at them briefly when they first arrived, but a couple of months ago I decided to read them properly and it was . . .'

'It was what?'

'It was really comforting to read all the things that people thought about Oscar, and it made me happy that he had had such an impact on so many people's lives. It made it feel like less of a waste.'

Rachel felt the snort of laughter leave her nose. 'Christ, they must be some bloody letters and cards, because I can't see his loss as anything but a complete tragedy – a great big waste of all that he could have been. And it's not fair.'

'No. It's not fair. I agree. But they helped me, nonetheless.'

'Well, good for you, James.'

'What, *that* makes you angry now? Listen to your tone! The fact that while you had fucked off to England and I was all alone, I took comfort from the kind words written by people who were trying to help – to reach out to us in our hour of need. *That's* a reason to sound a little off with me? Jesus fucking Christ!'

'Why does this have to be about you?' she cried. 'Why can't this be about how bloody unfair it is that my son was taken from me?'

'From us!' he corrected. 'From us! And that's kind of the problem here, Rachel. Or at least one of them. You are so wrapped up in your own grief, as if you are the only one who loved him and the only one who has had her life ripped apart, but you are not! You are not.'

'I am his mum!' she shouted.

'And I am his dad.'

They were quiet for a moment or two, looking at each other, both at a loss as to how to quash the flame of emotion that seemed to coat their interactions. The moonlight painted stripes of light on the bed linen and the cicadas chirped in time to the beat of their fractured hearts.

The bed felt tiny.

The room airless.

'There is no one else in the whole wide world who has the power to make me feel this way.' James spoke into the semi-darkness. 'I find you infuriating and you make my blood boil and I want to fix you, help you, protect you and run from you, all at once.'

'Which is the strongest feeling?' she asked with genuine curiosity.

He sighed and lay back on the pillows. 'Truthfully? I don't know, but I do know that whilst I missed you – and I did – I find your anger, your closed-off nature and your judgment almost too hard to deal with.'

'I can't apologise for that.' She knew he spoke the truth, but as she had said already, she was not yet transformed.

'No.' He sighed. 'I guess you can't. But don't take it out on me, Rachel. Because *that*'s not fair.'

'I'm sorry,' she whispered. 'I am. I find it so hard. My reactions are more like reflex than thought-out response.' Her tears beat the familiar path to her pillowslip.

Suddenly, James switched on the bedside light and reached for his dressing gown.

Rachel sat up. 'What are you doing?'

'Wait here.' He spoke as he left the room and she heard his footsteps on the stairs.

By the time he made his way back up, Rachel was agitated. He carried a pale-blue weekend bag with only one handle that she recognised as one she had thrown out some time ago. She wondered if he were packing to leave and felt the rise of panic in her gut at the prospect of him leaving her alone in this house of ghosts. *Was this what it felt like for you when I left?* She laid her hand flat on her stomach.

James placed the bulky bag on the mattress and sat behind it. He wasn't leaving. Instead, he dipped his hand into it and pulled out a handful of white envelopes, loose cards and folded letters. 'I want you to read some of these. They helped me and I think they will help you.'

'I don't want to.' She shook her head and pulled the duvet up to her chin, in the way Oscar used to when he too was trying to keep the monsters at bay.

'Please, Rachel!'

She shook her head again and sank down on the mattress with a bolt of unease firing through her very core. 'I don't want to,' she whispered.

'Why not?'

'Because.'

'Because what?' he pushed.

'Because it makes it real! It makes it so real and I am afraid it will drag me back to that moment, that second when you were looking up at me from the galley and you had two mugs of coffee in your hands and—'

She watched as he balled a fist and punched the leather bag, sending it flying on to the floor as the loose mail scattered where it fell. James stood and left the room, closing the door behind him.

And just like that, she was once again back to sleeping alone.

The two tiptoed around each other as they showered and dressed for the day ahead. They were courteous, but it was the civility of strangers. It cut her deeply and disturbed her psyche that they had come to this.

Where did we go, James? How did we crumble so easily without resistance?

She found the prospect of being in a church harder than she had imagined. She knew that some people – Cee-Cee included – took comfort from their faith and all that it might offer by way of the promise of reunion. But for her, anger – fanned by recent discord with James – was still crisp in her veins, and if there were a God, her question would be: What kind of God would take her little boy, smash her marriage and leave her feeling like this and why? Why?

Even the journey there made her heart race; there was something about attending a funeral that she feared – worried that witnessing the act of finality might be more than she could handle. Her legs trembled and as James drove along the South Road she considered asking him to turn left into the Reefs' car park, where they could sit out on the deck they loved, in a place studded with memories, high above the rocks, and remember Cee-Cee in their own way. But of course she didn't.

Today was not about her; it was about paying respects to the woman who had made their lives wonderful and whom Oscar had dearly loved and who had offered wise, wise words in her darkest hour. The woman who had taken up the reins and cared for James when he had needed it most.

Rachel looked at the bend in the road that came up from Horseshoe Bay and pictured young Cee-Cee walking along the verge in her cotton dress with her hand inside Willard's, feeling as if the whole wide world lay in her palm. This image alone was enough to make tears spring to her eyes.

James parked on Church Road, opposite the low, white chapel of St Anne's, which was simple and stunning. The sun glinted from the walls and it shone like a jewel against the backdrop of turquoise sky. Set on a slight hill with its graveyard snaking out towards the sea, with each plot immaculately tended, she thought it was the most perfect resting place for the woman who had spent every Sunday of her life worshipping here and who would forever rest in a piece of land within sight of the palm trees and the ocean of her island.

The inside of the building was just as she had imagined it from Cee-Cee's letters – cool and calming, with whitewashed walls and sweet-smelling cedar-wood pews. A high stained-glass window sat behind the altar, and candles flickered at either end of the sacred table. It was simple and uncluttered and yet no less atmospheric for that. Rachel could picture Grandma Sally in her floppy linen hat and Pastor Raymond standing at the front, preaching his messages of love and forgiveness, and she saw Cee-Cee stealing glimpses at Willard Templeton across the pews.

Slow organ music was playing and when the choir, dressed in white, began to sway with a low hum of accompaniment, Rachel felt the hairs on the back of her neck rise. Their clear, sweet sound rose up and danced around the rafters, falling like heavenly dust to lie on her shoulders. She and James took seats at the back of the church and watched as family, friends and neighbours of Cee-Cee filed in, the men wearing suits and dark ties and the women in dresses and hats. The floral displays were simple, various white flowers threaded with full-headed blooms of brightly coloured purple and pink hibiscus that looked and smelled wonderful. Hibiscus blooms full of colour quite unlike the ones that had wept away their very shade for the life of a baby boy.

James leaned over and whispered, 'Are you okay?'

She nodded her response, grateful for his attention and aware that she was crying with her eyes fixed on the altar. The priest in long white robes and with his hands pressed together in prayer walked in, and the music changed tempo to a more sombre piece. The choir sang loudly as Cee-Cee's pale wood coffin was brought in on the shoulders of six men, followed by a small troupe of women. All were crying, but none as loudly as a big-boned woman who walked along behind; she made more noise than all the others put together. She clutched her own single hibiscus bloom and swiped it under her nose, as if it were smelling salts. Rachel watched, fascinated, drawn to the bent old man who walked by the woman's side, patting her on the back and whispering, 'There, there, Clara. There, there. Time will heal. Time will heal.'

Rachel stared at the two who had shaped her friend's life, who had stolen her happiness and her chance of a family. She heard Cee-Cee's voice in her ear.

'My Clara?' I knew she was the greater loss, the one whose betrayal hurt me more because she was my best friend . . .

She took comfort from James standing so close and found it hard to listen to much of what was being said; her eyes were fixed on the narrow box that sat on the trestle by the altar, decked with white oleander and more bright-toned hibiscus.

Bones. Just bones.

Her mind inevitably wandered to the matter of death, and in her head, quite clearly, she heard Cee-Cee's voice, warm and calming as it always had been: *I am sad; sadder than sad and I won't ever stop. Not till I see him again in heaven. Because that is what I believe – that when you get to heaven, you get to gaze upon the thing you loved the most . . .*

I wish I believed that, Cee-Cee. I wish I believed in your God who could help me make sense of this nightmare in which I live. I wish I thought that one day I might go to a place called heaven and find my boy waiting for me. Because if I believed those things, I might not mind waking up every day. I might not still dream on occasion of jumping from a great height, knowing that peace awaits me at the bottom . . .

Only when James reached over and held her hand tightly did she realise that violent, gulping sobs had left her body, drawn from a place beyond her consciousness.

The service drew to a close and the family and loved ones made their way out to the churchyard. Rachel blinked as her eyes adjusted to the bright, blue day, in contrast to the dark interior of St Anne's. She was loitering on the dusty path of the graveyard when Clara and Willard walked out of the church, part of the wider crowd that moved slowly, and came to a standstill in front of her.

Rachel swallowed the many, many things she wanted to say to the woman whose image she had held in her mind for so long. This old lady, however, with tears streaking her skin, bore very little resemblance to the flighty, loud young thing that she had imagined.

Rachel smiled and caught her eye. 'I was Cee-Cee's friend,' she began.

Clara looked at her. 'She was my friend too,' she managed through a mouth contorted with sadness. Rachel saw Willard reach for her hand.

'Cee-Cee taught me so much.' Rachel spoke softly, and Clara and Willard seemed to tune out the hubbub all around and listen to her words. 'She taught me that bitterness lies in your very centre and, like a pit in a plum pudding, can taint the whole thing. She said forgiveness was better, sweeter.'

Clara cried noisily and searched Rachel's face. 'She said that?'

'She did.'

Clara scrunched up her lace-edged handkerchief and blotted her eyes. 'I miss her. I have always missed her. She was my very best friend.'

'I know.' Rachel smiled. 'And you were hers.'

Rachel and James took their leave, having paid their respects to the woman to whom they owed so much.

'Who was the lady you were talking to?'

'That was Clara. She and Cee-Cee were like sisters until Clara abandoned her – jealous, I think. Terrible. There were times in Cee-Cee's life when she really needed her friend and Clara just wasn't there.'

'Thank goodness for Vicky, eh?' He smiled.

'Oh God, I'm thankful for her every day.' She pictured her friend and missed her, wondering if she was at rewer. She felt an unexpected jolt of longing for that life far from here.

'And to think it used to be me you thanked God for.' He let this trail.

'Trust me, James, I don't thank God for much these days. Don't take it personally.'

'I am your husband. Bit hard not to take it personally.'

Rachel looked out of the window, feeling his words like a weight about her shoulders.

'I feel exhausted.' James changed tack as he pulled off his tie and threw it on to the back seat.

'Me too. That wasn't easy, was it?'

'No.' He looked ahead at the winding South Road. 'But I thought the service was good; there was a completeness to it, a feeling of closure that we haven't had.'

She sensed he was emboldened, able to speak without holding her eyeline.

'I guess that's part of the transformation I am still waiting on. Just the idea of a service . . .' She shuddered. 'I couldn't do it, James.'

They drove home in near silence and waited for the electric gates to whir open upon their return.

Once inside, the two made their way into the kitchen and James headed straight for the fridge. 'I don't know about you, but I feel like a drink.' He reached for the bottle of tonic and grabbed the gin from the cupboard before filling two tall glasses with ice, a wedge of lime and generous amounts of Tanqueray. He handed her a glass and they sat at the table where they had eaten hundreds of meals prepared for their family with love by Cee-Cee.

Rachel looked at the chair in which Oscar used to sit, kicking his legs back and forth.

Don't kick the chair, Oscar! It used to drive her crazy.

I don't want pasta! Can I have ice cream?

No! What do you think this is, a restaurant? Just eat the pasta!

I don't like it!

Then go to bed; how about that? I have had a very long day and I can't be doing with you being so fussy, not tonight. Go to bed!

'To Cee-Cee!' James raised his glass and pulled her from the painful memory.

'To Cee-Cee.' She did likewise and they both sipped.

'I liked the church. It wasn't too stuffy, felt nice.'

'Yes, it did,' she agreed, taking another sip of her drink and liking the clunk of the ice cubes.

'I didn't know her name was Cecilly.'

'I did.' She sipped. 'It's a sweet name. She told me that in one of her letters. They really are something, James; you should look at them.'

He laughed and shook his head. 'So what should I say to that? Refuse to read them? Hide under the duvet? Stomp my disapproval?'

She knew he referred to the blue weekend bag stuffed with words of condolence that he had no doubt secreted back in the garage.

'It's completely different!' She shook her head, in no mood to bicker with him.

'Yep,' he agreed, tapping the table with his fingertips. 'I guessed it might be. Just like a funeral for Oscar would be completely different.' He took another slug of gin.

'No, no, James!' she cut in. 'Please don't start with that again.' She felt the rise of terror in her throat at the very idea of a funeral, a service of any kind . . .

I couldn't do it! I couldn't let them bring an empty box into the room – or worse, a full one. I don't want to imagine my son's bones lying in it. I couldn't bear to hear other people crying who didn't love him as much as me. I can't show my sadness in such a public way. I would crack. I would break . . .

James stared at her. 'Rachel,' he began, his tone one of exasperation, and she got the feeling that all that had been simmering beneath his skin for the last few months was finding its way out of his mouth, possibly lubricated by the liberal consumption of gin. 'We can't keep having this conversation.'

'I agree. Neither of us wants to have this conversation. So let's not.' She knocked back the contents of her glass and went to the fridge to mix a refill. 'Do you want another one?' She lifted the bottle.

'Yes. Yes, I do.'

She heard the tension in his tone.

Three large gins on an empty stomach were what it took for her to feel a sense of calm wash over her. It had been a while since she had felt a drunken haze coat her thoughts and actions, and it wasn't wholly unpleasant. James sat in the chair, similarly slumped.

'I am a bit drunk, James.'

'Me too.' He smiled at her.

'I hate arguing with you.'

'Me too, but you drive me crazy! Life is so shit right now. It's just shit.'

'I know.' She hated the tears that fell, taking the edge from her drunken happy.

'I heard what you said to that woman – Cee-Cee's friend, Clara,' he whispered, his words spiked with emotion. 'And you're right, forgiveness is better, sweeter. We need to forgive ourselves. We need to understand that it was an accident, a terrible accident, or what will have been the point of Oscar's life? I have spent every waking moment torturing myself with all the things I might have done or could have done, and I know it needs to stop. It needs to stop now. We need to celebrate the seven short but glorious years we had with him. He was amazing, wasn't he? He was amazing and he was our boy.'

'He was.' She sobbed.

'And you know, it was his boisterousness, his inquisitive mind, his love of nature, all the things we gave him – those were the traits that took him off the boat. All those things made him special and we wouldn't have changed one single thing about him, would we?'

She shook her head. 'Not one.'

'I envy you, Rachel. When you were under the water you said you saw him. What wouldn't I give to see him one last time, just to get a glimpse of his little face.' He looked out of the window towards the ocean.

'It was wonderful. But I don't think it was real,' she whispered.

'I know, Rach, but that doesn't matter, does it?'

She shook her head. James was right. It mattered little whether it was real or a dream or the imaginings of a mind full of desperate longing; the result was the same: it was the start of a new dawn of healing. Oscar had said goodbye and he had looked . . . happy.

'I will carry that image in my heart for eternity.' Rachel turned to her husband. 'I know I could have been a better mum and that will haunt me, always. And I am truly sorry for what I nearly put you through that day, when I jumped.' She shook her head; even the memory of that day was painful.

'No, no, Rachel, you don't have to apologise to me and never doubt that as a mum, you were wonderful! The things I said before were rooted in anger, spite, wanting to hurt you because I was hurting and I was fucked up. I didn't mean it.'

'It felt like you meant it.'

'I am sorry. Please, I am sorry.'

'I'm sorry too,' she apologised. 'I'm sorry, James, that I was dismissive of your pain, unfeeling about your hurt.' She shook her head. 'I couldn't help it!'

'I know. I know.' He smiled briefly, as if glad of the acknowledgement, his mouth contorted with tears.

'It was like I had been stuffed into this small, dark box and all I could think about was how much I hurt and how scared I was and there was no room for anyone or anything else. And no one could hear me and no one could help me.'

'I could hear you. I could hear you, Rach, but you're right, I couldn't help you. I wanted to . . .'

'I know.' She stood and slipped into the chair next to his at the table. Leaning across, she rested her head on his chest, feeling his chin on her head. It felt nice. They both let their tears fall, unabashed. 'We are different shapes now, aren't we? I don't even know if we fit together any more, not like we used to. I have a piece missing. An Oscar-shaped piece; a reminder that I will never be whole but also that he was a part of me, a part of you!'

'Yes.'

She felt him nod his agreement.

'He was the best part of me, James, and you're right about forgiving ourselves. I feel guilty about the smallest of things. They keep me awake.'

'Like what?'

She sniffed. 'It sounds ridiculous . . .'

'Please tell me.'

She sat forward and tucked her hair behind her ears. 'I can't stop thinking about this one night when he wanted dessert but hadn't eaten his pasta. He wanted ice cream and I said no. I worry over and over about the fact that he might have gone to sleep hungry and I ask myself, what would have been the harm in letting him have a bowl of bloody ice cream? I wish I hadn't shouted at him and I wish I had taken him up a bowl of ice cream.'

She looked up at the sound of James laughing. It started as a wheeze and developed into a full-blown chuckle. 'Rach!'

'What? It's not funny!'

'No, Rachel, you don't understand.' He leaned forward and held her arm, until his laughter subsided. 'That night, I . . . I waited until you were in the bath and I took him up a big bowl of ice cream!'

'You did?' She felt the creep of a smile across her face.

'Yes!' He nodded. 'A bloody great big bowl of ice cream with marsh-mallows and chocolate sauce and all the trimmings, and I sat on the bed with him while he wolfed it down! He didn't go to sleep hungry. He went to bed chuckling, with a tummy full of ice cream and a face smeared with chocolate sauce.'

'I can't believe it! You have no idea.' Rachel shook her head, feeling the worry lift from her shoulders.

'I think that's how we parented, how we did it – together, filling in the gaps, giving him what he needed when he needed it. He was so loved.'

'By us and by Cee-Cee,' she reminded him.

'Yes. He had all three of us – a tag team.'

She smiled at the image. 'I feel . . .'

'What?' he coaxed.

'I feel lighter.' It was the only word she could think of to describe this new state.

'Yep. Lighter. I know what you mean.'

'Not better, not brilliant, not even happy, but lighter.'

James nodded. 'And that will do for now.'

'Yep.' She took a deep breath. 'That'll do for now. I love you, James.' The phrase flew automatically from her mouth. It was instinctive but no less true for that.

His instant tears were quite overwhelming. He swiped at his eyes with his fingertips. 'It's been a long time since you told me that, and I supposed you had stopped feeling that way and I understood. I did. Even though it was hard for me because I love you so much. I do.'

Rachel looked at him and saw the outline of a man who reminded her so much of someone she used to know. He looked like the man married to the girl who loved life, the girl who flung her arms around his neck in the shimmering water of Jobson's Cove and kissed his face, joy bursting from her with all that her wonderful life promised.

She is still there somewhere, cocooned . . . she thought, as her eyelids fell and she knew it was time to tread the stairs for bed.

◆ ◆ ◆

The house seemed warmer when she woke. Rachel had stirred in the night and noticed she slept with her leg cast over her husband's and it made her happy, this unexpected and comforting contact. It was still early and the sun streamed through the windows. The scent of coffee wafted from the kitchen. She slipped her arms into her robe and walked down the wide staircase.

The pale-blue leather weekend bag that she had last seen punched to the bedroom floor now sat on the tabletop. James had brought it in from the garage – she had to admire his tenacity. Rachel pulled up a seat and dipped her hand in, withdrawing a clutch of envelopes, cards and letters. She took a deep breath and opened a card with a picture of a tree on the front.

'*Everyone in class three will miss Oscar's smiling face. We have made a memory tree and every pupil wrote a special memory and hung it on the branches. Keeping you in our thoughts and prayers. Mrs Anderson.*' She read aloud.

The next card was plain, white with a small gold cross, the message short and sweet: '*Thinking of you, Mary and Ken Braithwaite.*' She didn't know who Mary and Ken Braithwaite were, but was grateful they had taken the time and trouble to write. Rachel kept going through her tears and her smiles, reading and absorbing all the wonderful messages of love and support for her and James and Oscar.

Her husband had been right; it did help. To know that her little boy had touched so many lives in his short time was a comfort. She fingered a note from Hank's mum that said simply, '*Hank wanted me to tell you that he cries when he thinks of Oscar, but then he laughs because he remembers something funny that Oscar did. I thought I should let you know.'* Rachel smiled. 'That's perfect, Hank. Thank you.'

Next she pulled out a letter, folded into three, but without an envelope. As she opened it James appeared and took in the pile of cards and notes. 'How are you doing?'

'I'm doing okay.' She looked at her newly showered husband and thought he looked younger than he had of late, as if well rested. He smiled at her and she knew him so well that this smile told her that this was going to be a good day. It felt as if some of the mist that had surrounded them had lifted and it was a welcome feeling.

'Coffee?'

'Yes, please.'

'You are reading them. I'm glad, Rach.'

She nodded, opening the letter; she laid it flat on the table. Reading quietly to herself, she let her eyes follow each word written in blue ink with a flourish, displaying beautiful penmanship that she instantly recognised.

Dear Mr and Mrs Croft, Rachel, James,

I write because sometimes I find the words that get knotted in your throat are smooth and ordered when you put pen to paper. I see your loss. I feel your loss and it takes me back to a time when I did not feel life was worth living. A time when my pain was such that I prayed for the angels to take me under their wing and relieve me from my burden. Of course they did nothing of the sort, their message loud and clear: Who are you, Miss Symmons, to think you can command the angels? So I lived a half-life. A quiet life. Until I met Oscar. He didn't care for my sadness. He didn't have time for my reflection, no sir. He ran at me and took my hand and pulled me from the gloom. He made me chase around that house playing games.

He brought me joy, that little boy who loved me. He made me love life again! All by loving him. You see, I thought I had been denied the chance to raise a child, but I had not. That chance was given to me at a time in my life when I had no right to expect it. Not that the joy was any less for that. So I thank you both, and I thank you for Oscar, and as God is my witness, if I can hold his hand and ease his path to heaven then that will give my life a meaning greater than I could ever have dreamed. With love to you, amen.

Cee-Cee

'Oh my! Oh, James!' she cried.

'Cee-Cee's letter.' He nodded his understanding as he placed the coffee mug on the table. 'I wanted to talk to her about it, thank her, but it never felt like the right moment.'

'I'm sure she knew how you felt, James.'

'Hope so. Drink up,' he urged. 'It's a beautiful day and we should go and get some fresh air.'

'I'll go shower.' She finished her coffee and made her way upstairs.

If they weren't out on *Liberté* it had always been their Sunday tradition to walk the shoreline before the heat of the day took hold, usually with Oscar running ahead, digging sand, flinging shells and pebbles out to sea or paddling in and out of the shallows.

Rachel lifted the hem of her cotton skirt and strolled along the water's edge of Horseshoe Bay, her feet sinking into the soft, darker sand, as the sun rose higher, turning the sky a pretty shade of turquoise.

'Paradise,' James commented as he looked towards the horizon.

'It was.' She stopped walking and stared out over the blue, blue sea. Loving the sound of birdsong, as if these winged creatures today shared her awakening sense of joy.

'But not any more?' James asked, as he sank down on to the sand with his elbows resting on his knees and his sunglasses now pulled down.

She sat next to him and wrapped her long skirt around her legs. 'We have lost what we had, James,' she whispered. 'We have lost everything, and when I was away it was easy to forget that we were wonderful! We were so wonderful together.'

'We were.' He nudged her playfully with his elbow.

'I have done a lot of thinking. I'm glad I came back—'

'Me too,' he interrupted.

'And I know that I'm still healing, still grieving. I suspect I always will be, and there's lots I don't know about what lies ahead. But the one thing I do know, James, is that I don't want this life. I don't want this life here without him in it. It feels hollow. It feels like a sentence. I see him everywhere and I can't cope with the reminders in every direction I look. In some ways it's comforting, but they hold me fast. I can't move on.'

She let her gaze sweep the beach and saw Oscar in his sun suit and hat, holding up a piece of seaweed. 'Look at this, Mummy!' She closed her eyes briefly and he had gone.

James ran his hand over his chin and took his time in asking the question they both knew loomed.

'Do you want to go back to Bristol?'

She nodded. 'I think I do.'

James reached across and took her hand in his, holding it tight.

'Do you want me to come with you?'

She took her time in answering. 'I think . . . I think I don't want to uproot you from your job, the house, everything that you have worked for.'

'None of it means anything without you,' he whispered, all playfulness now gone.

Rachel swallowed and held her nerve. 'I am still so confused, James, but I do know that when I was in Bristol I had the luxury of submitting to how I was feeling without having to think about you or anyone else, and I know that makes me selfish—'

'I understand. I do,' he interjected. 'And as much as it breaks my heart, I know that we are not the people we were; I know that we don't fit together like we used to.'

'I think I need to go back and try to find some clarity. I'm still trying to find my place in this new world. And that's all I know right now.' She wiped the tear that slipped down her cheek.

He brought their joined fingers to his mouth and kissed their hands.

'I wish you nothing but love, James, nothing but love,' she managed, emotion turning her voice into little more than a squeak.

'And I you, my beautiful girl.' He ran his fingers through her hair. 'Oscar's brilliant, brilliant mum. I love you, but I don't think it's enough right now.' He swallowed.

'I love you too, but I don't think it's enough right now either.'

Just as he had promised, her dad was standing in the arrivals hall waiting for her.

'Well, aren't you a sight for sore eyes.' He smiled. She stepped into his warm embrace and inhaled the familiar scent of his coat: petrol and glue. 'You look well, babber. A lot better. How's James?' he asked, and she was glad that her dad was kind-hearted enough to think of him.

'He's figuring everything out, Dad. Taking it one day at a time; like all of us, I guess. But getting there. It was good to spend time with him – a measure of closure, if you like.'

'And what was it like being in Bermuda again?'

'It was lovely in some ways. Cee-Cee's funeral was very moving and hard.' She pictured Clara and Willard making their way down the aisle of the church in which he had married Cee-Cee and spoken vows in front of her God. 'I feel like I've turned a corner, Dad. I know I can't let Oscar's death stop my life.'

She saw the look of shock on his face – yes, she had said it: *Oscar's death. Oscar died.* It didn't get any easier, but she knew it was necessary to make it commonplace; this was how she stopped the fear, moved past the hurt. 'I know I can't let it stop my life even though it has changed my life – changed us, changed all of us. James said we need to forgive ourselves and he is right.'

'He is.' Her dad nodded as they walked towards the car wheeling her suitcase. 'Hope you're hungry; your mum has made you a packed lunch.'

'Of course she has.' She smiled.

They drove along the motorway in amiable silence, just the way they liked it.

At her insistence, he stopped the car on the Gloucester Road, Bishopston. She had already emailed the agent and secured her flat for another six months – a breathing space, at least, where she could take this newfound energy, this cautious optimism and make a plan for the future. She decided to think six months ahead and to keep repeating this, see how far it took her. She even thought about buying a sofa and maybe even a bookshelf. This was progress in itself.

The pavement was busy and she took a moment to adjust to the crowds, the noise and the beep of tinny horns as traffic sat nose to tail going nowhere fast.

She pushed open the door of rewer and smiled. Glen was busy at the coffee bar, Sandra took an order from a table near the back and

Keith rang his bell from the kitchen. Glen turned and his face split into a warm smile.

'You came back.'

'It would appear so.' She kicked the floor.

'Do you still want your job?'

'I do.' She shoved her hands in her pockets. 'For six months at least, and then I might try to revive my old career.' *If I am strong enough . . . If I have forgiven myself . . .*

'Okay then. Six months? I'll take it.' He nodded. 'See you Monday.'

'Thanks, Glen.' She beamed at him.

'No worries. You look well.'

'I feel it.' She shrugged; it was still a novelty to admit to this.

'Oh, I've got something for you.'

She watched as he ducked down behind the long counter and resurfaced seconds later, walking towards her with his hand outstretched. 'I did my best. I didn't get all of it, but some.'

Rachel pulled her hand from her pocket, into which he dropped a small glass bottle with a dropper top that had once been home to vanilla extract. She shook the glass up towards the light and saw that it was a third full, packed with sand and one or two tiny crushed shells. The feel of it in her palm caused her stomach to fold. *That day . . . that moment, Oscar, when I realised you had gone . . .* She felt a little of her earlier optimism and energy evaporate.

'Oh, Glen!'

'I sifted it from the rubbish on the floor. Took me an age.'

Rachel stared at him, marvelling at how he had known instinctively what to do and how it would make her happy. She crept forward and kissed him on the cheek. 'Thank you. This means more to me than you can ever know. And, Glen?'

'What?'

'When you find the right person, you will feel overjoyed at the prospect of spending your life with them, not cornered. Love is about freedom, even if that means being apart.' She thought of her wonderful James and her heart flexed. 'It won't be about limping from one big event to the next; no one should choose drama. The mundane will be enough and you will feel happy in the everyday, happy now in the moment. And she will be very lucky to have you.'

'Thank you, Rach.' He took a deep breath and made a clicking noise with the side of his mouth. He had got the message, kindly and sincerely delivered: the girl who would be lucky to have him was not going to be her. She belonged to James, she belonged to Oscar, and a missing piece of her belonged to Bermuda.

'No, thank *you*.' She held up the little vial of sand and wrapped it tightly in her fingers.

'Don't mention it. It's just sand, right?'

'Yes.' She nodded. 'It's just sand.'

ELEVEN

Rachel sat back on her swivel chair and raised her arms above her head, twisting her neck to the left and right, as she did at the end of any long day spent behind her desk. She looked out of the picture window from where she had a perfect view of a bend in the river with the SS *Great Britain* docked to the left and the footpath, busy with walkers and runners alike, to the right. She glanced at the calendar on her pinboard where a neat red ring circled the date. It was hard to believe it had been one whole year since she had stepped nervously over the threshold and into the shiny glass building to begin her new job in digital marketing for the data-analytics company. In the last year her confidence had soared; it felt good to be back in the corporate saddle, where her identity was predominantly based on her senior role and no one looked at her with the cocked head and tight-lipped smile of sympathy. And even if it was only for a minute, it allowed her to forget her sadness. Each night, after a brisk walk home through the bustling city with her woolly scarf fastened at her neck and her thoughts thousands of miles away under an inky-blue, star-filled sky, she fell into her bed and often slept soundly. This in itself was a welcome relief after the insomnia of grief that had dictated her routine since losing Oscar.

Her wide desk was devoid of the photographs and personal touches that littered her colleagues' workspace. Not that she didn't carry permanent pictures of her family in her mind: images of Oscar laughing, Oscar swimming, and he and James together in the pool or on *Liberté*; images that sat behind her eyelids with every blink. But not having to respond to the inevitable questions that would arise from a photograph, or a memento of home, made life easier for her right now. And nearly two years since losing her boy, it was still all about trying to get through life, one day at a time, as best she could.

Her mobile rang.

'Hey, Vick.'

'How you doing?' Her friend cut to the chase.

'Okay. Just packing up.' She reached for her keys and handbag.

'Are you nervous?'

'Erm, a bit, yes.' She thought about the evening ahead. 'In fact, a lot. Very nervous. But also excited, if that makes any sense.'

'It does. Remember what I told you: try not to think about it too much, try not to over-plan or picture it, just go with it – and know that Gino and I and your mum and dad – all of us – will be right by your side. You've got this.' She spoke with conviction.

'Thanks, Vick. I feel weird about seeing James.' She swallowed the flare of nerves that made her feel a little lightheaded.

'Of course, but we are all so looking forward to seeing him that any awkwardness will be diluted.'

'Yep, I guess. Anyway, best go. I need to go home and change and whatnot. See you there?'

'You bet, and remember if at any time it feels too much or you change your mind—'

'I know – peaches and cream.' She smiled down the phone at her best friend. 'Peaches and cream.'

At home, Rachel stood in front of the full-length mirror in her bedroom and ran her palms over the calf-length navy frock, adjusting the cream ribbon bow at her neck and running her fingers through her shoulder-length hair.

'You can do this.' She nodded at her reflection.

Stepping out into the cold night air, she smiled at the student house opposite, where a new batch of Josh, Olly and Jaspers now lived in the street she called home. She had eschewed the offers of a lift from her parents, and even one from Peter, preferring to walk alone and gather her thoughts. She walked past rewer and looked in at the place, all closed up for the night. It was her favourite hang-out and still somewhere that, if the demand called for it, Glen would throw an apron at her and she would ferry plates of bacon and eggs from the kitchen to the tables with a fixed smile and a bottle of ketchup in her front pocket. She would forever love this little café and the people in it who had become like family to her, scooping her up when she had needed it the most and helping her get through the darkest of times. That little job had been a lifeline, enabled her to find her feet, filling her days and distracting her long enough to let the healing begin.

Rachel quickened her pace until she stood on the path, looking up at the flint-walled chapel where the sparkle of rain fell like gold in the lamplight. It felt a little magical and this made her happy. She pushed open the heavy oak door. Inside, the room was cosy. Candle flames lilted in the breeze and generous bundles of greenery set in sturdy vases had been placed in the deep window recesses and decorated the altar. It was perfect.

She looked at the pews that were starting to fill up with all the people she loved, sitting shoulder to shoulder. Sandra, Keith and Glen had taken seats at the back and she was touched that Keith, whilst still looking a little grumpy, had donned a dark suit and black tie. Vicky and Gino held hands; Francisco had been left at home with his gran.

Her mum, she noted, despite her pep talk only the week before, cried openly with a tissue pressed to her nose and this before the service had even begun. Her dad winked at her and placed his arm around his wife. Rachel smiled, reminding herself that grief had no blueprint; it was the right of everyone who loved her boy to mourn him in the way they saw fit.

Once the fog of loss had begun to lift, it had been an easy decision to hold the memorial service for Oscar, and it felt right to have it here in Bristol where her son had roots. She thought back to one of her regular calls to James. They were now able to discuss the minutiae of life without guilt and each sentence was offered like a gently rounded thing, rather than with the sharp barbs of anger and blame that had made previous words lodge in each other's breast, causing harm.

'Have you had your lunch?' she'd asked as she'd stirred a pot of soup on her stovetop.

'Not yet, might nip up to the Fairmont and grab a salad. It's a lovely day.'

She'd looked out of the window at the silhouette of chimney pots against the dark sky and tried to remember the bright glare of midday sun through the window and what it felt like to feel the warmth on her skin. 'Oscar would have me in the pool the moment he got home on a day like that.'

James laughed. 'Yep, you knew there was never any such thing as a quick dip; it was always a struggle to get him to come inside. Even when he was all pruney.'

They both laughed. It was a sad little laugh of happy memories tainted by the knowledge of what came next.

'His birthday's coming up,' James whispered.

'Yep, two weeks, three days.' She stopped stirring and placed the spoon on the countertop, her appetite suddenly gone.

'I don't know what I will do. Probably work late and just get my head down and then go home and drink gin.' He spoke softly.

'I'm thinking of taking the day off and pulling the duvet over my head and switching off my phone and sleeping, or at least pretending to.'

'That sounds like a plan.'

She knew he understood.

'I've been thinking, James, that maybe it's time we did something to mark Oscar's passing.' She took a deep breath, trying to read his silence. 'I don't know how you feel, but I was going to suggest that we have a memorial service for him, something . . .' She paused, listening intently to the silence on the other end of the line.

His response when it came was offered with the wobble of emotion she knew all too well.

'I think that would be the best thing, Rach; the absolute best thing.'

That had been a couple of months ago and here they were.

She shrugged off her coat and handed it to Vicky, who placed it on her lap, along with her own. Rachel waved to James's parents, happy they had made it. She walked forward and felt someone reach out and pat her arm. Looking down at the end of the pew, she stared into the face of the man she had not seen for over a year – her husband, her James. It was not only strange to feel the jolt of nerves for someone she was married to, but also odd to see him in this environment. It had been a long time since she had seen him in a winter coat. He smiled at her and she felt the spread of warmth in her chest, and something that felt a lot like relief.

Here you are . . .

He looked well, tanned of course, but he had filled out a little and seemed to have lost the sunken, sallow demeanour that had dogged him since that day.

'Hey, you.'

'Hey, you.'

They each took a second, examining the face of the other, once so familiar, now relearning the new bruise-like shadows and lines of age; the marks of grief that they wore like battle scars.

'This place is just right,' he whispered.

'I think so.' She let her eyes skirt the small chapel.

'Are you going to be okay?'

She nodded, feeling the swell of joy bloom in her gut simply because he was by her side, tonight when she needed him most. She had quite forgotten how his very presence, the proximity of him, made her feel safe, settled – and the force of it took her by surprise.

The little chapel was quiet; evening had been a good choice, the still of the night and the cloak of the dark contributing to the atmosphere of solemn thanks, given for a beautiful life in which she had been privileged to play a part.

Post the joyous rendition of 'All Things Bright and Beautiful' and with candles flickering, Rachel gave a small cough and stood behind the sturdy brass lectern, gripping the sides, grateful for the prop that kept her shaking hands steady. She spoke to the small gathering – people she and James loved and who loved them in return.

'I have been worrying over what to say,' she confessed, trying to control the quaver to her voice. 'I wanted to say how much we love and miss Oscar, but I don't know if I need to, as that feels like a given. He was a special little boy, an inquisitive, funny, smart little boy who was our joy. I know he is with us, part of us all, every single day. Our friend, our family member Cee-Cee, whom most of you don't know – but trust me, she was very special and important in our lives – she told me this: "Your family, your kin, that's all you have; it's all we have. Those in the present and those gone before, we all share the same things and we are bound."' Rachel paused and took a deep breath. 'And she was right. Thank you. Thank you, Cee-Cee,' she managed, looking up at the rafters of the chapel before letting her eyes fall to James.

He stood and the two passed in the aisle, she felt the lightest brush of his hand against hers and it sent sweet tremors of happiness through her very core.

She watched as he, too, steadied himself and looked out over the expectant faces.

'My wife once asked me if she thought it was possible to be too lucky.' He paused, and she pictured that night: she and James in the water with her arms wrapped tightly around him and the moonlight sending dappled shafts of light over the blue, blue sea. 'I told her this . . .' He stopped again, swallowed and fixed his eyes on her. 'You are my mate as well as my wife, and you are the best mum. Don't you worry, this life is just going to get better and better.' He did nothing to stop the tears that freely fell; this in turn triggered the tears of all who watched him with his head slightly bowed, standing at the lectern. James coughed and exhaled, before calmly saying, 'And it was true, Rach. All of it. There is no one else in the whole wide world Oscar and I could have loved as much. We were lucky. And I meant it, this life is just going to get better and better. From now on. We miss him, we will always miss him, but this is the moment. Better and better . . .'

The hymns that followed were sung with gusto and Rachel was glad others had taken up the mantle, as emotion prevented her from getting a note out. After the service she and James stood by the chapel door, issuing and receiving hugs and handshakes to all who had stood and given thanks for the life of their son. She found it almost overwhelming when her dad wrapped her husband in his big arms and the two stood together, heads on each other's shoulders, no words needed.

They had decided against a get-together afterwards, wanting the service to be as short and meaningful as possible without the distraction of booze and small talk. People understood and she noticed seemed keen to be alone with their grief, the depths of which had been stirred by the words sincerely spoken.

'That was as perfect as it could have been.' He looked down at her.

'Yes, yes, it was, and I am so, so glad you came all this way, James. It means the world, and of course it was only possible because you were here.' She felt a flicker of desolation at the thought that he would soon be heading back to his island home.

She saw him shiver. 'You're cold!'

'You could say that. It's bloody freezing.' He shoved his hands inside his coat pocket and hunched his shoulders.

'You're a Bermy boy now, not used to this chilly weather.'

He laughed.

'Would you like to come back to my flat? I have coffee and central heating,' she offered instinctively, as if it were the most natural thing in the world to want to spend time alone with this man.

James nodded and moved his elbow away from his body, leaving just enough of a gap for her to place her arm through. It felt comfortable, familiar and yet her heart pounded in her chest as nerves set in. Reunited, they walked side by side along the pavements, until they trod the stairs to her flat.

It felt strange having him in her little home. She watched as he slipped his arms from his winter coat and placed it on the back of the chair before taking a seat on the sofa, filling her little flat with his presence. Rachel put the kettle on, watching him from the doorway of the galley kitchen as he looked around the room. He was still as handsome as ever. She was struck by the way it felt to be in such close proximity to him, bringing to mind Gino and Vicky, laughing on the sofa, her dad with his arms around her mum's shoulders, even Peter and Julie, verbally jumping to each other's defence: couples, friends, lovers. Suddenly, she realised just how much she had missed being part of a two. James and Rachel. Rachel and James . . .

'Are you happy here, Rachel?'

'Oh!' The question caught her a little off guard. 'I am getting there. Mine is not a life I would have chosen, but it's my life and that's all there is to it. And I think happy is a stretch too far, but peace feels within reach. Yes, peace, that's the very best I can hope for. I am out of my cocoon and I'm doing okay.'

'Yep, that just about sums it up.' He sat back against the cushions. 'I know I am mending; my mind is sharper and I can now control my sadness, whereas before!' He threw his hands in the air and she remembered a phone call when he was in the bank, sobbing . . .

'Yes, sharper-minded, I agree with that, and I never really understood what Cee-Cee meant when she said you kind of learn to live with the pain, but you do, don't you?'

'Yes, you do.' He nodded sharply. 'It's like my body has swallowed up the whole experience and it sits inside me, always there, but I carry on.'

'Are you happy?' She returned the question.

He looked towards the window and answered slowly. 'Happy no, but better than I was. I am able to look at Oscar's life as a whole and I wish I wasn't able to; wish I didn't know about his last chapter, but' – he swallowed – 'it's as if my mind has now accepted that his death was part of his story. The seven years we had of him – his beginning, his middle and his end . . . He was ours and we loved him and we were lucky to have him.'

'We were lucky,' she managed. 'And thank you for what you said in the chapel, it was beautiful.'

'I meant it. And I keep thinking that if someone had asked me before he was born that if I knew in advance we would only get seven years but could choose *not* to have him, not to have this heartache, would I choose that?'

'Of course not.' She closed her eyes and answered for him.

'Of course not,' he confirmed.

They took a moment to analyse this truth. This painful, bittersweet truth.

'I sold the boat.'

'You did?'

'Yes. I had no desire to take her out and so . . .'

She nodded her understanding. 'I sometimes, in my less than lucid moments, think that the life in Bermuda carries on without me, as if

Cee-Cee and Oscar and you are in the house on North Shore Road and everything is as it was, and strangely it brings me comfort. I can picture you all there having a lovely time.'

He held her eyeline and there was a moment of silent contemplation for them both. She tried to imagine what it was going to feel like once he had returned to that house on the North Shore Road and the thought of him leaving caused something close to panic to rise in her throat.

'Except I am not there with Cee-Cee and Oscar.' He broke her thoughts. 'I am there on my own and I am not having a lovely time.'

She slipped down on to the sofa next to him. 'Are you lonely, James?' She felt bold asking.

He looked at her. 'I have been lonely since I stood in the galley with cups of coffee in my hands.'

'Me too,' she whispered.

James reached out hesitantly and took her hand into his. Her stomach flipped and it was as if electricity flowed from his palm to hers. It was warm, it was life-giving and it felt a lot like home.

'I miss you. I miss you so badly.' He spoke softly.

Rachel leaned in and placed her head on his chest in the place where she had woken and fallen asleep more times than she could possibly remember. And what she felt wasn't scary or jarring, but instead felt a lot like a beginning.

'You know, Rach, after everything we've been through, I don't need beaches, sunsets, yachts or a view of the sea. I don't need anything apart from moments like this, here with you.'

'Paradise.' The word slipped from her lips unbidden.

'Yes.' He tentatively kissed her scalp. 'Paradise.'

EPILOGUE

Rachel used her hip to open the glass door and unwound her woolly scarf; it was far warmer inside than out. It was late afternoon, the lunchtime rush was over and she took a seat at a table near the back.

'Be with you in a minute, doll!'

'Thanks, Sandra. No rush!' She hung her coat on the back of the chair and raised her hand in a wave, watching as the woman dealt with the customers sitting at the front.

'So why don't you just print what's available on a menu?' The girl was curious.

'My son thinks it builds a relationship between customer and staff, and look at us' – she touched her chest and then pointed at the girl – 'here we are chatting!' She leaned further in. 'But if you want my honest opinion, I think a menu would be better. Nearly eight years we've been open and you have no idea how many times I have to answer the same bloody question.'

'You are terrible!' Rachel smiled at the woman she held in such high affection as she rushed past her.

Sandra laughed. 'Yes, but the thing is I can be as terrible as I like; he's not going to sack me, is he? How can he, I'm his mum! And I work for free!'

'There are times when I would quite like to sack my mum.' She whispered the aside.

'Talk of the devil!' Sandra nodded towards the door as it opened and smiled at Brian, whom Rachel knew she had a soft spot for.

'Afternoon, Brian, Jean, did you pick her up all right?' Sandra hollered.

'Yes, of course. She's coming along now. She's had a lovely day at school, you'll be pleased to hear. But I'm not sure she was warm enough. She's only four, Rach, don't you think she should have a vest on?' Jean shrugged her arms from her coat.

'I think she's fine, Mum. You worry too much.'

'I daresay, but that's a mother's job. Isn't that right, Sandra?'

'Tell me about it. Check on!' she yelled towards the kitchen.

Brian took a seat at the table and unbuttoned his coat. He held his thumbs up to Sandra, who was miming a cup of tea over her customers' heads.

Jean tutted.

Rachel smiled.

It was all part of the pantomime, the tuts, nudges, teasing and nagging – part of the rich tapestry of behaviour that formed the warm blanket that kept them all safe and sound inside the family unit. She loved living in the same city as her mum and dad, realising how easy it was to work and live with their support.

It was even good to see Peter and Julie and the boys, on occasion.

Rachel felt her heart lift at the sight of her daughter, her precious little girl coming through the door with a large painting in her hand.

'Mummy!'

'Well, hello, Miss Cecilly. I hear you've been painting?'

Cecilly clambered on to her mum's lap and carefully laid her work of art on the table. 'It's a house.'

'Well, I can see that!' She winked at her dad, thankful for the steer from Cecilly, as she had been guessing it was a flower.

'That's my room.' Cecilly placed her little finger on a blob that could have been a window. 'And that's Oscar's room, even though he doesn't have a room here because he lives in heaven,' she stated matter-of-factly.

'Yes, he does.' Rachel took comfort that Oscar was now and always would be very much a part of their family.

'Can I have a drink, Mummy?' Cecilly called out.

'I'll get it! Coming right up, poppet.' Sandra swooped down and kissed the little girl, who added sparkle to all of their lives, even on the dullest of days, on the crown of her head.

'And what can I get for her dad?' Sandra smiled towards the door.

'Oh, nothing for me, thanks, I don't want to spoil my supper.' James patted his stomach as he entered and stared at his wife. Rachel felt her heart pulse with love for him: her beautiful, beautiful man, the father of her children.

'Oh, that's a shame. I've got a slice of fresh carrot cake with your name on it.' Sandra winked.

'Go on then.' He smiled and sat next to his wife.

'James!' Rachel sighed. 'I've cooked lasagne; you'd better eat it.'

'Don't worry, love.' Jean patted his arm. 'I've got Alka Seltzer in my bag. I'll leave you some.'

James smiled at his mother-in-law.

Glen came out of the kitchen. 'And I believe this is yours, madam.' He placed the orange juice in front of Cecilly.

'Thanks, bud.' James nodded in his direction.

'No worries, might have to miss five-a-side, James; can you let Gino know?'

James sucked his teeth. 'He's not going to be happy! You know the rule – you have to find a replacement or pay the fine!'

'I'll find a replacement. Christ, you'd think he'd let me off; we've got our final antenatal class.'

'When's your wife due?' Jean asked.

'Another three weeks.'

'Ooh, could be anytime!' James rubbed his hands together. 'It's so exciting!'

Glen exhaled through bloated cheeks. 'To be honest, I'm more scared than excited.'

'Don't be.' James dug the fork into the carrot cake that had arrived. 'You just have to go with the flow, take each day as it comes and go to sleep thankful every night.' Rachel and James exchanged a knowing look.

'Save some of that cake for Vicky, it's her favourite!' Rachel smiled at her husband, still thankful that he had packed up the good life on their little fishhook-shaped island and followed her to a Bristol suburb.

'James is right,' she advised Glen. 'Try not to overthink it. You need to let these little people be who they are going to be. They come into your life and you have to treasure every second you get with them. And all you can do is love them unconditionally. That's it. You will know what to do, instinctively, I'm sure of it.' Rachel nodded and felt the small weight of the bottle of sand in her pocket.

'Love them unconditionally, I can do that.' Glen clapped.

Her dad sat forward and spoke with uncharacteristic emotion. 'I think being a parent is all about loving your kids no matter how far away they are.'

Rachel closed her eyes and pictured her boy, swimming towards the horizon with a smile on his face.

'I think you're right, Dad; loving them no matter how far away they are. And learning how to take the rough with the smooth, one day at a time.' She held her daughter close and kissed her on the top of the head. Little Cecilly, named after the woman to whom she and James would forever be indebted, their darling Cee-Cee, who despite knowing what it felt like to be sadder than sad, had been so wise, so kind at a time when they had needed it most. She smiled fondly at the thought of her. 'And I guess never forgetting that, whatever happens, time heals. Time heals.'

BOOK CLUB QUESTIONS

1. Whose journey of grief did you most empathise/sympathise with – Rachel or James?

2. How did it make you feel, that moment when James and Rachel realise that Oscar is gone?

3. Which female character did you most closely identify with, Cee-Cee or Rachel, and why?

4. Did it add to or detract from the story to have Rachel and Cee-Cee's narratives interweaved in this way?

5. Did you feel it was right that there was no resolution over Oscar's disappearance?

6. Did the story make you want to visit Bermuda?

7. What one thing will stay with you from the book?

ABOUT THE AUTHOR

Photo © 2012 Paul Smith of Paul Smith Photography at
www.paulsmithphotography.info

Amanda Prowse likens her own life story to those she writes about in her books. After self-publishing her debut novel, *Poppy Day*, in 2011, she has gone on to author nineteen novels and six novellas. Her books have been translated into a dozen languages and she regularly tops bestseller charts all over the world. Remaining true to her ethos, Amanda writes stories of ordinary women and their families who find their strength, courage and love tested in ways they never imagined. The most prolific female contemporary fiction writer in the UK, with a legion of loyal readers, she goes from strength to strength. Being crowned 'queen of domestic drama' by the *Daily Mail* was one of her finest moments.

Amanda is a regular contributor on TV and radio, but her first love is, and will always be, writing.

You can find her online at www.amandaprowse.com, on Twitter @MrsAmandaProwse, and on Facebook at www.facebook.com/ amandaprowsenogreaterlove.